PRAISE FOR HILARY DARTT

"Author Hilary Dartt's debut novel – The Dating Intervention – contains every essential element that a fantastic, page-turner type book should contain: a deep sense of character, a near-tangible sense of place, and a captivating plot that moves quickly and fluidly throughout."

RACHELLE SPARKS

"I didn't want it to end! Hilary Dartt is a real talent!"

AMAZON REVIEWER

"Dartt's writing style is distinct, witty, fun, and heart-felt. She creates characters that feel like real people … Love it!"

BLOGGING & WRITING

ALSO BY HILARY DARTT

The Seedling Homestead Series

The Architecture of Vision

The Structure of Perfection

The Intervention Series

The Dating Intervention

The Marriage Intervention

The Motherhood Intervention

The Garden Club Series

Jasmine's Pact

Studying Sequoia

Just Holly

THE COMPOSITION OF ORDER

BOOK ONE IN THE SEEDLING HOMESTEAD SERIES

HILARY DARTT

ISBN: 978-1-950335-00-8

CHAPTER ONE

THE SIGNS WERE THERE, but Sarah Ward didn't see them because they stood outside the confines of her perfectly ordered world. Or, perhaps more accurately, she didn't see them because she wasn't looking.

It was the first Friday in June, one week before her only daughter's high school graduation, and Sarah Ward was accepting an invitation to a sex toy party.

"Please, just come," said her best friend Marcy Owens. "No pun intended."

She tittered, and Sarah couldn't help but laugh, too. They were running the audio for the graduation rehearsal, and Sarah was glad they were tucked safely inside the announcer's booth at the football field. Then she experienced a moment of panic. Was the mic on? She checked. It wasn't, and she let out a breath. Imagine that: her daughter's entire graduating class hearing Marcy's invitation.

She didn't want to go, not really. She had so much to do the next day.

"Wait," Marcy said. "Let me guess. Your to-do list for tomorrow is two pages long. Your day is planned out, to the minute, and it does not include an evening party."

Sarah nodded. It was true: she'd already written out her to-do list and planned her day hour-by-hour. But, she always left room in her schedule for unexpected events—like a sex toy party.

This event was particularly unexpected for two reasons: one, because it doubled as a bachelorette celebration for Marcy, who was marrying a man who went by Stevie (and how sexual could he possibly be?). And two, Sarah realized the moment Marcy invited her that she hadn't had sex with her husband in … well, in longer than she could remember. And she certainly hadn't touched or even looked at a sex toy since before Amelia was born.

After making some quick mental calculations, Sarah said, "All right. If I get up a little early, I can shift some things around to make time for it. I'll be there. But I'm not sure if I'll buy anything."

"Oh, live a little!" Marcy said, and Sarah blushed.

"I—it's been a while, Marcy."

"What? I thought you had lovemaking scheduled into your weekly routine like, three days a week or something. Surely you and Donny use toys to spice things up."

Where in the world had Marcy gotten that impression? Sarah and Donny hadn't done the deed three times a week since they were teenagers. In fact, Sarah thought, awareness dawning, they were intimate on Saturdays only, in bed, after dark. In the missionary position. And even those weekly sessions had tapered off recently, as Sarah, president of the Saguaro High School Parent-Teacher Association, planned graduation. Sarah made a mental note to stop neglecting her sex life. This thought process should have been the first sign something was amiss.

After all, she'd worked relentlessly to perfectly manage and balance every aspect of her life—marriage, motherhood, career, hobbies, and exercise. It was nothing if not predictable. Because after Sarah's early childhood, predictability was a sign of safety.

"I'll be there," Sarah said again. She nodded. And then she thought that perhaps she could revisit Sex Saturday after returning home from the party. She'd took her little spiral notebook out of her purse and added *Marcy's Party* and *Sex Saturday* to her list.

That evening when Sarah mentioned to Amelia that she was going to a party with Marcy the next day, Amelia's mouth dropped open.

"Mom," she said, her hazel eyes—Donny's eyes—wide. "Jess said she's having a *sex* party. She's completely traumatized that her mom is inviting other moms over to look at dildos. I can't believe you're *going* to that."

"Amelia," Sarah said, shocked enough that she put a hand over her heart. "I never thought I'd hear that word come out of your mouth. Anyway. I'm sure you know your father and I—"

"Oh, gross, Mom! I know you guys did it *once*! But the way you two act, I thought it was a one-and-done kind of thing. You guys don't even hold hands or kiss or anything. Stop talking about this!"

Sarah was stunned.

Amelia's words held some humor. But they also held truth … which, when Sarah looked back on this conversation, was the second sign something was amiss.

The next day, which was the Saturday six days before her only child's high school graduation ceremony, Sarah found herself sitting in Marcy's living room, surrounded by giggling women. And dildos of varying shapes, sizes, and colors, with varying features and vibrational capabilities.

"Ohmygawwwd! Does that one actually have *glitter*?" Zelda Bankowitz, who had twin sons in Amelia's graduating class, picked up the item in question and examined it. Then she pretended to put the tip of it in her mouth and, while making thrusting movements, repeatedly poked the inside of her cheek with her tongue.

"Whaddya think, Sarah? How about buying one of these, eh? Take it home tonight and…"

She held it up, wiggling its giant tip.

Sarah blanched. "That's, um, a little bigger than I prefer."

The room erupted in laughter.

"You know, that's what I thought when I first saw it, too," said Hailey, the adolescent salesgirl who didn't look old enough to drive a car, much less sell these scandalous items. "But then I tried it. And let me tell you—"

"Ohmygawwwd!" Zelda said again. "Honey, wrap one of these up for Sarah, here. She'll take it."

From across the room, Marcy stared at Sarah, her eyes full of mischief. Sarah just shook her head, one part amused and one part embarrassed.

An hour later, as Sarah prepared to leave, Marcy grabbed her bag, opening the top and peering in to peruse the contents. "Got everything?"

"You're invading my privacy!" Sarah shrieked, grabbing it back.

"I thought we did away with privacy years ago," Marcy said. "When Amelia and Jess were in the fifth grade and I asked for your advice on hormone treatment."

Seventeen years ago, the two had met at a playdate for a local mothers' group. They'd since been through everything together: parenting, and exercise regimes, diets, meal plans, wine drinking… and most recently, Marcy's divorce and subsequent dating escapades.

Sarah handed the bag back and Marcy peered into it.

"Ooh, you got the enhancement gel. Remember, exterior use only,"

Marcy said, and Sarah repeated what Hailey had said when she showed it: "Fire in the hooole!"

"You know, you didn't have to get the glittery dildo."

"I know," Sarah said. "But I thought it wouldn't hurt to, you know, give it a whirl."

As she drove home, Sarah visualized the list she'd made for the next day:

Wake up: 7 a.m.

Drink coffee.

Complete the next module in photography class.

Wake Amelia: 9 a.m. sharp.

Cook and serve breakfast.

Leave for soup kitchen: 10 a.m.

Return library books on the way home.

Chores: fold laundry, mop the kitchen floor, put dinner in the slow cooker.

Study: 2 p.m.

Sarah realized then that she was already turning into her subdivision and she hadn't even made it to three p.m.

It was time to switch gears, mentally. Sex. It had been so long since she initiated sex that Sarah wasn't sure exactly how to go about it. She didn't think Donny even realized Marcy's party was a sex toy party, so it was unlikely he was expecting her to come home bearing gifts.

Should she just hand him the bag? No, she should change into the lingerie she'd bought. She pulled into the driveway and noticed immediately that with the exception of Amelia's bedroom light, the house was dark. She wondered if Donny was already asleep.

If he was, should she wake him? Maybe she should save the sex toys for another night. Or, maybe that idea was actually an invention of procrastination. Sarah wondered why she was so nervous. They'd been married for two decades, and they'd been having sex for longer than that.

But, come to think of it, when was the last time they'd been intimate? How long *had* it been? Too long. In fact, it had been so long that doing so now would probably feel beyond awkward. How would he respond, tonight, when she produced the bright purple vibrator the consultant had said was, "Not only waterproof, but disappointment-proof, too"?

This was the moment Sarah Ward's realization began.

Standing in the garage, one hand on the doorknob to go inside and the other gripping a bag of overpriced sex toys, she realized she was terrified of what her husband's reaction would be. And if that wasn't a sign something was not quite right, what was?

The door flew open.

Sarah jumped back, and put her hand on her chest when she saw that Amelia stood on the other side.

"I heard the garage door," Amelia said.

Her gaze landed on Sarah's bag.

"Wow, Mom. That bag looks really full. Heavy. Like you bought some … *big* stuff."

Sarah felt her face start to burn.

"I can't even put into words how inappropriate this is," she said, even as a smile tugged at one corner of her mouth. "Shouldn't you be sleeping?"

"I waited up for you," Amelia said. "I wanted to see if you had fun at the party. It looks like you did. But that was only the beginning."

Sarah put her head down and brushed past Amelia into the house.

"Wow, Mom," she said again. "You're embarrassed. This is fun."

"This is *so* not fun," Sarah said, although the other side of her mouth was heading upward, too.

"So, are you going to, like, go seduce Dad right now?"

"Go to bed, young lady. We have a busy day tomorrow and you need your rest."

Squeaking with muted laughter, Amelia trotted up the stairs. Just before going into her room, she whisper-yelled, "Have fun, Mom!" and then, "This is so weird."

Sarah couldn't imagine what life would be like when Amelia left for college in a few short weeks. At the moment, Sarah was half-questioning her decision to sign Amelia up for a summer session. But it was all part of the master plan. Sarah had put in place every piece of the puzzle to increase Amelia's chances of getting a college scholarship. The hard work paid off. Amelia had a full ride to Northern Arizona University, where she'd be a member of the track team.

As she walked up the stairs to the bedroom she shared with Donny, Sarah thought about how she had carefully orchestrated every moment of Amelia's life to ensure she grew up into a kind, hard-working, determined young lady while making beautiful memories. And she'd gone so far as to cultivate new hobbies for herself (scrapbooking and Italian cooking) and to prepare for a new career (photography) so she'd have something to do when Amelia moved out.

But what she hadn't done was plan for the changes her marriage would go through. She'd just put it on autopilot, assuming it would remain the same forever. Yes, she'd planned bi-weekly date nights and weekly sex nights. But as Amelia got older and her schedule became more intense, those were the first to go by the wayside.

Before going into her own bedroom, she paused and took a deep breath. Darkness greeted her when she stepped inside. Donny was already asleep. Momentarily, Sarah considered scrapping the whole seduction idea. She could just slip between the sheets and pretend she hadn't just spent the equivalent of a weekly grocery bill on battery-powered toys and flavored lubricant. Strawberries and whipped cream. What had she been thinking?

If Donny woke up now, he'd see her there, frozen just inside the room. He'd barely be able to make out her silhouette in the dim light.

When was the last time they had sex?

Was it—no, this was impossible. They definitely hadn't done it in the past several weekends. Possibly even months. There'd been a statewide education policy conference in Phoenix, an orientation at Amelia's college, and, well, *life*. There'd been a track meet at one point, but no hot hotel sex on that weekend's itinerary. She'd insisted that Amelia stay in the hotel room with her and Donny, rather than in the room Amelia's teammates were sharing) so she'd be rested for the track meet. Sarah's hand made its way to her forehead as she ran backwards through all the recent weekends, weekdays, and months … and realized she couldn't even remember the last time she and Donny had acted like anything other than roommates.

She was torn: one part of her thought, *Something must be done about this, immediately*. She imagined leaping onto the bed at this very moment, straddling her husband, and having her way with him. The other part wasn't sure how Donny would respond. She imagined crawling into bed as quietly as possible and going straight to sleep.

But, the first part reasoned, if she did that, would they ever have sex again?

There was a third option: Sarah could sneak into the bathroom and call her sister, Margaret. Margaret would know what to do. She was an expert on all things related to the opposite sex—always had been. How many times had she advised Sarah on these matters? Exactly how to angle her head to get Donny to kiss her the first time, precisely what to say to let him know she was ready to go all the way, even how to convince him they should use the plates with scalloped edges at their wedding.

Donny's breathing remained even as Sarah tiptoed past him and into the bathroom. Then she realized she didn't have her phone. In all the excitement, she'd left it in the car. She could picture it there, now, tucked into the cupholder.

What would Margaret say if she were standing here now?

Get over it, Sarah. You've been with Donny since the beginning of time. Why wouldn't he want to have sex with you? Put on your big girl panties, get in there, and you-know-what your husband.

Margaret always used the f-word, which Sarah found amusing and appalling at the same time.

Smiling now, and with her confidence slightly bolstered by the imaginary pep talk from her sister, Sarah took off the practical jeans and sweater she was wearing and slipped into the lingerie she'd bought at Marcy's party.

She stood in front of the mirror. Her blond hair curled around her face and shoulders, and her eyes matched the cornflower blue of the see-through nighty. She'd spent enough time outside this spring that her arms were tan, and enough time at the gym that they were toned, too. Yes, her waistline had lost just a bit of that hourglass shape, but she was still trim and fit.

Why wouldn't her husband want to have sex with her?

If Margaret were here, standing in the bathroom with her, she'd say something about how Sarah was a fine piece of ass or how she looked totally—well, Sarah couldn't even bring herself to think of the word in its entirety. Maybe she could soften it: Sex-able? No, that wouldn't do. Sex-able didn't have quite the same ring to it. Anyway. It was time to pull out all the stops. Or something like that. Was there a bawdy way of saying that? Probably. She could Google it.

When Sarah found herself reaching for her phone, she froze. Not only was her phone in the car, but she recognized procrastination for what it was. She'd never get Donny in the sack if she hid in the bathroom Googling slang phrases for going all out. Sexing it up. She took a deep breath. Maybe a glass of wine would help. But she was in her lingerie now, and what if Amelia came downstairs while she was in the kitchen?

"I'm going to brush my teeth," she said to her reflection.

"Sarah," Donny called, then. She jumped. He was awake. "Are you okay?"

"Yeah," Sarah called back. "I'm fine!"

"You've been in there a really long time."

It was now or never. Although, she could brush her teeth. She *should.* Sarah closed her eyes and consciously relaxed her shoulder muscles. She opened the bathroom door. She closed it. Finally, she opened it again and marched into the bedroom, concentrating on her posture and her breathing.

Later, Sarah would reflect on this moment and think she should have researched synonyms for surprised. Shocked, astonished, amazed, bewildered … because Donny's expression, illuminated in the light from the bedside lamp he'd turned on, showed all of those things when he noticed what she was wearing.

The younger Donny would have practically jumped off the bed and come toward her at warp speed, eager to get his hands on her. But this Donny, after recovering from his shock, seemed uncertain of what to do. He remained motionless, his back against the headboard, his legs crossed at the ankles, his hands folded in his lap.

A tiny flare of anger went up in Sarah's mind, but she quickly snuffed it out, acknowledging it for what it was: fear of rejection. She lifted her arms, palms up, and said, "Well? What do you think?"

Donny cleared his throat. He uncrossed his legs and then recrossed them. "Wow."

The fear dissipated, just the tiniest bit. "Well, I guess 'wow' is good."

"It's been a while." He cleared his throat again.

Sarah nodded, feeling even more self-conscious. "I know. It has. Maybe I shouldn't have—"

She was smoothing her hands over her stomach, and managed to resist the urge to turn right around and go back into the bathroom. She could put on sweatpants. And have that wine.

"No," Donny said. "No, you should have. I'm just surprised, that's all. You look really nice, Sarah."

Finally, he did stand up. He approached her slowly, like she was a wild animal that might get spooked and take off. For some reason, this situation brought to mind the time when the four of them—Sarah, her sisters, and Donny—had found an injured rabbit at the base of the old cottonwood tree. It had lain so still they weren't even sure if it was alive. Then Donny walked toward it and it leapt into action, its back legs moving up and down so fast the children stepped back, startled. After that, he moved slowly, cautiously, closer, until he managed to sit down next to it. When he lifted it in his hands, the rabbit didn't even struggle.

He was standing in front of her now, and he took her shoulders in his hands. "You're so beautiful."

It came out in a whisper, which, for some reason, Sarah found very touching. So much so that she started to cry.

"What's the matter?" Donny pulled her against him, resting his chin on top of her head. As always, he tried to lighten the mood with a joke: "Geez, I've never seen anything like it: a wife who cries when her husband says she's beautiful."

Laughing, she tipped her head back to look at him. "It's not that. It's just that I feel like it's been way too long. We've both been so busy and you've been working so hard and Amelia's had so many practices and meets and—"

"Shh," Donny said. He kissed her, then, and a little flame started up at her center.

Well, this is nice, Sarah thought. It had been a long time since she felt that sensation. She kissed her husband back, relishing in the familiar-yet-unfamiliar feeling of his lips on hers. His hands were on her waist, bringing their hips together, and now they traveled up her torso and into her hair.

"Let's take this horizontal," he said.

It was one of their inside jokes, and it dissolved whatever was left of Sarah's awkwardness. Sarah backed Donny up to the bed, and he pulled her down on top of him. They kissed for a few minutes more, and then Donny flipped Sarah onto her back. His lips roamed over her neck and her collarbone, and then his hands came up her torso to cup her breasts.

She trailed her fingertips along his back. When she realized he was still fully dressed, she tugged his shirt up and over his head and tossed it off to the side. She could feel the warmth of his skin through the fabric of her lingerie. When she was trying it on in Marcy's bathroom, Marcy stood outside the door asking for detailed descriptions.

At one point, Sarah said, "I don't know why women spend so much on this stuff. We wear it for, like, a couple of minutes and then we take it off. I'm probably spending thirty dollars per minute on this one outfit."

"Then get something crotchless," Marcy said through the door. "You'll never have to take it off. If your hot and steamy sex session lasts for an hour, it's only a dollar per minute. That's a pretty good investment, if you ask me."

Despite her misgivings, Sarah had followed Marcy's advice and found something that not only had crotchless panties, but also was thin enough that the fabric over her breasts could slide easily down to reveal them. And not that she was watching the clock now, when her husbands head was between her thighs, but she thought she could make this last an hour. She ran her fingers through Donny's hair and urged him gently back up so they were face to face.

"I love this outfit," he whispered. "It's sexy *and* practical."

"I thought so, too," she said.

Sarah reached down between them and was surprised to find that Donny wasn't hard. Not even a little. Things down there were about as non-aroused as they could get.

"Everything okay?" she asked.

This had happened so rarely during their marriage that she wasn't quite sure what to do.

"Yeah," he said. "Just a bit rusty, you know. Like the tin man in *Wizard of Oz*. I need some loosening up."

Sarah nodded, but that feeling of unease had returned. Still, she was determined. She began stroking him, slowly and gently.

"Harder," he whispered.

She went harder, but still, nothing. His kissing gained ferocity, as if he were trying to will himself into being turned on. It didn't seem to work. The flame in Sarah's abdomen turned into a rock, heavy and solid.

"Donny?"

"Hmm?"

"Do you want to keep going?"

"Let's just give it a few more minutes," he said. "Out of practice."

He had stopped kissing her and had buried his face in her hair. She didn't know if it was because he was concentrating or because he was hoping the scent of her shampoo would turn him on. Her arm was getting tired and she felt stupid, here in her expensive lingerie, pumping away at a husband who obviously wasn't into it.

"It's okay," she said, trying for a reassuring tone. "We can stop."

Donny flopped onto his back then, and let out a huge sigh.

"I'm so sorry, Sarah," he said. "It's just—"

"It's fine," Sarah said, even though it wasn't. "You don't have to apologize. I know it's been a while. A long while. I probably caught you off guard."

"No, it's not that," Donny said. "I—"

"You don't have to explain," Sarah said. "It happens. I'm just used to you being such a, you know, stallion. But I guess we're getting older."

She sat up, patted him on the thigh, and went into the bathroom. For a moment, she imagined sinking down, her back against the cupboards below her sink. She imagined putting her head down on her knees and crying. Sobbing, actually. But she didn't do that.

Instead, her movements wooden, she removed the lingerie and put on her sweatpants. They were far more comfortable, anyway, and she'd worn them for hours and hours—days, even—which meant they'd yielded an excellent return on investment. She picked up the lingerie, holding it between her pointer finger and her thumb like it was a stinky sock. Then she dropped it into the trash can next to the toilet. When she went back into the bedroom, Donny was in bed, his back to her. If he wasn't actually asleep, he was definitely pretending to be, so she turned off the light on her nightstand and lay down.

Sleep came in snatches that night, and when it did, Sarah dreamed of her childhood home, the creek bubbling through the meadow and her best friend, Donny, laying next to her, the two of them staring up at the sky.

———

DONNY WAS GONE when Sarah's alarm went off at seven Sunday morning. Sarah knew before opening her eyes. She could feel his absence just as well as she could feel the sheets against her skin.

Sometimes he went for donuts on Sundays. But he almost always woke her up to tell her he was going. Didn't he? A sense of dread started to form, tightening Sarah's throat, and she swallowed. Then, telling herself the dread was a fabrication, she got out of bed.

She was on her second cup of coffee when Donny got home. He didn't even come inside, and, too nervous now to study, Sarah did what she did whenever she felt overwhelmed with nervous energy: she dusted and scrubbed and cleaned until the whole house shone. Donny loved a clean house. She vacuumed the blinds and even threw some of the drapes into the washing machine. She woke up Amelia and started the waffles. Donny loved waffles.

Finally, he walked in just as Sarah was taking out the trash, and they both froze. They did that awkward dance, where each of them tried to duck around the other, but they kept trying to go to the same side. Finally, Donny grabbed her upper arms and bent down just slightly so their eyes were on level.

"Sarah," he said.

"Donny," she said.

"Can we talk?"

"You're the one who ran out of here this morning." Nerves were making her grumpy.

He released her shoulders and looked down.

"Haven't you noticed that I've been getting up early, going for a run, almost every morning?"

Had he? "Have you?"

Exasperation made his voice sound tight. "Yes."

"I—"

"You hadn't noticed," he said. Now, something like dry amusement was mixed in with the exasperation. But when his eyes met hers again, she saw something else: hurt.

Upstairs, the shower turned off, which meant Amelia would be down any minute.

"Look," Donny said, inclining his head toward the stairs, toward their daughter. "This isn't really the ideal time to talk. But just give it some thought, okay?"

"Give what some thought?" Sarah was only half-pretending to be perplexed. The events of the previous night and this morning were making alarm bells sound in her mind.

"The fact that you don't notice me. That you haven't noticed me in … well, in a long time."

She nodded, opened her mouth to respond, and then closed it when Amelia came bounding down the stairs, her ringlets bouncing.

"Organic, gluten-free waffles," she said after an exaggerated inhale. "My favorite."

For the first time ever, Sarah thought she detected a bit of sarcasm. Donny raised an eyebrow at her and sat down at his spot at the table.

CHAPTER TWO

DURING THE NEXT SEVERAL DAYS, Sarah continued making her to-do lists. She continued playing the role of Amelia's mom, PTA President, Graduation Organizer Extraordinaire. She responded to texts, made phone calls, and picked up the stage decorations. She was absolutely immersed in a blur of of frantic pre-graduation activity.

Every so often, Donny's words—"give it some thought"—floated through her awareness, and she kept telling herself she'd think about what he'd said. As soon as she got through the next task. As soon as she got through graduation.

One evening, when Donny came home from work, Sarah noticed he looked tired. It had been so long since she asked how his day was that the words came out stunted and brittle. Just as he began to answer, Sarah's phone rang. It was someone at the high school, and Sarah figured it was about graduation. She held up her hand to signal for Donny to pause his story. She answered the phone, and before she knew it, Donny was walking away.

Now it was Friday, the day of Amelia's graduation. Things would certainly be better after this. They had to be. Her PTA duties would be over. Duties like putting the finishing touches on the candy leis each graduate would receive as part of the ceremony, which she was doing now. The truth was, crafting four hundred leis was taking way longer than she'd expected. It was the eleventh hour and she was scrambling to get them done before this evening.

"This project wasn't even my idea," she said out loud. No one was there to hear her, and she kept muttering. "It was Marcy's idea. And then, surprise! She was too busy to make them. Wedding plans. And now, here I am, making four hundred leis, alone. Only seventy-two more to go."

But this line of thought was a runaway train. It wouldn't do any good to let the resentment take over. She could have asked for help (or accepted the help other parents had offered), organized some kind of lei-making event or party. But it was almost as much work to do that as it was to just make the things herself.

Sarah sighed, and looked at the clock. Only thirty minutes until Margaret was scheduled to arrive ... which meant she'd probably show up in an hour. Which would still (barely) give them time to run their errands before heading to the high school for the graduation. They had to be early so they could get good seats while Amelia lined up.

"Mom? Are you okay?"

Amelia came bounding downstairs. She'd probably heard the tail end of Sarah's rant and now, found Sarah at the kitchen table, twisting a strip of blue cellophane between her hands. Sarah cleared her throat and looked at her daughter, who had the same crease between her eyebrows Donny often did.

"I'm fine, sweetie. Just running through all the things we need to get done today, before graduation."

"I made a list," Amelia said. She held up a piece of paper, decorated with doodles of hearts and graduation caps.

"All those life skills I've taught you are going to pay off in college," Sarah said, and the two of them said in unison, "Lists are a girl's best friend."

Even in her own funk, Sarah couldn't help but notice Amelia's energy seemed a little low. "What's wrong, honey?"

"I wish Auntie Hannah and Grandma were coming today. It's weird not having them here for my graduation."

"I know it is," Sarah said. "But you know Grandma can't travel this far, all the way from Wyoming to Arizona, and she can't be left alone. Aunt Margaret will be here in thirty minutes—"

"Or an hour."

"Or an hour, yes. And she will bring enough festive energy to make up for it. You won't even notice Auntie Hannah and Grandma aren't here. Plus, you're going to be so busy you wouldn't get to spend much time with them, anyway."

"You're right," Amelia said. "You guys would be up late chatting, and I'd be heading off to Grad Night right after dinner. But they'd stay the whole weekend, wouldn't they?"

"I don't know," Sarah said.

The doorbell rang, and Sarah looked at the clock again. Was Margaret actually—the door opened before Sarah even had the chance to finish her thought, and Amelia bounded over to greet her aunt.

"Aunt Margaret!"

"Amelia Bear! The graduate! How are you, sweetie? You look beautiful! Your hair! It's gorgeous!"

And just like that, Amelia transformed. Margaret had always had the ability to make people feel loved. Being in her presence felt like being wrapped in a warm blanket, one of those really soft ones with fake wool on one side. When Sarah had first come to live with Mama Katherine, Margaret and Hannah, it was Margaret who gave her the real sense of home. Now, her job as an architect kept her so busy they rarely saw one another. But when they did, it was a breath of fresh air on a clear spring day.

"And you!" Margaret said to Sarah, then. "Aren't you as beautiful as ever?"

They hugged, tightly, and then Margaret held her at arm's length.

"I can tell you're still going to that godawful gym. It's doing wonders for your muscles." She squeezed Sarah's shoulder. "Where's the man of the house? I saw his car outside, but he's ducking for cover, isn't he? All this hugging is just too much for Donny."

"I'll take a hug from you any day, Margaret." Donny came down the stairs now and wrapped Margaret in his arms, dwarfing her.

"It's good to see you, Donny," Margaret said. "Although I trust you'll be hiding in your bedroom tonight while Sarah and I sit around and gossip about all of our old high school friends."

"They're my high school friends, too," Donny said. "Maybe I'll crash your party."

He was smiling at Margaret, and Sarah wondered how long it had been since he'd smiled at her that way. Then, the moment was over.

"You bring a suitcase?" Donny said to Margaret.

"It's outside," Margaret said.

"And I'll bet you can't carry it," Donny said. "You had to charm some poor soul into loading it for you, right?"

"You're going to have to get married soon if you want to keep traveling, Aunt Margaret."

Only a trained observer could catch the tiny beat of silence between Amelia's comment and Margaret's response. But Sarah knew her sister, and she noticed Margaret's mouth snapped closed for the briefest second before she said, "It's my mega-watt smile. And now, I'm going to use it on you, Donny. Would you be so kind as to grab that suitcase for me and haul it upstairs? It's in the driveway. Then I'll do a quick freshen up before we head out for the big event."

"No rental car?" Donny said as he walked toward the front door.

"I grabbed a taxi," Margaret said.

"A taxi?" Donny said. "No hot rod this time?"

It was true—Margaret almost always rented something impractical, like a convertible roadster or a huge truck.

"Nope," Margaret said. "Decided to take a taxi." Then she smiled, too brightly, and said, "Thanks for taking it upstairs."

Sarah made a mental note to ask Margaret about the taxi and the over-bright smile, later, when they were alone.

"What is this?" Margaret said, motioning to the pile of cellophane and candy on the table.

"Candy leis," Sarah said, letting some irritation creep into her voice.

"Candy leis?" Margaret said. "For an entire army?"

"For an entire graduating class," Sarah said. She shrugged as if it were no big deal, and added, "I've got seventy-two left to make."

"Geez. Like you don't have enough to do, already."

"I know," Sarah said. "So since you're early, help me finish these so we can get out of here."

Again, there was an almost-unnoticeable pause and then Margaret said, "Let me just freshen up first. Long travel day."

Sarah nodded and resumed lei-making as Donny came back downstairs.

"Big day today, huh?" he said to Amelia. "I've got a meeting in an hour, but I'll see you at graduation. Okay? And do something about that hair."

He kissed the top of her head.

Amelia, all dimples, wild honey-brown curls, and adoration, smiled up at him. "Okay, Dad. Better not be late."

"Wouldn't miss it."

Sarah stared at Donny as he walked through the kitchen, and then she stared at the door after it closed behind him.

Margaret cleared her throat, startling Sarah out of her stupor. When Sarah looked at her, she realized her sister had noticed everything: Donny's quick exit, the lack of physical affection between them, and more than likely, Sarah's pensive mood.

The two of them had always shared a strange, almost-psychic connection, and even now, they had a quick unspoken conversation in which Margaret asked, *"What was up with that?"* And Sarah responded, *"What?!"* as if she didn't know what Margaret meant. Margaret rolled her eyes, pressing for more, saying Sarah couldn't get away with pretending something wasn't wrong. And Sarah conceded, but said they'd have to talk about it later. Margaret understood. After all, a woman couldn't talk about her marriage problems in front of her child.

That settled, Sarah said, "I'm so glad you're early. Have a seat."

For now, Sarah would tuck away the new train of thought regarding her marriage. She'd put it in the roundhouse and come back to it later. She had to focus on these leis, and on mothering and the first item on Amelia's list: *Stop at Full of Beans for a coffee.*

Next, they had to attend a quick PTA meeting about graduation, and then they'd go for lunch, and finally, Amelia would get her hair and makeup and nails done. Today, Sarah thought, would be full of memories Amelia could file under "Great Childhood" in her mental filing cabinet.

Sarah had more than enough negative childhood memories of her own, and she'd spent the last seventeen years ensuring Amelia would have as few as possible.

"Onward," she said, as much to her daughter as to herself.

Sarah didn't miss the looks Margaret threw her way throughout the day, between sips of coffee and bites of Romano's five-cheese pizza they ate on the restaurant's covered patio. She didn't miss the assessing gazes, either: Margaret watched her carefully as she drove through town, and as they got the callouses scraped off their feet.

Countless times, Sarah realized how grateful she was for Amelia's presence, and countless times, she reminded herself that Amelia would be gone this evening. So she geared up for the questions that were sure to come her way, as pointed as the looks and glances, and just louder than Margaret's unspoken thoughts.

They headed home to change for graduation, and after kissing both Sarah and Margaret on the cheek, Amelia ran upstairs to put on her dress.

"Want some iced tea while we regroup for the feature event?" Sarah said.

"Sure," Margaret said. "And then you can tell me what the hell's going on with you and Donny."

Sarah gulped.

"I heard that," Margaret said.

Sarah didn't bother denying it. She took down glasses—one of them chipped from the time Amelia dropped the cinnamon container on it while she was making cookies—and filled them with ice.

Margaret, her head in the fridge, said, "Don't you have a pitcher or something?"

"Top right," Sarah said. "It's blue. You gave it to me, remember? Housewarming present?"

"Right," Margaret said.

She extracted the pitcher, which she'd bought at an arts fair in Taos, New Mexico, and handed it to Sarah, who took her time pouring. If she took long enough, maybe she could avoid the conversation that was about to happen.

They sat down at the table, and Sarah started chattering. She talked about the ceremony, and said she hoped the kids would line up like they were supposed to. She talked about grad night and said she hoped no one would bring liquor on the school buses.

Mid-sentence, Margaret laid a hand over hers.

"What's going on with you and Donny?"

"What?" Sarah said, even though she'd known this was coming.

"You heard me."

Sarah felt her chin beginning to wobble, and she pressed her lips together.

"Is it that bad?" Margaret said. "How is that even possible? You guys are the couple of the century."

Before Sarah could respond, the door opened and Donny walked in. Sarah simultaneously wondered how her hair looked, and snatched her hand back from Margaret's. She stood up, and her chair made a loud scraping sound against the floor before tilting back.

"You're home early," she said, righting the chair and straightening her shirt, even though she was positive it didn't need straightening. "I thought you were going to meet us at the graduation. Everything okay?"

He nodded, and while he began emptying his lunchbox, she rushed over to the pantry and began getting out the ingredients for his daily snack.

"You don't have to do that, Sarah," he said. "I'm not hungry."

Hands full, she stilled. "Oh. Um, okay. I'll just put this stuff away, then."

Well, this was strange. She'd made him a snack every workday for the past twenty years. And he'd always eaten it. Hadn't he? After putting everything away, Sarah leaned a hip against the kitchen counter while Donny washed his hands. She could feel Margaret taking this all in.

"Everything okay?" Sarah said.

"What?" He turned off the water. "Yeah, it's fine. I'm just not hungry. Is Amelia all set for the big afternoon?"

"Yeah," Sarah said. "We took care of all the errands today."

She held up her hands and wiggled her fingers so he could see her fingernails. "Matching polish and everything."

"Great," Donny said, without really looking at her. "I'll go change."

Huh. Just last week, Sarah thought, this would have seemed like a perfectly normal conversation. But in light of the failed sexcapade, Donny's request for Sarah to pay attention, and everything she'd noticed during the past few days, Sarah thought it seemed strange and disconnected.

Minutes later, the four of them piled into Donny's car. Sarah insisted that Margaret ride in front, and she sat in the back with Amelia. Margaret's phone vibrated every couple of seconds, and she checked it each time, letting out little groans and big groans and finally vowing to shut it off for the entire weekend—just as soon as the graduation ceremony started.

"You're very popular," Sarah said.

"No, I'm not," Margaret said. "I just have lots of needy clients who believe my world revolves around them."

Sarah refrained from saying, "Well doesn't it?" because it did. Margaret was a workhorse. She was so in-demand that clients flew her from one side of the country to the other so they could meet with her in person, explain what they wanted built, and show her empty lots or old buildings they envisioned having remodeled. Margaret loved it. She was happy and fulfilled and didn't need a husband or children to make her more so.

Sarah, on the other hand, had wanted nothing more than to raise a family. Although she barely remembered the years before she'd come to live with Mama Katherine, she got flashes now and then, every single one infused with fear and chaos. She always imagined building a haven-like home and raising half a dozen kids, but she'd never gotten pregnant again after Amelia was born. And that was okay. She figured it was some message from God or the Universe that she would be a better mother if she just had the one child. She *was* a great mother, and she did build a haven for her family of three. She poured every single ounce of herself into that role.

Margaret's voice cut into her thoughts, then.

"Sarah."

Her sister's tone implied that she'd already said Sarah's name several times. Amelia was staring at her, and Donny watched her, too, in the rearview mirror.

"Sorry," she said. "Lost in my thoughts. What's up?"

"I just got a text from Hannah," Margaret said.

"And?" Sarah said. It was probably graduation-related. Sarah was infamous for not checking her text messages. She'd made a vow to herself that she wouldn't be one of those distracted parents who couldn't stop looking at her phone.

"Mama's sick," Margaret said. "Hannah's taking her to the hospital."

Amelia put a hand over her mouth. Donny glanced at Margaret, then at Sarah in the rearview mirror. Then he cursed when traffic stopped in front of him and he had to slam on the brakes.

"What kind of sick?" Sarah said. There wasn't any reason to panic. Not yet. People got sick all the time.

"Not sure," Margaret said as her fingers flew over the surface of her phone. She was, undoubtedly, grilling their sister for more details. "Unconscious. We won't know anything right away. Possibly a stroke."

"A stroke?" Amelia gripped Sarah's hand and Sarah thought it would be easy to give in to panic. But she wouldn't mar her daughter's high school graduation day with anxiety. She squeezed Amelia's hand in what she hoped was a reassuring way.

"She's on her way to the hospital," she said. "I'm sure she'll be in good hands there. Auntie Hannah will make sure of it."

When Margaret had used her personality to make Sarah feel like an immediate member of the Ward family, Hannah had ensured all of her needs were met from the moment she arrived on the doorstep, a cardboard box in her arms. She'd bossed Margaret into taking the box to the bedroom they'd share, and she sat Sarah down in the kitchen and made her a sloppy peanut butter and jelly sandwich. Sarah had cried tears of joy as she sat at that table for the first time, and Margaret had returned a few moments later to turn those tears into laughter. And Mama Katherine, half in tears herself, had wrapped Sarah in her arms and held her for a long, long time. It was all Sarah needed to feel like she was a part of something.

Sarah realized now that Mama had let her new sisters tend to her so they'd feel included, too. Mama always knew just what to do. She was a strong, sturdy woman and Sarah had always assumed she was invincible, immortal, even. Now, she was sick. She'd never been sick a day in her life. Taking a deep breath, and then another, Sarah reminded herself that the best thing to do was to remain calm. This was Amelia's graduation day.

She must not have fully convinced herself, though, because when they arrived at the high school and got out of the car, Donny put his hands on her shoulders and leaned down so they were eye to eye.

"Are you sure you're okay?"

She nodded. Then Donny did something completely unexpected: he hugged her.

"Mama Katherine is tough," he said. "Tougher than nails. She'll be okay."

Even while she internalized what he was saying, Sarah was thinking about how good he smelled, and how much she missed being intimate with him.

"I know she will," she said. "You're right. She's tough. And she wouldn't want us to spend today worrying."

Donny kissed the top of Sarah's head and she gave him one more squeeze.

———

"SO, BIG DAY, RIGHT?" Margaret sat at one end of the couch, her feet tucked up under her and her hands wrapped around a mug of tea.

"The biggest," Sarah said. She sipped her own tea, which was still too hot, and set it on the side table. "A visit from my sister, my daughter's high school graduation, and my mother in the hospital."

"Ha," Margaret said. "That last one is not the best but at least it was just dehydration."

"You really should join us for our trip up there this summer," Sarah said.

"I think I could fit that in," Margaret said. "I'd have to move some things around."

Sarah nodded, and already, she was thinking of ways they could help Mama Katherine. They could clean, and they could cook a bunch of freezer meals for Hannah so she didn't feel like she had to make twenty-one meals each week.

"Sarah, can I ask you something?"

"Anything," Sarah said, turning so she faced her sister head on. "You know that."

Margaret took a deep breath. "Is everything okay with you and Donny?"

Sarah blinked. "What do you mean?"

Margaret shrugged. "I mean, you guys seem so ... so platonic? Is that the right word? You're almost painfully polite to each other and I haven't seen you touch all afternoon, aside from that one hug after we got the text from Hannah. I mean, you guys used to hold hands all the time, or he'd swat your bottom or whatever. Now, today, it's just not the same. Did you have a fight?"

Sarah's initial reaction was to close off, or to say something like, "Of *course* we didn't have a fight," which was true.

She and Donny never fought.

She knew from experience that fighting between parents could make an entire family miserable. Her own biological parents had proven that, one drunken fistfight after another (that was one detail she did remember). When she was six and the social workers took her from their home, she vowed that she'd never fight with her husband. And when she first told her new mother, Mama Katherine, about her philosophy on relationships, Mama Katherine laughed and said, "You'll grow out of that, my dear."

But she hadn't. From the time she met Donny she had let all the little things go ... and weren't they all little things?

She'd seen some of her friends nitpick their spouses about food splatter in microwaves or dirty socks on the floor or clean laundry not put away. Marcy, who was now divorced, had constantly hounded her husband about his clothing choices.

Sarah never complained about the way Donny pushed trash down into the garbage can until it was so full she practically had to pry the bag out with a crowbar. She never complained about how he was almost always late coming home, or how he left unrinsed dishes in the sink rather than putting them in the dishwasher.

She'd rather let those things go than create a world where no one could ever do anything right. She'd lived in that world for six years.

"No, we didn't have a fight," Sarah said.

The fact that their marriage wasn't as romantic or passion-filled as it once had been wasn't a secret, not really. But saying it out loud, to someone else ... that would prove that Sarah had failed. She was the family woman, the marriage expert. For years, she'd been one half of Sarah-and-Donny. Saying, out loud, that that structure was crumbling (and it had to be if they couldn't even be intimate, right?)—would change everything.

"Wow, there's a lot going on in that pretty little head of yours," Margaret said then. "You didn't speak for, like, four minutes. It's amazing, I can practically see your wheels turning."

Sarah laughed. "Sorry. It's just that I can't remember the last time Donny and I had a conversation long enough to result in a fight, you know? I was noticing today that we haven't talked much lately. I was thinking about what it will be like when Amelia's gone. Strange."

Margaret nodded. "It seems—from what my friends say, anyway—that couples often lose their connection as their children get older. Parenting takes so much time and energy. Romance falls by the wayside."

"That's true," Sarah said.

"But if I know you, you scheduled regular date nights, right?"

Sarah couldn't help but feel like the was a dig as well as a compliment.

"Anyway," Margaret said before she could respond, "you're probably extra-busy. We dropped off that casserole at your friend's house earlier, and you were practically in charge of the graduation."

"Yes, I was," Sarah said. "But I planned it so that I wouldn't have to be involved on the day of."

"You had a walkie-talkie at your seat," Margaret said. "You were so busy checking in on everyone that you hardly had time to watch."

"But it was perfect."

"It was perfect. But it's a lot of, I don't know, time, a lot of pressure. It has to be hard on your marriage."

Not that Margaret knew anything about marriage. She was so focused on her career, it was like the spouse that couldn't talk back. But Sarah didn't say this, partly because it would be confrontational and partly because Margaret was sensitive about this issue. And partly because Margaret was right.

Instead, she said, "I should try harder."

Now Margaret laughed. "That's not quite what I meant. I think you're trying too hard at everything else. The answer isn't in trying harder, it's in putting more focus on your marriage. I think."

"It'll be better once Amelia goes off to college. This last year, senior year, has just been a whirlwind. Anyway. Enough about me. Tell me about work. Any cool trips coming up?"

"Actually, yes." Margaret shifted on the couch picked up her tea. "I'm going to Seattle next week, for a conference. And then, the following week, I'll be in Colorado to meet with a new client. And then the following week, I'll be in San Antonio."

"Wow," Sarah said. "You're such a jet-setter. I'm jealous."

"Gotta do it while I still can," Margaret said.

Her unspoken thought, that she had to travel now, before she was saddled with a husband and children, hung between them in the air. It was the one point on which they disagreed. It only made sense, considering where they'd come from. Margaret's own biological mother had given birth to her at fifteen.

"Her life was ruined before it even got started," Margaret often said as they were growing up. She was determined to have a career, to live a good life, before starting a family.

"That's wonderful," Sarah said. "Buy me a Christmas ornament in Seattle, will you? I've never been. And send me a selfie from the Space Needle."

"Oh, you know I will," Margaret said. "If I sent out Christmas cards, they'd be full of selfies I took at famous landmarks all year long. Nothing like the masterpieces you send out."

"Hardly," Sarah said, thinking she'd keep it a secret that she spent a small fortune having her cards professionally designed and printed each year. And that wasn't including what she spent on the photography.

"So," Margaret said. Her gaze was intense now, which made Sarah nervous. "I think you should initiate sex with Donny tonight. I think it's time. You should go in there, strip down, and tell him to take you like he did when you were teenagers in the back of Mama Katherine's pickup truck."

"Nice," Sarah said, remembering that awful, post-sex-toy-party failed session earlier that week. "I think I'm too old for that kind of sex."

"Are you?"

"Well, probably not. I just feel old."

"When is the last time the two of you bumped uglies?" Margaret said.

"Could you not use that phrase? It's awful."

"Fine," Margaret said. "It's just that I know how you feel about the f-word. When is the last time the two of you made whoopee?"

Sarah rolled her eyes.

"Wait," Margaret said. "Why aren't you answering?"

"I think I'm going to call it a night." Sarah stood up, leaving her mug on the table.

"Oh, don't you dare, Sarah Jane Ward. Don't you dare. Answer the question."

Sarah could feel a blush creeping up her neck. Margaret always had been a good interrogator.

"This is like that time you talked me into telling you where I'd hidden your stash of jelly beans."

"It is," Margaret said. "And do you remember the outcome?"

"I do," Sarah said. "It took you three hours, but I finally caved and told you, under threat of dismemberment."

"Don't make me take it that far. Sit down and answer the question."

"Wow, you have a great mom voice." Sarah sat. "That's going to come in handy when you have teenagers."

"*If.* Now answer the question."

"I—I'm not sure, honestly."

"Whenever you say, 'honestly,' I think you're lying," Margaret said.

"It's been a while."

"How long? A week? Two weeks? A month?"

This was worse than Sarah expected. And it was funny. Margaret thought a month was a long time to go without sex? The laughter bubbled up before Sarah could stop it. It started out as a giggle, then turned into a full belly laugh before morphing into a high-pitched wail.

Then, before Sarah realized what was happening, the wail turned into an actual cry. One with tears. Someone had told her once that laughter and crying fell close together on the emotional spectrum.

"What in tarnation?" Margaret said. It was one of Mama Katherine's favorite expressions, and the girls had always used it as a joke. Even now, it turned Sarah's tears into laughter again. Margaret scooted over so she was sitting right next to Sarah, and she put her arms around her.

"What's the matter? I was only teasing. I didn't realize this was so serious."

"It's not. It's not serious. I guess I'm just really emotional right now, with Amelia graduating and leaving for college and everything. Like I said, I just realized this morning that Donny and I have grown apart. And you're right—it's been way too long since we were intimate. Seriously, Margaret, I can't even remember the last time we made whoopee. I think it was after a track meet. Amelia stayed in a different hotel room, with her friend Jess. And Donny and I had sex that night."

"So that was this spring, right? Maybe within the past couple of months?"

Sarah laughed and shook her head. "No. Last spring. Amelia's junior year. It's been over a year."

After a beat of heavy silence, Margaret said, "Wow. This is worse than I thought."

Sarah started crying again, and Margaret said, "You absolutely must rectify this. You have to initiate, Sarah. Tonight. You and Donny are both busy and distracted. But a bit of sex will bring the focus right back to where it should be."

Sarah nodded. Maybe Margaret was right. Maybe she had some good advice despite her lack of experience in this area.

"Okay," she said. "I'll do it."

"Has he gone to bed?" Margaret said. "I thought he was going to come gossip with us, but he hasn't."

"Nah," Sarah said. "He rarely goes to sleep before eleven. He's probably watching TV in the bedroom."

"Perfect," Margaret said. "I'm going to go to bed, myself. And I expect you to report back to me in the morning. Or maybe I'll hear you through the walls tonight. After all this time, I'm sure you're not going to want to hold back once you get started."

"Ha. Okay."

They stood up, and Margaret wrapped Sarah in a hug. "I'm so glad I came. This has been good for me, and you obviously needed a pep talk."

"Obviously," Sarah said. "Sleep well. If you want to shower—"

"The towels are in the hall closet," Margaret said. "I know. Now go have randy sex with that good-looking husband of yours."

Sex wasn't in the cards, but maybe Sarah could talk some sense into Donny. Maybe she could make him see that she realized the error of her ways, that they could work on things…that she could change.

Sure enough, Donny was in the bedroom, laying on the bed, watching TV. It was some kind of sports talk show, and the hosts were discussing whether a golfer would play in an upcoming tournament. The first thing Sarah noticed was that Donny didn't even acknowledge that she'd come into the bedroom. This wasn't going well at all.

The announcers kept talking:

"Will, he's been nursing this injury for months, now. I'd imagine his doctors are going to advise him to take a break."

"Yes, John, but this tournament is important. It's a must-win if he wants to advance to next month's finals. I think he may just push through and take a break after this weekend."

Sarah cleared her throat. "What are you watching?"

It was almost comical, the way Donny looked over at her then. Like he hadn't realized she was there. But that was impossible. Surely he'd heard her open and shut the door.

"Just sports." He turned his attention back to the TV.

Well, that was obvious.

"How did you think graduation went?"

"Great," he said. "You did a great job."

"Do you think Amelia's having fun?" Sarah said.

"I'm sure she is."

"Donny," Sarah said.

"I'm sure she's fine, Sarah."

"Yes. Yes, I'm sure she is. But that's not what I—"

"You're going to have to get used to this when she goes away to college."

Well, this was going spectacularly.

CHAPTER THREE

SARAH WOKE up well before her alarm went off—and well before Donny woke up for his run—Saturday morning. She was tired down to her bones, tired in that way a person is post-event: after running and running for weeks, it was over. If she closed her eyes again, she'd fall into a deep, deep sleep and probably wouldn't wake up for lunch, much less breakfast.

But because Margaret was here, and because she'd promised to take her out on the town today, she dragged her body out of bed and went downstairs to make coffee. Once it had brewed, she poured herself a cup and sat at the counter, her limbs heavy and almost shapeless, like bags of flour.

"You've been up for an hour and you haven't even touched that coffee."

Sarah startled at Donny's voice, then picked up her mug and took a sip. The coffee was lukewarm, just this side of cold. Donny was dressed in his running gear, and he moved to the sink to fill a water bottle.

"Are those new shoes?" she asked.

"Um, not that new," he said. "Got them a couple months ago. I've put, maybe, two hundred miles on them. Remember, I asked you if you minded if I splurged on these?"

They were pretty spectacular, as far as running shoes went, rugged-looking and bright red.

"Ah," she said. "Now I remember. How do you like them?"

She couldn't believe this was the first time she'd asked. Five, even three years ago, she would have been waiting for him to get back from his very first run in a new pair of shoes, so she could hear all about them.

"They're great," he said. "I really like them. No more knee pain." He shrugged then. "Who knew it was that easy?"

When she smiled in response, Sarah knew her face looked like a grotesque mask, her lips pulled back from her teeth in a grimace.

"Look," he said. "Can we talk?"

"Always," she said, even though she'd just realized that wasn't true.

"This is going to be so hard to say," Donny said.

What? *What* was going to be so hard to say? What could possibly be so hard to say? This was really strange. He usually just came right out with announcements. They'd long had an agreement that they wouldn't dance around important issues. So what could be so big that he was afraid to say it?

Understanding rolled in, then, suffocating her. She knew what he was about to say. All the signs were there. He'd been taking his breakfast to go, coming home late, avoiding eye contact. The words were there, but she couldn't form them in her own mind.

Just as he inhaled to speak, Amelia, who was returning from Grad Night and had gotten a ride home with Marcy and Jess, came up behind Donny, grinning. Neither of them had heard her come in, but here she was, stumbling across a major disaster.

Sarah had to stop him. He couldn't say this in front of their daughter. He couldn't. It would break Amelia's heart, and she'd go off to college thinking that her safe place had shattered.

"Donny, you don't have to—"

"Just let me talk."

Amelia was frozen behind Donny. Sarah's eyes flicked over his shoulder to meet her daughter's, but couldn't resist coming back to rest on Donny's.

"But Amelia—"

"She'll be fine, Sarah. You've been a great mother to her."

"No, it's not that, it's—"

"I don't want to be married anymore."

The words came out in a rush, and Donny breathed hard into the silence that followed. The three of them stood there, stunned. Donny's chest moved up and down like he'd just sprinted around the block. A ringing started up in Sarah's ears.

"What?!" Amelia and Sarah said at the same time.

Donny's eyes flashed surprise and he spun around.

"Amelia," he said. "What are you doing here?"

"I *live* here, Dad."

She sounded so forlorn, Sarah wanted to cry.

"I just got home from Grad Night and walked in on *this*," Amelia said. "I don't even know what's happening."

Donny put a palm to his forehead. "I'm sorry, sunshine. I didn't mean for you to hear this conversation. Why don't you go on upstairs and go to bed. You've been up all night."

"Amelia," Sarah said, amazed that she managed to croak out any words at all. "Go on upstairs. Let your father and I finish this conversation, okay?"

Great. After everything she'd done, every nightmare she'd soothed, every organic lunch she'd packed, every school function she'd attended, her daughter would leave for college and begin her adult life as a broken person. It was the exact opposite of what she'd worked so hard for.

Amelia threw up her hands and ran up the stairs. She was such a good girl, Sarah thought, she didn't even slam her door.

Reason kicked in, then, and Sarah realized that hopefully, because she and Donny had done all of those things, this one setback would not ruin Amelia's life.

Still.

"You couldn't have waited just a couple more weeks?"

She practically spat the words at her husband, and he flinched as if they carried actual force. She didn't let him answer, though. Instead, she said, "Why, Donny?"

For a moment, he didn't answer. And it was only after a long span of near-silence, during which she could actually feel the kitchen clock ticking, that he spoke.

"It's been a long time coming," he said.

Sarah blinked. How was that even possible? Just like she'd striven to be a wonderful mother, she'd striven to be a perfect wife. She made him breakfast and lunch every morning. She ironed his work clothes every Tuesday night while they watched a TV show of his choosing. She had dinner on the table every evening when he got home from work. A healthy dinner, no less. And she made his favorite—meatloaf with mashed potatoes—at least once every two weeks. She cleaned the toothpaste out of his sink, for goodness' sake.

And while part of her was thinking, *What could possibly have gone wrong?* another part of her knew the answer. *This* was *a long time coming.*

Now, now that Donny had identified this problem, and shaped and sculpted into a Real Thing, and was holding it out in the light for Sarah to see, she couldn't stop looking at it. Donny had asked her to give it some thought. "It," being the fact that she didn't pay attention to him. And she'd meant to. But she'd just been so busy.

In the silent seconds that followed Donny's statement, Sarah ran through the past few days in her mind.

Each morning, Donny had walked through the kitchen and out to his car, grabbing the lunch Sarah had packed him on the way by. Each evening, he came home, ate dinner, and put on a show. Now, Sarah stifled a gasp as she became aware of the fact that there were none of the pleasantries, like, "Have a good day," or, "See you this evening," or, "You look nice today."

And, Sarah thought as awareness continued to dawn, this scenario wasn't unusual. When was the last time they'd kissed good-bye in the morning? Last week? No. Last month? Maybe. Maybe because it was Mother's Day and he'd given her the obligatory card, which he'd set on the counter, in the very same spot he'd placed every greeting card on every holiday for the past twenty years. She'd undoubtedly thanked him with a perfunctory, passionless smooch.

Her mind flashed back to their early marriage, where a morning good-bye kiss could turn into a full-on makeout session. Once, they'd even had sex right there in the kitchen, Sarah facing the counter, Donny's hands on her hips and his breath in her ear.

As Sarah finally took Donny's suggestion, though, she saw a completely different picture. Here were two people who lived together and who barely spoke a word to each other, much less shared a romantic moment.

"How can that be?" she whispered.

"You're—everything is just so—so perfect," he said. "It's not your fault, Sarah. I just feel like we've grown apart."

"But we talk every day."

Her hands were shaking now.

"I know. We do. And it's all so neat and tidy. You make my breakfast. You make my lunch. In the same lunchbox. Every day. You have dinner waiting for me."

Okay, so he was thinking of all the same things she'd thought of. "And these are bad things?"

"Yes. I mean, no. They're not. But we've lost any sense of real connection. Real passion."

Ah. "Is this about the other night? When I came home with new lingerie?"

Donny shook his head. "That was a symptom. Of a much bigger problem."

"A problem?"

Donny threw his hands up. "I can't talk about this right now. I didn't know Amelia was here."

There was something Sarah could dig her claws into. "I can't believe you made this announcement right now."

He pressed his lips together. "I didn't plan it this way. But as we were getting Amelia ready to leave for college, I just got to thinking that I can't pretend anymore. I can't lie to you. I can't go on a two-week vacation, visit your mom and sister, and pretend that everything's okay. Because it's not."

"So you decided it would be better to completely break our family apart before spending two weeks together in the RV."

"I admit, the timing isn't ideal."

"Well, that's for sure," Sarah said.

"I'm sorry, Sarah."

He turned to leave, and suddenly, Sarah felt like him walking out the door would seal their fate.

"Wait. Donny."

He stopped, and put his hands up on the walls of the alcove.

"I could be better. We could fix this."

Now, he shook his head. "I don't think we can, Sarah."

She wouldn't cry. Amelia could come back downstairs any minute, and if she saw Sarah crying, she would only be more traumatized than she already was. Now, Donny walked out the door. Sarah remained there, her hands knit together at her sternum, her body leaning just slightly forward as if it wanted to follow him.

———

"YOU DIDN'T DO IT."

Margaret came into the kitchen a few minutes (or was it a few hours?) later with a statement rather than a question. Sarah, who was still standing there, looking at the door, kept her eyes down, retrieved her coffee mug, and put it in the microwave.

Margaret went into questioning mode. "What happened? Was he asleep? He didn't refuse, did he? Did you chicken out?"

Sarah poured some coffee for Margaret and handed her the mug.

"I didn't chicken out." Sarah knew she should tell Margaret about Donny's big announcement now—get it over with—but she couldn't bring herself to say the words. Talking about it, admitting it, would somehow make Donny's decision irreversible.

"Remember that time when I was ten," Margaret said, "or maybe nine, and you wouldn't try that Tarzan jump off the rope swing?"

"How could I forget? You guys never let me live it down."

"Because we didn't want you to miss out on the experience. You've always done this, Sarah. You're a tiny bit afraid of something, you avoid it, and you miss out. You never even try."

"I think we both know I'm not afraid of sex with my husband."

"Don't twist this. It's not about you being afraid of sex. It's about you being afraid to initiate."

Fortunately, Margaret's cell phone rang. "We're going to revisit this," she said as she picked it up off the counter and answered.

Sarah watched her sister's face as she listened to whomever was on the other end. She was concentrating, chewing on her lower lip. Her black curls were wild around her head and she looked like some kind of angel with her pale skin and bright green eyes.

Margaret nodded, cleared her throat, and said, "Okay. Yes. Sarah and I were just talking about me joining them up there this summer. Before Amelia starts school. Right. Sarah was going to come after she and Donny dropped Amelia off. But now they're thinking of moving the trip forward. Tell Mama Katherine we love her, okay?"

She disconnected and put her phone down.

"Mama Katherine is asking about us," Margaret said. "She would like to see us, but doesn't want us to feel pressured to go up there. I'm busy with work, you're busy with Amelia. Et cetera. You know how she is."

"She doesn't want to inconvenience us and she'd never dream of asking us to come on her timetable."

"Right. Hannah's words, almost exactly."

"What are Hannah's words?" Donny had reappeared. Here he was in the kitchen again, sweaty and flushed.

As always, his coffee mug sat next to the coffee maker, a spoon in it. Had it been any other morning, Sarah would have automatically retrieved the creamer from the refrigerator and poured exactly a tablespoon of it into his mug before filling it the rest of the way with coffee.

Today, she didn't. Donny kept his eyes down and did it himself. Had it been any other morning, Margaret would have noticed the tension and stayed quiet. But today, for some reason, she didn't.

She said, "You're a very handsome man, Donald Ward."

Donny grinned at her. "Well, I have to say, I've been told that before. I mean, it's been a while, but your sister here used to think I was quite the catch."

Margaret arched an eyebrow at Sarah as if to confirm that Sarah should, in fact, get intimate with Donny. A pause. Donny sipped his coffee.

"I still do," Sarah said.

The conversation's energy had died, fizzled out like air escaping a partially-opened bottle of soda.

"So, Margaret," Donny said. "You're going to join us when we go see Mama Katherine before we take Amelia to school? Did I hear that right?"

"Yep," Margaret said. "Lucky you, you get to spend a solid couple of weeks with me this summer."

Donny smiled. "Can't wait. On another note, I've got lots to do today. Why don't you take my wife somewhere fun? Get her out of the house. She could use it."

Now, Margaret's eyes twinkled over the rim of her coffee cup. If Sarah could have seen her lips, she was sure they were twitching. "Oh, I think I can make that work."

His big announcement apparently having eased his anxiety, Donny jogged up the stairs.

"Well?" Margaret said. "Should we go and have some fun today? Donny's orders."

Two hours later, Sarah smiled at Margaret from across the space between the two massage tables in the couples' room at The Massage Station.

"This is heavenly," Margaret said.

It was. The room smelled like lavender and mint, and Sarah could hear water bubbling over rocks in a tiny fountain in one corner. The masseuse rubbed the past week's tension out of her shoulders, and she closed her eyes.

She'd bought a membership at The Massage Station years ago, but had often skipped her monthly sessions. She was enlightened enough to know that if she didn't take care of herself, she couldn't take care of her husband and daughter so she went to yoga and spin class, and she took her vitamins. But the massages were always the first thing to fall off the schedule. Now, she vowed that would change. There was nothing like being here, in the presence of her sister, having her muscles worked on, to soothe her frayed nerves.

Sarah found herself so relaxed she was almost asleep when Margaret spoke next.

"Do you remember the first time Mama Katherine got sick with the flu?"

"Yes," Sarah said. "I remember being terrified that she'd die and those social workers would send me back to live with my parents. I was so afraid I'd lose you and Hannah. I couldn't imagine being without you."

"You were so determined to nurse her right back to health," Margaret said. "At first, I thought you were taking it too far, sitting up all night to wipe her face with that washcloth. But then I realized you were just scared."

"Not scared," Sarah said. "Terrified. People died of the flu that year."

"I know, but Mama Katherine has always been strong."

It was true. When Sarah first laid eyes on Mama Katherine, she was intimidated beyond speech. The social worker had just driven her up the long driveway, under a sign that said, "Welcome to Seedling Homestead."

Sarah had asked what that meant, and the social worker seemed to think about it a moment before answering: "A seedling is a baby plant. And knowing your new mother, she considers this a place where people get what they need to grow."

This idea infused Sarah with contentment—until she saw Mama Katherine walk around the side of the big red farmhouse. She was tall and broad and scary.

The social worker encouraged Sarah to shake Mama Katherine's hand, but she towered over Sarah, her big hands imposing, and Sarah wouldn't come out from behind the social worker's leg.

So Mama Katherine got down on her knees and said, in a voice that was as gentle as it was commanding, "Come on out here, child. You're so beautiful. You shouldn't be hiding behind anyone. Come on, then."

Sarah had obeyed, clutching her stuffed rabbit against her chest so this woman, her new mother, couldn't get too close.

"I'm Katherine. You can call me Katherine. Or Katy. Or Mama K. Or Mama Katherine. For now, you don't have to call me anything at all. Come on inside."

That initial meeting got Sarah in the door, and over the next several weeks, she learned that Mama Katherine was a woman of her word.

"You do what she says," Margaret said, and Hannah added, "Or you clean out the chicken coop for a week."

At this, Margaret wrinkled her nose. "And she'll make you, too. I've cleaned it out three times, already."

When Mama Katherine tucked Sarah in that first night in the big red farmhouse, she said, "I promise you, sweetheart, I'll be your mother from now on. Okay? You'll never go hungry. You'll never go without clothes or shoes. And I can't promise you'll never feel afraid, but I promise to stand beside you and help you walk through that fear. It won't be at my hands, either."

Sure enough, Katherine, forever in her jeans and denim shirt, showed up at every school meeting and awards assembly. She fussed over the girls in her own brusque way, forcing them to wear double layers when it was cold and drink gallons of water when it was hot. These were things Sarah's biological mother had never done, never thought to do. It wasn't difficult for Sarah to adjust to being taken care of, and she tolerated this fussing better than either Margaret or Hannah.

Mama Katherine was a strong woman, who rose before the sun to make breakfast, then worked the farm all day, and then cooked and cleaned in the evenings. She seemed invincible.

And this—this life with a real parent and siblings and normalcy and routine—was like Heaven to Sarah. She went from being trapped year-round in a tiny, dingy apartment with rotting floorboards to roaming a five-acre farm barefoot, her new best friends shrieking with laughter as they ran through the tall grass.

So when the flu knocked Mama Katherine down that winter, Sarah panicked. And now, even though she was an adult with a daughter of her own, Sarah was panicking again. Mama Katherine was getting older. She wasn't actually invincible. She'd always seemed like some sort of goddess to Sarah, but the truth was that she was just a regular human. And she wasn't going to live forever.

And none of this was very pleasant to think about during a massage.

"Margaret," Sarah said, and her sister said, "Mmm?"

"Tell me all about your latest exploits."

"I thought you didn't approve," Margaret said, even though her voice had already taken on that dreamy quality of someone remembering pure sexual bliss.

"It's not that I don't approve," Sarah said. "It's just—"

"I know," Margaret said. "It's just that you don't think you could do it without getting attached."

"Something like that." It was really that Sarah had never been with anyone other than Donny, romantically or physically, and the thought of traipsing around the country, being with one man after another, seemed foreign and more than slightly uncomfortable.

"It's just sex, Sarah," Margaret said.

"I know. We've been over this. Just tell me a story."

"Fine." Margaret sighed. "The best one—well, recently, anyway—was Bear Mountain."

"If you're going to keep referring to these guys geographically, you really should take more care with the names of the cities where you work."

"Funny," Margaret said. "Anyway. Bear Mountain was an Internet find. His profile picture showed him looking absolutely gorgeous, and for once, he was even better in person. He had the most dreamy blue eyes. Like the Pacific Ocean in Mexico. Not the one in northern California."

"We've got to look at photos during lunch," Sarah said. "I've never seen the Pacific Ocean in Mexico."

"Yes, we do," Margaret said. "For you to get the full effect of that description. Anyway. Usually, we just go for dinner and drinks, and sometimes, as you know, we end up in a hotel room. But this guy, Bear Mountain, wanted to go for a ski lift ride. 'A dinner cruise,' he called it. Like, you ride this ski lift up to the top of the mountain and have dinner at the ski lodge. Have I ever mentioned that I get horrifically airsick?"

"You have. And I remember the post-donut airsickness when we flew to California."

"Well. So you can imagine my excitement when, over martinis at the bar where we met, Bear Mountain announces that he has a special surprise for me, and he holds up the tickets."

"I can only imagine your excitement."

"But I agree to go. I think it was that dreamy quality of his eyes. And the thought that it would be a short ride up. Anyway. So I agree to go, and we climb on, and we're going up. So slowly, right? And it's taking so long. And just when I think I'm going to start getting sick, Bear Mountain starts kissing me. I mean, like seriously making out on the ski lift. And all of a sudden, I'm not feeling sick. And when we get to the top and I'm breathless, either from the altitude or from the kissing, he says, 'I think we found the cure for your airsickness.'"

Sarah smiled. It did sound romantic. "And then what?"

"And then we went to the lodge and had giant steaks for dinner. And then we went back down the mountain. And that was it."

"No sex?"

"No, strangely," Margaret said. "No hot hotel sex. And it was the best one yet."

The massage therapists left the room, then, and Sarah wondered where the hour had gone.

"Can you imagine everything these women hear?" she said as they got dressed.

Margaret gave her a wicked grin and said, "I can. Which is why I totally lied to you just now. I totally had hot, kinky sex with Bear Mountain. Right there in the ski lift chair on the way back down."

Sarah shook her head. "I don't even want to know how you have hot, kinky sex on a ski lift."

"Oh, yes, you do. Now take me to lunch."

"I know just the place," Sarah said.

Margaret had insisted they take a taxi, which made Sarah a little apprehensive about Margaret's plans for lunch. Sure enough, as soon as they slid into the green velvet booth at Frank's Steakhouse, Margaret signaled for the waiter.

"I'll take two martinis, please. And keep 'em coming."

When Sarah wrinkled her nose and said, "It's not even noon," Margaret just smiled and pretended to check her watch. "It will be when they put the first round on the table. You've got to loosen up, Sarah."

Sarah shrugged. Piano music played over hidden speakers, white carnations sat in crystal vases on the tables, and Sarah had nowhere to be. "I suppose you're right."

"So," Margaret said.

"So," Sarah said, wondering what her sister was getting at.

"I think you need to spice things up with Donny."

Sarah's stomach lurched. The bartender, a black apron around her waist, delivered the cocktails with a flourish and Sarah picked hers up immediately.

"How do you know things are not spicy already?"

"It's so obvious," Margaret said. "There is about as much chemistry between the two of you as there are olives in this beverage. Which is not very much. You guys used to be so passionate. It was, like, electric. Back in the day. Now it's like the two of you are living parallel lives under the same roof. And you never, you know, *intersect.*"

Well, that was true, Sarah thought.

"But there are four olives in your martini," she said. "I've never seen that many in one martini."

"Oh," Margaret said. "I guess that's a lot. But you get what I'm saying. Anyway. What are you getting? What's good here?"

"The ravioli," Sarah said. She'd never even picked up her menu— she knew what she wanted. She loved the ravioli but rarely got it because she was always cutting back on carbs.

"I'll have the same," Margaret said.

"You don't eat pasta. It gives you gas."

"I know. I'll get a side salad."

"Okay. But I'm staying upwind."

"You know what?" Margaret said. "I'm getting you drunk. Right now. At noon-thirty. And then we are going shopping."

"What?" Sarah said. "Shopping?"

"Yes," Margaret said. "At that one shop downtown. The Big One? Is that right?"

"Ohmygod," Sarah said. "We are not. First of all—" she thought of the unopened toys she'd bought at Marcy's house, decided not to tell Margaret about them, and changed course "—that place is for kinky people, not regular people. And second of all ..."

Margaret snorted. "There is no second of all."

"Sarah. If you know your sex life has fizzled out, why wouldn't you try to fix it?"

This would be the perfect time for Sarah to admit to Margaret that Donny wanted a divorce. That he wanted to leave. That there would be no use for these toys. But she so rarely got to spend time with Margaret, and she didn't want to make it depressing.

So she said, "It's just so—so uncomfortable now. I'm forty. I thought those shops were for people in their twenties. You know?"

"Oh, I know, all right. Which is, Number One, why I'm getting you drunk. And, Number Two, why your sex life with your husband has completely fizzled out."

She signaled the server and asked for another round.

———

THE BIG ONE sat on Main Street, right out in the open between a flower shop and a boutique liquor store.

When she climbed unsteadily out of the taxi, Sarah snorted. "I never realized the correlation between these stores. Flowers, liquor, sex stuff."

"It's the triple crown of romance," Margaret said.

The outfits in The Big One's window were all leather and strings, and Sarah froze. "You know, I think we should just run next door and grab some wine. That'll have the same effect, won't it?"

"Hardly." Margaret grabbed her arm and steered her into the sex shop, where they came face-to-face with Sarah's friend, Marcy.

"Sarah, hi! This must be your sister. It's so funny running into you here. I know, I know, I just had that party, and here I am again! Just buying some last-minute essentials I forgot. You know, for the honeymoon. For Stevie and me."

Marcy held up a bottle of lubrication, and Margaret shot Sarah a sideways glance. Before Sarah could get a word in, Marcy went on: "I always thought you and Donny were such an amazing couple, and I guess this is how you've kept the flame burning, right? You shop here often?"

Margaret snickered. Sarah elbowed her.

"I don't, actually," Sarah said. She didn't mention that there was no flame burning in the Ward household. "As I said the other day, it's been a while."

We're actually here for my sister, who likes kinky sex on ski lifts.

"Your party the other night got me thinking, it might be fun to spice things up," she added.

She knew she'd come to regret using the very same words Margaret had used at lunch, but they tumbled right out of her mouth, and when they did, she couldn't help but notice Margaret's self-satisfied smile. Oh, well. Maybe there was something to her sister's madness.

"Well, I think I've got what I came for," Marcy said. She held up a giant purple dildo, and Sarah's mouth dropped open. Even Margaret gasped.

"It vibrates, and it swivels" Marcy said. "Six settings!"

"Oh, my," Sarah said. Then, realizing she should say something else, she said, "I'm so glad you found what you're looking for."

"You should see your face right now," Marcy said. "I'm totally kidding. This thing is huge. I'm still a beginner."

She looked around the store, then, and threw her hands up. "I have no idea where to start. And you forgot to text me those links so I could see what you were talking about at my party. You said it would be more cost-effective to buy it at a store."

"What was she talking about?" Margaret wanted to know.

"A—a cock ring?" Marcy said, and Sarah nodded. She blushed again.

"Ohhhh," Margaret said. "I think we can walk you through the cock rings. And Sarah, I think the classy lingerie is in the back of the store. Let's go, ladies."

For the next half-hour, the three of them examined toys, lotions, potions, and outfits. Marcy walked out with a bag stuffed with what she deemed "beginner items," and Sarah found a filmy outfit that Margaret promised would increase the "spice factor" in Sarah's bedroom.

"Do you think she calls him Stevie in bed?" Margaret wanted to know as soon as Marcy left them.

Sarah rolled her eyes, but answered truthfully. "I've wondered the same."

"Anyway. I'm so glad we did this. It will be like the first time for you and Donny all over again."

"I'm not sure if that's a good thing," Sarah said. "The first time with Donny was … well, it was over almost before it started."

"Okay," Margaret said. "The second time, then. Anyway. I don't need all the sordid details of the second time. I just want you to have a good time. And when he sees you in this outfit, you will."

Sarah didn't bother telling Margaret Donny wouldn't see her in this outfit. She didn't bother telling her that spicing things up was impossible at this point. She heard Mama Katherine's voice, then, saying that nothing was impossible. But reigniting the flame in the Ward bedroom was just about as improbable as things could get.

"I see your inner critic talking," Margaret said. "You're going to love this. Trust me."

CHAPTER FOUR

Donny was the first person Sarah met in her new life, aside from Mama Katherine, Hannah, and Margaret. It was her second day on the Seedling Homestead, and Mama Katherine had shooed the girls outside to play.

"You spent all day inside yesterday," she said. "And now you need some fresh air. Girls, give Sarah the tour, okay? And stay out of the creek."

The moment they got outside, Margaret and Hannah kicked off their shoes. Unaccustomed to being anywhere that bare feet didn't mean a high risk of disease (even Sarah's neglectful mother warned her of the dangers of stepping on rat droppings or used needles), Sarah left hers on. The girls shrugged at her, but didn't make a fuss about it.

"Want to see our tire swing?" Margaret said.

Sarah nodded, and the girls tore off across an open field. The tire swing hung from a huge cottonwood tree and looked like it had been there about a hundred years. It was the kind of scene you'd see in a book, Sarah thought, but she was living in it.

"Climb in," Hannah said to Sarah.

Margaret threw Hannah a dark look, probably because she'd wanted to go first, but she helped Hannah hold the tire steady so Sarah could get on. It was awkward, at first—she'd been on a regular swing only a handful of times and never on a tire swing. But once she was able to relax, and stop clinging to the rope for dear life, she felt a huge sense of joy expanding in her torso. This, this farm with the chickens and goats, this family with the mother and sisters, this was her new life. All of it—the farm, the family, the space, the trees, the sparkling creek, and the wide open sky—seemed magical.

So when Donny, a sunburned, barefoot boy with freckles across the bridge of his nose and a shock of blond hair sticking straight up off his head, splashed in, he seemed magical, too. Sarah could still remember that first impression: he was carefree and so, so full of life. She'd never seen anyone quite like Donny. The boys at her old school wore jeans and collared shirts and combed their hair. This kid wore overalls cut off just below the knees, and nothing else. The boys she knew avoided eye contact, unless they were whispering something mean about her stringy hair or holey shoes. But when the tire swing slowed to a halt (thanks to Margaret's insistence that she stop it so they could introduce Sarah and Donny properly), he marched right up to her and put out a hand to shake.

"You're the new sister," he said. "I'm Donny. Next-door neighbor and designated frog catcher."

Despite the fact that he was squinting, Sarah could see the bright blue color of his eyes.

"Where'd you come from?" he asked, and Hannah tried to shush him.

"Well, he ain't got no manners, that's for sure," Margaret said. She glared at him, and Sarah felt deep gratitude for her new sister's protectiveness.

"He *doesn't* have *any* manners, Margaret," Hannah said. She turned to Donny, then. "Let her be, will you? She just got here."

Donny shrugged. "Want me to spin you?"

When Sarah nodded, he grabbed the tire swing and started turning it, slowly. The rope shortened as it twisted, and soon Sarah was as high as Donny's shoulders.

"Ready?" he said.

"I think so," Sarah said.

Then, Donny, Margaret, and Hannah yelled, "Hold on tight!"

Donny let go of the tire, and it started to spin—so fast Sarah feared she'd lose her grip. She felt like screaming and crying and the tire kept spinning and Sarah surprised herself when she started to laugh. She'd never done anything just for fun before, just for pure joy. And she liked it. She liked it so much she asked him to spin her again and again until she thought she might throw up. The girls helped her down, and they all lay in the grass, staring up at the sky, for a long while.

Sarah had almost dozed off when Donny jumped to his feet and said, "Race you to the chicken coop."

All three girls jumped up, and Sarah ran as fast and as hard as she could, making sure to stay just behind her new sisters because she couldn't quite remember where the chicken coop was. It didn't matter, anyway, because just like that, Sarah became part of something real, something that didn't threaten to dissolve at any moment, leaving her alone.

———

AS THAT FIRST magnificent summer drew to a close and the start of a new school year approached, Sarah began feeling anxious. She knew enough to realize she'd lived in a cocoon for the past several weeks—a cocoon where the only visitors were Mama Katherine, Margaret, Hannah, and Donny. Going to school would mean breaking out of that cocoon and being surrounded by so many unknowns: new classmates, a new teacher, a new schedule.

Mama Katherine must have sensed her anxiety, because the weekend before the start of school, she declared a Family Shopping Day and took all three girls to the mall in Cheyenne.

"You girls have spent the summer in nothing but cutoffs and t-shirts, and I can't have you going to school looking like ragamuffins," she said. "We'll have to buy some dresses. And some nice school shoes."

Sarah had never been school shopping before. Well, that wasn't entirely true. Every once in a while, her biological mother would announce that it was time to go school shopping, and she'd take Sarah to the thrift store down the street.

After they browsed for a while, her mom would hand her several outfits, and Sarah would go into the fitting room and put them all on at once. "Layer it up," her mom would say. Then, they'd walk out of the store together.

So when Mama Katherine took Sarah to the department store, she did the same thing. This time, Margaret and Hannah insisted on crowding into the fitting room with her so they could examine each other's selections. When they saw Sarah layering the clothes, they seemed perplexed, to say the least.

"Just try one outfit on," Hannah said, her voice gentle. "Just one pants, and one shirt. Like this." She gestured to Margaret. "Or, just one dress, like this." She pointed at her own skinny, dress-clad frame.

In the fitting room, one leg halfway into her second pair of pants, Sarah froze.

"You mean, we pay for all this?"

Hannah and Margaret looked at each other, shared some kind of telecommunication, and then looked back at Sarah.

"Well," Hannah said. "Mama Katherine pays for it. You know. We don't have any more than we earn for doin' dishes and collecting eggs, and you know Margaret hates doin' dishes. But someone has to pay for it, don't they?"

Sarah nodded. "I suppose so."

Choosing clothes, trying them on, showing them off was a whole new experience for Sarah. At first, being the center of attention felt strange. But after a few twirls, and a few measuring looks from Mama Katherine, she decided she liked it. She decided right then and there that she loved wearing dresses. She loved the way the fabric brushed her knees. She loved the way the skirt moved from side to side when she walked. She felt pretty, and when Mama Katherine, Hannah, and Margaret declared that she looked pretty, too, she felt her throat constrict a little.

Mama Katherine took the girls out for milkshakes and they told Sarah all about the school: which bathroom to use (the one by the library—its locks worked and it wasn't missing a stall door), how to check out library books, and where the mean girls hung out. Even as they talked, Sarah pictured herself in her new dress and wondered what Donny would think of this strange new version of her.

———

MONDAY MORNING CAME QUICKLY. Sarah woke up before dawn, ready to go into the kitchen and forage for something to eat like she'd done every school day for as long as she could remember. But when she got there, Mama Katherine was already at the stove, flipping pancakes on her old iron griddle.

"Oh, good morning, sweetheart," she said. "I was hoping to surprise you all with pancakes, but you're up earlier than I expected."

If she hadn't realized it already, this would have been the moment Sarah realized that this life with Mama Katherine would be the exact opposite of her life with her first set of parents.

Margaret and Hannah came into the kitchen a few minutes later, each issuing a sleepy, "Good morning."

Pancakes had never tasted so good.

Mama Katherine said she'd walk the girls to their classrooms, but when they got to school, Hannah volunteered to do it so Mama Katherine could get started on the daily chores. Margaret insisted they walk Sarah first, "since it's her first day and she's probably the most nervousest," and Hannah said, "Well, if she wasn't before, then she is, now," but agreed.

Sarah had one sister on each side when she approached her classroom. And there was Donny, coming from the opposite direction. At the sight of her, he stopped walking. He dropped his brown paper lunch bag and didn't seem to notice.

Margaret giggled. Hannah shushed her. Donny closed his mouth.

Sarah said, "Good morning, Donny. You look nice."

And he did. He was wearing khaki shorts and a collared shirt, and his hair was combed into submission.

"You, too," he said, his voice quieter than she'd ever heard it.

"I guess we're in the same class."

He looked up at the number on the classroom door and back at Sarah. "Yep," he said. "I guess we are."

She was so relieved she thought she might cry.

"Have a great day," Margaret and Hannah said at the same time, each giving her a quick squeeze. "See you after school."

———

IF SCHOOL SHOPPING and first-day-of-school pancakes had seemed unusual, the greeting Mama Katherine gave the girls when they arrived home was even more so: a colorful vegetable tray, cheese and crackers, and glasses of juice sat on the dining room table.

"So? How was it? Is it going to be a great year?"

"Mama," Hannah said, her voice high with excitement. "You should have seen the way Donny looked at Sarah when he first saw her in her school clothes."

Mama Katherine looked at Sarah for confirmation, but before she could answer, Margaret piped up. "It was so funny, Mama. You would have thought he'd seen a ghost."

"Or a really pretty girl," Hannah said.

Mama Katherine raised her eyebrows and pursed her lips. Sarah blushed and looked down at her shoes.

"Maybe tomorrow I'll wear the jeans I brought with me."

"You'll do no such thing, Sarah," Mama Katherine said. "You felt so pretty in that dress. You *look* so pretty. You're just shining. If Donny Ward thinks you're beautiful, so be it."

———

SARAH AND DONNY remained friends throughout elementary school. They were at the top of the class, constantly competing for that Number One spot. They went against each other in the spelling bee, tied for first place in the science fair, and teamed up to lead student council.

By the time they were in the sixth grade, no one mentioned them separately any more. It was, "SarahandDonny," or "DonnyandSarah."

They shared everything from their lunches to their seats on the bus. So it only seemed natural that they'd share their first kiss, too.

It was the end of sixth grade's first semester and their teacher, Mrs. Luca, had assigned the two of them to carry chairs to a different, empty classroom. After their third or fourth trip, Donny sat down in one of the chairs. Sarah paused in the doorway, on her way out to get another stack of chairs.

"You coming?" she said.

"Sarah," he said, and she turned around and leaned against the doorjamb.

"What do you think about kissing me?"

The truth was, she *hadn't* thought about kissing him. Well, not much, anyway. Hannah was in high school now, and every once in a while, she'd mention that one of her friends had a boyfriend, or that she'd seen two people kissing in the hallway. And Margaret had had a few kisses of her own. To hear her tell it, kissing was a wet and sloppy experience. In fact, she seemed to be on some kind of search for the best kisser in junior high. If Sarah were to kiss anyone, Sarah thought, it probably would be Donny. But when she *had* thought of it, she'd felt a tiny bit uncomfortable. She didn't know how to kiss a boy. But, she couldn't say all this to Donny now, when he was sitting on that chair waiting for her answer.

So she shrugged. "I don't know."

He stood up and walked towards her. Her stomach reacted, not in the same way it used to when she saw her biological mom pouring vodka down her throat, but in a new way that felt like electricity. She stood up straight, and he grasped her upper arms.

"Want to find out what you think about it?" he said.

She licked her lips and nodded. He leaned forward. Sarah closed her eyes. She braced herself. And Donny's lips landed on the side of her face, between her right cheek and her ear. She opened her eyes and was surprised to see him smiling at her.

"I chickened out."

She smiled back. "Well, maybe next time."

———

SARAH DIDN'T HAVE to wait long for the next time. That same day, Donny found the courage to kiss her on the bus ride home. He'd chosen a spot near the back, and just as the bus pulled away from the curb at school, he said to her, "How about now?"

When she turned to look at him, he leaned in and planted his lips firmly on hers. It was, as Margaret had said, a wet experience. But it wasn't sloppy. And Sarah found that she enjoyed it. Her nerve endings picked up on every single detail and made a kind of photograph of the moment: the warmth of Donny's lips, the way the seat of the bus felt on her palms, the sound of the bus engine and the kids chattering.

In the years that followed, her memory would pull this photograph out every so often, and she'd again feel the wonder and excitement and nervousness of it.

———

BY THE TIME they reached high school, they were more inseparable than ever. They rode their bikes to school, took all the same classes, sat together at lunch, and did homework together before or after sports practices.

One night when all three sisters were sitting on Hannah's bed long after Mama Katherine had gone to sleep, Margaret asked Sarah if she thought she'd marry Donny.

"We've talked about it," Sarah said. "We've talked about how many kids we'll have and what we'll name them and where we'll live."

"But have you thought about where you'll go to college?" Hannah wanted to know. She was already enrolled in general ed classes at the local community college, and planned to become an elementary school teacher.

Sarah shook her head. "I figure I'll go, but I was waiting to see where Donny wants to go."

"Don't you want to, you know, sample other flavors?" Margaret asked.

"You mean, like *date* people?"

"Um, yeah. Like date people. Besides Donny, whom you've been dating since before you were dating."

"Why?" Sarah said, and her sisters dissolved into giggles.

"I guess we know the answer to that," Hannah squealed.

When the hilarity died down, Sarah said, "Do you guys think I should date other people? Sample other flavors? Whatever? I mean, what if I like this flavor?"

"If you're always eating Rocky Road ice cream, and you never try cookie dough ice cream, how do you know that you're actually missing out?" Margaret said.

"But if you're completely satisfied with Rocky Road," Sarah said, "then why not stick with it?"

"Or," Hannah said, holding up a finger, "maybe you take a break from ice cream all together and go to college."

"That's a mixed metaphor," Margaret said.

"It's more like a mix of metaphor and an actual example," Sarah said.

"I know," Hannah said. "I'm boring, and apparently not as clever as the two of you. I'm just saying, there's more to life than being with a man."

"So you don't want to get married, have kids, all that stuff?" Sarah asked.

It had never occurred to her that a woman wouldn't seek a spouse. Although, come to think of it, Mama Katherine seemed perfectly happy without one.

"Mama Katherine doesn't have a husband," Hannah said. "And she's perfectly happy."

"But she has us," Margaret said.

Then a thought struck Sarah and she said, "What do you think's going to happen when we all grow up and move out?"

No one answered.

"I wonder if she dated before we moved in," Margaret said.

Hannah shrugged. "I never thought to ask her."

"Let's ask her tomorrow," Margaret said. "And then Sarah can decide what to do with her life."

Hannah stretched, her arms above her head, and yawned. "It's getting late. I'm going to bed. Skedaddle, you two."

Later, as she lay awake in her own bed, Sarah thought about what her sisters had said. Maybe she should take a break from Donny and see someone else. Were she and Donny really "official" anyway? They'd never talked about it, or given themselves a label. Could they still be friends if she started going out with someone else? Who else was there? And what about in a couple of years' time, when they graduated from high school? Would she want to go to college on her own?

She drifted off to sleep, visions of unidentifiable high school boys lined up at the front door of the farmhouse, ready to take her to the movies, the ice cream shop, or the local diner, and her half-dream self scanning the line of them for Donny's face.

CHAPTER FIVE

THE ADULT, teetering-on-the-brink-of-divorce Sarah spent all of Saturday night half-dreaming and half-remembering. Donny slipped out of bed sometime around five and didn't come back. Finally, the blinding Arizona sun rose high enough to shine through the window across from the bed, scorching her eyes. Although she wanted to pull the covers over her head and stay there, she dragged herself downstairs.

"Wow," Margaret said when Sarah came into the kitchen. "You are certainly not as bright-eyed and bushy-tailed as I expected you would be. You look like death warmed over, actually."

Sarah sighed. "Thank you, Margaret. I really appreciate your honesty."

She poured herself a cup of coffee and sat down next to her sister at the bar.

"What happened? Donny keep you up all night after he saw you in that lingerie?"

"Hardly." Sarah put her elbows on the bar and her face in her hands.

"Did you chicken out again?"

"Can we change the subject?"

"Absolutely. What shall we do on my last day here?"

"Spend the entire day getting drunk."

Amelia came down the stairs just in time to hear that last bit, and Sarah jumped at the realization that Amelia didn't know she was keeping the impending divorce a secret from Margaret.

"Geez, Mom," she said, after giving Margaret a kiss on the cheek. "I don't think that's an appropriate activity for your teenaged daughter."

"You can be our designated driver," Sarah said. "We're just kidding, honey. How did you sleep?"

"Great," Amelia said. "I was exhausted. I'm still catching up from Grad Night, I guess. So what's the plan for today? Besides you getting sloshed. Which is totally weird, by the way. I've never even seen you have more than one glass of wine in a sitting."

Well, that was true.

"I know," Margaret said. "Why don't we spend the day downtown? We can shop, have a nice lunch, see a movie. Just keep it low-key."

"Shopping with Aunt Margaret is always an adventure," Amelia said to Sarah, her tone conspiratorial. "We'll bring paper bags to wear over our heads for when she embarrasses us."

"Come on, now," Margaret said, her lips twitching. "I'm not so bad. I make shopping fun."

It was true. Margaret did make shopping fun. The three of them headed downtown, where Margaret's antics distracted Sarah—mostly—from thoughts of Donny wanting to leave her.

Amelia drove, and when they found a parking spot along the main drag, Margaret hopped out of the car and into the street, making big arm motions as if she were an airport ramp agent, directing Amelia and her plane up to the gate. At lunch, she asked the server so many questions she had Sarah and Amelia in stitches:

"Is this pasta gluten-free?"

"Is this fish from the Pacific Ocean? I'm allergic to fish from the Pacific Ocean."

"Is this lettuce sourced locally? I eat *only* locally-sourced produce. Organic."

"How old is this chicken when it's butchered?"

"Is this beef grain-fed?"

"Which dish would you recommend? Oh, the lemon chicken? Does it have lemon rind in it? I can't eat lemon rind."

At first, the server seemed exasperated, but when he walked away from their table after Margaret settled on a garden salad, he looked amused. As was her style, Margaret insisted on picking up the tab, and she left him a huge cash tip and bustled them out of the restaurant before he could thank her.

In the movie theater, Margaret loud-whispered throughout the previews:

"Isn't that that Johnny Depp fellow? No? Harrison Ford? Are you sure? I thought Harrison Ford was a lot beefier than that."

"This movie looks terrible. All this romantic crap is just so unbelievable. Me? I prefer a good action film. One I can really sink my teeth into."

She crinkled her popcorn bag and took forever opening the plastic wrap on her candy. The people around them shifted uncomfortably in their seats and cleared their throats and Sarah, Amelia, and Margaret were giggling uncontrollably by the time the actual movie started.

They had so much fun, Sarah almost forgot to think about Donny. Almost. But the day came to an end and they had to return home. Which meant Sarah had to face her husband.

Sarah, Margaret, and Amelia were cooking dinner when Donny walked in that evening. To his credit, Sarah thought, he acted like nothing out of the ordinary had happened.

"How nice to come home to three beautiful women in my kitchen," he said.

He squeezed Margaret's arm and kissed Amelia on the cheek. Sarah half-expected him to give her a kiss on the mouth, but he didn't. He kissed her cheek, too, in the most chaste way possible.

She sighed, and Margaret must have noticed because she said, "Go on upstairs and put on your comfy pants, Donny. Your adoring female fan club will finish preparing your dinner."

"Yes, ma'am," he said, and he disappeared up the stairs.

"I wish you didn't have to leave tomorrow, Aunt Margaret," Amelia said.

Sarah felt the beginnings of a cry.

"I wish I could stay longer, too," Margaret said, "but it sounds like we'll all be together again before you go to school."

"What?" Amelia said. "We will?"

"You didn't tell her?" Margaret said to Sarah.

"I guess I haven't had a chance. Yes, Aunt Margaret's joining us in Wyoming."

Amelia, who stood at the stove sautéing vegetables, rotated slowly to look at them. Her eyes were wide, as if she didn't believe the news.

"It's true," Margaret said. "I've got a few obligations to take care of, and then I'll meet you there."

Amelia squealed. "I'm so excited!"

She left her post at the stove to hug her aunt, and then her mom, and then to jump around the kitchen, her arms raised. "I can't wait! Oh, I'm so excited! I can't wait! This is going to be so awesome!"

Her excitement was contagious, and Sarah found herself smiling again.

"Wait," Amelia said. "Mom, why are you crying?"

"I'm just happy," Sarah said. "It'll be so nice to have the five of us ladies together."

"And Dad, right?" Amelia said.

"Right," Sarah said. "And Dad."

"So when do we leave?" Amelia wanted to know.

"In a week," Sarah said.

"A week? A week! I can't wait!"

"Amelia, your veggies are going to burn," Margaret said.

"Oh! Right! My veggies!" She returned to the stove to stir the veggies, and every minute or so, she did a fist pump or a happy dance.

This trip would be good for all of them, Sarah thought.

———

IT WAS all Sarah could do the next morning to stop herself from pushing Margaret right out the front door. So far, she'd avoided telling her sister about the end of her marriage, but someone could spill the beans at any moment. Margaret had already said good-bye to Amelia and Donny, and she and Sarah waited outside for the taxi.

"You never said why you took a taxi," Sarah said.

Margaret, her eyes on a horizon interrupted by tall saguaro cacti and, behind them, mountains that looked like the spikes on a dragon's back, didn't answer right away. Sarah checked her watch, and despite all the thoughts swirling around in her own mind, she didn't miss the way Margaret's voice sounded clogged when she spoke.

"Multi-tasking," she said. "I used the drive time to do some work. Make calls, revise blueprints … share my genius."

"Huh," Sarah said. "Your clients are lucky you're so devoted."

"You're telling me."

The taxi pulled up then, and Sarah grabbed Margaret's suitcase and wheeled it over. Then, Margaret hugged her and although Sarah had willed herself not to make a fuss when her sister left, she burst into tears.

"What's all this?" Margaret said, holding her at arm's length.

"Do you have to go?"

"If I'm going to join you in Wyoming, I do," Margaret said.

Sarah nodded and used her index finger to wipe a tear from under her eye.

"Fine," she said.

Margaret laughed, just a little, and Sarah noticed her eyes were a little wet, too. Which was totally strange.

"Love you," Sarah said. "And thank you so much for coming out for Amelia's graduation."

"I wouldn't miss it," Margaret said.

They hugged again and within moments, Sarah was standing in her driveway, waving at the back of the taxi as it disappeared from sight.

CHAPTER SIX

ANOTHER COUPLE OF DAYS PASSED, during which Donny maintained his distance, Amelia packed her things, and Sarah distracted herself by working on the homework for the photography class she was taking. Somehow, they managed to avoid the topic of the impending divorce.

Now, it was almost time to leave for Wyoming, which forced Sarah and Donny to interact. As they packed the RV, she couldn't decide whether that was a curse or a blessing.

"When's the last time we took a trip in this thing?" Sarah said.

She was inside the RV, transferring food from a laundry basket to the refrigerator, and she tried to keep her tone light and conversational. Donny was up front, cleaning the inside of the windshield.

"Wasn't it that trip to the mountains in the spring? Late spring, wasn't it?"

"I think that was it," Sarah said. She searched her mind for something more to say about it, but came up empty, so she continued loading the refrigerator, stacking ready-to-heat pre-made meals on top of one another.

That trip had been over Amelia's spring break, now that she thought about it. They'd played hooky from everything else and taken what they thought would be one last family trip in Maude. They'd spent two days sledding.

Two full days of running up the mountainside and flying back down, taking breaks only to go back into the RV for hot chocolate or grilled cheese and tomato soup. There was nothing quite like sliding down the huge slide of nature's playground, cheeks stinging from the cold, fingertips numb. Sarah remembered now that she'd felt so alive during that trip.

"That was a good time," she said.

"Huh?" Donny said. Apparently his mind was on something else. "Oh, yeah. It was."

They'd all been so exhausted by nighttime that she and Donny hadn't even stayed up after Amelia went to bed, like they usually did. Typically, if it was warm enough, they'd sit outside next to a campfire. And if not, they'd sit inside and read together. And they almost always made love just before going to sleep. But not that trip, Sarah thought now. She went through her mental checklist as she added items to the fridge: hot dogs, ketchup, mustard, relish, buns.

Come to think of it, when was the last time they'd had sex in the RV?

"Huh," Sarah said, out loud.

"What?" Donny said.

"Oh, nothing," Sarah said. "Just thinking, that's all."

Finished with the food, Sarah went inside to get fresh towels and linens. She always changed them out at the start of a trip. Amelia sat at the kitchen counter, eating eggs and drinking—

"Amelia Jane Ward! Is that coffee?"

"Sure is," Amelia said.

"Since when do you drink coffee?"

Amelia shrugged. "I dunno. But I'm going to need it in college, aren't I? Aren't college kids always staying up late?"

"I don't know," Sarah said, and, thinking she'd rather it was coffee than beer, so she let it go.

"Where's Dad?"

"Cleaning windows."

"Did you guys already eat?" Amelia said.

"I made breakfast, but Dad wrapped his up and ate it while cleaning windows." She tried to make it sound like this was normal, but they both knew it wasn't. Although Donny had started taking his breakfast to go during the workweek, they usually ate together at the kitchen table on the weekends.

"He was really anxious to get those windows clean," Amelia said, her voice dripping with sarcasm.

Sarah said again, "He does love a clean window."

Donny walked in. He looked agitated.

"What's the matter?" Sarah said. "Is something wrong with the engine?"

She ran through a list of possibilities. Maybe there was an oil leak. Or maybe the spark plugs needed to be changed. Or maybe the radiator was acting wonky again. Although, he wouldn't know that yet, since he hadn't even started it up.

"Oh, everything's fine," Donny said, but he wouldn't look at her. "Good morning, sunshine," he said to Amelia. He bent to kiss her on the head. "I'm going to grab a quick shower."

"Okay," Sarah said. "Don't you want to sit down with Amelia for a few minutes?"

"I would love to," Donny said. "But I've got to run to the auto parts store to get new windshield wipers. Remember how the left one was disintegrating? I'd forgotten about that."

Sarah nodded. That sounded familiar. Donny left, and Amelia hopped off her barstool. "Jess asked if I'd go to the mall with her this morning. Is that okay?"

"Sure," Sarah said. "Just make sure you're all ready to go by two, okay? We wanted to get in a few hours of driving today before we stop for dinner."

"I'd better hurry up, then," Amelia said. She carried her plate to the sink. "I'm all packed. But I have a feeling this shopping trip is going to take a while. Jess has a date tonight."

"Oh yeah?" Sarah said. Neither Amelia nor her friends had shown more than a passing interest in guys during high school. "That's new. Who's the lucky guy?"

Amelia shrugged and paused at the bottom of the stairs. "Some guy she met at the coffee shop."

"Does her mom know?"

"I don't know," Amelia said. "But, I mean, we're going off to college in a few months, and you guys won't know when we're going on dates. Right? Do you think she should tell her mom?"

"Well, yeah," Sarah said. "I do. What if he's a creeper?"

"Oh, Mom," Amelia said. "You worry too much. What if he's a perfectly nice guy?"

With that, she bounced up the stairs, leaving Sarah alone with her thoughts and a brand new item to add to her List of Worries. Her only child—a daughter—was going off to college, and the List was growing:

What if she didn't eat right?

What if she drank too much?

What if she had a hard time making friends?

What if she was lonely?

What if she didn't like her classes?

What if she needed her mom?

What if she met a real-life creeper and went on a date with him and he murdered and dismembered her and threw her body parts into the ocean?

She was probably getting carried away. Amelia was going to college in-state, which meant there was no nearby ocean.

"Okay, I'm outta here!" Amelia came bounding back down the stairs, and Sarah jumped. "Jess is here."

"Okay!" Sarah said, her voice way too bright. "Have fun. And make sure her outfit isn't too, you know, revealing."

Amelia laughed. "Oh, Mom. You worry too much."

"It's my job," Sarah said.

Amelia kissed her on the cheek. "Bye. I'll be back by one-thirty."

As she walked out the front door, Sarah could have sworn she said under her breath, "Can't wait. Most awkward road trip ever."

SOMETIMES SARAH LOVED that her daughter was a teenager, and other times, she wished she could magically turn her into an infant again. Not that she enjoyed the sleepless nights, but an almost-adult noticed and vocalized things differently than a tiny baby did. Take, for example, the moment Donny pulled Maude away from the curb.

"Well, I'm checking out," Amelia said. "Please excuse me while I put in my headphones and pretend we're not the most dysfunctional family ever taking a road trip together."

She turned sideways in the dinette so her back was against the wall and her legs stuck out into the walkway, and she crossed her arms.

"That's a bit of an exaggeration, sunshine," Donny said.

Amelia shrugged and focused on the screen of her phone. Donny's eyes flicked from the rearview mirror back to the road. He always managed to keep his cool, Sarah thought. Under normal circumstances, Sarah would reprimand Amelia for speaking that way. But today, she sat stone-faced in the captain's chair behind the passenger seat.

Under normal circumstances, Sarah would be sitting in the passenger seat, at least for the first hour of their drive. Then, she may get up and sit at the dinette with Amelia so they could play cards or watch a video together. But Amelia wasn't quite herself—and Sarah couldn't blame her.

"I can't believe the two of you are acting like this is *normal*," Amelia said as they'd climbed into the RV a few minutes earlier. Sarah had thought of several responses:

"What do you expect me to do, Amelia? I'm in as much shock as you are."

"I'm not acting like this is normal. I have no idea how to act."

"Oh, I'm sorry. I'm busy being devastated. Tell me how you'd like me to act."

But she hadn't said anything aloud.

And now, here they sat, Amelia casting hateful glances at her and Donny, alternately, every thirty seconds or so.

Maude trundled along the highway, heading north through the high desert of Arizona, which was populated with juniper trees and scrub oaks and yellow grass. Donny tapped his thumbs on the steering wheel. Sarah let her thoughts drift. She imagined what her life would look like when they returned after taking Amelia to school. Life After Donny. LAD. It was a good acronym, anyway.

Where would they live? Although part of her thought both she and Donny had changed, fundamentally, part of her knew each of them was still the same person the other had fallen in love with. Donny would, most likely, offer her their house. Remaining there, though, in that cozy haven they'd called home, would cause her nothing but heartache as she remembered watching Amelia open her birthday gifts at the kitchen table, or singing along to cartoon soundtracks while making dinner, or practicing for the spelling bee just before bed.

Sarah's mouth dropped open when her mind began playing the memories of Life Before Amelia: she and Donny dancing in the kitchen when he came home early and interrupted her cooking, him chasing her around the house, threatening to swat her bottom with a towel, the two of them making love on the floor in front of a roaring fire.

Living alone in that house—with only memories to keep her company—would be absolutely unbearable. She'd have to move out, even if Donny said she could stay.

Donny's voice cut into her thoughts. "It's five-thirty. Should we stop for dinner?"

Sarah glanced at Amelia, who had fallen asleep, arms still crossed, headphones still on.

She shrugged. "I'm not hungry, and Amelia's sleeping."

This was the part where she'd normally jump up and offer to make him a sandwich; that was one of the main reasons they'd chosen a motorhome rather than a camping trailer. But she couldn't do it. She'd spent their whole married life jumping up to make him a sandwich—metaphorically—and look where it had gotten them.

"Okay," Donny said. "Let me know if you change your mind."

Sarah nodded. Donny drove. Amelia slept.

Because they were traveling north, the driver's side faced west. Sarah watched the sun make its way towards the horizon, silhouetting Donny's profile. It was fitting, she thought. Watching the lights go down on her marriage and her life. Her eyelids began to feel heavy, and she went into the bedroom to sleep.

Maude came rumbling to a stop, and the change in sound woke Sarah up. It was dark. The sun had finally gone all the way down. She checked her phone for the time and found it was well after eight. She looked out the window and noticed they had exited the highway and were about to turn onto a main drag, heavily populated with fast food restaurants and gas stations.

They usually stopped before dark. Maybe Donny hadn't found a campground or RV park because Sarah hadn't been sitting up front, scouring the Internet for the one with the highest ratings, best reviews, and good prices. She was usually the navigator. Or maybe he just hadn't wanted to stop. Maybe he just wanted to get as far as possible.

They'd taken several RV trips to Wyoming, and they'd found that while a leisurely trip took four days, they could make it to Mama Katherine's house in three if they hustled.

Mama Katherine.

Sarah didn't even try to muffle the groan that escaped, then. What would she tell Mama Katherine? What would she tell Margaret and Hannah? She had to hand it to Donny. Even though he'd inadvertently blurted out his revelation in front of Amelia, it saved them both the misery of having to make some kind of announcement.

"Mom?"

Another groan started low down in Sarah's throat, but she swallowed it.

"Back here."

Donny was pulling Maude into a gas station. Sarah sat up, then dragged herself off the bed and back to the dinette, where she slid in across from her daughter.

"Did you need something?"

"No," Amelia said. "I just wondered where you were."

Without speaking to either one of them, Donny parked at a pump and got out.

"Why doesn't Dad want to be married anymore?" she said as soon as he closed the door.

Sarah sighed, and the tears that had threatened all day finally broke loose like a dam had been blasted wide open. She put her head down on the table and cried.

"What's Dad doing?" Amelia said after a few moments, apparently choosing to ignore Sarah's misery. She obviously blamed Sarah for this. At least partially.

"What do you mean?" Sarah sat up. "I assumed he was getting gas."

"He went inside." Amelia handed her a tissue.

"He probably had to go to the bathroom," Sarah said. "You know he doesn't like to use the RV if it's Number Two."

In fact, it was a running joke. Whenever Donny went into a convenience store, Amelia would tease him about stinking up the bathroom.

Right now, it didn't seem so funny.

"Well, I hope he comes back," Amelia said. "I hope his desire to not be married doesn't mean he ditches us at a random gas station in the middle of nowhere."

"He wouldn't do that," Sarah said.

"Did you *do* something to him, Mom?"

"Why do you assume I did something, Amelia? This has been as much of a shock for me as it has for you, believe it or not."

"I mean, he's the one who said he doesn't want to be married anymore," Amelia said. "If you didn't do anything, why would he just up and leave you?"

Sarah shook her head and held up her hands. "Beats me."

"I always thought you were like, the perfect wife," Amelia said. Her voice had taken on a quality of awe. "I mean, you're always ironing his work shirts and making his lunch. You rub his shoulders after he has a long day at work. I brag about you to my friends. Now I feel like we've all been living a lie."

"I do, too," Sarah said. "I've spent my entire adult life trying to be the perfect wife, doing all the things that would create a happy environment for you. This is so out of the blue." Then something dawned on her. "And I shouldn't be talking to you, of all people. Sweetheart, this situation is not about you. It's not for you to stress about. Your dad and I love you very much. We just want what's best for you."

Other cars came and went, and Donny remained inside. Sarah

wondered what was taking him so long, or, if Amelia was right and he'd sneaked out the back door of the convenience store and run away. She had to keep herself busy, or she'd go crazy.

"You know what?" she said. "Why don't we organize this cabinet? We've been meaning to do it for ages."

"Go ahead," Amelia said. "I don't have the appetite for busywork."

"You know," Sarah said, "your life isn't the only one in upheaval right now. Could you have a little empathy, maybe?"

At first, Amelia didn't answer, and Sarah stood up. Emptying an entire cabinet while they were on the road probably wasn't the wisest idea. No matter where she set the books and videos, they'd undoubtedly slide onto the floor. But she couldn't lay on that bed a moment longer, and she couldn't sit here, staring at Amelia, or in the passenger seat, staring at the side of Donny's face or the unchanging landscape, without something to do.

She'd go crazy.

But when she began pulling books out of the cabinet and setting them in the captain's chair, she thought she might go crazy, after all. This was going to be a trip down memory lane. Here was *Anne of Green Gables*, which she and Amelia read together the summer Amelia was ten and they'd gone to Yosemite. Under towering mountains, they'd sat next to the campfire and read about Anne and her adventures on the farm at Avonlea while Donny played the guitar. And here was *Atlas Shrugged*. Donny had talked her into reading it aloud to him one fall when they drove to Zion National Park. That was just a few years ago and even Amelia had gotten wound up in the plot.

Sarah closed her eyes and leaned her head against the bottom of the cabinet. She had to sear these memories into her mind. They weren't going to make any new memories as a family. Although she wanted to be irrational, to scream and cry and bemoan the fact that Donny wanted to leave her, she thought stoicism might serve her better.

She jumped when Donny opened the driver's door.

"Sarah?" he said. "Are you all right?"

"I'm fine," she said. Her voice came out scratchy and she cleared her throat. "Just cleaning out this cabinet."

"Now?" he said. Maude dipped slightly when he sat down. He shut the door and started the engine.

"No time like the present."

"Okay," he said. He shifted into drive and they were rolling.

"Oh!" Amelia said. "That's where that copy of *The BFG* went! I was just looking for it the other day. I was going to bring it with me to college."

"Remember the nightmares it gave you?" Sarah said. "Are you sure you want to be alone in a dorm room after reading it?"

"Oh, Mom. I'm sure it won't give me nightmares again. I read that thing when I was a lot younger."

"Yeah," Donny said, and Sarah felt a little like he was intruding. "Like, last summer."

"Whatever," Amelia said, her tone playful. "I haven't had nightmares about the bone crushing giant since I was sixteen, at the oldest."

Donny laughed.

Sarah laughed.

Amelia laughed. But when her eyes caught Sarah's, she turned immediately sober.

Still, this tiny moment was like a crack in a cloudy sky, letting golden rays of sun shine through. Maybe Donny would change his mind. Maybe, if she perked up and acted like herself, he'd remember how great they were as a family unit.

"So, Dad. Tell us why you want to get divorced."

Or, maybe not.

Donny sighed. "Amelia, this is a conversation that should take place between your mom and me."

"Yes, exactly. But you brought me into it by making your big announcement when I was there."

"That was an accident," Donny said. "I'm sorry you overheard it."

"But I did," Amelia said.

"You should study law, not education," Donny said. "Some help here, Sarah?"

Sarah had returned to book sorting. "Amelia. Please."

"Fine," Amelia said. "Good talk."

Her sarcasm was almost laughable, especially because she rarely used it with her parents. But Sarah knew it came from a place of hurt. So she didn't reprimand Amelia. Instead, she continued pulling books down, making mental notes about where they'd read them:

The Great Brain: Washington state

Little House in the Big Woods: Flagstaff

The Lion, the Witch and the Wardrobe: Colorado

The Bridge to Terabithia: Utah

Sarah almost cried when she remembered Donny telling Amelia, "'Literature is the people who went before us, tapping out messages from the past, from beyond the grave, trying to tell us about life and death! Listen to them all!' It's a quote. I forget who said it, but that's why we read."

What had they been reading then? Oh, yes. It was *Where the Red Fern Grows*. That was a heartbreaker, for sure. And here it was, the exact copy Sarah had read when she was a kid. She added it to the growing stack of paperbacks.

Exhaustion overcame Donny at midnight, and he did something they'd done only rarely since they welcomed Maude into the family: he pulled into a truck stop. He parked alongside a truck whose trailer promised fresh produce, fast. Amelia had already made the dinette into a bed. She was still awake, though, reading a magazine. She'd been reading that same issue for a while now, and Sarah wondered if she was just pretending to read so she wouldn't have to socialize.

Sarah had finished sorting books, and she returned to the captain's chair, where she sat quietly, scrolling through her social media sites on her phone. Not that she had enough focus to even notice what she was seeing. She'd never been active as far as posting photos of herself or her family. She was too busy making a family and it all seemed so fake, so inauthentic.

The thought of where to sleep had run through Sarah's mind several times during this part of the journey and now, as Donny turned his chair around and stepped into the back of the RV, the decision became imminent. Would Donny want to sleep with her in the back bedroom? Or should she assume he didn't, and climb up into the overhead bunk?

"Well, this is awkward," she said.

"Oh, Sarah. We'll just sleep in our bed, like always," Donny said.

"Do you even want to sleep with me?"

"I've been sleeping with you for twenty years," he said. "Why would it be awkward now?"

Great. Now she felt like crying again.

"Besides," he said. "It's practical. I don't think either of us wants to sleep in the top bunk."

"Well, that's true."

"This is so weird, you guys," Amelia said. "I can't take it. I'm going to sleep."

While Donny leveled the RV, Sarah went into the bedroom and slid the door closed. She scrubbed her hands over her face, hard, and then started changing into pajamas. Her body felt stiff and she didn't know whether it was from sitting so long, or from sheer depletion. She pulled back the covers and got in bed. The sheets felt cold. How many times had they gotten into bed together, shivering, cuddling close to warm up? Countless times.

A few minutes later, Donny did join her. "Cold," he said.

"Yeah," she said.

He turned over, so his back was facing her, and fell asleep immediately—Sarah could tell from the way his breathing changed. Her own breath caught. She had spent the past twenty years memorizing everything about Donny. And now it was all over. All those things she knew about him—the way he liked his eggs cooked, the way his left eye changed shape when he was tired, the way he always forgot to trim the toenail on his right big toe—was she just supposed to put them in some kind of virtual trash can in her memory bank? It was impossible. This was impossible. Sleep was impossible.

CHAPTER SEVEN

DONNY, apparently eager to spend as little time as possible closed in an RV with his soon-to-be estranged wife and his angry teenaged daughter, made it to Mama Katherine's place in record time.

As he drove the RV under the weathered Seedling Homestead sign and down the long dirt road that led to the farm, Sarah felt relief and sadness so poignant they took her breath away. Sitting at the end of the two-track, it looked exactly the same as it always had: the red farmhouse tucked into the corner of the property, backed up against the mountain, the garden off to the left and the chicken coops and animal pens to the right, just next to the house.

Everything would be all right, now. This place, and the people in it, had served as a balm to Sarah's broken heart when she was a little girl, and had acted as a haven for her ever since. Although she dreaded telling Mama Katherine, Margaret, and Hannah that her marriage was over, she also needed a soft place to fall.

"It's so good to be here," she heard herself say.

If things were normal, she would have reached over to squeeze Donny's hand. But her left hand curled into a fist without her telling it to.

"It is," Amelia said, without any sarcasm.

Donny pulled the RV over to the left of the garden. Out sauntered John Wayne, the old herding dog Margaret had talked Mama Katherine into adopting more than a decade ago when Farmer Eddie's dog got loose and ended up having a litter of pups.

"Wow," Donny said as he rammed the shifter into park. "I can't believe John Wayne is still alive."

"Barely," Amelia said. This earned her a dark look from Sarah, who climbed out of her seat to greet the white-muzzled dog.

John Wayne grunted as he approached her on stiff legs. She bent down to scratch his neck, and he half-heartedly brought his hind leg up in a small scratching motion. Donny joined her and John Wayne nudged his hand, his tail wagging full-speed.

"Hi, old buddy," he said, and Sarah felt tears burn the backs of her eyes. Again. This was probably the last time Donny would see John Wayne. Never mind that it could very well be the last time she saw John Wayne.

Amelia knelt down to let the dog kiss her face, and she held his head in her hands for several moments.

"Well, there you are! And a whole day early, too!"

Mama Katherine came around the front of the garden, arms extended for hugging. Sarah didn't need telling—she rushed into those arms and allowed her mother to fairly crush her. It was only natural that in this moment, in this situation, memories would engulf her. When Sarah first arrived at the Seedling Homestead, Sarah was so uncertain of whether to trust her new mother that she hadn't allowed Mama Katherine to hug her for weeks. Mama Katherine had accepted this, but had gently touched Sarah on the shoulder, or smoothed her hair, every day.

Sarah's seventh birthday arrived twenty-two days after she moved in with Mama Katherine and the girls. She'd known it was coming, but she wasn't sure whether her new family knew. She woke up that morning with a strange mix of feelings: comfort that she didn't have to worry about her mother getting drunk and smashing her birthday cake while she tottered over to sing to Sarah; sadness that her first mother wouldn't be here to share the story of her birth, and happiness that this year would undoubtedly be different from the last. Margaret and Hannah were already up, apparently, because they weren't in bed with her—and they almost always crept in during the night.

For a moment, Sarah panicked: had she overslept? Would she miss breakfast? Mama Katherine insisted they eat breakfast, but they couldn't sit at the table until they were dressed with their hair combed. And if they weren't dressed with their hair combed by the time she served it up, they had to eat oatmeal and do extra chores that day. Sarah sat bolt upright, and then clambered out of bed to run to the kitchen.

That whole strange mix of feelings evaporated and was replaced by one overarching emotion: joy.

Her new family stood at the kitchen table, which was covered with a bright blue tablecloth. Atop that tablecloth sat a pile of gifts—wrapped in actual wrapping paper!—and a stack of pancakes so high Sarah thought it might topple over.

Hannah was trying to light a candle they'd stuck in the top pancake, and she froze when she realized Sarah was standing there, watching.

"Happy birthday, Sarah," Mama Katherine said then, her voice quiet, like she wasn't sure how Sarah would react.

Sarah ran the few steps to the spot where Mama Katherine stood next to the table, and straight into her arms.

In that moment, just as in this moment, Sarah felt so loved she could hardly feel anything else. Now, Mama Katherine was a bit older, a bit softer, but she was still Mama Katherine.

"Everything okay?" she said as Sarah squeezed her, held on for just a little too long.

"Of course," Sarah said, stepping back and trying to be nonchalant as she swiped at her tears.

Mama Katherine eyed her with no small amount of suspicion, and then she gestured for Amelia to give her a hug. "My, but aren't you all grown up?" she said. "I wish I could have made it to your graduation, sweetie. But this body's too old to make that trip. Still, I've got a present for you inside."

"Oh, it's fine, Grandma," Amelia said. "I understand. It was boring, anyway."

"And, Donald, how are you? You look exhausted. Come on in and have a beer."

He smiled at her—she'd been a second mother to him since Sarah moved in—and started to make his way towards the house.

"Oh, no you don't," she said, grabbing his wrist. "You give Mama Katherine a hug, young man."

He laughed, and, of course, obeyed.

"Now, Hannah's got some chili on the stove, and she and Margaret should be back soon. They ran to the store. So let's have a nice, cold drink and sit on the porch a while. We'll eat when they get home."

Not a minute later, Mama Katherine's old truck pulled into the driveway, and Hannah and Margaret climbed down. They shut their doors at the same time, and came running up to the house.

In the moment before Hannah squealed and lifted Amelia into a long, twirling hug, Sarah admired her tall, thin frame and her wild mass of blond curls. She put Amelia down and wrapped Sarah up.

"It's been way too long," Hannah said, and Sarah nodded because she couldn't speak.

Hannah held her at arms' length, then, and looked into her eyes. "What's up?"

Sarah shook her head and tried to send her sister some kind of telepathic message that this wasn't the best time to talk about it. "Nothing," she said. "Just tired. But so happy to be here. How about that beer?"

"Did I say anything about beer?" Mama Katherine teased. Sarah knew they always kept dark beer in the fridge, and stocked up when anyone visited.

She felt the tension begin to leave her body as soon as she stepped inside. Everything in the house looked as it always did. Some things don't change, she thought as she followed Hannah to the kitchen. She heard Donny asking Mama Katherine about his old property, which his parents had sold when Donny's job took him to Arizona. They'd moved to be closer to Donny, Sarah, and Amelia.

After Hannah handed out the beers—and an iced tea for Amelia —they returned to the front porch. Sarah and Amelia sat in the porch swing, and Hannah, Margaret, and Mama Katherine took three of the rockers. Donny remained standing, shifting from one foot to another.

"There's an extra chair here, Donny," Mama Katherine said. "No need for you to stand."

"Thanks," Donny said, "but I've been sitting for three days straight. I think I'd like to walk on over to the old place, check it out."

In the past, Sarah would ask if he wanted company, and he'd accept. They'd stroll, hand in hand, down the hill and across the creek —the old log bridge was probably still there—to his childhood home. But this wasn't the past, so she sipped her beer and watched him go, alone.

"The place looks nice," Sarah said.

"So, spill," Hannah said.

"What?" Sarah said. Her gaze landed on Margaret and she said, "So. How was your trip out here?"

"Well, it was a doozy," Margaret said. "What a trip! Thunderstorms over Texas, wind storms over Kansas. I couldn't get out of the airport to save my life. I thought I was going to miss this family reunion."

"But then you sweet-talked an airline attendant into putting you on standby," Amelia said.

"How did you know?"

"You're always sweet-talking someone," Amelia said. "It's your specialty."

"This is true. And now, my darling niece, I'd like to sweet talk *you* into getting me another beer."

"Say no more," Amelia said.

"Wow," Sarah said. "I wish I could get her to do her laundry as cheerfully."

"So, how are things?" Margaret said. "What did I miss?"

"Hannah made chili," Sarah said, in what was probably an obvious attempt to postpone talking about herself.

Mama Katherine shot her a look and said, "It's almost ready. We can eat any time."

"We should wait for Dad," Amelia said, returning to the porch and handing Margaret a beer.

"Oh!" Margaret said. "Where *is* Donny?"

"Went to have a look at his old place," Mama Katherine said. "Here, let's sit. We can wait a while. That chili's only getting better, the longer it simmers."

Hannah cleared her throat and looked at Sarah. Sarah's stomach swirled. "What's the matter with you?" Hannah said. "You're not acting like yourself."

"Dad's leaving her," Amelia blurted out.

Sarah felt embarrassment rush to color her face as she looked first at Amelia, then at Hannah, at Margaret, and finally at Mama Katherine.

"Is it true?" Mama Katherine said.

"Unfortunately, yes," Sarah said. She took another drink of her beer and then threw one hand up. "And I know you're going to ask me why, or what went wrong, but I have no idea."

"It's because she makes him breakfast," Amelia said.

Her expression turned sheepish when Sarah looked at her. "You were eavesdropping?"

Amelia's gaze dropped to her lap. "Not intentionally. I just walked in, and—"

She looked up and shrugged.

"Amelia, I'm so sorry," Hannah said.

"You know," Amelia said, "I think I'll join Dad for that walk. This is going to be weird."

"Actually," Sarah said. "Stay. We can talk about this later."

Amelia nodded and looked away, and Hannah, always the one to smooth things over, said, "So. Amelia. Tell us about your graduation."

Even though she'd just told Mama Katherine it was boring, her eyes lit up. "It was great. The band played live music before, and we all lined up and we were dancing. It was so much fun."

As her daughter talked, Sarah used her feet to rock the swing back and forth, back and forth. She let herself get lost in the rhythm as she breathed in the fresh mountain air and listened to her daughter chatter away. She stared out at the scene before her, the never-ending landscape in its deep shades of green and brown and blue. At one point, she looked over and caught Mama Katherine staring at her.

"Trying to read my mind?" she said quietly.

Mama Katherine just smiled a sad smile, and reached over to squeeze her hand. Sarah squeezed it back, and they sat there, holding hands and rocking, while Hannah kept the spotlight on Amelia and her graduation and plans for college.

As she talked, Sarah's mind wandered to her husband. Her soon-to-be ex-husband. Was what she'd done so terrible that he couldn't stand to be with her any longer? Maybe he was already seeing someone else. Would he have moved on that fast? She doubted it. How could he blame her for wanting the best for their daughter?

And look at her now. Sarah glanced over at Amelia, who was deep in conversation with Hannah. She had grown into a responsible, caring young adult, whom Sarah was confident could take on the world. Sarah sighed.

Hannah noticed the sigh—she noticed everything—and she pierced Sarah with a glare. "So. It's later."

Sarah jumped. Then she realized what Hannah meant, and she sneaked a glance at Amelia. "Can this wait until even later?"

"Can what wait?" Margaret said.

"Dad's leaving Mom," Amelia said. "And I suspect Mom doesn't want to talk about it when I'm here."

"The lingerie didn't work out, then?" Margaret said.

"Ha," Sarah said. "No."

In what was surely a case of divine timing, Donny came walking up the driveway, his hands in his pockets. For just a split second, all the women stared at him when he stopped at the bottom of the stairs. The silence lasted a just a beat too long. Donny broke it with a stuttered hello, and Hannah jumped into action.

"Oh, Donny! Hi! We were just waiting for you to get back so we could eat. Chili's on the stove. Want another beer?"

Before he even had a chance to answer, Sarah said to Mama Katherine, "So tell us about your new neighbors. The ones who moved into Donny's old place."

"It's a young family," Mama Katherine said. "Two parents and a flock of little boys. They all look almost exactly the same, with their curly brown hair and those freckles. It took me a couple of weeks to figure out that there are five of them. Anyway, real nice couple. Matthew and Heidi. And the boys are Luke, John, Paul, James, and Simon. Luke might be about your age, Amelia."

Mama Katherine went on, talking about how the smaller boys had come over one afternoon, asking if they could use the tire swing. Mama Katherine was so delighted to have children around that she ran inside to make cookies for them.

"It's just so nice to have little ones around the house again," she said.

Another beat of silence, as both Hannah and Margaret rolled their eyes. Sarah knew they both felt pressured to start families, and she felt a bit sorry for them.

Then, as they ate dinner, Sarah couldn't help but feel a little bit sorry for Donny. The small talk wasn't quite enough to smother the awkwardness that had sprung up. This had to be hard for him, showing up here with her, knowing their split would eventually become a topic of conversation.

It reminded her of one dinner in particular, during their teenage years, when Donny became the center of attention thanks to a comment about women being less capable of completing farm chores.

The girls had ribbed him something fierce, and Mama Katherine had said, "Donny, son, you're a rose in a bed of thorns."

The adult version of this went a little differently. Rather than ribbing him, her sisters asked him a few questions but mostly pretended he wasn't there. For his part, Donny mostly looked at his chili and commented once or twice on how good it was. Finally, everyone finished, Donny volunteered himself and Amelia to do the dishes, and the four Bradley women went into the living room with a pot of Mama Katherine's strongest tea.

"Okay, sister," Margaret said before Sarah had even finished sitting down on the couch. "Spill it. What in tarnation is happening here?"

Hannah giggled at Margaret's use of Mama Katherine's favorite phrase, but the air in the room was still heavy. Even though she'd just sat down in her rocking chair, Mama Katherine stood up to pour the tea.

"Well," Sarah said. "You heard what Amelia said. Donny's leaving me. That's all there is to it."

"What do you mean, 'That's all there is to it'?" Hannah said. "Surely he said why."

Sarah sighed, and Mama Katherine handed her a cup of tea. "It's all right. You can tell us."

"I know," Sarah said. She felt her chin quiver and she took a sip of the tea. It was still too hot and Sarah flinched. "I know. It's just—I'm not sure what to say."

Margaret shrugged. "Tell us what Donny said."

That was as good a start as any. So Sarah told them. She did her best to be precise, to give her mom and sisters the word-for-word reason Donny had given her. When she finished, she sighed and said, "So. There you have it. My husband wants a divorce because I've tried too hard to be a good mother."

To say the members of her little audience were stunned would be an understatement. For a long moment (maybe two long moments), no one spoke. Sarah could hear Donny and Amelia talking quietly as they did dishes. She could hear them turning the water on and off as they rinsed, and cabinet doors opening and closing as they put bowls and spoons away.

Hannah's eyebrows drew together. *Good*, Sarah thought. *She's angry.* Mama Katherine, always calm, always taking things in stride, simply raised her eyebrows. *She's waiting to see what happens next.* And Margaret, bless her, lifted a hand, in a *Stop* motion.

"Wait," she said. "What?"

"He actually said that?" Hannah said.

Mama Katherine just watched, her focus shifting from Sarah to Margaret to Hannah and back to Sarah as they all waited for her to answer.

"Well," Sarah said.

"I knew something was up when I was there," Margaret said.

"You don't have to sound so triumphant about it," Sarah said.

"It's not that," Margaret said. "It's just that something felt, I don't know, off. I thought you were just on the rag, or something."

"So what did he *actually* say?" Hannah said.

Mama Katherine sipped her tea. In the kitchen, Donny and Amelia had started singing *Brown Eyed Girl*.

"Well," Sarah said. This time, no one jumped in, so she kept talking. "He said, basically, that I've been too attentive, too dutiful, made too many meals. I've lost my spark. I am no longer any fun. And he can't think of spending the rest of our lives together."

Her voice cracked on this last bit, and she took a gulp of her tea, wishing for something stronger.

"We're going to need something stronger," Mama Katherine said.

She went to the bar and took down a bottle of brandy, then poured a healthy dose into each tea cup.

"I mean, hasn't he said anything before?" Margaret said. "He wouldn't just let things go to the point of no return, would he?"

Sarah pressed her lips together. Had Donny said something? Was it possible that he had tried to clue her in, and she'd missed the signs? It was possible, she thought, remorse spreading through her consciousness like oil spreading over water.

"I'm sure he did," Sarah said.

Still chatting, Donny and Amelia came out of the kitchen and towards the living room. Sarah saw the twin smiles die on their faces when they felt the air there, heavy with the weight of this conversation.

"I was going to run Amelia into Walker for some ice cream," Donny said, his voice just a little too loud. "Does anybody want anything?"

"You taking the buggy?" Mama Katherine said. The buggy was actually an off-road vehicle, what Mama Katherine referred to as a golf cart on steroids, and they used it for quick trips into town.

Donny cleared his throat. "I was, if that's okay."

Usually, no one asked permission to take the buggy—they just took it.

"It's always okay, Donny," Mama Katherine said. "As long as you bring us a big tub of ice cream. Double chocolate fudge, right ladies?"

"Right," the three sisters said in unison.

Donny nodded, and he and Amelia walked out.

"Well," said Mama Katherine, and Margaret and Hannah said, "Well."

"The real question is," Mama Katherine said, "what are we going to do about this?"

"Mama," Sarah said. "I don't think there's anything we *can* do. I think we just soldier on. You know? He's already made up his mind."

"Has he?" Mama said.

"I mean, he wouldn't have said something, otherwise," Sarah said.

"Anyway. I just wanted to tell you. We can stop talking about this, now."

She didn't miss the glance Margaret threw at Hannah, nor the one both of her sisters shot at their mother. But she let it go. She was done talking about this.

"So, Margaret," she said.

"So, Sarah," Margaret said. She stretched her legs out in front of her, then tucked them underneath herself on the couch.

"Where are you off to, next? What's your next big project?"

"You know," Margaret said. "I'm thinking of taking some time off."

"What?" Sarah and Hannah said at the same time.

Again, Mama Katherine kept quiet, just waiting to hear what Margaret would say next.

"Have I ever told you that all my doctors' appointments happen to fall at the same time each year? In the same month, I have my regular annual exam, my eye doctor, my dentist. I always end up taking a whole day off, anyway."

"A whole day off," Hannah said. Sarah giggled.

Margaret shrugged. "So I thought I may as well take a whole week off."

"A whole week," Mama Katherine said. She whistled, long and low.

"What?" Margaret said. She looked around at them, and Sarah thought she seemed perplexed. "I never take time off. You guys know that. So a week seems like a long time. I mean, even when I went to Amelia's graduation, I only took off work for a day. Remember, Sarah? I flew in Friday morning and left Sunday."

"Why don't you just go all in and take, like, two weeks off?" Hannah said.

"That makes me uncomfortable," Margaret said, and they all laughed.

"Seriously," she said. "I wouldn't know what to do with myself."

"That is just crazy talk," Hannah said.

"Do you ever take time off?" Margaret said.

"Every summer," Hannah said. "You know it's hard to take time off during the school year."

"But do you ever go anywhere?" Margaret said.

"Nah," Hannah said. "I don't want to leave Mama alone while I galavant around the world."

"You know I can take care of myself, Hannah," Mama Katherine chimed in. There was an edge to her voice, Sarah thought. She resented the idea that Hannah felt like she had to be taken care of. "I could manage without you for a week if you wanted to vacation. I'd love to see you have a nice adventure."

"You would?" Hannah said.

"We all would," Margaret said.

Hannah looked at Sarah, who confirmed by nodding. "We would."

"Have you guys talked about this?" Hannah said.

"No, no," Margaret and Sarah said, which, Sarah thought, made it seem like they had. Well, they may have. On occasion.

"You have," Hannah said. There was a twinkle of humor in her eyes, but not a big one.

"It's just that you're so fun," Margaret said. "And it seems like you just stay cooped up on the farm all the time. You're missing out."

"Am I?" Hannah said. "Because I feel like I'm enjoying the peace of living this way. It's perfect."

Sarah could understand that. Hannah had always liked routine. She'd always liked calm. She was the one who color-coded her closet and organized and reorganized the cabinet under the bathroom sink.

"But don't you ever, you know, long for adventure?" Margaret said.

Hannah shook her head. "Nope. Not one tiny bit. I like routine. I'm perfectly happy here."

Sarah had asked her before whether she wanted to get married one day, and have kids. She'd always wanted Amelia to have cousins. But Hannah remained steadfast: she wanted to stay on Seedling Homestead and take care of Mama Katherine. She had no desire to have a family of her own. Margaret didn't, either. Jet-setting wasn't really conducive to raising a family.

"We should go on an adventure together," Margaret said.

"Uh oh," Sarah said. "I can see it. She's doing that thing she does. She's got an idea and she won't be satisfied until we agree to take part in it."

"Like that time she talked you two girls and Donny into hiding in the cornfield until way past dark, and then pretending to be ghosts?" Mama Katherine said.

"Yes!" Hannah said, and Sarah said, "but you weren't even scared because you were so mad! You and Donny's parents had been looking for us."

"For hours," Mama Katherine said. "I was so mad I could have spit."

Donny's voice cut in: "But Margaret, in all her charm, talked you out of your temper."

Sarah hadn't realized he and Amelia had returned.

"She always was the sweet-talker," Mama Katherine said, smiling up at Donny.

He held up the gallon of ice cream. "I'll grab some bowls."

Amelia sat down on the floor at her mother's feet. "What other mischief did Aunt Margaret get you into?"

"What about the time Mama Katherine got us all dressed up for family portraits?" Sarah said.

"Yes!" Hannah said. "And then she talked us into catching crawdads while we waited for Mama Katherine to finish morning chores!"

"Yes!" Sarah said. "Mama Katherine was so—"

"I could have skinned the three of you alive. Oh, my blood was boiling."

"Did Aunt Margaret talk her way out of that one?"

"Oh, no. There was no talking her way out of that one," Mama Katherine said.

"So what did you do about the portraits?" Amelia said.

Sarah giggled. Hannah stood up and walked over to the fireplace, where she took a framed photo off the mantle. She handed it to Amelia and sat back down.

"It's my favorite," Mama Katherine said. "It's a complete disaster, but it's the best portrait I have of the three of you. It shows you exactly as you were: adventurous, mischievous, and always covered in dirt."

Sarah put her hand out and Amelia handed her the photo. In it, the girls stood on the bank of the creek. Margaret, her black curls wild around her head, like a halo, had mud up to her elbows and caked onto her knees. Hannah, who always tried to stay clean, had a big smear of mud on her cheek, like she'd brushed her hair out of her face at one point. And Sarah leaned on a stick they'd been using to catch the crawdads, her hair sticking out in every direction. Mama Katherine stood just a few feet away, looking at her daughters with a smile that showed exasperation, pride, and a deep, deep love.

They'd had so much fun that day, Sarah remembered. The photographer Mama Katherine hired had followed them around for an hour or two.

"Just play," the woman said. "Do what you'd normally do."

As a result, Mama Katherine had a photo album full of memories from around the property: the girls pushing each other on the tire swing, feeding the chickens, walking down the road with John

Wayne's predecessor, Ringo … all while they wore the white dresses Mama Katherine had bought them.

"I don't know what I was thinking, buying you girls those white dresses," Mama Katherine said now. "One of my dumbest moments, that's for sure."

"I think it was brilliant, Mama," Hannah said.

"Yeah," Amelia said. "All Mom has for portraits are fancy ones. Even the photos she called, 'candid' are actually staged. She rearranged the background of every photo before she pressed the button."

Sarah shrugged. It was true.

"And now you have a lifetime of beautiful memories," Donny said. He'd come back in at the tail end of the conversation, carrying bowls of ice cream on a tray.

"You're missing one," Margaret said, and Donny said, "I'm going to call it a night. I'd love to stay up and chat with you ladies, but I'll admit I'm feeling outnumbered. I think I'm going to sleep under the stars."

It wasn't uncommon. Donny often pulled out a bedroll and slept outside when they were here.

He was fond of saying, "There's nothing like the stars in the Wyoming sky."

After he handed out the ice cream, he headed outside.

Mama Katherine used her spoon to point to the front door, through which he'd left, and said, "That man has loved you since he was a little boy, Sarah, and he still does."

Sarah could feel Amelia's posture stiffen against her legs.

"Mama, I think it's over. No use trying to rekindle a fire that's gone completely out. I'm going to have to move on, and you are, too."

CHAPTER EIGHT

The Walker Farmer's Market was a bustling hive of activity on this Saturday morning, and Sarah allowed herself to bask in the energy, to let the live music, the piles of produce, and the scents of coffee and handmade lavender soap soothe her. They were almost like medicine, and Sarah found her spirits lifting.

"I smell the almonds," Margaret said. "Where's that booth?"

They'd spent every summer Saturday here as children, getting underfoot as Mama Katherine sold the fresh flowers she'd grown in her garden. And every summer Saturday, Margaret scrounged up enough change to buy a paper cone full of almonds.

"It's right there," Hannah said, and even in her distracted state, Sarah noticed a strange tone in her voice. She glanced at her oldest sister, who gave her a pointed look, implying that Margaret should have known the almond booth was right in front of them. Sarah just shrugged, and they made their way over.

"I always find those things kind of disappointing," Sarah whispered as they approached. "They smell so good. But they never taste as cinnamon-y as that."

"More for me," Margaret said.

While she paid—and chatted up the vendor, a short, stocky man with a missing top canine tooth—Sarah continued to survey the Farmer's Market. She was surprised to see some of the same booths that had been here thirty years ago. There was the hand-dyed wool yarn, wound into colorful spools and spilling out of baskets older than Sarah was. And just beyond that stall, Sarah saw the man who made and sold goat milk products like soaps and lip balms and hand creams. She remembered wrinkling her nose over the idea of goat milk soap, but it had become kind of a trend, after all.

"Did they add a flea market?" she said to Hannah, whose eyes were roaming the scene, too.

"Pretty much," Hannah said. "They're calling it an antique swap or something, but it's pretty much just junk, from what I can tell."

"One man's trash," Sarah said.

"Right," Hannah said.

By now, Margaret was saying good-bye to the almond vendor, and the three of them made their way down the main row, between piles of fresh kale and pyramids of shiny apples.

They came to the antique swap booth, and although both Margaret and Hannah ignored it, Sarah steered them closer.

"I want to check this out," she said.

Hannah made a harrumphing sound. "If you want to see this, you oughta join me in the shed and help me go through Mama's stuff. She has tons of junk you could peruse. I've already taken about ten loads to the thrift shop."

Margaret, her mouth full of almonds, chortled.

Sarah was only half-listening as she explored the booth, examining old treasures. Here was an antique sugar dispenser, ceramic with a bold floral image painted on one side. And here was an old metal top, the kind with the plunger. If Amelia was still a little kid, Sarah would have bought it for her. She set it down and picked up a metal recipe box. It was white with red and yellow flowers, and the word *Recipes* printed on one side.

It completely clashed with her kitchen, but wasn't that the point? She'd be needing a new kitchen soon. That thought made her heart beat faster, and not in a good way.

She looked over at her sisters, wanting to gain their approval before she handed over her cash, but they were involved in a serious-looking discussion with the man who sold red-leaf lettuce. So she bought the box, tucked it into her purse, and rejoined them. Without acknowledging her, they kept talking. But they did fall into step beside her, the rhythm easy and natural.

Margaret was admonishing Hannah for getting rid of Mama Katherine's things without consulting them, and Hannah was defending herself, saying she couldn't wait forever for the jet-setting Margaret and the super-mom Sarah to come help her. Sarah saw her point, so she didn't interject.

All three women stopped short when they heard a familiar voice: Donny's. It came from just behind the fresh berry booth, and although he was hidden from view, his words carried easily.

"Yeah, we're separating," he was saying. Sarah's breathing ceased, and she heard a woman's voice, pressing for more.

"Ohmygod, I always thought you guys were the perfect couple. What happened?"

"It's just time, you know? I mean, we've been together since we were kids and the marriage just kind of lost its magic."

Then, the woman's voice again: "I am so sorry, Donny. I really am. But I'm just so glad we reconnected. I have to admit, I always had a thing for you in high school."

There was a brief lull in the conversation and Sarah wasn't sure whether to interpret it as an uncomfortable silence or some silent affirmation that Donny's feelings were mutual. Margaret gripped Sarah's wrist. Hannah was holding her breath.

Then the woman laughed and said, "But you never had eyes for anyone but Sarah, did you?"

All three sisters exhaled.

The woman kept talking then, babbling, which Sarah took to mean that the silence had been an uncomfortable one: "Well, here's my business card. You know, just in case you end up in the area and need a, you know, contact."

"Thanks, Carrie," Donny said. "It was nice to see you."

The situation couldn't possibly get more awkward unless—Donny slipped between the two booths and came face-to-face with Sarah and her sisters. Sarah was relieved to see him in escape mode, but at the same time, she didn't want to face him.

"Oh, uh, hello, ladies," he said.

Sarah was too stunned to answer, but fortunately, Margaret stepped in. "Hello, Donald," she said.

Then, Hannah steered them away like a trio of motorboats, leaving Donny to bob in their wake.

"Did you hear that?" Margaret hissed when they were out of earshot.

"Oh, I heard it," Hannah said.

"He was actually telling someone about the d—"

"No one said anything about the D-word," Sarah said.

Hannah peered around Sarah to make eye contact with Margaret, who shook her head as if to warn Hannah off of trying to talk sense into a crazy person.

Sarah, throat aching with pent-up emotion, whispered, "It's just so much harder to hear him saying it, out loud, to someone else, you know? The fact that he's telling a virtual stranger makes it seem so much more real. Like it's imminent."

"Isn't it?" Hannah said in a voice so gentle that it unleashed Sarah's tears.

Sarah swiped at her cheeks and said, "I don't know."

She didn't say any more as they ferried her back to the parking lot and Mama Katherine's old farm truck. The smell—metal and an engine that ran just a little too rich—was reminiscent of Sarah's childhood at Mama Katherine's house and therefore, it was comforting. Margaret took the dreaded middle seat, a gesture of goodwill that warmed Sarah's heart but also made her think her sisters thought her split up with Donny was inevitable.

Hannah coaxed the engine to life, and as the old truck rumbled down the road, Sarah rolled down her window, letting the cool mountain air rush over her skin.

Was divorce imminent? Or could she change the course of what was happening? As if Margaret could read her thoughts, she took Sarah's hand and squeezed it.

Sarah, wishing for her camera, let her eyes follow the jagged edges of the mountaintops against the pristine blue backdrop of the sky. Before today, Donny's intention to end their marriage hadn't seemed real.

But hearing him say the words, aloud, when he thought she wasn't there … it was the proverbial knife to the heart. Yes, that might be a tad dramatic, she thought. Suddenly, though, the idea of Donny leaving was a real thing. No longer an amorphous, intangible idea, the unavoidable truth stood before her, its height and breadth obscuring everything else.

Everything, that is, except for the emergence of a new determination. Sarah would make things right. Her relationship with Donny had grown and thrived for three decades, and she wouldn't stand by and let it crumble to the ground within a matter of days.

She would repair her marriage. She just had to figure out how.

————

HANNAH PULLED the truck into the driveway and John Wayne walked out to greet them. Sarah gave him a scratch behind the ears, and he ambled off.

"I'm just going to put my purse in the RV," Sarah told her sisters, "and then I'll be in."

When she set her purse down on the table, a clunking sound reminded her about the recipe box she'd bought. That was a silly purchase if ever there was one, she thought, but she'd been caught up in the moment.

She took it out of her purse and opened it. A stack of dividers stood neatly inside, their tabs splotched and greasy as if someone had thumbed through them countless times.

Sarah always loved hearing other people's stories, and she wondered who had owned this recipe box. Who had flicked through it in a hurry to find a quick dinner recipe to feed hungry children? Or to find a perfect meal for company?

As she tilted the tin box to look at the red-and-yellow flower design, she felt something shift inside. Underneath the index cards, she found a small notebook.

It had a plain brown paper cover and a spiral spine, and it looked like it had been well-loved. A coffee stain had made one entire corner of the notebook a darker brown, and the pages there were wrinkly. There was an oil stain just below the center of the cover, and finger-print smudges and a dent where someone had held the book as they read.

Sarah opened the book, and was surprised to see it was a journal. Handwriting—a woman's, judging by the way the cursive swirled and swooped neatly on the lined paper—spread over the inside cover and the first page. Still standing in the RV's entrance, she started to read.

———

IF YOU'RE READING THIS, there's one thing you should know: it's something George Sand said. Now, to tell you the truth, I don't know who George Sand is. But is that really important? Not for the matters of this story. I saw this quote in a book once and it stuck with me. Good old Georgie, he said:

———

THERE IS ONLY one happiness in this life, to love and be loved.

———

THERE. What do you think about that? If you'd said that to me ten, even five years ago, I would have disagreed. I would have said that adventure is happiness. Helen Keller once said, Life is either a great adventure, or nothing. Or something like that. I would have said fun is happiness. It is, isn't it? I would have said so many things. But if there's one thing I've learned it's that love makes everything an adventure. Ergo (I've always wanted to use that word), love is happiness. I think Mr. George Sand was onto something.

Anyway, if you're reading this, you found my journal. Serendipity.

I started this journal—well, never mind. You're going to keep reading, right? You'll get all the main info, like who, what, where, when, why, and how as you go.

But here's something you won't know until you get to the end. Which is why I'm putting it here, at the beginning (and you've got to read this in order). You won't know when you start that this has turned into a beautiful love story. In its early stages, it looked more like it might be a tragedy, or even the tale of an epic, bloody battle. As it unfolded, though, it turned into something incredible, something amazing, something so far beyond what I'd expected it to be.

I'm an old woman now. And if you asked me one thing I've learned (I know, you didn't ask, but I'm going to tell you anyway—it's one privilege of being an old lady—that and peeing when you sneeze), I'd tell you this: good old Georgie was right. Love is happiness. Love is everything.

Now ... happy reading.

———

WELL, Sarah thought, she was in her mid-thirties and according to the author of this notebook, she'd already experienced life's only happiness. Love might not last a lifetime with Donny, but it would with her daughter. Maybe that was the real reason people had children—to ensure there was someone to love them well into old age and even after. She rubbed her eyes, which stung with fatigue. Intrigue beat out the emotion and exhaustion and she slid down into the dinette, spread the journal open on the table, and kept reading.

———

JUNE 2: My thirtieth birthday

———

AN ARRANGED MARRIAGE. In this decade. You'd think our society would have risen above such barbaric practices by now (the California Sandpipers even managed to win the national hockey championships—it doesn't even snow in Los Angeles, where they're based), but apparently not. So today I marry Philip Carlisle, Junior, the third, or something like that. Okay, it's just Philip Carlisle, Junior. Poor guy doesn't know what he's getting, I'm sure. He is probably expecting a demure bride. Little does he know. I would be laughing if I weren't terrified. Daddy probably thinks this is the only way to ensure I'm married off and out of his hair—and not doomed to a life as a spinster as I approach the ripe old age of forty. In fact, I know that's what Daddy thinks.

It's almost unthinkable that in just a few hours, I will pledge my unending devotion to a man I met only yesterday. I understand Daddy's reason for wanting us to get married (besides saving me from becoming a cat lady), but the whole thing is just so … archaic. Philip's father, Jack, has been Daddy's rival for as long as I can remember. Each of them owns one of the biggest apple orchards in California. They've been neck-and-neck for years, each of them the other's only competition. Until last year. A businessman came in and scooped up a handful of the smaller orchards, effectively taking over a third of the apple growing operations in this area. The only thing to do, Daddy said, was to join forces. It was the first thing Daddy and Jack have ever agreed on.

Because they wanted to make sure the partnership stuck and carried forward onto future generations, "Like a marriage," Daddy said, they decided it would be a good idea for an actual marriage to take place. Philip is Jack's prickly, brooding son, whose moodiness has apparently ruined any other prospects for marriage. And I'm Daddy's only daughter, the soon-to-be cat lady.

Since Daddy and Jack have always been rivals, Philip and I have rarely had the opportunity to talk. I've caught glimpses of him at big industry meetings. I'm going to be honest, here. After all, it's just you, Journal. (Speaking of that, maybe I should give you a name. I'll think on that.) He is definitely good-looking. Nice strong chin, clear blue eyes, and straight white teeth. Although I'm pretty sure the only time I've ever seen them straight-on is when he sneered at me. He has large hands, which I'm sure bodes well for our future sex life. Because as you can imagine, Daddy and Jack want grandchildren. They've made that perfectly clear.

Anyway, yesterday's "introductions," as our fathers called them, were unpleasant, to say the least.

Philip seems as unhappy about the idea of our impending nuptials as I am. We shook hands. His palm was warm and dry, and he had a good, firm grip. None of that clammy fish palm from my husband-to-be. I admit, that was a huge relief. He was polite enough, to be sure. And his smile was quite cool. Oh, he's also uncommonly tall. Which I like. I'll have to look up at him whenever we talk. What he lacks in personality, he makes up for with those serious eyebrows. Ha! I jest, Journal (I really do need a new name for you. How about Pauline?).

I'm sure there's a personality in there somewhere. Locked away beneath that stony exterior. He didn't even laugh at my joke about serving apple pie at our wedding.

Now, Pauline, you may be wondering why, even after the California Sandpipers won the hockey championships (which, I daresay, does more to signify the evolution of humans than the Civil Rights Act), I must be forced to marry this young man. And why he must be forced to marry me, because, let's face it, a 30-year-old professional woman is still considered outside the norm, isn't she? (She is, Pauline, in case you haven't been keeping up with social structures.) He's probably afraid I'll go without a bra. Which I won't.

Anyway, here's the answer: Daddy has promised that if I marry Philip, he will pay for me to hire a housekeeper and a cook. Now, this may sound like small beans. But Daddy knows how important my career is to me, and how important a nice home is to Philip. If I can hire a housekeeper and a cook—which I'd never be able to afford on my salary—I can continue working. It's worth it, if you ask me.

And Philip? Couldn't he refuse? I suspect he can't. I suspect, after seeing him at so many meetings and in so many press events, standing right next to his dad, that his family's orchard is as important to him as my career is to me. I'm sure his father has threatened to give the orchard to one of his siblings if he doesn't get married and put this merger through.

I have to admit, even though I've put on a brave face for my friends, particularly Shirley, since Daddy first broached the subject of an arranged marriage, I'm terrified. This is either the beginning of something great, or the beginning of the end.

Okay, that was a bit dramatic. But that's how I feel. Wish me luck. I've got to put on my bridal gown. Me. In a bridal gown. Can you believe it?

The fathers have decided on a new name for our merged orchard (without any input from us): Golden Delicious Orchards.

Hazel Rickshaw Carlisle. I hate to say so, but it has a nice ring to it, don't you think?

———

SARAH CLOSED the journal and placed one hand on top of it. In the history of the National Hockey League, she thought, the California Sandpipers had won the championships only once, and that was fifty years ago now. (The team dissolved a few years later, and it was no wonder. How could a team named after a beach-faring bird ever expect to win big?) If Sarah had her timing right, the modern-day Hazel was probably in her eighties.

Wow. Sarah wished she could find this Hazel Rickshaw Carlisle. She'd love to ask whether things had worked out with Philip, and if so, what she could do about her own marriage.

CHAPTER NINE

THAT NIGHT, Sarah woke up at two a.m., Wyoming's nighttime chill creating goosebumps on her arms. Donny, who said he'd just about frozen the night before, slept next to her in the RV's narrow bed, his breathing calm and even. How could he sleep so peacefully? A tiny, mean part of her, fueled by hurt, wanted to turn over roughly, or to shake him awake and demand to know where everything had gone wrong.

But she didn't have to. Donny woke with a start, a sharp inhale breaking through the near silence. Normally, she would ask him if he was okay, whether he'd had a nightmare. But for now, she remained quiet.

"Are you awake?" he whispered, then.

Sarah didn't answer.

"Sarah. I can tell you're awake."

She sighed, loudly, but cut it short—and resolved to sleep inside from now on—when she remembered Amelia was sleeping just a few feet away.

"We need to talk," Donny said.

"I can't have this conversation in a whisper."

"Then just listen. I'll talk."

At her sides, Sarah's hands gripped the comforter. She nodded, knowing he could hear her head rubbing against her pillow.

"I'm sorry," he said.

Maybe he was going to take it back. She didn't speak.

He went on, "Anyway. I know you're upset. This probably comes as a surprise to you."

She nodded.

"I'm really sorry I didn't say something sooner. Okay? It's just that, for a while now, I've been feeling—I don't know—alone in this marriage."

How is that even possible?

Sarah's mind pointed out all the ways in which she'd been a model wife: the breakfasts and lunches and dinners and ironing and pre-dinner cocktails and shaved legs. He didn't even know about the times she'd declined invitations for girls' nights out, or weekend trips with other moms. He didn't even know how she purposely set her alarm to go off fifteen minutes before his so she could make fresh coffee for him. He didn't even know she hated French Roast! She hated French Roast and she'd been making—and drinking—French Roast every morning for the past two decades. For him. All in the name of being a good wife. And here he was, saying he felt alone in this marriage.

"What do you mean?" Her words came out in more of a croak than a whisper.

"I've lost you, Sarah."

Had she imagined it, or had his voice actually broken?

"What do you mean?" she said again.

"It's—it's like you're a cardboard cutout of the person I married."

What happened to that, "It's not you, it's me," cliché?

"It happened so gradually," he said, and in the dim light of the half-moon, she could see him put his hands on his forehead. "I mean, we used to have so much fun together, didn't we? Remember that time when Amelia was a baby, and Margaret came to stay, and she watched Amelia while we went out for ice cream? And then on the way home, we stopped at the grocery store to get something—something you never thought you'd be shopping for. Was it maxi pads? Those big granny ones? Remember that?"

In the dark, Sarah smiled. She did remember that. She'd been absolutely mortified to have to buy those overnight maxi pads, but she'd run out of the ones the hospital nurses sent home with her, and she still needed them. Donny, the hero of the night, said, "I'll grab them for you. I'm a man! My wife just gave birth to a beautiful baby girl. I'm not ashamed that she needs granny pads!"

But when they actually walked into the store, his bravado disappeared. While Sarah browsed through the huge selection of maxi pads, Donny perused the next aisle, poking his head around the end cap every few moments to see if she was done. Then, when she finally nodded and gave him a thumbs-up, he dashed over to where she stood and tried to take the package from her.

That's when he realized she was actually holding half a dozen packages. Later she'd explain that if they bought a bunch now, they wouldn't have to repeat this process. With Donny's speed coming in, and with the expectation that she'd be holding a single package, he fumbled them and dropped them, sending bright pink boxes of maxi pads bouncing down the aisle. Naturally, this put them both in stitches. Even while they laughed, they did their best to remain quiet, to not attract the attention of other shoppers. Giggling silently, they began collecting the maxi pads.

Naturally, an old lady chose that moment to walk down the aisle, and she looked at them with an expression so startled that both Donny and Sarah completely lost control. They clutched each other's arms, laughing, tears streaming down their faces.

Looking back on it now, it didn't seem quite as funny. But, Sarah reminded herself, they were drunk on lack of sleep, high on this new, powerful love for the tiny miracle they'd created together.

"I remember," she said.

"And what about when we took Amelia to the County Fair for the first time?"

Oh, that had been awful. Well, for a short while. And then they'd turned it into something fun. Sarah, in all her excitement over sharing the fair experience with Amelia, had insisted they go on that spinning ride that presses people's backs against a wall.

"If you want to," she said to the seven-year-old Amelia, "you can turn your body upside down while you're spinning. It's gravity. It's so neat!"

Unfortunately, Amelia didn't share her mother's iron stomach. She didn't enjoy the ride at all, and ended up puking all over the ground as soon as she escaped from the spinning pod. Then she cried, because her stomach was too tender for her to enjoy the cotton candy they'd promised her. They went home, but not before Sarah sneaked off to buy a cotton candy, which she smuggled to the car under her shirt. Amelia was too disappointed to notice. The next day, they had a cotton candy party, complete with homemade fair games and prizes. Of the three of them, Donny probably enjoyed that cotton candy party the most. He ran the games, and played his role with such enthusiasm.

That night, Donny and Sarah had out-of-this-world sex. Now, the details of the fair and the cotton candy party might be a little fuzzy, but she remembered that sex with absolute clarity.

"Then everything became so serious," Donny said, forcing her back into the present moment, back into the darkened bedroom of the RV, back into the final weeks of her marriage. "It was like everything was too significant to be fun. After that cotton candy party. The new Sarah would insist on dye-free, organic cotton candy. Which they don't make. So our poor kid was relegated to organic graham crackers while everyone else had candy bars. Instead of just reading with Amelia, we had to read certain books that had the right word count or phonics or whatever. And instead of just playing with her, we had to hit all these milestones. Our date nights turned into life planning sessions for our daughter. And it's not that I haven't wanted to give her the best possible life. You know I have. It's just that nothing was *fun* anymore."

Shock hit Sarah in the back of the neck and radiated through her body. What was he saying?

"Everything I've done was to provide a good foundation for Amelia," Sarah said. Her mouth was suddenly very dry.

"I know," Donny said, his voice taking on an urgent quality. "I know it has. And I'm not saying there's anything wrong with that—"

"But you are. Because you're saying you don't want to be married anymore."

He turned toward her now. "I just feel like we've lost each other."

She turned onto her side, facing away from him. "Don't you think we can find each other again?"

Now he sighed. Again. "I've been trying to find you, Sarah. And the Sarah I fell in love with is gone."

There were so many raw emotions buzzing around inside Sarah's body: fear, hurt, anger, confusion. There were so many questions:

Why hadn't he said something before this?

Why hadn't he told her, so she could try to find him again?

Was it a crime to do everything possible to create a good life for their daughter?

Would things have been different if they'd had more children?

Was he telling the truth?

Was there another reason he didn't want to be married?

And then, the biggest question of all, the one that rose into her consciousness just before she fell asleep: Could any of what he said possibly be true?

Sarah woke before Donny and Amelia the next morning, just as the sun emerged from below the horizon. She pulled the journal out from under her pillow, and read it in the dusky pink light of the sunrise.

———

JUNE 3: One day after my thirtieth birthday (and my wedding)

———

DEAR PAULINE (YES, I think we're going to stick with that—I like it),

———

IT'S OFFICIAL: I'd like you to meet Hazel Rickshaw Carlisle. That's me.

I have to admit, I felt really beautiful in that wedding gown. And I think I surprised Philip Carlisle, Junior, too. His eyes just about popped out of his head when he saw me. It wasn't one of those Big Moments you hear women talk about, since it was a courthouse wedding and not a church wedding. There wasn't an aisle and nobody was playing the Bridal March.

And I know you've been wondering about this, Pauline: yes, we kissed to seal the deal.

It was perfunctory. Not the most passionate kiss I've ever experienced.

But there was a zing, Pauline. I felt it. From that point of contact down to my toes. A little zing.

My parents hosted a nice luncheon for us afterward. I think my friends came mostly out of curiosity. The luncheon was fine—Mother served shrimp cocktail, which is my favorite. Then, we went to dinner at the club, with all of our parents. The mood was quite celebratory, but I think that was related more to the marriage of our family businesses than to the marriage of Philip and me. But that's not what I want to tell you about.

Obviously, our parents were expecting us to consummate our marriage last night. Our wedding night. Yes, Daddy and Mother, an arranged marriage to the son of our longtime rival, who is also a complete stranger to me, is very romantic. You'd better believe I was anxious to hop into bed, to lose my virginity to him.

I jest. (You'll find that I jest quite a lot. It drives Mother crazy.)

Philip's parents insisted that we stay at their orchard. It sounds rather hokey, but the truth is that it's a beautiful property. In the olden days, they had a full stable there, and they've since converted the barn into a cottage. It really is adorable. They did it all up for us: fresh flowers in crystal vases on almost every surface. Well, on every surface except the bed. Ha. Champagne in a bucket on the kitchen counter. A quiche in the refrigerator, complete with instructions for reheating it in the morning.

Anyway. Pauline, I was so nervous. Did I mention that? I know, I know, I put on a brave face. I acted like it was no big deal when Shirley brought it up. But I was terrified. Truth be told, I envisioned myself in a chastity belt on more than one occasion.

There was no need. When we walked into the barn-cottage, Philip shut the door behind us with a kind of showmanship. At first, I thought he was going to tear off the beautiful suit Mother bought me for the dinner party. But he didn't.

Instead, he looked me right in the eye, gave me the most—okay, the ONLY —genuine smile he'd given me thus far, and he said, "Stop looking so nervous, Hazel. I'm not going to tear off that suit." (It's like he knew exactly what I was thinking, Pauline!). He said, "Let's get to know each other, shall we? Have a seat."

He opened the champagne, poured it into flutes, and sat down across the table from me. Then, he proceeded to ask me questions. And not just shallow questions like what my favorite food is, although he asked those, too. But he wanted to know what big dreams I have, what big fears I have, and whether I really like apple pie. He seemed genuinely interested in my answers.

Did you know he's terrified of cats?

Anyway, I may never fall in love with Philip Carlisle, Junior, but I think this is going to turn out okay.

———

"WHAT ARE YOU READING?" Donny's morning voice was rough and scratchy. There had been a time when hearing just a couple of words in that voice had turned Sarah weak in the knees with desire.

"Oh, just this old journal I found at the flea market."

"Somebody was selling a journal?"

"It was inside a recipe box."

"You bought a recipe box?"

Sarah shrugged. She closed the journal, and immediately started to get up.

"I'll make breakfast," she said.

Donny sighed, and Sarah wondered what was wrong with making breakfast. The floor was cold against the bottoms of her feet and she walked as quietly as she could so as not to wake Amelia. She got out the bread to make toast, and the fact that it was whole wheat reminded her of what Donny had said the night before.

Yes, since Amelia was born, she'd eaten a pretty healthy diet. When other kids in her class brought potato chips and cookies for lunch, Sarah brought carrot sticks and grapes. When she begged her mom to pack leftover Christmas cookies, Sarah always said, "You can have one when you get home. After dinner. If you eat all the vegetables."

Was there something wrong with wanting their daughter to be healthy? Sarah thought as she cut the toast slices in half, narrowly missing her own finger with the knife.

Now that she was thinking about it, though, when had Amelia stopped asking for treats? When was the last time they'd had *dessert*?

It had been eons. The next time they went to the store, Sarah thought as she cracked eggs into a pan, she was going to buy something sweet. She'd march right in and buy a candy bar. Or a pre-made pie, as laden with preservatives as it was. Or something. A giddy feeling expanded inside, and Sarah stifled a laugh.

She set their plates on the counter. She'd typically wait for Donny to join her, but this morning, thinking consideration had gotten her into this mess, she picked hers up, sat down in the captain's chair and began to pile eggs onto her toast while she thought about Hazel. Was she still alive? Did she realize her journal had been given to a thrift shop? Sarah made a mental note to do an Internet search of the local white pages. Donny walked out of the bedroom and picked up his plate, then slid into the dinette. They ate in silence.

Then the nostalgia hit.

Hazel Rickshaw Carlisle's love story hadn't started off with much fanfare. But Sarah's had. Because she and Donny had always known they'd get married, he had years to plan the perfect proposal. Not only that, but he knew her well enough to plan one she'd love. How he still managed to surprise her, she'd never know.

They were seventeen. *Seventeen!* Sarah thought now. Amelia's age.

Sarah glanced at her daughter, who was still asleep (or feigning sleep) in the bunk over the cab. Amelia's main interests were teen magazines and bowling. How in the world had she, Sarah, thought she was ready to commit to a lifetime of love at that age? Well, she had been, but apparently Donny hadn't. If he'd waited until she was twenty-five to propose, maybe things would have gone differently. Serious Sarah would have already shown up on the scene, and he'd have been mentally prepared for organic fruit in place of cotton candy. Cotton candy! Of course she wouldn't let Sarah eat cotton candy.

Anyway. Sarah shook it off. There was nothing wrong with

insisting their daughter eat healthy. They'd given her a really strong foundation for future health. And there was nothing she could do about it now.

Yes, they were both seventeen when Donny proposed. But he'd been planning the big day since he was fourteen, saving the money he earned from mowing neighbors' lawns, feeding their horses, and changing the oil on their cars. He borrowed a tractor and a driver—Mr. Brooks, an old farmer who lived a few acres over—and told Sarah he had a surprise for her.

When she first saw Mr. Brooks and the tractor, with the little trailer attached, she stopped short. She didn't know what she was expecting, but it wasn't this. For some reason, she found herself feeling a little nervous when she saw Mr. Brooks's knowing smile. She took the hand he offered and stepped onto the trailer.

Donny had planned an elaborate hay ride that took them past the spots where they'd shared significant moments. Mr. Brooks drove them past the tire swing where they first met, along the creek where they fished for crawdads, down the road where he and her sisters taught her how to ride a two-wheeler. As they rumbled past each stop, he pointed it out, but other than that, he seemed very quiet. Subdued.

Finally, Mr. Brooks pulled up at the base of the willow tree where they often picnicked. He stopped the tractor. The sun was going down, and its golden light shone through the tree's leaves. Donny led Sarah off the trailer, and Mr. Brooks drove away with a tip of his hat. Sarah laughed, watching as the tractor trundled away from them.

When she turned around, Donny was staring at her in such an intense way, she gasped.

"Is everything okay?" she said.

"Always," he said. He cleared his throat and took off his hat. "Sarah."

"Donny." She giggled.

He took both of her hands in his. "When I first saw you on Mama Katherine's farm, standing there with Margaret and Hannah next to the creek, I thought you were an angel. I thought you were a vision from Heaven. When I realized you were real, I knew I wanted to be with you for the rest of my life. When I heard you laugh that first time, when I spun you on that old tire swing, I knew I would do anything to protect you. To hear that laugh over and over again."

Sarah stood there, staring at him, breathless. He used one hand to remove something from his pocket. He held it up between them. It was a ring. A gold band with a tiny glittering stone on top.

"Sarah Jane Ward, nothing has changed. Except that I'm old enough to ask you. I still want to be with you for the rest of my life. I still want to protect you. I still want to hear that laugh over and over again. Will you do me the honor of being my wife?"

Serious Sarah, the grown-up version of the girl who had responded to Donny's proposal with a nod and a hug and yes, a few tears, looked down at that same ring, which had been on her finger ever since. When she did, a tear escaped from under her eyelid and landed on the surface of her plate, beading up and sparkling in the sunlight.

———

THAT AFTERNOON, Sarah and Amelia pulled weeds in Mama Katherine's enormous garden. Sarah paused every half-hour or so to photograph a baby tomato or a giant caterpillar or a nest of bird's eggs. Sometimes she paused for longer than she should, because she was rearranging the backgrounds of her photos: adjusting the position of a leaf, relocating a rock that didn't quite match, turning an egg so that its speckles showed more prominently.

That's when it hit her: rearranging the backgrounds of her photos was symbolic of her need to control every aspect of her life—and Donny's and Amelia's. She wasn't composing photos ... she was composing order. But life wasn't all about order.

Donny's reappearance—glasses of lemonade in hand—cut her musing short. Sarah sat back on her heels to drink hers.

"I gave the truck a once-over and it needs a few belts and an oil change," he said. "I'm going to run it into town, to that auto parts store. Do you want to come?"

The invitation was meant for Amelia, Sarah knew, but she immediately saw her opportunity.

"Sure," they said at the same time.

Amelia threw her a look so dark Sarah almost laughed. They finished up their lemonade, Amelia ran the glasses back into the kitchen, and the three of them climbed into the cab of the truck.

"We should fill her up," Sarah said, hoping her candy-bar-buying mission wasn't too obvious.

Donny just nodded, and a few minutes later, pulled into the gas station.

"I think I'm going to run in," Sarah said to Amelia when Donny got out. "Want anything?"

Amelia shook her head. "Why are you going in?" she wanted to know.

Sarah didn't admit she was going in so she could buy sugary treats. She wanted to surprise Amelia. So she just shrugged. "I don't know. Just wanted a little pick-me-up."

"You never go in," Amelia said.

"Well, I'm going in, now," Sarah said, noticing her voice was a bit snappy and instantly regretting it. "Do you want something, or not?"

"I already said I didn't," Amelia said, her tone echoing Sarah's. "I just think it's weird you're going in."

Sarah reminded herself that everyone's nerves were on high alert after Donny's announcement, and she took a deep breath. Donny had set up the gas to pump, and he was now walking into the store. She'd just sneak in behind him, buy the candy, and get back to the truck. Then, when they were on the road, she could present both Amelia and Donny with the bounty. She nodded.

"Mom?" Amelia said. "Are you okay? You're—I don't know. You're acting weird."

Sarah flashed her daughter a smile in response, and descended onto the pavement. It had been years since she'd gone inside at a gas station. Her strict schedule meant she rarely had time, and she hated using the bathrooms at these places. Plus, practicality didn't allow for extra snacks. She always packed fruit and cut-up veggies and cheese so she wouldn't have to buy processed foods when they were on the go.

"Wow, Sarah," she mumbled to herself as she walked across the parking lot. "You really *are* inflexible."

She stopped outside the doors and squared her shoulders. Still, when she stepped in to the air-conditioned building, she froze. Smells and colors and sounds assaulted her. Signs hung from the ceiling, promoting gallons of soda for just a few cents, or pounds of hot dogs for a dollar. Over the loudspeakers, advertisements blared. This was complete sensory overload. Had these stores always been like this?

"Wow," she said.

Keep moving, Sarah. The candy was easy to spot. And there was so much of it. She had no idea what to buy. There was the traditional stuff—regular chocolate bars and those peanut bars with caramel. But there was also new stuff in brightly colored packaging that promised to be exponentially better than all the old stuff.

Fortunately, she recognized a childhood favorite: a 100 Grand bar. She snatched up three of them and marched up to the front of the store. She'd hoped to get back to the truck before Donny saw her, so she could surprise him, too, but this line was incredible.

A familiar thought flared up: *And this is why half of America is obese.* But she fought it off. There was nothing wrong with a treat now and then. Besides, no one in this line was obese. One guy was even holding a pre-packaged salad. They sold *salads* in these places?

"Sarah?" Donny was beside her, then. "What are you doing in here?"

With a guilty smile, she held up the three candy bars. "Just getting us a little treat?"

He blinked. "Sarah. Just because I said the thing about the cotton candy doesn't mean—"

She staved him off. "You were right. It's about time I lightened up. Do you still like these?"

"I don't even know what to say," he said.

The line moved forward.

"Did you know they sell *salads* at these places?" she said.

"Um, yes?" Donny said. "I did. Truth be told, they're not very good. But they've sold salads for quite a while."

"Huh," Sarah said.

"How long has it been since you walked into a convenience store?" Donny said.

Sarah shrugged. She didn't want to admit how long it had been. "Eons."

"I guess so."

They didn't speak as the line moved forward again, Sarah paid, and they walked back to the truck. After Donny replaced the fuel nozzle and twisted on the gas cap, Sarah handed him his 100 Grand. He gave her one more quizzical look, and accepted it with a, "Thanks."

When Sarah presented Amelia with the candy, Amelia looked at Donny as if to ask if her mother had lost her mind. Then she shrugged and said, "Thanks? I think?"

"You're welcome," Sarah said.

She climbed in next to Amelia and opened the candy. It was only then that she noticed Donny and Amelia hadn't opened theirs. "What are you guys waiting for?"

"I'm scared," Amelia said.

"Scared of what?" Sarah said.

"Why did you buy these, Mom?"

Sarah took a bite of the bar. "Ohmygosh this is so good."

"I think you've lost it," Amelia said.

Donny, who had been watching her carefully, as if this might be a trap, said, "I'm going for it, Amelia. I think you should, too."

Amelia shrugged and opened hers. Donny let out a moan of satisfaction and started the truck. Sarah lifted her camera and without stopping to check the background, she snapped a shot of Amelia, grinning mouth full. Sarah couldn't be certain, but she felt like, in that moment, something shifted.

CHAPTER TEN

A QUICK INTERNET search for *Hazel Rickshaw Carlisle, Wyoming,* turned up few results. Sarah didn't know what she'd been expecting, but it was more than this. Then she remembered that Hazel and Philip hadn't married here in Wyoming—they'd been in California.

Mumbling as she did it, Sarah changed *Wyoming* to *California* and tapped "Search."

Hannah came into Mama Katherine's kitchen, where Sarah was sitting at the table.

"What are you mumbling about?" she said.

"Oh, nothing," Sarah said. She put her phone down. This whole thing was silly, anyway.

"You're wearing your concentration face," Hannah said. She sat down next to Sarah.

"Just doing a little Internet research, nothing important. I know you wanted help sorting through Mama Katherine's stuff today. I was just finishing my coffee."

She held up her coffee cup, which was empty and had gone cold a while ago.

"I'm scared, Sarah," Hannah said, and Sarah was surprised to see tears in her sister's eyes. "I'm scared Mama Katherine is going to die."

"Are you scared she's going to die, or are you scared about what will happen after she dies?" Sarah said.

Hannah nodded. "I'll be alone. You know? I've spent my entire adult life taking care of her."

Now, Sarah nodded. She and Margaret had discussed this at

length. Hannah had her teaching job, and her students. But she definitely didn't have a social life.

"Maybe now is the time to start branching out," Sarah said. "Can't you join some kind of group, or club, or something?"

Hannah laughed. "Yeah. Spinsters Anonymous."

Sarah thought about Hazel and her arranged marriage.

"Maybe you should start dating."

"I hardly have time for that," Hannah said. "And besides. Have you seen the men in this town?"

"I guess not," Sarah said. "Is it bad?"

Hannah's nose wrinkled. "Pretty much the worst."

"I'm going to find you a man."

Hannah just shook her head, dismissing the idea. "First, find me some boxes. They're in the laundry room. I'll get some tape. Let's get packing."

Mama Katherine's garden shed was the scene of many teenage shenanigans, Sarah thought. Specifically, it was one of the places she and Donny had sneaked off to when they wanted to make out.

Which, she realized now as the wooden door creaked open to reveal a cloud of dust and curtains of cobwebs, was pretty gross. Still, the memories made her smile: when they were fourteen, Donny dared her to go into the shed and stay there for three minutes—three full minutes—even though she was terrified of the resident Daddy long legs. At the two-minute mark, he came in and said, "I'll bet I can distract you for the final minute."

That third minute passed so quickly Sarah couldn't believe it. In fact, maybe they'd stayed in there even longer.

Now, Sarah and Hannah stood side by side, surveying the neat rows and stacks of Mama Katherine's cardboard boxes. Each one was labeled with something semi-humorous: *The worst years of my life— 1958-1959, The Year of My Most Horrible Haircut (1955), Junk from my Hobbit-like apartment.*

"Have you ever talked to Mama Katherine about her life before kids?" Sarah said.

"I've asked her about it, but she seems to want to keep it private," Hannah said.

Sarah nodded. She'd experienced the same.

"Doesn't she want to help you with this?" Sarah said. "Or did she just give you full executive power?"

"She said she trusts me," Hannah said. "She said it's all old junk she put here when she first moved in, and she couldn't care less if we throw it in the trash, box by box. I guess I'm the one who wants to weed through it and make sure we're not throwing away anything important."

Sarah had heaved a box off the top of a stack, and pried open the lid. She pulled out the avocado-colored ceramic base of a lamp and cringed. "Like this?"

"Maybe we *should* just be tossing these boxes in a Dumpster," Hannah said. "But I just can't bring myself to do it."

"Where's Margaret, anyway?" Sarah said. "I was going to say this will go faster with two of us working on it. But it would go even faster if she were here."

"I don't know," Hannah said. "She's been a bit mysterious since you all got here, hasn't she? She keeps disappearing."

"I didn't even notice," Sarah said. "I've been so wrapped up in what's gone wrong with Donny, and—I just haven't noticed."

Fortunately, Hannah didn't ask her what else she'd been wrapped up in, and just shrugged. "I'm sure she's just trying to get work done while she's here. She so rarely takes time off."

"True," Sarah said. "You know, since she's not here now, I think I'll give her this lamp as a gift. So she doesn't feel left out."

Hannah snorted. "Great idea. Let's get to work."

For the next hour, the two of them went through boxes, unearthing the strangest combination of belongings: books and hats and old dolls and dishes. They sorted the items into new boxes: trash, donations, and stuff to ask Mama Katherine about.

"Does it seem like she just threw stuff in these boxes in a hurry?" Hannah said at one point.

"It does," Sarah said. "Like the house was on fire and she had to get out as quickly as possible."

"She's never been excessively neat and tidy, but this is over the top, even for her."

Sarah shrugged. "I've never had to pack up my things before, so I don't know what it's like. But I guess I'll find out in a few weeks."

"So you and Donny are really over?" Hannah said. "That seems impossible."

"Oh, it's possible," Sarah said. Without warning, she burst into tears. "I can't blame him, Hannah. I've been awful. It's no wonder he wants to leave."

"What?" Hannah said. "You've been, like, the perfect wife and mother. Any man would be lucky to have you."

"Did you know, I bought a candy bar the other day, and Amelia thought I was losing my mind?"

"Well, you've always been health-conscious. There's nothing wrong with that."

"I rearranged the backgrounds of my *photos*! I've been a controlling maniac, that's what I've been!"

"But who can blame you?" Hannah said. "Your early years were so chaotic. That does something to your hard wiring. You just wanted to create a peaceful environment."

"I know," Sarah said, her voice more of a wail than anything. "But that doesn't mean I was any more bearable to live with."

"But Donny's known you forever. He knew your past. He knew what he was getting into," Hannah said.

"It got worse when we had Amelia," Sarah said. "And then I took it too far, for too long. And now it's too late."

"Is it?" Hannah said.

"Obviously," Sarah said. "You heard him at the farmer's market. He told someone—a stranger—that we're splitting up."

Hannah worked in silence for a few minutes. Finally, she said, "I'm no expert on relationships, Sarah, but I think it says something that he's here with you."

"Yeah," Sarah said. "It says he's a good father."

"It says more than that," Hannah said.

Sarah just shook her head. After another hour and probably two dozen more boxes (including *All The Pink Stuff From My Childhood Bedroom* and *The Horrible Dresses Mother Gave Me That She Couldn't Bear For Me To Throw Away*), Sarah and Hannah called it quits.

Hannah said she wanted to spend some time researching new lesson plan ideas for the upcoming school year, so Sarah escaped to the RV to read Hazel's journal.

———

JUNE 10: Wedding + one week

———

DEAR PAULINE,

———

THIS MARRIAGE THING is going to work out perfectly. So far, Philip has pretty much left me alone. We share a bedroom in our new house, but he hasn't slept in it yet. I do wonder where he's sleeping. He's let me come and go as I please, without asking many questions. Okay, without asking ANY questions. He is quite disinterested. Which is good. I suppose.

And I've been able to spend lots of time at the office. Advertising is THE industry to be in, Pauline. I'm right on the cutting edge. And I think they're going to make me a senior copywriter soon. That would be so amazing!

Here's what I've learned about marriage in the past week:

Philip's favorite dinner food is spaghetti. Our cook, Betty, makes great spaghetti. Hey, that rhymes.

I love having a cook.

Only one week has passed, but in that week, I've finished moving all my things into our new, beautiful house. I'd never stopped to think of what I'd bring into my "adult" life and what I'd leave behind. Is it silly that I wanted to bring my jewelry box? The one with the dancing elephant inside? Daddy thought that was such a clever thing, to have an elephant inside of a jewelry box. I wonder what Philip would think of it. I haven't shown it to him and I probably won't. I'm sure he would find it childish.

Shirley is coming for a visit this weekend. I'm excited to show her around Golden Delicious Orchards.

I'd better sign off for now. I have a big team meeting tomorrow at work. I've been working hard on some ad copy and I am hoping they'll choose my headline. If I can get them to use just one piece of my copy, that's like getting out of the starting gate. Then I'm on the track with the rest of those fellows.

I can assure you, Pauline, my copy is worlds ahead of any copy that Maximillian Duff has put together. But I'd better go polish it up, just to be sure.

———

JUNE 17: Two weeks since Philip and I tied the knot

———

DEAR PAULINE,

———

THEY MADE ME SENIOR COPYWRITER! I knew it! I just knew I could do it. And you should have seen Maximillian Duff's face! That expression! Yes,

Max, dear, women can write, too. Stuff that bewildered expression right—well, you know, Pauline. Right where the sun doesn't shine.

Shirley came for a visit over the weekend. We had a lovely time. Even though I'd made it perfectly clear that the marriage between Philip and me is more of a business arrangement than anything else, she had so many questions about what it's like to be married. Obviously, she asked about the sex. When I said, "What sex? There is no sex, Shirley," she seemed absolutely blown away. Shirley's still in the Virgin Club with me.

Then, she seemed surprised when he wasn't around for most of the day, and even more so when he didn't sleep here.

Even though it doesn't bother me that Philip and I are strictly business, I had kind of an epiphany. And aren't diaries the place for epiphanies? Oh, but you know you're more than just a diary, Pauline.

My epiphany is something like a question: Is this all there is?

Yes, I'm thrilled about being made senior copywriter. And I'm thrilled that Daddy's business will continue to thrive. It's his legacy, isn't it? And it will be mine, too. Apple pies as far as the eye can see.

I know that technically, you don't have a memory, Pauline, but remember last week when I said Philip was disinterested? And I said it was good? Philip does let me come and go as I please, and he seems perfectly content when I go to work early or come home late (if a girl wants to keep her senior copywriter position, that's what she has to do).

It is good. It is wonderful.

But ...

I realized when Shirley was here that if nothing changes, I will live my entire life in a loveless marriage, working full-time. Oh, sure, I can leave my own legacy with the advertising! My copy is in the ads that will sell nylons and beer and potato chips for huge companies. Thousands of people will read my words.

But here's the thing: I have no one with whom to share that excitement! You see, I came home from work the other day, after I was officially promoted, and Philip wasn't there. Betty had left early—she left a lasagna in the refrigerator (I think Italian is her specialty)—which meant I was alone in the house.

I called Mother, but you know how Mother is about these things. Okay, maybe you don't know. Mother doesn't care whether I have a career. I mean, she wants me to be happy, but mostly she indulges my excitement like I'm living in some kind of fantasy world. ("Oh, yes, darling, that's a lovely pet unicorn you have.") She'd be excited if Philip and I ever had children, but seeing as how we don't exchange more than a handful of words each day, I am not sure how we will ever get around to exchanging—well, you know.

I'm getting off topic.

Here's the thing, Pauline: Is this all there is?

Ten years from now, even five years from now, will I come home to an empty house, eat Italian food cooked by someone else, and go to bed alone, without ever telling anyone about my day? Without ever sharing the excitement of a particularly good headline or motto? Things would be different if I'd remained unmarried and returned home to my empty apartment.

This seems like a boring existence. I am not miserable now, but I fear that I may become miserable as time passes. And I'm scared.

Now. My daddy didn't raise a whiner. My mother didn't raise a quitter.

So you know what I'm going to do, Pauline? I'll tell you.

I'm going to make Philip interested. I'm going to make him fall in love with me. And I'm going to fall in love with him, too.

———

JUNE 18: Two weeks + one day since we said our vows

———

HI PAULINE,

———

A GOAL CAN'T BECOME reality unless there's a plan to make it so. That's why I've developed a plan for winning Philip's heart. The first step is to get to know him. I know, it's almost ludicrous to think that I've got to get to know a man with whom I'm already living, to whom I've already made a lifetime commitment.

I'm breaking that step down into smaller steps.

First off: Observation. I'm going to watch Philip, take in everything I can. I'll memorize his mannerisms, learn his habits, and discover his secrets.

Second: Immersion. We'll have to spend more time together. Maybe I can take a day off and spend it with him, at the orchard. We've been eating dinner together, but our conversations have been mostly small talk. I'll have to change that.

Third: Adventure. There is nothing like adventure to bring two people closer together. I'm not sure, yet, how to create more adventure in our lives, but I have a few ideas brewing.

I've heard people talk about soulmates. Well, I've mostly heard Shirley talk about soulmates. But I don't think there has to be one single soulmate for each person. I believe that two people who are a good fit can fall in love. Like Mother and Daddy. I'm out to prove it.

———

JUNE 20: Day Two of the Grand Experiment

———

STAGE ONE: Observation

———

PHILIP CARLISLE IS A VERY good-looking young man.

———

THAT IS ALL.

———

JUST KIDDING, Pauline.

———

WELL, he IS a very good-looking young man. He is so tall. And his hands are broad. His chin is strong and manly. His eyes are the most interesting color. They're blue, like I said before. But they're almost gray.

But that is not all I've observed about him.

Philip is very tidy. His shirt buttons always line up just so with his pants button. His side of the closet is very organized: shirts all at one end, lightest to darkest. Pants at the other, lightest to darkest. His belts hang in between his shirts and his pants, and he keeps his shoes in their boxes (I thought only women did that).

Philip likes to have a bourbon every evening before dinner. I had witnessed this before, but I hadn't witnessed that he always uses three ice cubes. Not two, not four, but three. Every time. He says the bourbon makes him feel relaxed after a stressful day.

Naturally, I asked the follow-up question, which was: What makes your days stressful? (It's the kind of thing I'd ask an advertising client, Pauline. So being a professional woman comes in handy in marriage, after all! Mother said it would doom me to a life of spinsterhood. But look.)

And he played right into my little plan: he agreed to let me join him for a day at the orchard.

Philip's favorite food is meatloaf. I know. Not very adventurous (rest assured we'll do something about that). As I mentioned previously, he likes Italian (thank goodness, since that is all Betty seems to make). But I learned that he prefers German food. I think I will give Betty a day off and make him some schnitzel. I actually don't know what schnitzel is. But I'm going to make it. Mother has a German cookbook, to be sure. Or those wonderful pretzels. I wonder if Philip likes beer.

Come to think of it, I should start a list of questions to ask Philip.

I'll start one on the next page and add to it. Hold on. I'll be back in a minute.

———

QUESTIONS TO ASK Philip

———

JUNE 20

———

WHY THREE ICE cubes in your bourbon?

    Do you drink beer? If so, what kind?

    Do you prefer dogs or cats?

    How old were you when you lost your first tooth?

    Do you like apples?

    As a child, what did you want to be when you grew up?

    Do you want any children?

    How often do you cut your toenails?

    What is your favorite book, ever?

    If you could spend one day in a different city, where would you go?

    What is your favorite childhood memory?

———

OKAY, Pauline. I'm back. Whew! I came up with ten questions to ask Philip and I had to stop myself there. I don't want to overwhelm him.

Further observations about Philip:

At dinner, he wipes his mouth after every bite. He doesn't eat breakfast. He always leaves the house two minutes before he says he plans to. I don't know if he actually plans to leave two minutes earlier than he SAYS he plans to, or if he just happens to be ahead of schedule. Every day. If I were Philip, I would just set my alarm clock to go off two minutes later in the morning.

Oh! One more thing before I sign off for the day: I discovered that Philip is sleeping in a spare bedroom. I find it a little strange that he never told me where he'd be sleeping, and that he just gave me the master bedroom by default. I suppose he didn't want me to feel out of place. But this is interesting.

I've got to sign off, now.

Hopefully, the next time I write, I will have begun putting my plan into action.

The next step: Immersion.

CHAPTER ELEVEN

WHEN SARAH WALKED into the living room later that evening, she wished she'd told everyone she was going for a night walk. But Donny had already claimed that activity, and Amelia was asleep the spare bedroom Mama had insisted on clearing out when nighttime temperatures dropped to the forties. Which meant Sarah was forced to socialize. Margaret was sitting on the floor with her elbows on the coffee table, and Hannah sat on the couch. Mama Katherine sat in a side chair, her feet on the ottoman, legs crossed at the ankles.

Before Sarah could even sit down, Margaret said, "Did you really fix the background of every candid photo you took of Amelia?"

Naturally, Sarah thought as she flopped down on the couch next to Hannah, *Margaret had to come back to that.*

"Not every one," Sarah said. "Sometimes the background looked fine on its own and I'd leave it alone."

"But, why?" Margaret wanted to know.

"I don't know," Sarah said. "I guess … well, partly because I knew I'd be sending those pictures to you guys. You know? And to Donny's parents. I didn't want anyone to think we lived out of laundry baskets sometimes. Even though we did. And because I want Amelia to look back on these photos and remember that we had a nice family life. She grew up in a nice house. You know?"

At first, no one responded.

Both Hannah and Margaret looked at Mama Katherine, who looked at each of them in turn and then back at Sarah.

"This is one of the reasons I never wanted kids," Hannah said.

"Way too much pressure. You're afraid people are judging you based on the backgrounds of your photos."

"Not judging me," Sarah said, but she didn't supply an alternative because she didn't have one.

Margaret chimed in: "I didn't have kids because of what we're seeing here, with Sarah and Donny."

She apparently missed the warning glare Mama Katherine shot at her, because she continued, "I mean, I thought they were the world's perfect couple. You know? I mean, they were probably voted 'Most Likely to Be Married Eighty Years From Now' in our high school yearbook, weren't they? Things can be going along so splendidly, and then, out of nowhere, they just fall apart."

"Thank you for reminding me of my failure, Margaret," Sarah said.

"I wasn't," Margaret said. "I didn't mean it like that."

"They haven't fallen apart," Mama Katherine said.

"But we have, Mama," Sarah said. Her voice cracked. "Your optimism can't fix this."

"Your pessimism definitely won't."

Both Margaret and Hannah gasped, which would have been funny under different circumstances. And while what Mama Katherine said might be true, Sarah thought, the words still stung.

Sarah waited a long moment before speaking, but when she did, her voice was strong. "Mama, he said he wants to leave. Maybe if he'd said something earlier, maybe if he'd given me a chance, I could try to fix this. But it's already over."

Mama Katherine stood up, and not for the first time this visit, Sarah noticed how much older she looked. The lines around her eyes were deeper, even when she wasn't smiling. She looked thinner and somehow smaller. And right now, she looked a little angry, too.

"What have I told you girls for years?" she said. "I've told you that people don't give you chances."

"You make your own chances," all three sisters said.

"That's right," Mama Katherine said. "And if your marriage is important to you, Sarah, then don't you dare wait around for Donny to give you a chance. You make your own chance, right now."

Mama Katherine excused herself and went to bed, her gait a little slower than it had been the last time Sarah saw her. Hannah had been right to ask them to come now. Still, while Mama Katherine might be getting older, physically, she hadn't lost her fire. She was like the flower of an Angel's Trumpet: beautiful but deadly.

Fatigue overcame Sarah as soon as Mama Katherine went into her bedroom. Hannah and Margaret floundered around for something to talk about, and the conversation dipped into several surface-level topics like the garden and the chicken coop. Margaret was yawning a lot, and Hannah kept teasing her about it.

"I'm going to call it a night," Sarah said.

She couldn't help but notice that her sisters looked relieved. They'd probably be as happy as she was that she was leaving. She knew her negative energy was exhausting.

"Sarah," Hannah said when Sarah reached the entrance of the living room.

Sarah turned around.

"We love you. No matter what happens or how this turns out. Okay?"

Before Sarah could speak, Margaret said, "And you haven't failed. Not at all. You've raised a beautiful, charming, smart, independent young lady. And that, in and of itself, is a success. If you do that one thing right, then you've succeeded."

"Thank you for saying so."

Sarah ducked out of the room quickly, hoping to get outside and into the cold air before her sisters could see her cry. She didn't want this trip to turn into a pity party. In an effort to ground herself, she focused on the tangible: the walkway's gravel crunching under her feet, the breeze brushing over the skin on her face. There, that felt better. Amelia wouldn't notice if Sarah didn't come to bed for a while.

She knew Donny's walk would take him down along the creek, so she chose a different route, making her way towards the back of the property where the mountains rose into the sky, black against deep blue velvet. She'd always sought solace here. When flashbacks disguised as nightmares woke her in the middle of the night, she found her way to this path, to its near silence, its comfort.

At her favorite spot, a human-shaped dip in a foothill just a stone's throw from the house, Sarah laid in the grass, her hands behind her head. The moonless sky glittered with stars.

Once, when she and Donny were thirteen or so, they'd lain in this very spot watching a meteor shower.

"Did you know they say that when two people witness a shooting star together, their souls become one?" Donny said then.

"No," Sarah said. "I didn't know that. But what happens when they see, like, a hundred shooting stars together?"

Donny hadn't answered, then, but he'd taken her hand and laced his fingers with hers.

Sarah smiled at the memory, but her smile faded when she saw a shooting star arc across the sky, its tail dissolving into the darkness while she stood here alone. What did *that* mean? She got up at that point, and made her way back home, where she sneaked into bed beside her daughter.

———

"MOM? ARE YOU AWAKE?"

Sarah wasn't awake. It had been well after midnight when she came to bed. And judging by the slant of the sun coming through the window, it couldn't be much later than six a.m.

Sarah groaned. "I am, now," she said. Then she turned on her side and flung an arm over her daughter. "But I'm going back to sleep."

"Wait. Mom? Can I ask you something?"

"If you must."

"Why doesn't Dad want to be married anymore? I know it's not about you making him too many breakfasts or forcing me to eat organic cotton candy. It has to be something bigger than that, right?"

Sarah knew she had to choose her words carefully. How many articles had Sarah read that said children of divorced parents always blamed themselves for the split? Sarah sighed and sat up, leaning back against the headboard. Amelia put her hands behind her head and focused her gaze on the ceiling.

"First of all," she said, "you have to know this has nothing to do with you."

"Yeah, yeah," Amelia said. "That's something all divorced parents say."

Hearing the word, *divorced*, out loud, made Sarah feel sick. She folded her hands over her stomach and tipped her head back.

"That's because it's true."

"Whatever."

"You asked, Amelia. Do you want me to answer, or do you want to argue about things parents say?"

Sarah rarely spoke this harshly. Usually, she'd say something sweet —too sweet—like, "Oh, Amelia. That's not very nice." In response to her stern voice, though, Amelia gritted her teeth. Sarah could see the muscle flexing in her jaw.

"Fine. Answer."

"Fine. Your dad and I have been together since we were practically kids. And I think the bottom line is that we've grown apart. We're different people than we were as teenagers. I mean, everyone evolves, right? Maybe the two of us evolved in opposite directions. And maybe he was just the first to notice it."

"So you're just going to let him leave?"

"What choice do I have, Amelia? He's already made up his mind."

"Stop saying my name. You only say my name when you're angry."

"I'm not angry, Am—I'm not angry. I'm as perplexed as you are."

"You mean he didn't even tell you why he wants to leave?"

Sarah sighed. What could it hurt to give her daughter a little insight? She was a young adult now and she had a right to understand there were lots of dynamics at play.

"The answer he gave me was a variation of what I just said. About us growing apart."

"A variation?"

"Yes. Want breakfast? I can smell bacon cooking. Grandma's probably making her famous bacon pancakes."

"Which smell delicious," Amelia said. "But what did Dad say, *exactly*?"

"Is it important?" Sarah said.

"It is to me."

"Okay," Sarah said. "First of all, I had no idea. I feel blindsided by this."

Amelia looked over her shoulder, raised an eyebrow. Sarah shrugged in response. "I didn't realize he was so unhappy. For so long. Dad said I've lost sight of myself and I'm not the same person I used to be. But apparently, I've slowly morphed into a boring version of myself. It's been a long time coming."

"You *have* gotten boring, Mom. You used to be so much fun. And then it's like, in your quest to become Super Mom, you lost that spark."

Ah. So Amelia agreed with Donny. Which meant she blamed Sarah for the impending divorce.

"What do you mean?" Her voice came out in a squeak.

"I mean, think about how we used to spend our weekends. We'd go ride bikes or go for a hike or bake cookies. But as I've gotten older, our weekends have been scheduled, like, down to the minute. So I'll be prepared for college or adulthood or whatever next steps there are. We volunteer at the homeless shelter. We grocery shop. We have scheduled 'social' time, but it's usually going to see a movie you deem educational or to eat at a restaurant you believe is cultural. It's like you're so worried about checking off all the boxes that you've forgotten how to just *be*."

A long silence followed. Sarah had no idea what to say. A tiny, reasonable part of her could totally understand where Amelia was coming from. But most of her was beginning to feel indignant. Keeping her voice low and quiet required a gargantuan effort.

"So I'm being punished for doing my very best to ensure you're a well-rounded human being as you enter adulthood?"

"No, Mom," Amelia said, exasperation lighting up her voice. "It's just that you're not really Mom, or Sarah, anymore. You're Super Mom. And that's it. I mean, when's the last time you and I just went out and had fun? Besides when Aunt Margaret visited? Really. Think about it."

Sarah did, and the results of her internal search were disappointing. She went over weekend after weekend, combing through activities, and all she turned up were memories of events she'd carefully designed to enrich Amelia's life somehow.

"Ooh!" Sarah said. "What about that time we went to fly kites at the kite festival?"

Amelia sighed. "Wow, Mom. That's the best you can do? First of all, that was, like, three years ago. And second, do you remember how, when we got home from the kite festival, you made me do a mini research paper on kites?"

Oh. That was true.

"It was just so you'd learn more—"

"About kites. Yes, I know, Mom. 'It's science! In the real world!' And it's fine. But it's just an example."

"You know," Sarah said. "I think I've lost my appetite. I'm going to go for a walk."

Just like she had as a teenager, Sarah slipped out the back door. Only, doing so at twelve minutes after six in the morning was a lot different than doing so at eleven p.m.

"What do I tell Mama Katherine?" Amelia had said a few minutes earlier as Sarah laced up her hiking boots.

"Just tell her I went for a walk. She'll understand. And tell her to save me some bacon pancakes."

Sarah loved summer mornings in Wyoming. The air had just the slightest edge to it, and the breeze was still calm and gentle. She walked down to the creek, where the early morning sunlight sparkled on the water. John Wayne must love summer mornings, too, because she hadn't made it more than a few yards when she heard his collar jingle behind her. He fell into step with her.

"Hi, buddy," she said, and he looked up and gave her a doggy grin, almost as if to return her greeting.

She had to admit to herself that she still felt angry about the things Amelia and Donny had said. Everything she'd done for the past seventeen years was designed to give Amelia the best possible chance at a successful and happy life. And now she was being punished for it. Not only did Donny think she was boring, but Amelia blamed her for him thinking so. On another level, Sarah was upset that Donny hadn't said anything while there was still time to salvage their marriage.

She walked along the creek's edge, like she had millions of times as a child. The earth was soft under her feet. John Wayne's paws left prints. There was the tree where Donny had put up a rope swing one summer. All four of them had used that thing every day and they went back to school that fall with mosquito bites and sunburns and scraped knees. And there, just across from the tree, was the spot where the beaver had built its dam year after year. The kids had watched the beaver babies scampering around on it the summer after the rope swing. Sarah smiled as she remembered naming the babies: Chewy, Nibbles, and Chomper.

Would she let Amelia play on the rope swing and lure baby beavers to within arm's length?

Probably not. She'd be afraid Amelia would contract West Nile Virus from mosquitos near the rope swing, and any number of diseases from the baby beavers.

Although Sarah knew she'd done nothing but be the best mother she knew how, she also had enough introspection to realize that there might be some truth in what Donny and Amelia said: they used to have so much fun. And then day by day, year by year, Sarah had managed to suck that fun right out of their lives.

It started with a ban on cotton candy. Then it was quashing Donut Sunday because she didn't want Amelia having too much sugar. And when the school sold ice pops after lunch on Fridays, Sarah told Amelia she could take apple slices to school as a substitute: she shouldn't be eating all the dye in those frozen treats.

John Wayne ran ahead of Sarah and then stopped to drink from the creek. As she passed, he picked up his pace again.

And what about things with Donny?

Their lives were filled with frivolity and playfulness—at first. But as

Amelia grew into toddlerhood and then childhood, Sarah took her role as Amelia's Mother increasingly seriously. As she did, she lost sight of her role as Donny's Wife. One year they'd had Amelia's birthday party at the nearby gymnastics facility. Donny chased Sarah around the gym, catching her and carrying her to the foam pit, where he'd dump her in. She'd be laughing so hard she could barely climb out, and he'd throw her back in. The following year, they'd hosted the party at home, so Sarah could control the decorations. Then, the next year they returned to the gym, and when Donny grabbed Sarah around the waist, she pushed out of his embrace and told him she had to set up the food.

"Are you deep in thought, or did you sleep as badly as I did?"

Donny came around the bend in the creek, his bedroll slung over his shoulder. Sarah jumped. She'd expected to encounter animals out here—elk, bison, birds—but not humans. God, he was handsome, even though he looked bone tired. He was so tall and his shoulders were so broad. He rarely wore t-shirts, but he was wearing one now and his biceps stretched the fabric tight. John Wayne growled once, but it was halfhearted.

"Just going for a walk," Sarah said.

"Bit early, isn't it?"

"Amelia woke me up."

"She always did have trouble sleeping on vacation," Donny said. He scratched John Wayne behind the pointy ears for a few seconds, before the dog lay down at Sarah's feet.

Sarah nodded, but she didn't meet his eyes. She'd fretted over that, too, checking out books from the library on how to get your child to sleep, nighttime anxiety, and problems related to lack of sleep. Of course, Amelia always made a quick recovery.

"And I'll bet Mama Katherine's making her famous bacon pancakes," he said.

"I could smell the bacon cooking when I left."

"How on earth did you get out the door with that smell following you?"

"I know," Sarah said. "That smell hypnotizes you. You can't help yourself. You'd be seated at the table right now if you'd slept inside."

She hadn't meant anything by it, but the words hung in the air like a curtain being dropped between them.

"Well," Donny said. "I don't want to miss them. We all know Margaret will wolf those things down like candy."

Sarah nodded. "Save me a couple, will you?"

"Will do," Donny said. "Have a nice walk."

Sarah walked for a while longer, and the sun rose higher into the sky. She didn't see any wildlife, but she did see Farmer Eddie, who came walking down the road with his dog, Susan, who happened to be one of John Wayne's litter mates. Sarah lifted a hand at Farmer Eddie, and he nodded at her from a distance. When he was within talking distance, he said, "Well, what a beautiful sight on this beautiful morning. I haven't seen a Bradley girl on my morning walk in I don't know how long."

He strode right up and hugged Sarah, and she hugged him back, surprised to feel the bones in his shoulders and back. She'd always thought Farmer Eddie was ageless, just like Mama Katherine.

"Yeah," Sarah said. "I'm the early riser of the bunch, that's for sure."

As they stepped apart, Sarah felt Farmer Eddie examining her just as she was examining him. The skin on his face was leathery from years of being in the sun, but his eyes twinkled at her just as they'd always done.

"Can Susan and I join you for a few minutes?" he said.

"Sure," Sarah said. "I'd love that." She felt like she should point out that he'd be backtracking, but she didn't.

As they strolled, the dogs trotted ahead, side by side.

"Saw your husband this morning."

"Yeah? You know he likes to sleep under the stars whenever we're here."

"Nothing like it," Farmer Eddie said.

"True. There's also nothing like a warm, soft bed."

Farmer Eddie grunted. "What's troubling you, Sarah?"

"Why do you ask?"

"I know a troubled young lady when I see one."

"I'm hardly a young lady anymore."

"But," Eddie said, lifting a hand, pointer finger extended, "you'll always be a young lady to me. I've known you since you were. And I know a troubled expression when I see one."

"It's nothing," Sarah said. "Just a transition, that's all, with Amelia going off to college and everything."

"Amelia going off to college, already? Wow. That happened faster than green grass through a goose."

"You're telling me," Sarah said. "How are things on the farm?"

"Well," Eddie said. "Whatever's going on with you and Donny will blow over. Don't you worry. As for things on the farm, they're just fine. Same as always. You know, I like to keep things simple.

Not much has changed around here, and that's just the way I like it."

"Yeah," Sarah said. "There's something to be said for that."

"Speaking of things that don't change," Eddie said, "let's head on back to your Mama's place. I know she's making those bacon pancakes this morning and I certainly don't want to miss them. I hear Margaret's in town and Lord knows we've got to be quick."

Mama Katherine didn't seem the least bit surprised to see Farmer Eddie when he and Sarah came into the kitchen.

"Good morning, you two," she called. "I've just got to run back and switch over the laundry. I'll be right back."

Farmer Eddie took off his straw hat and hung it on a peg by the side door. Sarah wracked her brain, trying to remember how often he'd been over for meals and whether this level of comfort should take her by surprise.

Was it possible—no, Mama Katherine always told the girls she didn't need or want romance. If anything, Mama Katherine and Farmer Eddie shared a friendship of convenience. Each of them lived alone, now. Mama Katherine could cook and Farmer Eddie could repair things, and they probably had some sort of informal agreement wherein she fed him and he helped out around her farm.

That conclusion went right down the drain when Margaret shot Sarah a "what in the world" look, one eyebrow raised, head tilting towards Farmer Eddie, who was now helping himself to a cup of coffee. Hannah, who stood at the kitchen counter with Donny and Amelia, didn't seem surprised at all. She just called out, "Good morning, Eddie, good morning, Sarah," and went about buttering her pancakes.

Sarah looked back at Margaret, and the two of them shrugged. So what if he came over for breakfast once in a while?

But when Eddie took two plates out of the cupboard, piled each one high with pancakes, and started buttering those pancakes, it became clear that he did more than come over for breakfast once in a while.

Sarah waited for him to sit down with Hannah, Amelia, and Donny, and then she went into the kitchen. Margaret, in a not-so-subtle move, sauntered in and whispered, "What in the world? Have you ever seen Farmer Eddie take plates out of our cupboard?"

"No," Sarah said. "Have you?"

"No," Margaret said. "Do you think—"

"No," they both said at the same time.

"But," Sarah said, "he buttered her pancakes."

"I think he's doing more than buttering her pancakes, if you know what I mean."

"Girls," Mama Katherine said as she came back into the kitchen carrying a basket of clean clothes. "Stop yammering and get your pancakes dished up while they're still hot."

"Okay, Mama," they both said.

As they did, Margaret whispered, "We're going to have to corner Hannah later and ask her about this. Because she's acting like it's totally ordinary."

Sarah nodded. "Only, she hasn't said anything to either of us about it."

"Exactly," Margaret said.

After breakfast, Mama Katherine asked Farmer Eddie to look at something in her chicken coop, which, apparently, Margaret found as suggestive as Sarah did, because Margaret caught her eye and they both covered their mouths with their napkins. Amelia, who'd helped cook breakfast, asked if she could go for a walk, and Donny went to take a shower.

Sarah, Margaret, and Hannah shared clean-up duty.

"So..." Sarah said, letting her voice trail off as she stacked plates in the sink.

"Mama Katherine and Farmer Eddie," Margaret said, making it a statement rather than a question.

Hannah, who was rinsing dishes and putting them in the dishwasher, sighed. "I didn't know whether to tell you."

"Wait!" Margaret said. "So it's true? It's a thing? I was kind of joking. I never thought—"

"You never thought she wanted romance?" Hannah said.

"No!" Sarah said. "She always said—"

"I don't need a man to validate my existence," Margaret and Hannah said, their voices perfect imitations of Mama Katherine's drawl.

"So how long has this been—you know ..."

"Happening?" Hannah said, moving her eyebrows up and down. This only produced more giggles.

"Yeah," Sarah said.

As Hannah had emptied the sink, Sarah had filled it with more dishes, and Hannah started scrubbing them.

"Well, let me tell you," she said. "I've only seen the evidence of things *happening* for the past couple of weeks. But from the looks of it, it's been going on longer than that. I think they might have been doing some, you know, *afternoon delight*, or whatever you want to call it, while I was at school."

"You're teaching long division to a bunch of fourth graders and our mom is doing multiplication." Margaret, who was cleaning the counter with a rag, laughed at her own cleverness and Sarah just shook her head.

"You haven't asked her about it?" Sarah said.

She took a sponge over to the table and started wiping up crumbs.

"I mean," Hannah said, "I've wanted to. But it's really none of my business, is it? She never asks me about my love life. So I feel like I owe her the same respect. You know?"

"You've never had a love life, Hannah," Margaret said. Then she sucked in a breath, obviously wishing she could take the words back.

"I know," Hannah said. "I know I haven't."

"But that's none of our business," Sarah said, looking pointedly at Margaret.

"Right," Margaret said. "It's not."

"Anyway," Sarah said. "Do you think this thing between Mama and Eddie, whatever it is, is a good thing?"

"I think so," Hannah said. "I mean, they've known each other forever. We know he's a great guy. And she seems so comfortable around him. They're both adults."

"True," Sarah said.

"Well, it's certainly interesting," Margaret said.

The kitchen was clean and the dishes were done. "Well," Sarah said, "I'm going to go get some clothes out of the RV. And this thing between Mama and Eddie? I think it's neat."

CHAPTER TWELVE

QUESTIONS TO ASK *Philip*

———

JUNE 20 - UPDATED JUNE 28: Ten days since launching the Grand Experiment

———

WHY THREE ICE cubes in your bourbon? Two don't keep it cold. Four water it down. (Yes, he has experimented.)

Do you drink beer? If so, what kind? Yes. Schlitz. (Have never heard of this, Pauline. Must research.)

Do you prefer dogs or cats? Dogs. (Maybe we should get a dog. Something to consider.)

How old were you when you lost your first tooth? Four. (Yes! Four! Rollerskating accident.)

Do you like apples? Yes. (Especially Gala.)

As a child, what did you want to be when you grew up? A veterinarian.

Do you want any children? (I skipped this one, Pauline. I was too shy to ask it. But it did lead me to thinking about sexual intercourse. Go ahead, Pauline. Gasp. I can practically hear it.)

How often do you cut your toenails? Every Tuesday.

What is your favorite book, ever? The Lion, the Witch and the Wardrobe.

If you could spend one day in a different city, where would you go? San Francisco. (He's never been. Neither have I.)

What is your favorite childhood memory? The harvest at Dad's orchard. Sitting in carts of apples, testing them, while all the hustle and bustle of apple picking went on around him. (I admit, Pauline, this is one of my own favorite childhood memories. So we do have at least this one thing in common.)

———

NEW QUESTIONS: June 28

———

WHY DO you always leave two minutes before you say you're going to? Do you plan that?

What is your worst fear?

What is your favorite color?

What is your least favorite dessert? (You can learn a lot about a person, Pauline, by hearing the answer to this question.)

Who was your favorite teacher? Why?

What was your favorite subject in school?

What is your favorite holiday?

———

HANNAH'S VOICE interrupted Sarah's reading.

"Speaking of 'things'," she said, and Sarah, who was sitting in the captain's chair just inside the RV's open door, "You've been doing a lot of this thing lately. Every time I walk by, I see you with your nose in that thing."

"You do? I have?"

"Yes and yes."

"Huh," Sarah said. She closed the journal and put it on her lap.

"What is it?" Margaret's silhouette joined Hannah's in the doorway.

"I didn't realize you were here, too," Sarah said, her voice sounding more accusatory than she meant for it to.

"We're stalking you," Margaret said, and Hannah added, "We're worried about you, Sarah."

"Why, because I'm reading this journal? Or because my husband is leaving me?"

Hannah and Margaret looked at each other.

"Both," they said at the same time.

"What is it?" Margaret said again.

"It's a journal."

"*Your* journal?" Hannah said.

"No," Sarah said. "Hazel's."

"Who in the world is Hazel?" Margaret said.

"The author of this journal," Sarah said. "I found it. In that recipe box."

"The one you bought at the farmer's market?" Hannah said.

Sarah nodded. She was tempted to pick up the journal and hold it close to her chest, to protect it, but she refrained.

"What's got you so intrigued about it?" Margaret said, and Hannah said, "Yeah, what's so great about it?"

"It's just interesting, that's all."

"Huh," Hannah said, and Margaret said, "Can we read it?"

"Yeah," Sarah said, drawing the word out. "I suppose so. But I'm right in the middle of a good part."

"A good part?" Margaret said to Hannah, and Hannah replied, "It must be a riveting journal."

"It is," Sarah said. "In fact, I'll read you the note on the inside of the front cover."

While Margaret and Hannah made themselves at home, sliding into the dinette, Sarah flipped to the front of the journal. She cleared her throat and started to read.

———

"IF YOU'RE READING THIS, there's one thing you should know: it's something George Sand said. Now, to tell you the truth, I don't know who George Sand is. But is that really important? Not for the matters of this story. I saw this quote in a book once and it stuck with me. Good old Georgie, he said:

———

THERE IS ONLY one happiness in this life, to love and be loved."

———

MARGARET LOOKED UP AT SARAH. "George Sand was a woman, did you know that?"

"No," Sarah said. "I never thought to look it up."

"She was a French novelist in the eighteen hundreds. Anyway."

She motioned for Sarah to keep reading, and she did.

———

"THERE. What do you think about that? If you'd said that to me ten, even five years ago, I would have disagreed. I would have said that adventure is happiness. Helen Keller once said, Life is either a great adventure, or nothing. Or something like that. I would have said fun is happiness. It is, isn't it? I would have said so many things."

———

"I LIKE THIS—WHAT did you say her name was?" Hannah said.

"Hazel," Sarah said.

"She sounds like my kind of woman," Hannah said.

"Keep reading," Margaret said.

———

"BUT IF THERE'S one thing I've learned it's that love makes everything an adventure. Ergo (I've always wanted to use that word), love is happiness. I think Mr. George Sand was onto something.

Anyway, if you're reading this, you found my journal. Serendipity.

I started this journal—well, never mind. You're going to keep reading, right? You'll get all the main info, like who, what, where, when, why, and how as you go.

But here's something you won't know until you get to the end. Which is why I'm putting it here, at the beginning. You won't know when you start that this has turned into a beautiful love story. In its early stages, it looked more like it might be a tragedy, or even an epic, bloody battle story. As it unfolded, though, it turned into something incredible, something amazing, something so far beyond what I'd expected it to be.

I'm an old woman now. And if you asked me one thing I've learned (I know, you didn't ask, but I'm going to tell you anyway—it's one privilege of being an old lady—that and peeing when you sneeze), I'd tell you this: good old Georgie was right. Love is happiness. Love is everything."

———

"WELL, sounds like she went a bit batty after one too many adventures," Margaret said.

Still, her eyes were wet with tears.

"Are you actually tearing up?" Sarah said. "I'm quite incredulous. That's not like you at all."

"I don't know," Margaret said. She used her pointer fingers to flick the tears away and then said, "So. You're reading this journal for inspiration."

"Precisely," Sarah said.

"Well, does she know what she's talking about?" Hannah said.

Sarah shrugged. "I mean, I think so. I haven't gotten to the tragedy part yet. And I'm so curious about who this Hazel woman is. Do you think she'd want her journal back?"

"We could find her," Margaret said. "But she left that message in the front. So I think she meant for it to get passed on."

"True," Hannah said.

"But aren't you curious?" Margaret said to Sarah. "After all the reading you're doing, you probably feel like she's your new best friend."

"I do," Sarah said.

"Well, we'll leave you to it," Margaret said. "And I'll just do some quick, preliminary research."

———

JUNE 29: Day One of Immersion

———

LET THE IMMERSION BEGIN!

———

YES, Pauline. I'm hiding in the bathroom as I write this. I don't know why, but I don't want Philip to know about you. Not yet, anyway. He probably thinks I'm in here primping. For what? you might ask.

I am going to the orchard with Philip today. We will ride in together. I asked Betty to pack us a picnic lunch. Perhaps I should have asked Philip what he usually does for lunch, so as not to mess up his daily routine, you know, but I thought eating together would give us time to talk. A man's got to eat, right?

Shirley always says that if you can keep a man fed, rested, and loved up (yes, those are Shirley's words), then you'll have a happy husband. Although, I'm not sure if she's an expert, considering she's not married.

I'll write more later, Pauline. I really do need to primp now. Ha!

———

EVENING ENTRY

———

HI PAULINE,

———

WELL, I'm back. What a day! It was so busy I actually joined Philip for a pre-dinner bourbon to relax. Three ice cubes. Betty made us a delicious fried chicken dinner and I ate three pieces of chicken! I was ravenous.

So. Today went well. I have a good feeling about this, Pauline. You know, as soon as I put my mind to it—to making Philip fall in love with me—I started to see the possibilities. I started to feel the chemistry. The orchard employees all believe we married for love. They don't realize our parents considered both of us spinsters. So naturally, we were inclined to behave that way when I visited the orchard today. And when we did, I began to feel a tiny spark.

When we first arrived, Philip told me to wait in the car while he came around and opened my door. What a gentleman! Then, he offered me his hand, and he kept holding my hand as we walked to the office. You probably remember that I said I didn't want to ask Philip the question about whether he wanted children. And because it was so scandalous, you probably remember me saying that thinking about procreating got me thinking about —well, about procreating. Sexual intercourse.

When Philip and I were holding hands, I paid careful attention to the way his skin felt against mine. When we walked up and down the rows of trees together, I noticed the feel of his hand on my lower back. I've dated before, and other men have touched my lower back. But I've always known I'd remain a virgin until marriage. Then, when it looked like I'd never marry, I gave up on the idea of sex.

Now that it's a possibility, though, my nerve endings are on high alert. Mother would say, "Get your mind out of the gutter, Hazel," although I suppose thinking about sex with your own husband doesn't really qualify as "in the gutter."

It was fun and enlightening to watch Philip at work. He obviously loves the employees, and they love him right back. He calls each of them by name, asks after their families, and smiles all day long. He's genuinely happy in this business. In his element.

And tonight at dinner, we had so much to talk about. He told me stories about the orchard, about the people there. We laughed and laughed. And there was some electrifying eye contact, Pauline. I mean, there were a few pauses in the conversation, and we filled them by just looking at each other, smiling. I don't know if I've smiled that much in months. He still headed off to the guest bedroom to sleep, and I'm still alone in the master bedroom as we speak (or, should I say, as I write).

But I have a feeling things are moving forward between us.

––––––

SARAH CLOSED the journal and set it on her lap. Was it as simple as making a decision, like Hazel had done?

Could she just *decide* to win Donny back? Naturally, a million thoughts zoomed through her mind, then: doubt-filled whispers all saying variations of the same thing: *Donny's already made up his mind. It won't work. He's done. You'll just get hurt in the end.*

When Donny told Sarah (and Amelia) that he wanted out of this marriage, he had sounded resigned. Certain. But could she change his mind? And would she? Would she set out to do it without knowing how things turned out for Hazel and Philip in the end?

Actually, what had Hazel's message said? The one written on the inside cover of the journal? Even though she'd just read it to her sisters, Sarah looked again, her eyes landing on certain key phrases:

––––––

THERE IS ONLY one happiness in this life, to love and be loved.

––––––

YOU WON'T KNOW when you start that this has turned into a beautiful love story. In its early stages, it looked more like it might be a tragedy, or even an epic, bloody battle story. As it unfolded, though, it turned into something incredible, something amazing, something so far beyond what I'd expected it to be.

———

I'M AN OLD WOMAN NOW. And if you asked me one thing I've learned (I know, you didn't ask, but I'm going to tell you anyway—it's one privilege of being an old lady—that and peeing when you sneeze), I'd tell you this: good old Georgie was right. Love is happiness. Love is everything.

———

SARAH RAN her fingers over Hazel's handwriting. For Hazel Rickshaw Carlisle, things had started out with a decision: with a choice to make her husband fall in love with her. And in her own words, they evolved into a beautiful love story.

Was it possible that Sarah's own love story, the one where Donny played opposite her, wasn't over yet? Was it possible that they'd come to the end of one chapter and needed to pen a new one?

A feeling—something like hope—started to blossom in Sarah's stomach, unfurling like a new flower until she could feel it in her throat. It was possible. She and Donny had fallen in love once, and they could fall in love again.

Right?

"Right," she said aloud.

There. She'd made the decision. She felt like she should do something to celebrate this occasion. It seemed so big. And yet, there was nothing to do now except move forward.

She grabbed some clothes and stepped out of the RV, where she found Amelia walking up the road with a strange smile on her face.

"Hi, honey," Sarah said. "What's up?"

"Oh, nothing."

Well, *that* sounded suspicious.

"How was your walk?"

Amelia clasped her hands together behind her back and looked at the ground, exactly as she had when she was five and she sneaked and ate the lollipop Sarah had left on the kitchen counter. "Fine," she said.

"See anything interesting?"

"I met a couple of those neighbor boys Grandma was talking about," Amelia said without looking up. "Simon. And Luke."

Even though Amelia's face was down, Sarah could see a furious blush making its way up her cheeks. This was interesting.

"And?"

Amelia looked at her feet. "They seem nice."

Normally, with images of her own biological mother dancing, drunk, through her mind, Sarah would say something designed to ward off unwanted pregnancy. Sarah's own mother had told her countless times that she was the result of an unplanned pregnancy, conceived on a drunken night, never wanted. But Amelia wasn't Sarah's mother. Amelia was her own well adjusted person, as she'd reminded Sarah a million times when Sarah prohibited her from going on dates.

"Any of them cute?" Sarah said.

Amelia hadn't been moving, so to speak. But nevertheless, she froze. Slowly, she raised her gaze to meet Sarah's, that blush still going strong.

She looked at the ground again. "Luke," she said, her voice a squeak. If it were even possible, her face became even more red.

"He's the one Mama Katherine said was your age?"

Amelia nodded and tucked a strand of hair behind her ear—another nervous habit. "We just … talked … for a few minutes. And then he had to go. Chores, you know. Said his mom makes him muck the horse stalls every morning."

"What did he look like?"

Amelia's eyes widened. She obviously hadn't expected this line of questioning. "Um. Well, he has curly brown hair, like Mama Katherine said. And freckles. He's tall. Taller than me. And he. Well."

"Well, what?"

Amelia looked at the ground again, and Sarah found herself on the verge of laughter. *See? I can be fun.*

"Tell me, Amelia."

"I can't. You'll be mad."

"I promise I won't," Sarah said. "I'm turning over a new leaf. I'm going to be more easygoing."

"He wasn't wearing a shirt." She blurted out the words as if they had a mind of their own and she couldn't contain them.

Sarah raised an eyebrow.

"Mom! You said you wouldn't be mad!"

"I'm not mad!"

"But your eyebrow."

Sarah ran a forefinger over the offending eyebrow to smooth it into its normal position.

"I'm just surprised," Sarah said. "You don't usually tell me these things."

"Well, this is why!" Amelia said. "You said you wouldn't be mad, but you're raising your eyebrow. That's your mad face."

Sarah couldn't help it, now: she burst into laughter. Hysterics, actually.

"What's so funny?" Amelia stomped one foot.

"It's just," Sarah said on a gasp. "It's just so cute, that's all. I love that you're sharing with me."

Now Amelia raised an eyebrow. It wasn't an angry expression, Sarah thought. It was more of a what-the-heck-is-happening-here expression. Sarah took a deep breath and forced herself to stop laughing.

"So. Tell me about this shirtless Luke character. Did he have nice muscles? Was he witty? Clever? What do you even *like* in a boy, Amelia?"

———

WHEN AMELIA and Sarah went back into the house, they found that Donny had gone over to Eddie's to help him repair some siding on his barn. The women spent the rest of the morning in the garden, weeding and harvesting. No one said anything out loud about how much work there was to do.

No one except Mama Katherine, anyway.

"Well, we had such a wet spring," she said more than once. "These weeds are just popping up willy nilly."

Sarah grunted in what she hoped sounded like agreement, but she thought it was a strong indicator of Mama Katherine's failing health that she'd let her garden go this badly. And where was Hannah in all this? Hannah was here to take care of Mama Katherine. She should have noticed the garden needed tending.

"So, Amelia," Margaret said, breaking into Sarah's thoughts. "I hear you met one of the neighbor boys this morning."

Amelia, who was kneeling between rows of tomato plants, weeding the beds, stilled. She stood up and wiped the hair off her forehead with a gloved hand. She turned to glare at Sarah, who gave her a blank look in return.

"Where'd you hear that?" she said to Margaret.

Margaret shrugged. "I didn't. But you just confirmed it."

Her face had been slightly pink from the afternoon heat, but now, once again, it turned a furious red.

"Which one was it?" Margaret wanted to know.

"Luke," Amelia said. Her voice was nothing more than a mumble, and she crouched back down, busying herself with the weeds.

"Nice day," Mama Katherine said. Sarah wasn't sure whether she was oblivious to Margaret needling Amelia, or she just wanted to change the subject.

"It is, Mama," Hannah said. "Look how many tomatoes there are. I think we could make a tomato salad. Amelia, honey, why don't you grab a basket and harvest some of those tomatoes. The plants can barely stand up, they're so heavy."

Amelia trudged off to the planting table and when she returned, Hannah said, "Sarah, let's go inside and make some nice lemonade. How does that sound? The rest of these ladies can pick tomatoes and onions, and oh, my, look how many cucumbers there are. Have mercy. Pick those too, Margaret. We'll add those to the tomato salad."

Sarah thought Hannah's voice sounded strange, and when Hannah grabbed her arm in a vice grip to steer her into the kitchen, she knew her hunch was right on.

As soon as they were inside, Hannah let go of her arm and leaned against the counter.

"Everything okay?" Sarah said.

"I'm so mad, I could just—I don't know, I could just cry."

With that, she burst into tears.

The plan Sarah had been hatching—to tell Hannah about her decision to make Donny fall in love with her again—fizzled out as she wrapped her arms around her big sister.

"What in tarnation?" Sarah said, infusing her voice with as much of Mama Katherine's accent as she could.

This provoked a little laugh from Hannah, who straightened up and sighed. Sarah handed her a handkerchief.

"I'm just so mad."

"I got that."

"Did you see that garden?"

"I did," Sarah said. "We all did."

"Do you know how many times I tried to go out there and work in it?" Hannah said.

"I most certainly do not," Sarah said.

"Too many to count. I asked Mama Katherine what I could do to help. I could see the weeds growing, but she said she was taking care of it. I don't know what in tarnation she was actually doing out there, but I can assure you, it wasn't taking care of that garden! And now the three of you—you, Margaret, and Amelia—are probably thinking I haven't been taking care of Mama Katherine."

"I admit," Sarah said, "I did wonder why you let it get so out of hand. But I can understand now why it happened. I'm going to start making the lemonade, since that's why we're in here."

Hannah nodded. "It's just been so much, Sarah. I didn't want to tell you and Margaret—didn't want to worry you." She sniffed and blew her nose. "I feel like I want nothing more than for Mama to feel independent, you know? Like her usual self. But I spend all my time running around, creating the illusion that she's independent. For her. Maybe for me!"

Sarah poured water into the tea kettle and set it to boil on the stove. She ran her pointer finger over the handle, remembering the Christmas when she'd given it to Mama Katherine. It was probably the ugliest tea kettle in America, Sarah thought now, with its illustrations of fat pigs and cows and its checkerboard border. But Mama Katherine had exclaimed over it like it was a brand new diamond ring.

While Sarah took down a pitcher and glasses, Hannah went on: "I can't keep up with it all. Appointments, shopping, taking care of the farm, and making Mama think she's really doing well. It's too much."

"I think you need something stronger in your lemonade."

"I think I do."

"Look," Sarah said. "What if I stayed with you for a while?"

"What?" Hannah paused halfway through measuring sugar into the pitcher.

"I mean, with Amelia going to school, and Donny, well, leaving me, this would be the perfect time for me to stay and help you. I thought I'd made the decision to try to win him back, you know?" The water had come to a boil. Sarah turned off the stove, and as she poured the water into the pitcher, she said, "But maybe this is a sign. Maybe it's a sign that I need to come back home."

"Wait," Hannah said. She handed Sarah a spoon to stir the sugar into the water, and she went to work filling a bucket with ice cubes. Sarah thought she was tossing those cubes into that bucket with a little more force than the situation warranted. "You're telling me you'd made the decision to win Donny back?"

"Mm-hmm."

"When did you make that decision?" When Sarah saw Hannah's air quotes, she knew she was in trouble.

Sarah sighed. "This morning."

"Wow, you really stuck with it."

"Wait. What is that supposed to mean? He wants to leave me, Hannah. My decision was probably nothing more than a dream, an illusion."

"What decision?" With her typical impeccable timing, Margaret had chosen to come inside at this exact moment. Sarah cringed. "Oh, I see. It's a secret, is it? You know how much I've always loved a secret."

"You hate secrets," Hannah said, and Sarah said, "You never let secrets stay secrets."

"True," Margaret said.

"Remember that time you thought I was keeping a secret from you and you went into detective mode and realized it was actually a birthday present I was working on for you?" Hannah said. She added lemon juice to the pitcher, and Sarah kept stirring.

"Ah, yes," Margaret said. "The great photo collage. I ruined that one for myself."

"Yes, you did," Sarah said. "And remember that one Christmas, the one where you—"

"The one where I sneaked into Mama Katherine's closet and looked at all our presents beforehand?"

"Yes," Hannah said.

"And Mama Katherine put all our presents under the tree without wrapping them," Sarah said.

Both Hannah and Sarah said, "I was so disappointed."

"I'll admit," Margaret said, "that wasn't one of my brightest moments. However, I'm an adult now, and I will not be deterred from hearing more about the secret decision you were talking about, Sarah."

"Oh," Sarah said. "That."

"Yes," Margaret said. "I'll get out some glasses and a tray while you dish."

"She made the decision to try to win Donny back," Hannah said.

Sarah shot her a dirty look.

"What?" Hannah said. "You were going to tell her anyway. Now it won't be long and drawn out. But, not to worry, because she has already made a new decision, which is to un-make the first one."

"What?" Margaret said. "That doesn't make sense."

"Hannah needs help around here," Sarah said, "and I thought that after dropping Amelia off at college, maybe I could just stay here for a while."

"Hannah needs help?" Margaret said. "I didn't realize the phrase, 'I need help' was in her vernacular."

"I don't *need* help," Hannah said. "I'm just feeling a bit overwhelmed, is all."

Mama Katherine's voice came in through the open door. "Lemonade almost ready, you three? I don't know how many girls it takes to make lemonade, but I'm getting thirsty."

"We're comin,' Mama," Hannah said. "Where's that tray, Margaret?"

"I can't find it," Margaret said.

Hannah sighed, pulled the tray out from the very cupboard where Margaret was searching, and began setting the glasses on the tray in quick, jerky movements.

"In that case," Margaret said. "Why don't I stay and help out? Sarah, you have a real life back in Arizona. I have no attachments. Easier for me to stay."

"I—"

"That way," Margaret said, "you can work on winning Donny back."

"Good idea," Hannah said. She hefted the tray and walked outside, her two younger sisters following her like little ducklings.

CHAPTER THIRTEEN

After a huge spaghetti dinner involving lots of table wine, the women settled in the living room while Amelia and Donny played checkers in the kitchen.

"So," Margaret said. "Hannah and I have read the journal. Just up to the part where you are now."

"And? What do you think?" Sarah said.

"I wish we knew who this Hazel person was," Margaret said. "She turned thirty the same year the California Sandpipers won the hockey championships, which would mean she's in her eighties now."

"I wonder if she's still alive," Sarah said. She immediately regretted it, because Hannah's face blanched. Mama Katherine was in her eighties. "What did you think of her plan, though?" Sarah said.

"I think it's a sign," Margaret said, and Hannah, who didn't believe in signs, threw her a dark look and said, "Or, it's a nicely-timed piece of inspiration."

"Inspiration for what?" Sarah said.

"To go full-immersion," Margaret said.

"To win Donny back," Hannah said.

"What's this?" Mama Katherine said.

Sarah sighed. "Never mind, Mama. I'm afraid it's a lost cause."

"What's a lost cause?"

"She'd made a decision to try to win back Donny's love," Hannah said. "And then, at the farmer's market, we overheard Donny telling some woman that they were splitting up, and she decided it was a lost cause."

"But," Margaret said, "we don't think it is."

"I think she should carry on, and do everything she can to convince Donny to stay," Hannah said, and Margaret said, "Me too."

"I agree," Mama Katherine said.

"Well, I'm grateful for your opinions," Sarah said. "Really."

"Lay off the sarcasm," Hannah said. "Want a chocolate?"

"Please," said Margaret, Sarah and Katherine.

"Sarah," Mama Katherine said. "Is this marriage important to you?"

"Yes!" Sarah said. "The most important."

"Then why wouldn't you try to fix things? I know my daughter, and she wouldn't let her man walk off into the sunset without even trying. Imagine watching him walk away, knowing you hadn't done everything you could to keep him here."

"Imagine me doing everything I could, and having him leave anyway."

"This is why I don't get attached," Margaret said. Hannah glared at her and passed her the little bowl of chocolates.

"That man will not leave you, if you remind him why he loves you in the first place," Mama Katherine said.

"I don't even know why he loved me in the first place," Sarah said.

"You know," Hannah said, "it's almost like the two of you were pre-destined. You met so young, and committed to each other so young, that it was, like, a *given* you'd be together."

"Not that there's anything wrong with that," Margaret said when Sarah's eyes narrowed.

"No!" Hannah said. "Not at all. But I wonder if that's why you neglected your marriage once Amelia was born."

"I neglected my marriage?" Sarah said, her voice shrill. "Do you really think so?"

"You've all had enough therapy to know what happened, there," Mama Katherine said. "Your biological mother failed you, Sarah. You spent your first few years in complete chaos. So when you had your own daughter, you rebelled against chaos and seized control of the situation. You were determined not to make the same mistakes your mother did. You wanted to give your daughter everything. Everything. And you have."

"But in doing so," Hannah said, "you stepped away from your marriage for a while."

"But you were the best mother to me," Sarah said to Katherine.

"Ah," said Mama Katherine. "I was a good mother to you, wasn't

I? But I made my own mistakes. I dedicated myself to you girls. I don't regret it, not one bit. But I do wonder if I did you a disservice by avoiding romance all those years. God knows I love a good man, and I did have…needs. But you never saw me in a marriage. You never saw me being both a wife and a mother. So you never learned that, yourself. Nevertheless, we're here, now. And in your case, Sarah, I think we all know you need to fight for your marriage. If something's important to you, you don't fly the white flag. You fight. Understand?"

When Sarah nodded, Mama Katherine stood up. "Well, since you girls were all so upset about my garden today, why don't you go work on it now? I'm going to bed."

"Moonlight gardening," Margaret said, standing up. "Sounds romantic."

"Yeah," Hannah said, standing up as well. "Why don't you and Donny tackle those weeds, Sarah?"

————

IT'S NOT that Sarah and Donny's first kiss—the one in the backseat of the school bus—was particularly titillating, but it did open the gate. It was like neither of them could get enough of the other. They were insatiable.

After that, they kissed every chance they got. Donny showed up daily between second and third periods to walk Sarah to English class, and they'd stand outside the door and make out until the bell rang, at which point he'd break away, smiling broadly. She'd duck into the classroom, where Mrs. Geigher would give her a stern look. Donny would run down the hall to P.E. His long, easy stride was still etched into Sarah's memory. At lunch, they'd kiss between bites of food.

"I love the turkey sandwich you brought today," he'd say, and she'd say, "I think you should bring Ranch Doritos tomorrow, too."

They met up after their final classes and kissed in greeting, Donny pulling Sarah against him like it had been weeks, not hours, since they'd seen each other. Passersby would say things like, "Get a room," and "Give it a rest, you two," and "Stop sucking face," but this only made Donny laugh against Sarah's mouth and Sarah's fingers curl more firmly around the back of his neck.

On the weekends, they'd finish chores and then sneak away to their secret meeting spot: the loft of Donny's parents' barn. There, they spread blankets on the floor and lay side by side for hours. Sometimes they'd talk about palm reading or their future children. Sometimes they kissed until they were breathless.

Sarah remembered one winter afternoon when she surprised Donny with homemade chocolate chip cookies and a Thermos of hot chocolate. She set them up on a tray in the loft before he arrived. They spent several hours playing gin rummy, drinking the hot chocolate, and eating the cookies. After she beat him four times in a row, he moved the tray out of the way and tackled her gently, laying her down on the blankets and kissing her until her head spun. For the first time, his hands found their way to her breasts, and she groaned in pleasure as the new sensations shot from one end of her body to the other.

By the time they were sophomores in high school, sex was imminent. At least, both Donny and Sarah thought it was. But the universe —and Mama Katherine—seemed to have other ideas.

One morning at school, Donny approached Sarah before the first bell. She was at her locker, and when her friends saw him approach, they melted away. Sarah thought they were probably tired of watching (and hearing) all the kissing.

"Good morning, beautiful," Donny said, and Sarah shut her locker and leaned her back against it.

Donny put one hand on either side of her head, and gave her a long kiss that earned a few whistles from other students.

"I have an idea," he said when he drew away. "I'll tell you about it at lunch."

He kissed her one more time, quickly, and practically skipped off down the hall. Donny's "idea" distracted Sarah throughout first period math and second period biology. She could only imagine what it was. Spring break was approaching. Maybe it had something to do with that. During the past week or so, the school counselors had started talking to the sophomore class about college as they created their schedules for junior year. Maybe he wanted them to go to college together.

After second period, Donny was waiting just outside Sarah's classroom, leaning against the wall in the hallway. When she approached him, he pulled her close. "You smell so good. I can't wait to tell you my idea."

Then he took her hand, walked her to English class, and kissed her on the cheek. Sarah spent third and fourth periods wondering which smell he was referring to. Was it her shampoo? She'd sneaked some of Hannah's fancy stuff this morning because she'd run out of her own.

Or was it Margaret's body lotion? She'd sneaked some of that, too, but not because she'd run out. She just liked the way it smelled.

She knew she could ask Mama Katherine to buy her her own body lotion, but she was afraid her sisters would tease her about buying it for Donny. Truth be told, though, isn't that exactly what she'd be doing? Better to buy it for Donny than to sneak it for him.

Finally, *finally*, the lunch period rolled around … and Donny was nowhere to be found.

Sarah couldn't believe it. She stood there in the quad, arms at her sides, turning in a slow circle. He wasn't in his usual spot, over by the gym with his friends. And he wasn't in their usual spot, next to the giant pine tree. So Sarah walked over to where her girlfriends were sitting, on the big steps in front of the multi-purpose room. She sat down and began to eat, wondering where in the world Donny had gone.

Finally, *finally*, he showed up, just as the end-of-lunch bell rang. He emerged onto the quad from the direction of the student parking lot, and Sarah wondered if he'd actually left school during lunch. Immediately, his eyes found hers and, expression serious, he made a beeline for her.

Sarah couldn't help but laugh.

"Wow," she said. "You're on a mission, aren't you?"

"I was. Mission complete."

"Where'd you go? I waited all through lunch to hear your big idea, and then you weren't here. The bell just rang."

"I went to a secret location, which I can't disclose."

"Are you coming, Sarah?" Amy Shepherd, Sarah's best friend, had already started walking towards their photography class.

"Go ahead," Sarah said. "I'll be right behind you."

When she turned back to Donny, his stare was intense. He took both of her hands in his and said, "I want to make love to you, Sarah."

This was hardly the way Sarah had imagined Donny asking her to have sex with him. Or the place, either. Still, everything went quiet around them. It was like they were standing on a tiny, silent island while the rest of the world swirled around them. Somewhere in her awareness, Sarah knew the other students were laughing, giving each other high fives, shouting fake insults across the quad.

But all she could see, all she could hear, was Donny.

"When?" she said.

The way he was looking at her, she half-expected him to say, "Right now," and start removing her clothes. But he didn't. He said,

"Tonight," which, to Sarah's fifteen-year-old mind, meant almost the same thing. The time span between "right now" and "tonight," she knew, would feel at once like an eternity and a half-second. Sarah swallowed and licked her lips. Her heart was beating a million miles per hour.

"Will you?" Donny said, giving her hands a gentle squeeze.

She nodded.

During fifth period, line segments and angles couldn't even come close to competing with Donny's proposal for space in Sarah's mind. Would sex with Donny be everything she'd imagined it would? How would it even work? Sarah knew the mechanics, obviously. She'd grown up on a farm. But what would they do? Would they kiss, first? And for how long? Where would they go? It seemed like losing your virginity was a big deal, and she didn't want it to happen in the back-seat of a car like it had for Margaret. This was a special occasion, and it should feel special, shouldn't it? Speaking of feeling, what would sex *feel* like?

"Miss Bradley," said Mr. Schneider, then. "I do believe your mind has been transported to another planet. By aliens, perhaps? Now, you know my stance on alien life forms. But I need you to talk those guys into letting your brain return to geometry class so you can answer my question."

DONNY WAS WAITING for Sarah after sixth-period P.E. She emerged from the locker room still wearing her gym clothes just as she did every Friday. For the first time, she felt self-conscious in the blue sweat shorts and gray t-shirt. Why hadn't she showered and changed back into her regular clothes?

But Donny didn't blink an eye. He just grabbed her hand and headed for the parking lot as if this were any other day.

"So. Remember how I said I had an idea?"

"Yeah," Sarah said, drawing the word out.

"I know. You're thinking I already told you."

"You did," Sarah said, feeling her face grow warm. Talking about sex, really talking about it, in the daylight, felt as terrifying as it did exhilarating.

"But I didn't tell you my plan."

"There's a plan?"

"Yeah," Donny said. "Of course there is. I want our first time to be special. Don't you?"

"Of course I do," Sarah said. She stole a glance at him and saw that the tips of his ears were pink.

"So," Donny said. "The plan."

"The plan," Sarah said.

"It's a surprise."

"What? You just acted like you were going to tell me." She punched him on the arm, and he flinched. They both laughed and some of the tension dissipated.

"Wait and see," he said. "I'll be at your window after Mama Katherine goes to bed."

Well. That would give Sarah plenty of time to shower and change into regular clothes. By now, they'd approached Margaret's car, an old Datsun that only barely managed to get them all from home to school and back again. And Margaret walked up right behind them.

"Hey, guys," she said.

Sarah froze. Donny froze. Had she heard them? If so, would she tell Mama Katherine? Yes, she'd already had sex with Jeremy Rigdon. But she was Sarah's big sister. Would she feel like she should try to stop them?

"Hey," Donny said.

"Hey," Sarah said. Donny elbowed her, and she realized too late that her voice had been way too cheerful.

But if Margaret had overheard them, she didn't act like it. She made small talk throughout the seven-mile drive, never once even hinting that she had an inkling of their plan.

"See ya, Donny," she said when she pulled up at the entrance to his driveway.

Donny shrugged at Sarah when he got out of the car. Margaret was silent as she drove up the road to the farmhouse, and Sarah assumed they were in the clear.

Of course, the afternoon dragged as Sarah completed her chores: laundry, mucking out the chicken coop, and feeding John Wayne. She even did some extra dishwashing, just to keep busy. All the while, her thoughts drifted to Donny, to his idea, his plan.

"You're productive today," Mama Katherine said, more than once.

"You never saw a very busy person who was unhappy," Sarah said. It was a quote Mama Katherine had used frequently throughout the girls' childhoods, and Mama Katherine laughed in response.

"Not that I mind," she said. "I appreciate the help. But I expected you'd be with Donny, it being Friday, and you're done with your chores."

Sarah concentrated doubly hard on scraping off the tiny bit of pasta that had hardened onto the baking dish after they ate up the tuna casserole.

"He's going to come over later, I think," Sarah said. Then, remembering he'd said he'd be over after Mama Katherine went to bed, she quickly added, "Or maybe not."

"Hmm," Mama Katherine said. "I made his favorite peach cobbler for dessert. Maybe you should run over and let him know."

Sarah nodded. "Maybe I will."

But she was too nervous to see him before she *saw* him, so she pretended to get distracted with a project that wasn't due for three more weeks. Then it was dinnertime.

The feelings of excitement and nervousness and anticipation coalesced in her stomach and she barely ate the chicken salad Mama Katherine had made.

"Everything okay, Sarah?" Mama Katherine said halfway through dinner. "You've done nothing more than move that salad around on your plate since we sat down."

"Fine!" Sarah said. "It's fine. I'm just not that hungry for some reason."

The clock ticked and tocked and ticked and tocked, slower than ever before.

Thankfully, Hannah jumped in with a discussion she'd had in one of her college classes, something about whether video games containing violence are appropriate for children. While Hannah had argued that *obviously*, they weren't, there was a particularly outspoken guy in her class who thought they were.

"He's so cocky," Hannah said, "and he hasn't even spent any time around kids. I have no idea why he's in the early education program."

"So let me guess," Margaret said. "You guys got into it. Locked horns."

Mama Katherine smiled a knowing smile, and Sarah realized she knew where this was going. She smiled, too.

"He has the hots for you," Margaret said. "I'll bet he doesn't even believe what he was saying. He was probably just trying to get your goat, so to speak."

"Is he handsome?" Mama Katherine wanted to know.

Hannah's mouth formed a little *o*, and Margaret burst into laughter.

"I knew it! He *is* crush-worthy!"

"Sounds like he does have a thing for you," Mama Katherine said.

"No!" Hannah said. "Impossible. He's so … such a … he's a city kid. You know? He'd never be interested in a country girl like me. He said as much, in high school."

"In high school?" Sarah said. "You didn't tell us you have a past with this guy."

Margaret nodded, smug. "It's that mega-hot Tanner Lucas, isn't it?"

"Did you just say, 'mega-hot'?" Hannah said.

"He *is* mega-hot," Margaret said.

"Well, regardless," Hannah said. "He'd never be interested in me."

Mama Katherine shrugged, and Sarah said, "But I think he is. Tell me this. Who spoke first during the debate today? You or him?"

Hannah waited a moment before speaking, and as she did, realization dawned on her face. "I did."

"I knew it!" Margaret said again. "He was trying to get your goat. He likes you."

"I agree," Sarah said. "So I think next time, you should let him speak first. And then you debate what he says."

"Isn't that leading him on?" Hannah wanted to know.

"Nah," Margaret said. "It's just friendly flirting. And there's nothing wrong with that."

Mama Katherine stood up. "I agree. Invite him over for peach cobbler the next time you get into it with him."

"Well, I never," Hannah said. "I never."

Finally, the table was cleared, the dishes were done, and the house was buttoned up for the night. Margaret had a "study date," which Sarah knew meant she was going to make out with some guy under the bleachers or something. Hannah had a study date, which meant she was meeting with a girlfriend at Walker's only coffee shop, where she'd get an herbal tea and talk about whether video games with violence were appropriate for children—and whether that crush-worthy city kid would show up at class the following week. And Mama Katherine was going to read a book in bed.

Which left Sarah alone to wait for Donny.

She wasn't sure *how* to wait. Should she wait in bed? She pulled the covers back and slid under them. No, this was weird. She was still fully clothed. She had to get up to open the window, anyway. And even if she left it open for him, he'd come in here to find her wearing her shoes in bed.

She got up and took off her shoes. She could sit on top of the covers and read. That would certainly look more natural, although she knew she wouldn't be able to concentrate on any words on any page, right now. The pacing started automatically. She walked along her bed, from head to foot, and back again, trailing her fingertips along its surface.

Then she froze. Why hadn't she thought of wearing something sexier under her clothes? Not that she owned anything remotely sexy. She could borrow something of Margaret's, or Hannah's. Of the three of them, Margaret was the most well-endowed (Hannah's words, not her own).

Both Hannah and Sarah were string-bean thin, as Mama Katherine liked to say, but Margaret was compact and curvy. When she felt self-conscious about the size of her breasts, Mama Katherine had taken her on a special shopping trip to buy bras that offered support and beauty. Now, her lingerie drawer overflowed with silky fabrics of every color, lined with lace and satin.

While the lace would look fine on Sarah, the cups would be anything but overflowing. She chuckled a little at the image. Her own bras were a practical collection of skin-tone colors and t-shirt-friendly fabrics.

"I could wear the tan bra with the front clasp, or the tan bra with the back clasp," she said aloud. "Or, I could wear the white bra, or the other white bra."

Then she had a thought, and a little thrill ran up her spine. What if she was naked when Donny knocked on her window? That would be sexy, right? Sarah nodded, and began unbuttoning her jeans. As she pulled them over her hips, she anticipated Donny's hands there. As she removed her t-shirt, she could almost feel his fingers on her skin. Why hadn't they done this sooner?

She stepped out of her underwear and folded them carefully. Not that Donny would notice if she left them on the floor. Then she unhooked her bra and folded it, too. Finally, she slipped under the covers to wait.

Under normal circumstances she would have drifted off to sleep. But not tonight. Covers up to her chin and eyes darting to the window every time a tree branch scraped it or an owl hooted, she waited.

Finally, she heard it: Donny's tap on the window. She sat straight up, clutching the covers to her chest. Then she remembered he'd seen everything under those covers, and she let them drop away. She got out of bed, mustered up as much confidence as she could, and walked over to the window.

In all her excitement about this plan, she'd forgotten how much the window groaned when someone opened it. Still, she told herself, the sound didn't go on for very long. From the outside, the window was high enough that Donny couldn't see anything lower than the top of Sarah's head. But once he climbed inside and realized she was naked, his eyes widened. So did his grin.

He stepped forward and without touching her body, he kissed her long and slow. Every single one of Sarah's nerve endings started to buzz, vibrating in the way Sarah imagined atoms and molecules did.

"Hi," Donny said when he finally pulled away.

"Hi," Sarah said.

"Well, you look nice," he said. "That birthday suit looks good on you."

"Why, thank you. I'd like to see your birthday suit, as well. If you don't mind."

It took Donny less than three seconds to undress, and he gestured, palm up, at the bed. They both climbed in, and Donny pulled the covers up over their bodies. One of his hands caressed the side of her face, and he looked at her so intensely her heart squeezed.

"I know I've already, you know, seen every part of you," Donny said. "But it's different seeing you like this. All at once. You're so beautiful, Sarah."

"Wow," she said. "I think even my toes are blushing."

"Let me check."

And so it was that Mama Katherine gave two quick raps on the door before walking into Sarah's room to find Sarah naked in bed and Donny under the covers.

———

NOW, more than twenty years later, Sarah laughed at the memory as she collected the courage she needed to ask Donny to do some moonlight gardening with her. Mama Katherine had *known*, somehow, that Donny was coming over. She must have, because her face didn't show one iota of surprise when she saw the lump under Sarah's covers.

She'd simply said, "Sarah, why don't you package up some peach cobbler for Donny to take home. Now."

And then she'd walked out.

At first, Donny moved in slow motion as he collected his clothes. It was shock. But then, they started laughing, giggling uncontrollably as they both got dressed. Sarah had tears of laughter streaming down her face as she retrieved the cobbler. When they kissed good-bye, plans foiled, they were still laughing. The sex had happened—obviously— but it hadn't happened that night.

Now, Sarah could hear Amelia chattering away as they cleaned up the checkers. Although she hated to interrupt their conversation, she also knew she needed to take action if she wanted to implement Hazel's plan in her own life.

She walked into the kitchen and Amelia stopped talking. Donny looked at her and raised his eyebrows, as if to ask what she needed.

"Good game?" Her voice came out in a kind of croak.

"I beat Dad," Amelia said.

Donny shook his head. "Sad, but true," he said. "If our daughter employs the same strategic thinking in college as she does in checkers, we won't have anything to worry about."

Those words—*our daughter*—made tears spring to Sarah's eyes. The fact that there was still an "our" in all this gave her hope.

"Mama Katherine asked if we'd do some gardening this evening," she said. She wondered if he could hear the emotion in her voice.

There was a tiny beat before Donny answered. "Sure."

"Can I, uh, skip out on that? I told Luke I'd text him tonight."

Sarah's mind flashed, immediately, to the attempted lovemaking session Mama Katherine had interrupted. She wondered if Amelia would do something like that. Had Luke planned to show up at Amelia's window tonight?

No, she was putting too much thought into this. They'd only just met.

"Yeah, I think that'd be okay," Sarah said, as if she hadn't planned on trying to find a way to ask Amelia to leave her alone with Donny so they could talk.

———

IF SARAH WERE to assume Hazel's plan was successful (and she did assume that), then maybe Sarah should follow the same steps Hazel had taken. Stage one was Observation. It was where Hazel got to know Philip and all of his habits. Sarah figured she could skip this, since she'd been observing Donny Ward for practically her entire life.

She already knew that he removed his socks and put them on the living room floor every evening at 8:34 p.m. She already knew that he took his coffee black and didn't like iced tea. She already knew that he loved eating those huge salted pretzels and hated seafood. His favorite color was orange and his lucky number was fourteen. His lucky charm was a tarot card he'd gotten at the county fair the summer he turned fifteen. It predicted he'd live a rich life. He still kept it in his wallet, behind his drivers license.

Donny's eyes were the exact color of coffee—coffee in a mug with a tablespoon of milk. He loved soda but not the diet stuff. He'd watch the *Star Wars* movies over and over again. His favorite book was *Where the Red Fern Grows*.

So, Sarah decided, she would skip straight to Stage Two: Immersion.

The first step: getting Donny's help in the garden. She knew he wouldn't turn her down. He loved Mama Katherine.

"Even though we all spent hours out here today," Sarah said as they walked into the twilight together, "there's still so much to do. It's really overgrown."

"That's surprising," Donny said. "Mama Katherine never lets her garden get out of hand."

"My thoughts exactly," Sarah said. "I think that's part of why Hannah's so worried about her."

"Makes sense," Donny said.

It was strange, Sarah thought, to have this level of comfort with someone while simultaneously feeling like he was a stranger. Always the gentleman, Donny held the garden gate open for Sarah. She ducked past him, not missing the pine-tree scent of his cologne as she did. Sarah had assumed they'd work side by side, but as soon as she knelt down in the soft dirt next to the corn stalks, Donny went to the other end of the garden, near the onions.

They weeded in silence for a few minutes. Sarah reveled in the sounds of a summer evening: bugs whirring around, a mixed-up rooster crowing, a nearby tractor making what was probably the last trip around a field. Meanwhile, she casted about for something to say to Donny.

———

SO, do you plan to move out as soon as we get home?
   Where will you live when you leave me?
   How did you fall out of love with me?
   Why didn't you tell me sooner?

———

NONE OF THOSE WOULD DO.

"Nice night," she said.

"It is," he said.

"It's finally cooling off," she said.

"Yeah," he said. "It was a scorcher."

When had their conversations been reduced to small talk?

She remembered discussing the potential for alien life and arguing over whether cats made better pets than dogs.

"Donny?"

"Yeah."

"Do you still think about whether aliens exist?"

"That's a funny question."

"I know," Sarah said. "Forget it."

"Do you?"

"Not really," Sarah said. "I was just thinking about that one night."

"The night when we both sneaked out and had a campout under the stars?" Donny said.

"And talked about aliens."

"That was a fun night," Donny said, and Sarah thought she detected a little wistfulness there. "Didn't you burn your hand when we were making s'mores?"

Sarah chuckled. "I'd forgotten about that part. I think that's what gave us away to Mama Katherine."

"And she put the lock on your window and told my mom."

They worked in silence for a while, and Sarah thought about whether she should tell Donny she intended to make him fall in love with her again. Maybe it would be better to just do it. She probably shouldn't tell him. He may be more likely to resist, to tell her he'd already called it quits.

"Sarah?"

"Yeah?"

For the smallest fraction of a second, she thought he might say he'd changed his mind, that he wanted to stay with her, that their time together wasn't lost.

But then he said, "I'm really sorry. About everything."

Donny slept under the stars again.

CHAPTER FOURTEEN

INSTEAD OF SLEEPING, Sarah sought solace in Hazel's journal. She curled up on the back porch with it, and read by the light of Mama Katherine's old flashlight.

JULY 3: One month + one day since The Big Day (our wedding, of course)

TOMORROW IS JULY 4. You could have looked at today's date, Pauline, and figured that out for yourself. Haha. Just kidding. Anyway. Philip and I have decided to throw a huge Independence Day celebration. The apples won't be ripe, but the orchard is such a beautiful setting with the leaves flared out and the apples growing and the house as a backdrop. We'll have dinner and drinks and dancing. People can set off firecrackers, and I am almost positive we'll be able to see the big fireworks display from town.

While I've done most of the party planning—organizing caterers, sending out invitations, and deciding on the menu—I look forward to seeing how Philip and I work as a team tomorrow. If setting up for a party isn't Full Immersion, I don't know what is.

You probably don't care what we're eating, but here's the menu:
Pineapple chicken
Miniature quiches
Cheese logs with fancy crackers

Deviled eggs

A fruit tray with yogurt dip

Black forest cake (for dessert)

And champagne cocktails to toast our country's birthday just before the big fireworks display.

(No, don't be silly, Pauline! I won't be cooking any of this. Betty will prepare it in the morning and I'll simply set it out.)

Tomorrow's to-do list includes setting up tables and chairs, decorating the tables, stringing lights (which we probably should have done today, but oh, well), and raking the rows between the trees. I'd like to set up the patio, too, with plenty of seating.

If everything falls into place, tomorrow could be quite romantic, Pauline. I'm looking forward to it. But—I'm exhausted just thinking about it. Off to bed.

JULY 4 - NOON (5 hours until the party begins)

OH MY DEAR PAULINE,

I HAVE SAD, sad news: Philip and I are not going to fall wildly in love. This marriage will never work. We are a terrible team. I wish you were a human, Pauline, and you could have seen how catastrophically we work together. I am not even sure whether catastrophically is a word, but if not, it should be. We decided that it would be best to start by raking the leaves from the rows between the apple trees.

It's a beautiful day, Pauline. Not quite as humid as it has been here in previous years, and therefore not quite as hot. I was ready first, so I went out and started raking. I raked and raked, and before long I'd cleared an entire row. Where was Philip? I needed a drink so I went inside to get one and I found him sitting at the kitchen counter, talking on the phone. He was on a call. A work call. I mean, I know he runs the place, but I needed help, Pauline! We'd agreed to start raking and he said he'd be right out and he just didn't come out. Nor did he think about putting his caller on hold to alert me that he'd be a moment. Several moments, actually.

After he hung up, he apologized (I'm sure he noticed me huffing about the kitchen). He said the phone rang, he answered it, and he got caught up talking to someone who'd called about a big order. A potential big order, I should say.

We finished the raking, and we decided to go ahead and set up the tables. We each took an end, and disaster struck. We tried to navigate our way from the shed to the orchard, and we hit that table on every possible obstacle. Who even knew you could run the end of a table right into a tree? He'd say, "left," and I'd go left, and he'd say, "I meant MY left," and I'd overcorrect and before we knew it we were both so frustrated!

I needed a break from the madness, which is why I sit here now, writing to you. Pauline, we've been "working" for five hours and we have set up only four out of twelve tables. I can't see any way we can finish by five p.m. I'd better go give it my best shot, though, because we have guests coming. And even though we may make an atrocious team, there may still be romance ahead. I hope I have time for a shower. Or, at least, to brush my teeth.

———

JULY 4 - 11 P.M.

———

OH MY DEAR PAULINE,

———

THINGS TURNED out even better than I'd hoped. We may not work well together, and we may never put on another party together, but there were definitely … ahem … fireworks tonight. I'll tell you more, later. Philip is waiting for me to join him on the patio.

———

SARAH CLOSED the journal and sat in the dark for a few moments, listening to the chirping of crickets and the loud croaking of what was certainly a huge bullfrog. Hazel had given her an idea. July fourth was approaching, and it would present a great opportunity for Sarah to reconnect with Donny. She was sure her sisters would help, and the timing would be just right so that they could take Amelia to college after that (Sarah had signed her up for a summer session so she could get her feet wet—what had she been thinking?).

A party would give them a joint cause to work on, and it would be so good for Mama Katherine. In the dark, Sarah nodded to herself. Then she gathered some clothes and went back inside, to the bedroom she shared with Amelia.

Her daughter was sleeping, her breathing even and her body still. Sarah changed into pajamas and slipped into bed.

"Mom?"

"Yeah?"

"Can we talk?"

Sarah's entire body filled with dread in the half-second that followed Amelia's question. She probably wanted to talk about Donny. Or, more specifically, about Donny leaving Sarah. And Sarah didn't know what to say about it. But she'd always told Amelia that she could talk to her about anything, hadn't she?

"Sure."

Amelia rolled over, put an arm around Sarah's waist, and squeezed. "Don't worry, Mom. I don't want to talk about Dad. I'm just going to let the two of you work that out."

On a sigh of relief, Sarah laughed. "Okay. What is it, then?"

Amelia flopped onto her back. "It's that guy I met. Luke."

"Oh, yeah? What about him?"

"Nothing."

Sarah was glad it was dark so Amelia couldn't see her smile. "So you want to talk about nothing?"

"Ha," Amelia said. "I mean, it's nothing specific. We just had such a good time, walking."

"Yes, walking sounds quite fun."

"Mo-om," Amelia said. "I just mean that we got along so well. He's not like the guys I've met back home, you know? He was actually interested in what I had to say. Did you know he did a Science Fair project every year of elementary school and junior high?"

"I didn't know that," Sarah said. "But that's impressive."

"It is," Amelia said.

"What else?"

"Well, he's going to start raising horses."

"That's fun," Sarah said.

"He asked if I was named after Amelia Earhart. He's the first guy to ever ask me that."

"Why don't you invite him over for Fourth of July?"

"Okay," Amelia said, drawing the word out. "Are we doing something?"

Sarah told Amelia about her plan to propose a party. "But I haven't run it by your grandmother or your aunts, yet."

"I'm sure they'll be excited."

"I don't know," Amelia said.

"What do you mean?"

"I mean, Aunt Hannah has seemed stressed since we got here. And Aunt Margaret—she's acting weird. She keeps sneaking off to talk on the phone. I don't know if she has a secret long-distance boyfriend, or what. And she seems distracted. Haven't you noticed?"

"Honestly, no," Sarah said. "I've been distracted, myself. I noticed Hannah, but I thought we'd help get the house in order and that would make things better. I did notice Margaret's been on the phone a lot, but I assumed it was work-related. She's seemed like her normal self."

"Watch her tomorrow," Amelia said. "And then tell me what you think. Even so, I think the Fourth of July party is a fantastic idea."

CHAPTER FIFTEEN

MARGARET CONFIRMED Amelia's observations the next morning at breakfast when Sarah proposed the Fourth of July party.

"I don't know," she said, looking down at her plate and swirling a piece of sausage around in her syrup.

Amelia looked at Sarah as if to say, "I told you so," and Sarah looked at Hannah, whose own expression showed pure surprise.

Then Hannah and Mama Katherine said in unison, "Well, I think it's a great idea."

"It just seems like a lot of work, is all," Margaret said. She was still looking at her plate.

"But, Aunt Margaret," Amelia said, "you're, like, the queen of parties."

"I know," Margaret said. "I know I am. But there's just so much to do around here."

"Has an alien Aunt Hannah taken over your body?" Amelia said.

"Body swap," Hannah said. Her tone said she was joking, but as she looked at Margaret, the line between her eyebrows said she was worried.

"No," Margaret said. "It *is* a great idea. It's just—it's a great idea. Let's do it. It'll be fun. And Farmer Eddie can come."

"It doesn't have to be big," Mama Katherine said, nodding. "We'll just invite Eddie, and the Suttons, and maybe a few other families. And that's it. Okay?"

"And Donny, Amelia, and I will do most of the work," Sarah said.

"Okay? You just be here, sharing that sparkling personality with all of our guests."

"Okay," Margaret said. She looked at each of them in turn, offering a smile that didn't quite pass muster. Later that morning, Sarah cornered Hannah in the laundry room.

"Has Margaret said anything to you?" Sarah said.

"She's said lots of things," Hannah said. "And wow. This reminds me of the time you trapped me in here, trying to get me to hide your late-night tryst with Donny. You were ruthless then, and I'm scared now."

"That was important," Sarah said, "and this is, too. Amelia said Margaret's been acting weird."

"Like what?" Hannah said.

"Like, sneaking off to talk on the phone, acting distracted, things like that."

"It's Margaret," Hannah said. "You know she has a crazy social life. I'm sure she's just keeping up with it while she's here. You know?"

Sarah nodded. "You might be right. But the more I think about it, the more I think something's wrong. Let's watch her."

"Okay," Hannah said. "But I'm sure it's nothing. Although—"

"What?" Sarah said.

"I noticed some other weird stuff. Like, at the Farmer's Market, when she didn't see the almonds. And there've been a couple of times when she's looking for something that's right in front of her, and she can't find it. She's probably just distracted. I'm sure it's nothing."

"Let's just make sure we're sure," Sarah said.

Before they could say anything else, Donny appeared in the doorway. "What are you two ladies doing in here, having some kind of top-secret meeting?"

Hannah beamed at him. "Yes, actually. We are. You missed breakfast, you know. Let me make you a plate while I tell you about our plans for you over the next week."

"Should I be scared?" Donny said.

"Absolutely," Hannah said. "That's why, after I make you breakfast, I'm going to run out to the farmer's market."

She squeezed Sarah's arm and herded them into the kitchen. While Sarah washed dishes, Hannah flipped a few pancakes, plated them alongside some sausage, and hurried out of the house.

"How'd you sleep last night?" Sarah asked as Donny ate.

She leaned against the kitchen counter, coffee mug in hand. John Wayne laid at her feet, ears perked and head tilted as he waited for Donny to toss him a scrap. Donny obliged him, even though Mama Katherine had always reprimanded the girls for giving him human food.

"Fine," Donny said. "It got a bit chilly."

Were they really talking about the weather? There were so many other things she wanted to say to him: "Something's wrong with Margaret," "I'm scared for Mama Katherine," "I don't want you to leave me." Even John Wayne found this depressing, despite the fact that he'd just earned a piece of sausage. He got up, stretched, and left the kitchen.

Sarah had spent so many years trying to protect Donny from the stressors in her own life that she had reduced them to conversations so surface-level she barely even knew what he thought any more. They talked about schedules and homework assignments and weekly menus. But they had not talked about fears or hopes or politics or even where to go for vacation. Sarah just soldiered onward. She may mention a fear that Amelia would get drunk at a party, or her hope that their daughter would get into college. She'd tell Donny about a vacation but only after she'd already decided where to go ... which choice would provide the best experience for Amelia.

"How did you sleep?" Donny said.

"Donny?"

Done with his breakfast, he put his plate in the sink and started looking at the magnets on Mama Katherine's refrigerator. Now he turned to look at her. Sarah found the eye contact almost surprising. Not that they never made eye contact, she thought, but it felt for the first time like she was really seeing him. She wondered if he noticed, if he could feel the shift. He was waiting for her to speak.

"When did we stop talking?"

A long moment passed. He didn't look away. Sarah didn't, either.

He still held his coffee mug, and he looked down into it, briefly. He pushed away from the counter and poured himself a refill, then held up the pot in an offer to do the same for Sarah. She nodded, remembering the way they used to spend so many early mornings: with travel mugs of coffee, they'd walk for what seemed at once like minutes and hours, just talking and talking.

"I don't know," he said, finally, and Sarah felt a twinge of disappointment, until he went on. "The realization hit me one day. And when it did, I also realized things had gradually slipped away. It's like, when you go to the beach. And you're holding a handful of sand, with your fist closed. Dry sand. And it just falls out of your hand. If you're not looking, you might not even notice it's happening. Then you open your hand, palm up, and there's just a tiny bit of sand left. Right?"

Numb, Sarah nodded. "Which day was it? The day when you realized your hand was empty?"

"*Almost* empty," he said. "Amelia was fifteen or so."

Sarah gasped, involuntarily. "It's been three years?"

Donny nodded, staring into his coffee again. "It's been three years."

Sarah busied herself drying dishes, hoping he'd elaborate, and he did.

"It was that day when Amelia went with Payton to the water park. Remember that?"

"I remember."

"I wanted to take you out that day. You'd been so busy with all the PTA stuff and the end-of-year dance and everything. You'd been so distracted. And I was busy at work, too. So I thought, Amelia's going to be gone all day. She's going to be having a blast. The two of us could spend the day together. We could go for a drive, maybe go to the bookstore, have some lunch. You know?"

"And I ruined it." Sarah's vision was blurry with tears. Robotically, she started putting away the dry dishes.

"You didn't ruin it," Donny said. "But every time I tried to talk about something, you—"

"I talked about Amelia and Payton. I was so worried about them. Which was silly, because they were fine. But I imagined them being accosted by creepy men or even drowning or choking on their lunch or—"

"Or making friends with girls who'd smuggled in vodka in water bottles."

Sarah laughed. Now, with that day well behind them—and completely safe and successful—it sounded absurd.

Donny smiled, but his expression looked sad. "That was the weekend I was considering that promotion. Taking it meant so many things for us, and so did not taking it. I needed to do some soul searching, and who better to do it with, than you? But you were—"

"I was in Crazy Mom Mode," Sarah said.

"Yeah," Donny said.

Her natural inclination was to defend herself, explain her behavior. But she waited.

"I wanted so badly to talk to you, Sarah. You were my compass. And I felt like I'd lost you. And to make matters worse, it didn't seem like you even noticed."

"Donny, I—I am so sorry. I remember that day, too."

"Why didn't you say anything sooner?"

"I tried, Sarah," Donny said. "I tried. I understood—I understand—your desire to spend as much time as possible with Amelia. I understand you wanting to be a great mom. And you are. That's why I'd bring up date nights when she was busy with friends. Even when you did agree to go out, you always insisted on being home before she planned to, in case she needed us. When I wanted to talk about something, you'd always steer the conversation back to Amelia. And I felt like I couldn't fault you for that. 'I'm sorry, Sarah, but I'm falling out of love with you because you're too good of a mother.' That hardly seems fair."

"But how could I know it was bothering you, if you didn't tell me?"

"I tried to tell you," he said. "But you'd always change the subject."

She wanted to ask, "Well, why weren't you more forceful about it?" But she didn't, because she knew. She knew he was right. She could remember several times when he'd started to say something, and she'd given him a brush-off apology and then tried to listen to what he was saying while simultaneously worrying about Amelia. So she nodded. "I did do that," she said. "I didn't mean to push you away."

"I know," he said.

Feeling like she'd probably squeezed all the juice out of this conversation, Sarah decided to introduce the Immersion Phase.

"We're having a Fourth of July party," she said.

"You are?" he said.

"*You* are, too."

"I am?"

"Well, naturally, the Bradley sisters need your help."

"Naturally," Donny said. "And I'd be glad to offer my services."

"Want to ride into town later? I thought we could get some new flowers from the nursery, plant them in Mama Katherine's big pots, spruce the place up a bit."

"Sure," Donny said. "If we can stop at the hardware store. Free popcorn."

"Old habits die hard," Sarah said. "I'd love to."

———

AFTER BREAKFAST, Sarah went into the RV to grab a change of clothes. For the first time in as long as she could remember, she carefully considered her options for an outfit. She lifted a pair of khaki pants out of the drawer, and almost recoiled at the sudden memory of a photo Amelia had snapped one Easter when she wore them. "Unflattering" was putting it mildly. Why hadn't she thrown them away at once? Because, with their elastic waistband and many pockets, they were useful. Functional.

"Ugh," she said.

In her mind, she labeled those khaki pants "Trash" and dropped them onto the floor.

Then she pulled out a pair of jean capris. Donny had commented—several years ago—that she looked great in them, and she realized now she hadn't worn them since. What had she been thinking? She'd been thinking the faux pockets were impractical. In fact, she'd thrown them in on this trip only as a backup pair.

Sarah shook her head.

She'd brought several unisex track t-shirts from Amelia's high school days, but she slid their hangers to one side of the RV's closet in search of something more feminine. There was the shirt she'd worn the last time they went on a date for their anniversary. Their fifteenth anniversary.

Now, she gasped. That was years ago. Why had she forsaken celebrating their anniversaries, their marriage?

It was craziness.

Pauline—Hazel's journal—was tucked into the corner of the closet, and Sarah decided to bring it inside with her. Maybe one of her sisters would want to do some research this afternoon while she and Donny went into Walker. Before going inside to shower, though, she read another entry.

———

JULY 5: The day after our FIRST KISS!!!

———

PAULINE!

———

WE KISSED! Philip and I kissed and it was the most wonderful experience! Now, Pauline, I've kissed and been kissed before. But it was never like this. Remember last night, when I said there were fireworks? And then Philip was waiting for me to join him on the patio? Well, the fireworks between Philip and me started before the actual fireworks started.

Yes, we're a terrible table-moving team. But by the time we'd gotten all the outdoor furniture set up, we were laughing and joking about just how terrible we were. Philip had me in stitches. He's so FUNNY, Pauline!

He'd say, "Hey, Hazel, I have an idea. When I want you to go to your right, I'll say, 'Go to your left!' And when you want me to raise my end of the table higher, just tell me, 'Hey Phil, lower your end of the table, would you please?'"

We were in tears, Pauline! From laughter!

And then the guests started arriving before we'd even put up the lights. But it didn't matter. It didn't matter because we were having so much fun. The table-moving experience seemed to open some door I didn't even realize was standing closed between us.

We've always agreed that, in front of other people, we should act like a "normal" married couple. But last night, it didn't feel like acting.

As you know, we were entertaining, so things were really jovial. It felt so natural when Philip touched my arm or squeezed my hand.

And then there was A Moment, Pauline. It happened when our friends the Lewises left us alone at the meat and cheese tray. Margie Lewis said to Carl, 'Carl, let's go get another drink, shall we?' and then she winked at me. They walked away.

Philip turned to me and he said, "Well, how do you like that, Mrs. Carlisle? We're alone."

He tucked a strand of hair behind my ear, and he left his hand there, just below my ear, and he was looking at me so intensely. He looked at my mouth. Just like you see it happen in movies. He's never done that before. Even on our wedding day, Pauline, he didn't look at me like that.

I knew he was going to kiss me. I just knew it. And then I think he lost his nerve, because his lips twitched and he said, "Well, our tables turned out okay after all, didn't they?"

And then the Lewises were back and The Moment was over. After that, I couldn't wait for everyone to leave, so I could kiss Philip senseless. I was noticing the way his mouth looked so full and his shoulders looked so broad and his smile looked so warm.

Everyone did leave ... eventually. Ha! It was a great party and people lingered. When they were all gone, I ran inside to freshen up. That's when I last wrote, Pauline, and Philip was waiting for me on the patio.

I went back outside. And there he was, leaning against the railing. When he saw me, he smiled, and it was so genuine, so heartfelt, that I couldn't help but smile back. It was completely involuntary, like your heartbeat (not yours, Pauline. Obviously).

I said something about it being a great party, and he agreed. He handed me a glass of champagne and we toasted. And then, he cupped the back of my head with his free hand and said, "I've been wanting to do this all night."

He kissed me, right then and there.

And it was wonderful. It was so nice. I actually couldn't believe it. It felt so—natural! And so breathtaking at the same time. How is that possible? I think we're on the way to having a real, actual marriage.

———

SO HAZEL and Philip had finally kissed. Sarah felt giddy with that new-love feeling. It *was* possible. When Hazel had first married Philip, she hadn't thought they'd fall in love. But they were. They were falling in love. Hazel had set out to make Philip love her, and it had worked.

Bolstered by the story of Hazel and Philip's first kiss, Sarah gathered up her sexy jean capris and the anniversary-date-worthy tank top and went back inside to get ready. She and Donny were going to buy flowers, and what was more symbolic of new beginnings than that?

———

SARAH HAD to stop herself from saying, "Nice day," as Donny drove Mama Katherine's old farm truck down the long country road to town.

It *was* a nice day, the sun shining brightly, throwing all of summer's colors—flowers in beds, puffy white clouds in the blue sky —into sharp contrast.

In a way, it seemed wrong to mar this beautiful picture with her worries, but Sarah reminded herself that not sharing her worries is what had led her to this place—the place where her husband wanted to leave her.

So she said, "Have you noticed Margaret acting—I don't know, strange?"

Donny drummed his thumbs on the steering wheel, his expression thoughtful. "I didn't want to say anything."

"So you have."

"She's just—well, *subdued*, I guess."

"Why didn't you want to say anything?" Sarah said.

"I don't know. You've already got enough on your mind, with Amelia going to school and Mama Katherine struggling like she is. To tell you the truth, I thought maybe Margaret was just stressed, too."

"Yeah," Sarah said. "Maybe that's all it is."

She'd almost forgotten how astute Donny could be, how tuned into the nuances and layers of moods and situations.

"Still," they said at the same time.

"It's not like her to be sneaking into other rooms, getting on her phone when she thinks we're not paying attention," Sarah said.

"Maybe she has a new boy toy. You know how she can get."

"Did you just accuse my sister of having a boy toy?"

"I guess I did," Donny said. "I mean, it's never a boyfriend or a beau or 'her man,' is it?"

Sarah laughed. "I guess not."

"We're here," Donny said.

He pulled into the nursery's parking lot and Sarah felt her heart rate pick up. "I used to love this place," she said, almost involuntarily.

A tiny brown building, made to look like some kind of woodland cottage, served as the entryway and office. To the right, rows and rows of flowers lined an expansive patio. Sarah could smell the wet potting soil, the bags of fertilizer stacked off to one side. Morning dew stood on petals, sparkling on yellows and reds and purples.

Being here, side by side with Donny as he pushed the cart up and down the narrow rows, felt almost normal. It was nearly impossible to believe that he planned to end their marriage after this, to leave her. Nearly. Although they talked companionably, trading opinions on red versus purple and tall versus short, Donny never touched Sarah, or paused to smile at her like he once would have.

On the outside, Sarah conveyed confidence and ease. On the inside, she felt panic setting in. How could she possibly fix this? Donny would undoubtedly feel strange if she suddenly started acting like pre-parenthood Sarah. Or would he? How would the pre-parenthood Sarah act in this situation? She'd touch his arm, give him a quick squeeze around the waist. Maybe she'd even caress his backside and say something suggestive about *later*. At this, she almost laughed out loud. That would give Donny a scare—if she suddenly started rubbing his ass after abstaining from doing so for years.

She sighed.

"Everything okay?" Donny said.

"What?" Sarah said, then, before he could repeat himself, she gave him a bright smile. "Yes! Everything's fine."

I'm just trying to figure out how to touch you again.

She'd have to do this in baby steps. If she could just commit to one step per day, she could eventually get from brink-of-divorce to happy-together-again. First: get comfortable with casual touching.

"I think we've got enough flowers to plant the entire five-acre homestead," he said, gesturing at the cart, which was so heavily laden Sarah blinked. She hadn't realized just how many flowers she'd stacked on there.

"Did you want to get anything else?" Donny said.

"I think this'll do it." Now she did laugh out loud. Donny laughed out loud. Their eyes met and she felt a sense of connection. She was tempted to touch his arm, to squeeze his shoulder, to do something to acknowledge the moment. But then the moment was gone and Donny marched the cart up to the register.

"Well, Jiminy Cricket," Mama Katherine said when she saw the load of flowers in the bed of the truck. "You didn't say we were turning the whole place into a flower garden."

Margaret whistled, and Hannah said, "I have no idea how we're going to get all of those in within the next week."

"We may have gotten a little carried away," Sarah said.

"'We'?" Donny said. "I was just pushing the cart, Sarah."

That comment felt so much like their old banter that Sarah felt a new stirring of hope. Now, she thought, would be an excellent time to reach out and touch his arm. Or give him a playful punch. But again, the moment passed before she had a chance. Donny was sliding trays of flowers out of the truck and Mama Katherine was directing him to set them on the ground at intervals.

"Looks like the two of you had a successful shopping trip," Margaret said to Sarah when Donny followed Mama Katherine across the yard with two trays of snapdragons.

"I know," Sarah said. "We spent a small fortune."

"That's not what I meant," Margaret said.

"Yeah," Hannah said. "It feels like the vibe has shifted a little bit."

"The vibe?" Sarah said. "Are you turning into a hippie on us?"

"No," Hannah said. "But it does, right Margaret?"

"Right," Margaret said. "The vibe has definitely shifted."

"Tell us about it while we get the tools," Hannah said.

As they always had, Margaret and Sarah followed Hannah's lead, falling into step behind her.

"There's nothing to tell," Sarah said.

Typically, Margaret would say something here, whether it was to make a bawdy comment or to push Sarah for more information. When she remained silent, Sarah decided this was the perfect opportunity to say something about her strange behavior since arriving at the farm.

Hannah wrenched open the door to the shed, and Sarah said, "Margaret, is everything okay?"

An untrained eye would have missed it. But as the youngest sister, Sarah had spent her entire childhood and most of her young adulthood studying her older sisters. Margaret went deer-in-the-headlights for a fraction of a second and Sarah knew. Something was wrong. And it was just like Margaret to hide it from them. She recovered quickly, flashing them a smile before offering a quick, "Yes! Everything's great! Oh! And I meant to tell you: I did some research on Hazel Rickshaw Carlisle. It looks like she just disappeared off the face of the earth at a certain point. I found her information in a couple of Census reports, and then, about forty years ago, poof! Nothing."

Then she shrugged and ducked into the darkness of the shed.

Sarah looked at Hannah, whose expression only confirmed what she was thinking. Margaret emerged with a couple of shovels and handed one to each of her sisters. "Now, get to work! I'll grab a few more tools."

"This conversation isn't over," Hannah said.

"You're going to have to spill it, sister," Sarah said.

"Spill what?" Margaret said, and Sarah and Hannah exchanged another look.

With the warning firmly in place, they went to plant flowers. Margaret and Hannah claimed the flower beds in front of the house, which left Sarah planting in the back.

As she made her way along the walkway that led into the house, she noticed Donny and Mama Katherine huddled together, talking in low voices. When they heard her coming, they both jumped.

Donny's face flushed, and he took the shovel Sarah offered him. Their fingers brushed, but it was accidental. Sarah couldn't mark that off as a friendly touch.

Mama Katherine cleared her throat. "Donny and I were just talking," she said, loudly.

"I saw that," Sarah said.

"We were just discussing whether to alternate colors lining the walkway."

"Oh, okay," Sarah said. Without making eye contact with either of them, she set her shovel down and went to turn on the hose. "What did you decide?"

Now Donny cleared his throat. "We, uh, didn't."

"Hmm," Sarah said.

"Well, that's settled," Mama Katherine said. "Let's alternate."

Donny nodded. "Sounds good."

"I'll leave you two to it." Mama Katherine walked away, and Donny watched her go, a small smile on his lips.

"Well," Sarah said. "Should we start planting?"

She wet the dirt, and then, working on opposite sides of the walkway, they used their shovels to turn the earth. During Sarah's childhood, Mama Katherine had always kept this area planted with flowers, but it was obvious from the way the ground was hard-packed that she hadn't done so in a long time. Hannah had every right to be worried, Sarah thought. Suddenly, she felt guilty for not coming home more often, for not offering to help Hannah more.

As if he could hear what she was thinking, Donny said, "I'm glad we're here, Sarah."

Unbidden, and unexpectedly, tears flooded her eyes. All she could do was nod.

It was dinnertime before Sarah finally worked up the courage to touch her husband. They'd worked all day, pulling out weeds, churning up flower beds, and planting flowers. Amelia joined them mid-morning when she woke up.

She raked up piles of leaves and weeds and trimmings, pausing every so often to check her phone. Several times, Sarah caught her grinning and wondered if she was texting with the mysterious Luke Sutton from across the way.

Her question was answered when Luke showed up with his own rake and shovel, his muscular arms rippling in a tank top. He said hello to everyone, as if they were old friends, and began working right away.

Sarah caught Donny's eye, and they grinned at each other. For the next couple of hours, Sarah watched her daughter flirt, obviously overcome by Luke's charm. The two of them chatted away, raking and shoveling and moving the rocks and bricks from previous renditions of the yard.

Hannah put Mama Katherine in charge of refreshments, and she made sandwiches and lemonade for lunch. By late afternoon, everyone was slightly sunburned, but the yard looked like an oil painting, all bright colors and tidy containers.

"I think we'll have a big barbecue for dinner," Mama Katherine said. "I've got a bunch of meat that needs cooking up, anyway, and we can throw some corn and potatoes on the grill, too. Easiest thing we could do, after all our hard work today. Donny and Sarah, drag the grill over here, would you, please? Maybe get it cleaned up?"

Sarah knew what she was doing, and she surmised that Donny did, too. It was the same thing she used to do when the girls fought: she'd give them some project to work on together, and they'd go from "bickering like two wet hens" to being "two peas in a pod" (Mama's words).

Still, neither Donny nor Sarah would argue with her. Wily old fox.

"Amelia, you and Luke can drag some tables and chairs over here," Mama Katherine said, then. "We'll eat outside. Margaret and Hannah, come on inside and help me season this meat."

Alone with Donny again, Sarah noticed for the first time that he'd taken off his shirt and was wearing an undershirt. How had she forgotten how sexy he was? His shoulders were so muscular, and right now, they were covered in sweat and dirt and he looked so … manly. Sarah found herself licking her lips, unconsciously.

"Where is the grill?" he said, then.

Sarah realized she had no idea. "Should we check the shed?"

As they walked over there together, a film reel of memories played in Sarah's mind. When she and Donny were teenagers, the shed was brand new. Since Hannah, Margaret, and Sarah were all driving by then, the garage was full of cars and Mama Katherine had needed somewhere to put all the gardening supplies. So, she'd installed the shed. And Sarah and Donny had taken full advantage of the dark, quiet, private location. Several times.

The modern-day Donny pulled open the door and whistled.

"Well, it's not the haven of our youth, is it?"

So he'd been remembering, too. And it was true: the corners were now fuzzy with cobwebs, and Sarah couldn't shake the feeling that creepy crawly creatures lived in there, too. She wouldn't be caught dead getting naked in here, now.

This thought made her giggle, and when she did, Donny laughed, too.

"Oh, to be young again," he said.

Although he'd meant it as a joke, she was sure, Sarah detected quite a bit of wistfulness in his voice. This wistfulness gave her the courage to reach out and touch him, to close the space between them. She put her hand on his shoulder, then ran it down his arm to his hand. She squeezed, briefly, and said, "We had some good times, didn't we?"

Sarah was surprised that he squeezed her hand in response, and she wondered whether it was just a reflex. She let go and pointed at the grill, which stood against the opposite wall. "Well, there it is."

As they maneuvered it out of the shed, lifting it over flower pots and sliding it past tools and scrap lumber, Sarah thought about Hazel and Philip, and how Hazel had said they made such a bad team when they set up the tables for their Fourth of July party.

Sarah and Donny had always made a good team, and they barely had to speak to accomplish the barbecue-moving feat. If Hazel and Philip had overcome the initial bumps and potholes on their road to love, then couldn't Sarah and Donny overcome these?

By the time they got the grill up and running, everyone else had come back outside. Mama Katherine had set a huge platter of meat on the table, Margaret and Hannah held platters of potatoes and corn, and Amelia and Luke had brought out chairs for everyone.

Although at this point, the yard wasn't shining like it would be on the Fourth of July, Sarah could see the potential.

"Drinks!" Mama Katherine said. "Sarah and Donny, you two go grab some beverages."

As they stepped into the cool shade of the house, Sarah stopped, waiting for her eyes to adjust. Donny ran smack into the back of her, and grabbed her waist from behind. Just when she was thinking how amazing it was that the contact felt so natural, he jerked his hands away as if it had burned him. While she remained silent, stunned by this turn of events, he barked out an awkward laugh.

Unsure of how to react, Sarah walked straight into the kitchen to retrieve drinks.

"Where's that old drinks bucket?" Donny said, apparently having regained his composure enough to speak.

"It's in the pantry, top shelf," Sarah said. She refrained from adding, "Where it always is," because she knew the biting tone in her head was a result of nothing other than her own hurt.

She took bottles of beer and soda out of the fridge and transferred them into the bucket. He pulled the ice tray out of the freezer and poured the cubes over the drinks. When they'd filled the bucket, Sarah bent down to lift it up.

"Let me," Donny said.

Where he once would have gently nudged her aside, this time, he stood clear back until she released the bucket's handles and straightened up. She followed him outside.

Luke had already started grilling the meat and it sizzled, sending out aromas that made Sarah's mouth water. More than those aromas, though, Sarah noticed that Amelia had placed herself right next to Luke's elbow and the two of them were looking at each other, smiling. Donny set down the bucket, and then turned around to give Sarah a meaningful look. So, he'd noticed their daughter flirting, too.

"Hey, you two," Donny said, then. "Careful, or you'll burn the meat."

Luke jumped. Amelia, eyebrows drawn together, gave Donny a reproachful look, and Hannah laughed, the sound loud and musical. Mama Katherine clucked, and said, "Now, now."

Sarah assumed she was going to say something to Amelia and Luke about the six-inch rule, but instead she turned to Donny and said, "I seem to remember a certain someone burning one particular birthday cake because he couldn't keep his hands off the birthday girl."

Donny blushed a red so deep Sarah thought *he* might catch on fire. It was her Sweet Sixteen, when he'd insisted on making her favorite strawberry cake. Mama Katherine wasn't feeling well that day. She'd come down with a summer cold and even though she said making the cake would be "no trouble, no trouble at all," Donny had stepped in, saying that of course he'd make it, and that Mama Katherine should take a nap so she could enjoy the festivities. She'd obeyed, and Donny had mixed up that batter with the efficiency of a pro. Then he'd put it into the oven, forgotten to set the timer, and started doing things to Sarah that made her toes curl, right there in the kitchen.

Now, Sarah's own face blazed with heat. She looked around to take a quick inventory of reactions and only then did she notice that Margaret was missing again.

"Where's Margaret?"

Donny, relieved at this shift in attention, said, "I don't know. She was out here with the corn a minute ago. I've never known her to disappear when the beer shows up."

Suddenly, Margaret breezed out of the house. "Were you talking about me? My ears were burning. Did someone say beer?"

Donny pulled one out of the bucket, dried it off, and opened it, and when he handed it to her, she gulped half of it down in one go.

Sarah looked at Donny, who looked right back at her, eyebrows raised. Yes, something was definitely going on with Margaret.

"Wow," Hannah said. "Must have been thirsty."

"Yard work," Margaret said, wiping her mouth with the back of one hand. Still, she didn't make eye contact with anyone before she wandered over to poke at the steaks on the grill.

———

DONNY AND SARAH were the only ones left around the fire pit. Margaret, after downing three beers during the span of dinnertime, claimed exhaustion and went to bed. Hannah said she had some mending to do, and followed Margaret in. Sarah hoped she'd try to get the scoop on all the strange phone calls and disappearances. Mama Katherine took John Wayne for his nighttime stroll. Amelia declared that a walk sounded like a great idea, and she and Luke had disappeared into the dark, too.

"You think it's okay that we let Amelia go with Luke tonight?" Donny said.

She'd been wondering the same, but had fought off thinking about it in a new effort to let go. Not only would Amelia's going off to college force her to let go, but she'd also held on so tightly she'd ruined her marriage.

So even while her mind was going a million miles per hour, imagining all the terrible things that could happen to Amelia (Luke taking her virginity and then breaking her heart, Amelia getting mauled by a bear on her way home in the dark), she took a deep breath and said, "I think it's fine. He seems like a nice kid. She's responsible. And we gave her a curfew. How much can happen in two hours?"

"How much, indeed," Donny said. "I seem to remember that at that age, quite a lot can happen in two hours."

"When we were teenagers, quite a lot could happen in a tenth of that time," Sarah said. "For both of us."

"True," Donny said. "The life of a teenager, right?"

The day's tension seemed to melt away, then. At least, momentarily. For Sarah, a new realization dawned: when they were teenagers, they could make sex a long, lingering experience, if they wanted to. Or, they could make it a fast adventure, where they both reached their destinations in a matter of minutes.

As they grew older, though, reaching that destination took longer and longer, even when they planned a quickie. At first, that wasn't true of Donny. He was as eager as ever, complimenting the curve of Sarah's hip or the color of the skin just inside her thigh as he explored her body. It was Sarah who grew impatient, who always had something else to do, somewhere else to be. Donny would nibble on her hip bone, and she'd urge him upward so they could join.

Sarah knew Donny mistook this as passion at the beginning. But at some point, he'd undoubtedly recognized it as what it was: an attempt to hurry things along, to check "intercourse" off a to-do list that wouldn't get out of the forefront of Sarah's mind.

Initially, she'd been relieved when he stopped trying to turn their lovemaking into a long, drawn out process. So much so that she'd barely noticed when he stopped trying to do any lovemaking, at all.

"Wow," Donny said. "You went quiet. What happened?"

"I don't know," Sarah said. "Just thinking, I guess."

"About Amelia?"

"About us," she said. "I was just realizing how much things have changed."

And I was wondering if I could change them back.

"Us, as teenagers, was a long time ago," Donny said.

"I know," Sarah said.

A few nearby crickets chirped, and other than that, the evening was silent.

Finally, Donny said, "Want to go for a walk?"

What did that mean? Did it mean he wanted to rekindle their teenage romance? Did it mean he wanted to talk about rekindling their teenage romance? Or did it mean he just wanted to go for a walk? Most importantly, did it matter? He was inviting Sarah to spend time with him.

She stood up and stretched. "Sure. That'd be nice."

They fell effortlessly into step with one another.

Once they turned out onto the main road, Donny said, "So did you know I took that promotion?"

Sarah stopped walking. "You did?"

"Yeah," Donny said, stopping next to her.

"I—I don't know what to say."

"Congratulations?"

She started walking again. He did, too.

"Well," she said. "Congratulations."

She wanted to ask why he hadn't told her. But the truth was, she honestly couldn't remember whether he'd told her, or not. She remembered him trying to talk to her before he decided, that weekend when she was in Crazy Mom Mode and couldn't make the mental space for him. But had he come home the following week and shared the big news?

Surely he hadn't. She would know. She would remember. Wouldn't she?

"Thanks," he said.

"So. Um. How's it been going?"

"It's been going okay," he said. "I didn't think I'd like managing people. But they're good people, you know? I should have known that, since I'd worked with them for years. It's different, though, being someone's co-worker, someone's equal, as opposed to being their supervisor."

"I can imagine," Sarah said. "Why'd you decide to take it?"

Although Sarah thought Donny should have anticipated that question—it seemed like a natural progression of the conversation—he seemed unprepared to answer it. His feet slid along the gravel, just like they had when he was a kid and didn't want to 'fess up about where he'd gotten an extra piece of candy or why his pants were muddy when he'd promised to stay out of the creek.

"Why don't you want to answer?" she said.

"I took it because the pay's so good," he said. The tone of his voice, the finality of it, made Sarah think he was thinking, *There. That's a sufficient answer.*

"But we didn't need more money. And didn't you say it was going to be stressful?"

He had said that, she remembered that much.

"True," Donny said. "Both are true. We didn't need more money, and I did say it was going to be stressful. I've just been tucking the extra money away in savings."

"I haven't seen our balance increase. Are you sure the bank's recording your deposits? Maybe you should go in when we get back."

Donny made a weird sound in his throat, like he was choking. Sarah recognized this, too: he'd been found out. Here was another slice of the conversation he had wanted to avoid.

"I opened a new savings account."

Without telling me?

Why did you keep it a secret?

What are you going to do with the money?

"Oh. I see," Sarah said.

"I'm sorry, Sarah. I just felt like this would be easier. You know, if you didn't know."

"If I didn't know what?"

"I'm saving up."

"Saving up?" Sarah said, her tongue stiff in her mouth. "For what?"

"To buy a house."

The words sank in quickly, settling right in the pit of Sarah's stomach.

"A house?" she said.

"Yes," Donny said. "A house."

"But—"

"I want to move back here, Sarah. Back home."

"You're moving? You've already planned this?"

"Well, I—no. I hadn't. I hadn't planned it until we came back here and I realized this is where I want to be."

The unspoken words hung there between them in the dark. *Without you.*

Sarah couldn't speak, so she did the next best thing: she turned around and headed back toward Mama Katherine's. She walked quickly, without taking notice of all the things she had just a few minutes ago. The crickets, the gravel crunching, the twinkling stars—they'd all just provide an even richer setting for her memory whenever she thought back on this moment.

Donny, moving?

It meant so many things. It meant there was no getting him back. It meant he'd decided. When Amelia had a break from college, she'd have to choose between them.

This was a disaster.

Even while Sarah marched down the driveway, she half-listened for Donny's footsteps. She half-expected him to follow her, to explain her pain away. But he didn't.

John Wayne greeted her when she came into the yard, his friendly bark-and-howl cracking with old age. At first, Sarah didn't notice Mama Katherine was standing at the side door, her hand on the knob. When she did, she jumped.

"You startled me," she said, then hurried to brush away any signs of tears.

"Now," Mama Katherine said. "Do you want to tell me what's the matter?"

At first, Sarah resisted. She was a grown woman, she thought as she stood there in the pool of light from the entryway. She couldn't come crying to her mama every time something didn't go her way. Mama Katherine had her own problems to deal with. She was getting older, undoubtedly facing the end of her own life. Something like this wasn't actually that big of a deal, when you put it in context, Sarah thought. She should just go inside and go to bed. Like Mama Katherine was so fond of saying, things always look better in the morning.

"It's Donny, isn't it?"

Caught.

Sarah found that she couldn't speak, so she nodded, instead.

"He plans to move out here when we get back home."

"Come here, honey." Mama Katherine opened her arms and Sarah rushed into them.

"I'd made this plan, you know, to win him back, to convince him that he could still love me, that we could still work. But it obviously failed. I don't know what to do."

"I know it feels like the end of the world," Mama Katherine said.

This brought on a fresh round of tears.

"It's not," Mama Katherine said. "I assure you, it's not. In fact, let me tell you a story."

She patted Sarah's back and then released her. "Come on inside."

CHAPTER SIXTEEN

Mama Katherine insisted on making tea. While she did, Sarah sat at the kitchen table, her head in her hands.

"I've never told any of you girls this," Mama Katherine said a few minutes later, sliding a cup of tea between Sarah's elbows and sitting down next to her. "But I suppose it's time."

Curiosity sufficiently piqued, Sarah sat up and wrapped her hands around the teacup. Mama Katherine didn't speak right away. She blew into her tea and Sarah watched the steam rise.

"A long time ago," Mama Katherine said, and Sarah said, "In a galaxy far, far away."

Mama Katherine smiled, and her eyes looked sad. "Kind of. Anyway. A long time ago, before Hannah—so thirty-some-odd years ago, forty now. My, how quickly time passes. I was in love. So in love."

"Wait," Sarah said. "You were? I thought you'd sworn off men. 'I'm an independent woman, girls. And I don't need a man or anyone else telling me how to run this farm.'"

Mama chuckled. "Well, that's true. I was an independent woman. But now that I look back on it, I think I said that to protect myself, to heal my own broken heart."

"I think you're getting ahead of yourself," Sarah said. "Start from the beginning."

Mama Katherine nodded. "Things turned out so much differently than I'd expected. I thought my story was a tragedy. But—although it turned out differently from what I expected, it's turned into a grand adventure. An epic love story."

"An epic love story?" Hannah said. She'd come into the kitchen, now, too, and was filling her glass of water at the sink.

"Sit," Mama Katherine said. "I'd like you to hear this story, too. Where's Margaret?"

As if on cue, Margaret came in, next, rubbing her eyes. "Geez, you all are night owls."

"Get a cup of tea and sit," Mama Katherine said.

Margaret obeyed, and Mama Katherine said, "I was just telling Sarah the story of my one and only love. Aside from you three, of course."

"What?" Margaret said. "There was love?"

"There was," Mama Katherine said. "Believe it or not."

"Why have we never heard this story before?" Hannah said.

"Why, indeed," Mama Katherine said. She sighed. "I think I kept it from you because I never wanted you to blame yourselves for my heartbreak. Goodness knows the three of you had enough going on, I didn't need to traumatize you with the mistaken belief that I missed out on romance because of you."

"Which means that you did," Sarah said. "Right?"

Her sisters nodded, and Mama Katherine waved them off. "Not at all."

After a beat of silence, during which all three women waited, rapt, she said, "I was married."

All three women gasped as if she'd told them she was a bank robber.

And while Sarah knew millions of questions were swirling around in each of their minds—*What happened? Where is he now? Why didn't you tell us?*—no one said anything. Mama Katherine's eyes took on a dreamy quality, and she said, "I was a beauty back then."

"You're a beauty now." Sarah reached out and squeezed her mama's hand.

"Well, age has made me a bit rough around the edges, I'll be the first to admit."

"Nonsense," Hannah said. "You're as beautiful now as you've ever been."

"Oh, my girls," Mama Katherine said. "You're so good to me."

Margaret stood up. "This moment calls for a real drink." Then she sat back down. "Get us one, will you, Sarah?"

Automatically, Sarah stood up to obey. She almost missed the way Hannah was looking at Margaret, as if she were a puzzle they were trying to build, using an upside-down picture as a guide.

It *was* strange that Margaret hadn't gotten the drinks, herself, but Sarah was so absorbed in the beginning of Mama Katherine's story that she hadn't paid the moment much attention. Still eager to hear it, she grabbed four tumblers and a bottle of brandy out of the liquor cabinet. Once she'd poured generous shots and passed the tumblers out, she settled down in her spot again.

Mama Katherine raised her glass. "To love," she said.

Sarah almost burst into tears.

"So," Mama Katherine said. "I'll spare you the gory details of the beginning of the story. But once we finally fell in love, we did everything together. We built and planted my garden. We rode horses. We had picnics. We made love. Frequently. You want to talk about passion …"

Here, she paused, and Margaret snickered. "That's something I never expected to hear you say."

Mama Katherine gave Margaret a smile that bordered on wicked, and went on: "Now, you remember me saying I never thought I'd get married, right? I mean, in those days a woman as tall as I was had a hard time finding a man."

"As tall as you were *and* as feisty," Sarah said.

"Yes," Mama Katherine said. "Exactly. And I was near spinster age by the time Lady Fortune tipped the scales. Anyway, I never wanted children."

Sarah, Margaret, and Hannah gasped again. Mama Katherine chuckled and then, her expression somber, she looked at each one of them in turn as she said, "But you know that changed. Obviously."

"Obviously," they all said.

How could a woman be such a good mother, so kind and nurturing and selfless, if she didn't want children?

"I was a career woman," Mama Katherine said. "I was hungry for it. I thought, at the time, that having children would ruin my life. So when I ended up pregnant—with Hannah's older brother, Benny—"

Now, the room went absolutely silent. Mama Katherine kept talking, as if, now that she'd finally let this story out, she couldn't stop its telling.

"I was devastated. He was a beautiful boy, Hannah," she said, almost as an aside. "You have the same eyes, the same chin. Anyway. I gave birth to Benny, and immediately hired a nanny for him. At first, I was resentful of him, of all the work he required and all the attention my husband gave him. Don't get me wrong—I loved him. I wanted the best for him. I did everything I thought good mothers did: I rocked him at night, I made his baby food rather than buying it in jars, I made sure he got proper sleep and his nursery was clean."

Sarah glanced at Hannah and saw that she had tears in her eyes.

"But I didn't pay him much attention. I was so busy," Mama Katherine said, with a roll of her eyes. "I still hate myself for that. But as he got a little older, and started to smile and interact, I started to actually enjoy him. He looked just like his daddy, right down to the little ridge on the bridge of his nose, and the way his eyes crinkled when he smiled. He had the chubbiest cheeks and hands. You could see the dimples around his mouth and on his fat little knuckles. Anyway. One day I came home from work and our property was quiet. Eerily so. Even though there was nothing different about that day—I'd often come home and everyone would be inside, getting ready for dinner—a heaviness had settled in and I could feel it as soon as I got out of my car. Inside the house, Benny's nanny was crying. It was a horrible, weeping, mewling sound. I knew, right away."

Mama Katherine paused and took a sip of her brandy.

"Benny loved to climb. He'd climb anything he could: the stairs, the dining room table, the trees on our property, any equipment we had in the yard. Well, that day, he was napping, and the nanny was in the kitchen getting things ready for dinner. It was a roast. I can smell it to this day. It was still in the oven when I walked into the house. Benny woke up from his nap, climbed right out of his crib, and wandered outside. He was supposed to be sleeping. He wandered into the path of a work truck, and it ran him over. Killed him instantly."

No one spoke. Sarah thought about how Mama Katherine had kept this secret for so long. Did Hannah know? A quick glance at her pale, stricken face revealed that she didn't. Mama Katherine had held this secret close. She'd tucked it inside her heart, hiding it from all of them and probably from herself, too. A lone cricket took up chirping outside, breaking the thick silence in the room.

"It ripped his dad and I apart," Mama Katherine said. "There was so much guilt, on both sides. So much pain. It was unbearable. We couldn't look at each other without thinking of Benny. We couldn't speak without talking about what happened. I took the blame. I never wanted babies in the first place and maybe this was God's way of punishing me. I preferred my career over motherhood and maybe Benny being snatched out of my life was a lesson of some kind. I never said any of this out loud, but one night, Benny's father did, and I found out he felt the same way. I asked him what he wanted for dinner, and he just lit into me. He let me have it. He told me, 'I can't believe you're asking me what I want for dinner. For dinner! Our son is dead. Dead! And it's your fault. You never wanted him! If you'd been here, you would have saved him. But you weren't. And now he's dead. And you're asking me what I want for dinner.'"

Sarah was positive that being on the receiving end of those harsh word had hurt. They were an accusation, a condemnation, as much as they were a confirmation of Mama Katherine's own thoughts.

"But it wasn't your fault," Hannah said, her voice a near whisper. "Those things happen. The same thing could have happened if you were home with him."

Mama Katherine nodded, but her expression said she didn't believe it. She used a forefinger to wipe a tear from under her eye.

From the way Margaret leaned forward, elbows on the table, eyes focused on Mama Katherine's, Sarah could tell she was anxious to hear what happened next. And so was Sarah. When did Hannah enter this picture? Had Katherine ever spoken to her husband again?

"So what happened?" Hannah said.

"I left," Mama Katherine said. "I left, and I never looked back."

"But—" Hannah said.

"And when I moved away, I found out I was pregnant with you."

She didn't say as much, but Sarah wondered if that discovery had terrified Mama Katherine.

"Didn't he try to find you?" Margaret wanted to know.

Mama Katherine shrugged and finished off her bourbon, setting the glass down gently. "I suppose that's a story for another day. But I'm telling you this because when things ended between me and your father, Hannah, I was devastated. I thought my world was going to end. And then you came along. And then you, Margaret, and you, Sarah. I feel so lucky, beyond lucky, to have experienced that deep, deep romantic love, even if it was only for a short time. But when it comes down to it, raising you girls was the most important thing I ever did. By far. There is more to life than marriage, Sarah. And you've done a damned good job of raising Amelia. The love you and Donny have for each other? It matters. It gave Amelia the foundation she needed to blossom into such a lovely young woman. When I first left my husband, I was just broken. Shattered. But life went on. I planted new roots, here at the Seedling Homestead. I vowed never to fall in love with a man again, but I fell in love with the three of you. And look what a beautiful life I've had. I'm sitting here today, at my own kitchen table, surrounded by my three grown daughters. I couldn't ask for more, could I? Now. I'm exhausted. I'm going to bed."

She stood up, and the three sisters watched her move off towards her bedroom. Margaret pushed the bottle of bourbon across the table to Hannah, who refilled their tumblers.

Mama Katherine paused before heading down the hallway, and said, "All this to say, Sarah, that although the end of your marriage may feel like the end of your life, it's not. It's certainly not. There is so much more, and you just have to be open to finding it."

Sarah nodded. Intellectually, she knew Mama Katherine was right. She was young. She could start a new career if she wanted to. She'd already gone back to school for photography. But emotionally, she couldn't believe she'd ever rise from these ashes. She felt broken and shattered and frankly, irreparable.

"Good night, girls," Mama Katherine said. Then she was gone.

"I take it you didn't know that story," Sarah said to her sisters.

"I'm in shock," Hannah said.

"Do you want to talk about it?" Margaret said. "I mean, you have a dad. That's pretty crazy, right?"

"I always knew I had a dad, Margaret," Hannah said.

"Well, I know that," Margaret said. "But—"

"I need some time to take this in," Hannah said. "I need to think about it."

Margaret opened her mouth, like she had more to say, and Hannah said, "Can we change the subject?"

"Donny's been saving up to buy a new house for himself," Sarah said. "Here, in Wyoming."

It was almost comical, the way both Margaret's and Hannah's mouths dropped open as they simultaneously looked at each other and then back at Sarah. Hannah reached across the table to squeeze Sarah's hand.

"Which is the worst possible thing he could do," Sarah said. "When Amelia gets breaks from college, she's going to have to decide which of us to visit. I'm going to have to move out of our house— Amelia's childhood home. That's the backdrop for so many of her memories. And the worst part is, there's nothing I can do to stop him."

"It'll be okay," Hannah said. "She's a strong girl, Sarah. Yes, this will require an adjustment, but she's starting a new phase of life. And she'll still have all those great memories in her mind."

"And in your perfect photos with their neatly arranged backgrounds," Margaret said.

Hannah snickered, and Sarah said, "I think that bourbon is going to your head."

CHAPTER SEVENTEEN

*J*ULY *12: One week since our first kiss*

———

I KNOW, *I know. It's been an entire week since I wrote, Pauline. And I'm sure you have missed me. The truth is, Philip and I have spent practically seven straight days copulating. It was The Kiss That Broke The Ice. So far, we have had sexual intercourse in bed, in the living room in front of the fire, and in the kitchen. Oh, and in the shower. The shower, of all places. Philip called in sick so we could spend time together. Yes, Pauline. "Spend time together" is code for "have sexual intercourse all day long."*

I told him, "You can't call in love sick." And he said, "Actually, Mrs. Carlisle, I can. I'm the boss."

Which, I suppose, is true. I love it when he calls me Mrs. Carlisle.

We're planning a vacation together, this fall. To Zion National Park. It's supposed to be beautiful, Pauline. We're going to camp there.

I'm so glad I made the decision to make Philip fall for me. I know it took some aligning of the stars, or some Fate, or a sprinkle of magic, but it was so worth it. We're having so much fun together.

Okay, I've got to sign off. Can you believe that even while you're laying around in bed all day, the dishes still pile up?

Well. We had to eat, didn't we? To fortify our bodies. Ha!

Goodnight, Pauline.

———

OCTOBER 10: Four months since we said "I do"

———

PAULINE,

———

WE'VE JUST SPENT the most wonderful week in Zion National Park. I can't believe Philip took a week off at this time of year, during the harvest! "Adventure can't wait, Hazel!" he said to me.

Utah is stunning, Pauline. Absolutely beautiful. We decided that we must buy an RV so that we can camp all the time. Anyway, the leaves were just starting to turn and the water was so clear and the mountains were just breathtaking, spiking into the sky.

I wish you could have seen it, Pauline. I wish you were a human. Ha! I took lots of photos and when I have them developed I will share them with Shirley. But let's face it: she's not as good of a listener as you are.

There is nothing quite like hiking to the top of a mountain with your husband, and taking in a view worthy of the gods. We'd stand there, out of breath, holding hands, and just look at it. It's like God was saying, "Behold!" and we had no choice but to ... well, behold!

Anyway, we've planned another trip, already. We'll go to the beach this winter. It's only a couple of hours away, and we've both been there before, but not together. Obviously.

I'd better get going, Pauline. I told Philip I'd help him catch up on work when we returned. Tata for now.

DECEMBER 15: The day we found out

———

BIG NEWS, Pauline! We're going to have a baby!

(Why aren't you responding, Pauline? Your silence is confirmation of my worst fear: that I'm not meant to be a mother.)

I'll admit, I was as surprised as you are. I mean, Philip and I hadn't really discussed having children, you know. We were shell shocked after being married, initially, and we've only just broken that in. But when this all started out, I'd said Adventure would be the third phase of my project—and what is parenthood, if not an adventure?

I'll admit, I feel (no small amount of) trepidation about becoming a mother. I've just begun to break the barrier at work and motherhood will undoubtedly slow my momentum. Being able to sling martinis with the guys gave me some leverage. Helped me fit in, you know. I am positive a pregnant belly won't do the same for my camaraderie with the men.

It's not that I don't have wonderful footsteps in which to follow, Pauline. My own mother set a stellar example. The problem is, she also set a standard to which I'm not sure I can measure up.

Is it a boy, or a girl? I wish you could tell me.

Although I am scared out of my wits, I also can't wait to see whether this baby has Philip's eyes or my chin. Or Philip's dimples (have I mentioned that he has the most adorable dimples?) or my nose. (I hope the poor thing doesn't get my nose.)

We're having a pre-Christmas dinner tonight to celebrate and to make the announcement to our parents. I'm positive they'll be overcome with joy. They never expected us to have children, I'm sure of it. And they'll be so happy to have an heir, someone to carry on the Carlisle-Rickshaw Family Orchard name. If I don't talk to you again, Pauline, Merry Christmas!

AUGUST 7: One month after the birth of Baby Carlisle

HE'S HERE, Pauline … and I've realized my worst fear. I'm a terrible mother. We haven't come up with a name for the baby. Why, you ask? Because, Pauline, I've been so busy. I'm busy trying to stop his crying. Or, when he finally falls asleep, I'm busy trying to catch a wink, myself.

I think the baby can sense my unease, Pauline. Perhaps he felt it when he was in the womb. I wasn't as excited as I should have been. He's content as can be when Philip holds him, but as soon as I come within a seven-mile radius, he starts screaming his tiny head off. I've never seen a face turn so red so quickly.

Baby Boy Carlisle was born a month ago, on July 7. He's perfect in every way. Ten fingers, ten toes, and his eyebrows! They're adorable and fuzzy and he already draws them together as if he's perplexed or angry. Or maybe he's just thinking.

And to see Philip with the baby, Pauline! I'm falling in love with him all over again. He's such a wonderful father. He walks the halls with him when he's restless (which is pretty much all the time) and has been such a supportive husband, too, bringing me water when I'm nursing and massaging my shoulders after I've held the baby for a long time.

But still, something feels off. I can't quite put my finger on it. And I hope it doesn't ruin my baby's life. I don't know who in the world thought I'd be a competent mother …

———

SARAH HID IN THE RV, devouring Hazel's writings, looking for some kind of proof that her own marriage could survive the tragic turn it had taken. After all, Hazel had said her own story looked like a tragedy and wound up a love story.

So far, nothing about the Carlisle marriage seemed truly tragic, but the most recent entry did carry a definite sense of foreboding.

Sitting at the dinette in the RV now, Sarah closed the journal and set it on her lap. Then she closed her eyes and put her head back against the wall.

It had been three days since Donny announced he was saving to buy a house, and Sarah had managed to avoid talking to him for all three of them. When he came into a room, she found an excuse to leave it. When he returned home from errands or the long drives he'd begun taking, she locked herself in the bedroom or the RV, or took a really long shower until he found an activity with which to busy himself.

She had to survive for only a few days more. Then it would be time to take Amelia to school, and she could make her way back to Arizona while Donny returned here, to Wyoming, to make his new life. Without her.

There was a knock on the door then, and Sarah jumped. Her first instinct was to hide the journal, but Margaret had already opened the door and was coming up the steps.

"Whatcha doing?"

Sarah froze.

"Just getting some clothes."

"You've been spending an awful lot of time, 'just getting some clothes,'" Margaret said. "And it looks like you're sitting at the dining table. Which, I happen to know, is not where you keep your clothes. Whatcha doin'?"

Sarah held the journal up and looked at it as if she'd just realized it was there, in her hand.

"Again?" Margaret said.

"Still," Sarah said.

Margaret climbed into the RV and sat across the table from Sarah. "If you're so interested in it, you should be doing more research to find out who this Hazel person is. Or was. Whatever."

"I thought you were doing that. You're so good at research."

Margaret shrugged. "I've been busy."

"I've noticed," Sarah said. "And you still haven't told us what you've been so busy doing. All these disappearances, and then all the questions you were asking Mama."

Margaret froze, just momentarily, barely long enough for Sarah to notice. "Ah. Just work stuff."

She shrugged, and the movement was so herky-jerky, so awkward, that Sarah knew she was lying.

But before she could say anything about it, Margaret said, "Did it ever occur to you that Donny buying a house here doesn't necessarily signal the very end of things?"

One part of Sarah's brain recognized the distraction for what it was, and the other part grasped onto this topic with the fervor of desperation.

"How could it not?" she said. "He's been imagining buying his own house. Without me. He didn't even consult me about it. He's been squirreling away money. Money that amounts to tens of thousands of dollars. And he never once mentioned it to me. I am fairly confident that's a sign he doesn't want to involve me in the decision-making process."

"Maybe he could be persuaded to want to involve you," Margaret said.

"I don't want to have to persuade him," Sarah said.

"So why are you still reading this thing?" Margaret held the journal with one hand and used the thumb of her other hand to flip through the journal's pages before sliding it across the table to Sarah.

"I guess I just wanted to see how it turned out. From the moment I read the very first entry, I felt a connection with this Hazel person. I mean, she named the journal. Pauline. And when she writes, I can hear her voice. She's become like a friend to me."

Hearing the words come out of her own mouth, Sarah realized how silly they sounded and she laughed out loud.

"So what's happened?" Margaret said.

"Well, you could read it for yourself," Sarah said.

"Just give me the gist."

Sarah did—explaining the arranged marriage and Hazel's plan

and the Fourth of July party and the trip to Zion and the pregnancy and the birth of the unnamed baby.

"That does sound pretty fun, except for the unplanned pregnancy," Margaret said. "And I notice you're copying her Fourth of July party idea."

"Yes," Sarah said. "And I thought it would be good for Mama Katherine, too, to have everyone over. You know how she loves that."

"I do," Margaret said. "And I think it's a spectacular idea."

CHAPTER EIGHTEEN

"This is where you plan to bring out the big guns, right?" Hannah looked very conspiratorial as she smirked at Sarah. "This is where you use your sharp wit and amazing good looks to win Donny back?"

Mama Katherine had put the two of them in charge of baking cupcakes. She insisted on homemade, and wanted a batch of each chocolate and vanilla. Now, they stood side by side at the kitchen counter, stirring batter in Mama's big mixing bowls.

Sarah blew a stray piece of hair out of her eyes. "Well, that was my original plan. I was going to bring out the big guns today, but I think it's pointless, now. So I'll probably just relax, have a beer, and enjoy myself this evening. No stress, no pressure, no big guns."

Hannah stopped stirring. "You don't mean to tell me you're quitting. I mean, I know you'd said you un-made your original decision, but I thought that was just self-doubt talking. You can't possibly be quitting."

"Quitting what?"

"Quitting in your quest to save your marriage."

"Quitting before I'd even gotten started, I'd say," Sarah said. "Hardly counts as quitting."

"You know," Hannah said. "Our mama didn't raise a bunch of quitters."

Sarah had to laugh. "I know she didn't. But there's a difference between quitting, and conceding gracefully when you know you've lost."

"Huh," Hannah said, then in an abrupt change of subject, she said,

"Have you managed to hear any of Margaret's top secret phone calls?"

"You mean, have I eavesdropped on our sister, who is an adult and certainly deserving of some semblance of privacy?"

"Yeah," Hannah said. She was now lining cupcake pans with the foil liners Mama Katherine said would make the cupcakes festive. "Have you?"

Sarah stared at Hannah, her mouth open. "Absolutely not." After a pause, she added, "I tried. But I couldn't hear her."

"Well, I have," Hannah said.

"What? You're supposed to be the mature one, and all that. And you've been eavesdropping on our sister? That's like a kid trying to eavesdrop on her parents to find out if Santa Claus is real."

"Well, not exactly," Hannah said. "I thought something was wrong."

"And? What did you find out?"

"See?!" Hannah pointed a measuring cup at Sarah. "You want to know, too!"

"I disagree with your methods. But yes. I want to know, too."

Margaret walked in, stopping the conversation in its tracks. "Do I hear bickering in here?"

As she had since they were children, Margaret dipped a finger into the batter in Sarah's bowl and popped it into her mouth. When Sarah started to protest, she used her other hand to grab a taste of Hannah's batter, too.

"I love raw batter," she said.

"We know," Hannah and Sarah said.

"Hey, does one of you want to come into town with me?" Margaret said.

"I thought we'd run all of our errands yesterday," Hannah said. "So we wouldn't have to brave the last-minute Fourth of July madness."

"I know," Margaret said. "But I forgot to grab the paper plates and stuff. Plasticware. We don't want to be washing dishes all night."

"True," Hannah said. "We don't. I'll go, if Sarah finishes the cupcakes."

She threw Sarah a look so filled with meaning Sarah stifled a giggle as her sisters walked out of the kitchen, the two of them whispering with one another. Just as Sarah was starting to wonder what they were whispering about, they reached the threshold of the front door and Margaret turned around and called, "Mama Katherine didn't raise a bunch of quitters, Sarah."

Sarah smiled and, shaking her head, began scooping batter into the cupcake pans.

Then Mama Katherine came in, wiping the sweat from her forehead with a handkerchief. "It's a beautiful day," she said. "But I think I should spend some time inside where it's cool before we kick off this party."

"You should," Sarah said. "You can monitor my cupcake scooping."

Mama Katherine sat down across the counter from Sarah, and Sarah got her a glass of water.

"You know, Sarah," she said after taking a long drink. "I didn't raise a bunch of quitters. You may think all is said and done because Donny planned to buy a house, but I think you're wrong. I'd hate for you to give up now."

"Geez," Sarah said, trying to infuse her voice with something that could pass for humor. "What is this? The Call-Sarah-a-Quitter Brigade?"

Mama Katherine gave her a wry smile. "Never, Sarah. It's the Don't-Give-Up-On-Your-Marriage Brigade."

"But Donny's given up on it. So it's a waste of my energy to keep trying. Instead, I should be focusing on how to move on."

"I disagree," Mama Katherine said.

"You're not the one who—"

Mama held up a hand. "I'm worried about your sister."

"Margaret?"

"Hannah."

Sarah felt a little jolt, and then a swarm of butterflies in her stomach. This was unexpected. "Hannah?"

"Yes," Mama Katherine said.

"But, why?"

Had Hannah been acting off, too? Sarah had been so wrapped up in her own failing marriage that she hadn't even noticed. Hannah was always the sensible one, the no-nonsense sister whose feathers were hard to ruffle. Not much seemed to bother her.

"Well, I'm getting older. I'm not going to be here forever."

"I hate that thought." Sarah put the cupcake pans into the oven and set the timer.

"I know, Sarah. But it's a fact, isn't it? We all die. I think there's a quote about that. How we all start dying the moment we're born."

"Uplifting."

"Right," Mama Katherine said. "Anyway. When I'm gone, what

will Hannah have?"

"She'll have her job," Sarah said. "She loves teaching."

"That's true. But is that enough for her?"

"I always thought it was," Sarah said. "She seems happy, doesn't she? Fulfilled?"

"She does," Mama Katherine said. "But your sister, she's a nurturer. She needs to take care of someone. And when I'm gone, who will that be?"

"Her students?" This was making Sarah uncomfortable. She didn't like thinking about Mama Katherine dying, and she didn't like thinking about Hannah coming home from work to an empty house, day after day after day. A little shiver ran up her spine.

"You're right. She'll always have her students. But ..."

"What are you getting at, Mama? You want us to encourage her to find a boyfriend, or what? I don't think she'll take kindly to that."

"Not a boyfriend, necessarily."

"What, then?"

"I'm not sure," Mama Katherine said.

"A girlfriend?"

"No ... Not that I know of, anyway. Just promise me that you'll look out for her, check in with her. You know?"

"Mama. You're not going anywhere just yet," Sarah said.

"I know," Mama Katherine said. "But promise me, anyway."

"Fine," Sarah said. "I promise."

"Fine," Mama Katherine said, her tone of voice mimicking Sarah's. She stood up. "Now, let's get this party started. I think, if we bring out the big guns, we can make progress towards winning Donny back."

Sarah opened her mouth to speak, but Mama Katherine raised a hand. "I've got work to do."

As she counted down the hours to the Fourth of July party, Sarah thought about what it would actually look like to win Donny back. She'd have to flirt with him, wouldn't she?

In one of Hannah's first college classes, she had to give a "how-to" speech. She chose "How to Flirt," and practiced over and over again with Sarah and Margaret as audience members.

"It's in the tilt of your head," she'd say, "and the fluttering of your eyelashes."

Sarah wondered how much of that speech Hannah remembered. Not only could Sarah get some tips for flirting with her husband, but also she could get a handle on how often Hannah had actually used these tips over the course of her adulthood. And, if she could get

Hannah alone, Sarah could find out she Hannah had heard when she eavesdropped on Margaret.

Hannah and Margaret returned from town just as Sarah was taking the cupcakes out of the pan so they could cool for frosting.

"Good, you're back," Sarah said when they walked into the kitchen. "I could use some help frosting these cupcakes."

"I'll make my exit," Margaret said. "You know I hate frosting cupcakes."

"Can't. Take. The. Stickiness!" Hannah and Sarah said at the same time.

Ever since Margaret was a little girl, she'd hated frosting. She didn't mind getting dirty in the mud or playing in the creek, but if something felt sticky, she'd throw a fit.

Hannah, who seemed to sense that Sarah wanted to talk, alone, said to Margaret, "Why don't you set up the plates and plasticware outside next to the grill?"

"You don't need to tell me twice," she said. She grabbed the bags from the store and headed outside.

"So," Sarah said. "She's gone. Dish."

"It's something with her health," Hannah said. "She's been saying things like 'referral,' and 'specialist,' and she's been asking to make appointments. I've heard her talk about stuff being covered and deductibles."

Fear took root in Sarah's belly, and bloomed quickly into an invasive plant, curling its tendrils into her lungs and down the tops of her thighs.

"Did you bring it up when you went to the store just now?"

Hannah shook her head.

"What should we do?" Sarah said.

Hannah, eyes wide, shrugged. "I don't know. I don't know what we can do."

"I mean, should we ask her?"

Hannah laughed. "Um, tell her I've been eavesdropping and ask her what's going on?"

"I mean, yeah. Just say you overheard her. Or something."

"Don't you think she'll be mad?"

Now, Sarah shrugged. "I don't know. Does it matter?"

"Maybe she's waiting to tell us when she gets more information. Especially with everything that's going on with you and Donny, she doesn't want to—"

Again, with uncanny timing, Margaret came back inside, stopping

Hannah's voice in its tracks.

"Doesn't want to what?" she said.

Sarah and Hannah exchanged a quick glance, and Sarah was positive Margaret noticed.

"Maybe Mama Katherine doesn't want to do the grilling," Sarah said.

"I'm sure she doesn't," Margaret said. "Ask Donny to do it. He doesn't mind."

Sarah nodded, and then said, "Speaking of Donny. Hannah, do you remember that speech you gave in college?"

"How to Flirt?" Hannah and Margaret said.

———

WITH A CRASH COURSE in flirting under her belt, Sarah pretended to wander over to the patio where Donny was laying steaks on the grill. Inside, though, she was making a beeline. When she approached, Donny turned to face her, and she angled her head slightly down so she was looking up at him through her eyelashes.

"Everything okay?" he said.

"Yeah," Sarah said, brushing her hair out of her face with one hand, doing her best to look nonchalant about it. "I just thought you might be thirsty. I was bringing you some water."

Now she produced a bottle of water from behind her back and offered it to him.

"Thanks," he said, taking the bottle from her. When he did, she made sure to hold onto it just a little too long, as Hannah had instructed. When Donny lifted an eyebrow at her, she wondered if maybe this flirting instruction was just a little too juvenile. Which made her giggle.

She hoped the sound was alluring, but she feared that it bordered on maniacal. Without warning, Hannah appeared at her side. "How's it going?" she said, too loudly.

"Fine?" Donny said. He'd been around the Bradley girls long enough to know when something was off. "How are things going with you, Hannah?"

Sarah gave Hannah a dark look, and Hannah smiled even more brightly.

"Sarah, can I talk to you for a minute?"

"Let me know if you need anything else," Sarah said to Donny. "Anything at all."

Hannah rolled her eyes, grabbed Sarah's wrist, and towed her off to a spot a safe distance away from the grill.

"You're being way too obvious," she hissed. "Your flirting skills are horrible. You look like a college co-ed trying to get free drinks."

Sarah felt her face flush and Hannah laughed, pulling her into a hug.

"Listen," she said. "Act more … natural. I mean, you look like you have a bug in your eye."

"That was me, batting my eyelashes," Sarah said. "Like you told me to."

"Don't get defensive," Hannah said.

"Hey," Sarah said, "Have you ever used this stuff? You know, in your own life?"

"Who, me?" Hannah said.

"Yep."

"Nope," Hannah said. "I was like one of those people who gives everyone parenting advice, yet has never had children. Only, it was about flirting."

"Did your advice work?"

"Yes, and I'm quite proud of it. I've played matchmaker to many long-lasting couples who are now very much in love."

"Aren't you smug?" Sarah swatted her sister on the arm. "And okay. I'll stop looking like I've got a bug in my eye."

"Please do."

"Okay, but stop watching me. You're making me self-conscious."

"How can I coach you if I don't watch you?"

Sarah sighed, and Margaret materialized behind Hannah's shoulder. "Remember that time when we were in high school, and she wanted to coach me as I flirted with Jackson Riverdale? Remember that?"

Before Sarah knew it, all three of them were in a half-collapse, holding onto each other's shoulders, laughing.

"That was so awful," Margaret said, her voice a squeal, and Sarah said, "I can't believe you were doing what she said to do! You just followed right along while she marched you to your dating grave."

"That was so mean," Margaret said, and Hannah, tears streaming down her face, said, "Well, you used up all my hair spray that morning and I couldn't fix my hair. I was upset."

"You—" Margaret gasped for air, still laughing. "You humiliated me."

"You deserved it!" Hannah said.

Sarah remembered that day with such clarity, as the three of them had replayed it over and over again for anyone who would listen; Margaret with her face twisted into an angry expression (save for the slight quirk of her mouth) and the other two girls in hysterics.

"And she told me to copy everything she did," Margaret would say.

"And then," Sarah would say, her voice a crescendo of hilarity, "she started rubbing her hands all over her body."

Hannah would nod and demonstrate, her hands roaming from her throat to her shoulders to her neck, and then, right down her torso.

"And she just *did* it," Hannah would shriek.

"She was just talking away, to Jackson Riverdale," Sarah would say as Hannah's face became redder and redder. "And rubbing herself."

Apparently, the grown-up Sarah thought now, the scene only became funnier over time.

"Ah," Mama Katherine said. She had walked up just as Margaret had recreated the body-rubbing moment. "Reliving the Jackson Riverdale experience, are we? Again?"

"Now that's all I'm going to be thinking about when I'm talking to Donny," she said.

"Perfect," Margaret said. "And if you want, I can stand behind Donny and tell you what to do."

"Oh, please do," Sarah said. "Since apparently Hannah here, expert that she is, thinks I'm failing."

"I don't," Hannah said. "You just seem unnatural, that's all."

"As unnatural as rubbing her hands all over her body while she talks to Donny?" Margaret said, putting herself into hysterics again.

"All I can do now is to walk away," Sarah said.

"Just act natural," Mama Katherine said.

This was the kiss of death: all three girls hooted with laughter. With the shrill sounds following her, Sarah left them and walked back over to where Donny stood at the grill.

"It's good to see you laughing," Donny said. "It's the Jackson Riverdale story again, isn't it? I saw Hannah doing the hand movements."

"Poor guy," Sarah said. "You've probably heard that one a million times."

Donny chuckled. "And seen Hannah reliving it."

"Never gets old," they said at the same time.

"So I guess everything's okay with Margaret, if she's reliving the Jackson Riverdale incident?"

"Ha," Sarah said. "Who knows? It's still a mystery. Investigation is ongoing. How's your water?"

How's your water? *It's water.*

Donny held the bottle up and examined it. "Fine," he said. "It's water."

"Right."

While Donny poked at the steaks with the metal tongs, Sarah looked around at the yard. "The flowers really do look nice."

Donny surveyed their work. "They do," he said. "You have such a good eye. I never would have thought to plant them in layers like that."

"Thanks," Sarah said. "I'm thinking of taking up gardening again. You know, when we—when I get back home. All this planting made me realize how much I miss it. And with Amelia gone…"

"I used to love it when you gardened," Donny said.

"You did? You never said so."

"Well, you've got to understand, Sarah. There came a point when I'd give you a compliment and you'd find some way to complain about whatever it was I was complimenting. So if I told you that I liked your garden, or your flowers were beautiful, you'd say something like—"

"Like, 'Thanks. It takes up so much time,'" Sarah said, and Donny nodded. With yet another realization dawning now, Sarah went on, "'I actually don't even like gardening. Gardening is stupid. There's dirt. And I have to water my flowers.'"

"Something like that," Donny said.

"Wow," Sarah said. "I really was awful."

He wrapped a hand around her bicep and gave a quick squeeze. "Not awful," he said. "Just—not yourself."

"Oh, no," Sarah said. "I was awful. I'm so sorry."

Donny set down the tongs and crossed his arms. "Did you even notice you were awful?"

"Wait. I thought you just said I wasn't awful."

He grinned. "You were awful."

"I didn't notice," Sarah said, and then added, "Well. I *mostly* didn't notice. Looking at it now, I can see that I was awful. From, you know, your perspective. At the time, I felt like I was doing the Super Mom thing, you know? And anything that stood in the way of me focusing entirely on Amelia?" She swiped her pointer finger across her neck.

He laughed. "Can't fault you for that."

There was an awkward pause then, because faulting Sarah for that was exactly what Donny was doing by leaving her, and they both knew it. Donny dropped his arms and picked up the tongs.

"Steaks look good," Sarah said, then, remembering she'd promised herself she wouldn't be reduced to small talk, she added, "Well, Amelia's turned out pretty well, anyway."

They both looked over to the table, where Amelia and Luke were setting up cups and plasticware. Luke was trying to teach Amelia to juggle the red plastic cups, and she kept dropping them. They were both laughing.

It reminded Sarah of the afternoon she and Donny had spent skipping rocks. Well, she corrected herself, he'd skipped rocks, and she'd tried to do so … with no luck. Every time she tossed a rock, it would sink straight down to the bottom of the swimming hole, without skipping even a single time. Donny was a good teacher, and a great sport, and tried over and over to explain the technique. "It's all in the flick of your wrist," he said, or, "Keep your elbow in. You look like a chicken, and you've never seen a chicken skip rocks before, have you?"

Although Sarah was tempted to bring this up now, she also knew Donny would be wary if she did. They couldn't rebuild their marriage on their shared past.

"She has turned out well, although she's a terrible juggler," Donny said. "Good thing she won't need those juggling skills in college."

"Not to worry," Sarah said. "I'll teach her to skip rocks."

"Over my dead body," Donny said. "I won't have you teaching our daughter The Chicken."

Ah, so he remembered, too.

"Fine," she said. "Then you'd better teach her."

Sarah and Donny watched as Amelia and Luke finished setting the table. Every thirty seconds (or maybe even more frequently, Sarah thought), Luke did something to make Amelia laugh.

Sarah made a growling sound. "It's going to be hard for her to leave him."

"First heartbreak," Donny said. "It's good to get it under her belt now."

Was there a subtext? Did he mean that it was better to experience heartbreak at seventeen than to do so at thirty-seven?

"Hey, I smell burning," Sarah said. "I think your meat's done."

Donny jumped, and turned around to take the steaks off the grill. As he laid them on a platter, he said, "You weren't awful, Sarah. You just became so distant. I felt like I lost my best friend."

Sarah took the platter from him so he could fill another one.

"I know," Sarah said. Then she shrugged one shoulder. "I *was* awful."

Mama Katherine had seated Sarah and Donny side-by-side at family dinners for years, and they took their usual spots automatically. Margaret brought Sarah a beer and winked as she handed it to her. This made Sarah suspicious, and when she took her first sip she realized Margaret had spiked the beer with a shot (or two) of tequila. Under normal circumstances, Sarah would pass the beer to someone else, but this evening, she decided to drink it herself.

After the first few sips, she felt any hard edges turning soft, and she winked at Margaret across the table. Margaret gave her a thumbs up, and then, in a move way too obvious, lifted her chin at Donny as if to say, "Go on." Sarah smiled and shook her head, and Donny leaned over to whisper, "What is your sister doing?"

"I think she laced her beer with tequila, too."

"Too?" Donny said.

"Yeah," Sarah said. "She definitely laced mine. Taste it."

Donny took the beer, tasted it, and grinned at Sarah before handing it back. Then he shook his head, just as Sarah had done a moment ago, and she wondered how many mannerisms they shared. They would have been one of those old couples who dress the same. That is, if she hadn't messed things up.

Throughout the rest of dinner, the beer-and-tequila worked its magic, warming Sarah's core and loosening her limbs. Relaxed and gaining confidence, she concentrated her efforts on flirting with Donny, letting their fingers touch when he passed the salad dressing and leaning up against him to ask him for the butter.

"What do you want to bet Mama's going to make us play charades?" Donny said.

"Oh, she is," Sarah said. "I'm not betting against you on that one."

"She hasn't made us play in, like, years," Sarah said.

"Yeah," Donny said. "Because you never wanted to. You always had to help Amelia get to bed."

Wow. It seemed like Donny finally saying something about Sarah's behavior had opened the flood gates.

Sarah pressed her lips together, then inhaled sharply and said, "You're right."

Charades had always been a family favorite. When Amelia was really little, Sarah and Donny put her to bed before the adults played. But as she got older and her bedtime got later, Sarah insisted on carrying out the entire bedtime routine, even if a game of charades was in full swing. Amelia absolutely wasn't allowed to stay up late to join in. At first, everyone went on without her. But they also said it wasn't as fun when she didn't play—watching Sarah and Donny play on the same team was like watching some kind of phenomenon, and it had become a favorite part of the game. So after Sarah ducked out a few times, the rest of them just stopped playing.

"Let's play now," Sarah said to Donny.

"Are you sure?" he said.

"Yes," Sarah said. "I'm sure."

I want to see if we still have that connection, if we can still be a phenomenon together, one last time.

Before Donny could answer, Sarah said, a little too loudly, "I think we should play charades."

All the conversation at the table stopped. People exchanged glances: Hannah and Margaret, Mama and Amelia, Farmer Eddie and Luke.

"What?" Sarah said. "We used to love charades."

"I thought you hated it," Amelia said.

If it were even possible, the table became quieter than it had been just a second before.

"What?" Sarah said. "I love it. I *love* it!"

"Somebody get this woman another beer," Hannah said. "Beer's bringing the Real Sarah back."

"Well, that stings," Sarah said. "But I'll forge ahead."

"It was the tequila," Margaret said. "Thank the tequila. I'm game. Let's play."

"But first," Sarah said, "tell me why you thought I hated it, Amelia."

On the spot now, Amelia blinked. "Oh, never mind. It's nothing."

Mama Bear crept forward in Sarah's mind, warning her not to embarrass Amelia. But tequila said this question deserved to be answered. So Sarah said, "It's not nothing. I won't be mad. I promise."

Amelia sighed, a sound so heavy Sarah's heart broke a little. But tequila made Sarah raise an eyebrow, and Amelia said, "It's just that, whenever you'd put me to bed when everyone started playing, you'd seem so … I don't know. Just forget it, okay?"

"Well, I can't, now," Sarah said, making her best effort to infuse her voice with patience. "You're leaving me hanging."

"Yeah," Margaret said. "You're leaving us hanging."

"Well," Amelia said. Luke nudged her with his shoulder. "You seemed so agitated. So annoyed. Like you couldn't believe they were playing charades *again*. I remember I asked you once, what was wrong, and you said, 'Nothing, Amelia. Nothing. It's just that some people have important things to do.'"

"I said that?" Sarah said, and when Amelia nodded, her movement jerky and uncertain, Sarah said, "Of course I did."

Now, everyone stared at Sarah. She could hear real, actual crickets chirping, as the sun was sinking into the horizon. She took a deep breath. Why hadn't she realized playing charades *was* an important thing? That this time they had together, with Mama Katherine, with Amelia, was so fleeting?

"Well, that was stupid and I take it back," she said, forcing a laugh. "Let's play now."

After the table-clearing bustle that followed, they sat down to play charades. Mama Katherine separated them into their usual teams, pitting Sarah, Donny, Amelia, and Hannah against herself, Margaret, Luke, and Farmer Eddie.

"You go first, Sarah," Margaret said, then. She handed Sarah another beer. "Let's see if you've still got it."

Sarah took a sip, tasted tequila, and said, "Oh, I've still got it."

She stood up, which she hadn't done since dinner started, and the world tilted, just a little. She blinked.

"Want me to drink that beer for you?" Margaret said.

Sarah waved her off, took a swig, and marched to the end of the table to draw her first card: Romeo and Juliet.

"Well." She blinked again.

"Ooh," Margaret said. "She's stumped. This is looking good for The Ducks."

"The Ducks?" Luke said. "Is that our team name?"

"I'm not stumped," Sarah said. "I'm thinking, that's all."

"She's stumped," Margaret hissed.

How in high Heaven could she act this out? She could pantomime killing herself, but that wouldn't convey the depth of the story, would it? She could pantomime killing herself and someone else. But that would just be confusing.

She had to act out being in love. But how? She couldn't do it alone. Then she got an idea. But could she do it? It would take guts, that's for sure. But didn't a person need guts when she was trying to save her marriage?

Emboldened by alcohol and an audience hungry for whatever she was going to do next, Sarah made up her mind.

She marched right up to Donny, took his head in her hands, and kissed him on the mouth. She kissed him like she hadn't kissed him in ages: long and deep and with every ounce of her focus.

Then she stood up and plunged a dagger into her heart.

Donny didn't miss a beat. Just like he would have in the past, he called out, "Romeo and Juliet!" as soon as Sarah's body crumpled to the ground.

Sarah, still laying behind Donny's chair, wished she could see her sisters' faces now. Margaret would be looking at her with a sly smile on her face, and one eyebrow raised. Hannah would, undoubtedly, be in shock, her mouth hanging open and a smile in her eyes.

Triumphant, Sarah stood up, took a bow to a smattering of applause, and sat back down in her seat, all the while avoiding eye contact with everyone, but especially with Donny.

———

HE'D KISSED HER BACK.

Sarah was sure of it. When she first planted her lips on Donny's, he froze. She'd expected that, and because he didn't pull away, she deepened the kiss. Within a mere second, he was kissing her back. His tongue was in her mouth and his hands were on her wrists.

She thought, well, that's a relief, before standing up to pantomime killing herself. They didn't look at each other for the rest of the game, unless one of them was acting out a card. As always, their team won. Amelia acted out a skunk, Donny drew a birthday party, and Hannah got race car driving.

By the end of the game, Sarah was glowing, and apparently, it was noticeable.

"Wow, Sarah," Margaret said. "You look so smug after that win. I think you should make the root beer floats."

"That's not smug," Hannah said. "That's the good, old-fashioned rosy-cheeked look of someone who just, you know—"

Sarah, afraid someone was going to say something about her kissing Donny, started to interject, but Mama Katherine saved her. "That's the good, old-fashioned rosy-cheeked look of someone who just had fun. Let loose. I'm so proud of you, my dear."

Her last words were laced with sarcasm, which stung a little, but Sarah brushed it off. Kiss or no kiss, she had enjoyed playing charades and she wondered why she'd gone so long without doing so. Although, the kiss was an added bonus, she thought as she stood up to go into the kitchen.

Someone had the foresight to put the root beer mugs in the freezer, and just as Sarah was lining them up along the counter, the side door squeaked open and slammed shut. She didn't have to turn around to know it was Donny. Terrified that he was going to bring up the kiss, her first instinct was to cringe, but fortunately good sense stepped in and stopped her. Instead, she adjusted the mugs, making sure they were all positioned in exactly the same way.

"I count eight mugs, there," he said.

Well, that's not what she'd been expecting him to say.

"Yeah," she said, moving to retrieve the ice cream from the freezer. "Eight people, eight mugs."

"Wait," he said. "You're having one?"

She shut the freezer and turned to face him, still holding the tub of ice cream.

"Well, why wouldn't I?"

Donny smiled at her, then, and she realized she hadn't seen a genuine smile from him in—well, she didn't know how long it had been. Longer than she could remember, that was for sure.

"I have no idea, Sarah," he said. "I never could figure out why you'd skip out on root beer floats. You love those things. Or, you *did*."

"I skipped out on them?"

Now his mouth dropped open. "Um, yeah. Every summer, when Margaret and Hannah would make them, you'd say something weird about not wanting one. You haven't had one in years. The first time you turned it down, I thought you'd maybe had too much wine and didn't feel well. The second time, I thought you were watching your weight, you know? That was the summer you kept talking about how you needed to join the gym. And then you did join the gym. And then you never had a root beer float again."

"Wait," Sarah said. "That's true."

"I know," Donny said. He took the ice cream from her, set it on the counter, and peeled off the lid.

She found the scooper in a drawer and he leaned against the counter while she scooped. "Did that alien invade my body, like, for years?"

"I thought so," Donny said. He got the root beer out of the pantry and twisted the lid off.

"Wow," Sarah said. "I can't believe I haven't had a root beer float for *years*. Literally, years!"

"It's a tragedy," Donny said. "But the good news is that you're coming around."

He gestured at the mugs, then started pouring soda into each one. And even when he was finished, and the two of them carried the floats outside, he didn't say anything about the kiss.

An hour later, Sarah said to Donny, "Geez, you'd think my having a root beer float was the first day of Armageddon, the way everyone made such a big deal of it."

Mama Katherine had volunteered the two of them to walk Farmer Eddie home, and they were walking back now in the darkness. Donny chuckled. "I know. But to tell you the truth—"

"I know," Sarah said. "Everyone's surprised I let my hair down."

"You're a lot better-looking when you let your hair down," he said. "Figuratively."

She laughed. "Not sure whether I should be charmed or offended."

It would have felt natural to link her arm through his, but Sarah refrained, instead linking her own hands together behind her back.

"It's true, Sarah," he said. "I think we've all missed the old you."

"Is it possible that I was just, you know, evolving, as I got older?"

She was genuinely curious, but she also felt that even asking the question might seem like she was making an excuse.

"De-volving, more like," Donny said.

"Wow," she said. "You're not holding back, tonight."

"I'm kidding," he said. "I mean, maybe you were evolving. If you want to call it that. But in most cases, it really did seem like someone else had taken over your body."

"Really?"

"Really."

They walked along without talking for a few moments, and Sarah could hear the night sounds she loved so much: the crickets, and the creek running nearby. The breeze rustled the leaves of the willow trees, and from somewhere far away, a bird gave a quiet hoot.

"I missed root beer floats," Sarah said. She was talking about more than root beer floats, and she wondered if Donny knew that.

"I can't imagine you didn't," Donny said. "But, look. Now you've had one and all is right with the world again."

Is all right with the world?

Sarah thought of the kiss, of the way he had responded to her so willingly. Then she thought of the play she'd been acting out—Romeo and Juliet—and she remembered it ended in tragedy, with both lovers dead. She shivered.

"Cold?"

"Nah," she said. "Just got a chill, that's all."

CHAPTER NINETEEN

"IF HE'S NOT BRINGING it up, then I'm certainly not bringing it up, either," Sarah said to her mom and sisters the next morning. They sat around the kitchen table after breakfast. Since the four of them had cooked, Donny and Amelia had gone outside to feed and water the chickens and collect eggs. As soon as the door had shut behind them, Margaret had pounced, wanting to know if Donny had said anything about the Romeo and Juliet kiss.

When Sarah said he hadn't, everyone else's eyes got big.

"He didn't say a word?" Margaret said.

"Not a word."

"So what did you talk about when you took Farmer Eddie home?" Hannah wanted to know.

"Root beer floats, mostly. Alien invasions."

Mama Katherine gave a little chuckle. "You haven't had a root beer float in years."

Sarah held up a hand. "Believe me, I heard about it. I don't know what I was thinking."

"Thus, the alien invasion," Margaret said. "A health-conscious alien invaded your body."

"That's right," Sarah said. "I don't take any responsibility for my lapse in root beer float drinking."

"What else did you talk about?" Hannah said.

"Nothing, really," Sarah said. "Do you think I should have brought up the kiss?"

"Let it lie," Mama said.

"Yeah, let it lie," Margaret and Hannah said.

Sarah looked down into her coffee mug. "Okay. It just feels so strange to not say anything."

"You'll get over it," Hannah said. "Speaking of not saying anything, Margaret, why don't you say something now about all the sneaking around you've been doing?"

Margaret's green eyes widened and she sat up very straight. "Me?"

"You're the only Margaret in here," Sarah said, aiming to maintain a casual tone of voice even though she was surprised Hannah had just come right out with the question.

Mama Katherine nodded. "You've been sneaking around?"

Even though she'd run out of coffee several minutes ago, Margaret raised her mug to her lips and tried to take a drink.

"You've never been much good at hiding things," Mama Katherine said. "Out with it."

When the girls were little, Sarah and Hannah could never count on Margaret to steal cookies from the kitchen or keep from revealing booby traps or surprises. They learned early on that they had to keep her in the dark until the need for secrecy had passed. Her expression was always a dead giveaway, which was probably why, even after taking a fake sip of coffee from her empty cup, she was holding that cup in front of her face.

"I've got all day," Sarah said.

"Me, too," Hannah said.

"I don't," Mama Katherine said. "You all know I'm going to have to use the toilet soon. I can't go more than an hour without peeing these days. Ah, the joys of getting old."

Something about Mama's comment rang a bell in Sarah's mind, but Margaret spoke again before she had a chance to dial in on what it was.

"It's nothing," Margaret said. "I don't want to worry you."

"So it *is* something," Hannah said. "Otherwise you wouldn't be worried about worrying us."

Sarah said, "Good point," and Margaret said, "Well, that's true."

"Go on, then," Mama Katherine said.

"Well, they're not sure, exactly," Margaret said.

"Who aren't?" Sarah, Mama Katherine, and Hannah said at the same time.

"The doctors," Margaret said. "I've got to get a third opinion."

"A third opinion about what?" Sarah said.

Margaret looked at the tabletop. "Dr. Lane thinks I may have retinitis pigmentosa."

"What's that?" Hannah said. "Is this the part where we should get worried?"

"Probably," Margaret said, her voice cracking just the tiniest bit. "I am."

"What is it?" Mama Katherine said.

Margaret took another deep breath, then looked at each of them in turn before saying, "The short answer? I'm going blind."

Sarah was stunned. How could Margaret, a visionary with an eye for beauty, possibly live life as a blind person? It didn't seem fair.

Just like Sarah couldn't imagine living her life without Donny, she couldn't imagine Margaret living without her sense of sight. It was worse for Margaret than for anyone else. She wasn't yet married; so did this mean she'd never see the face of the man she'd eventually fall in love with? Did this mean she'd never see what her own children looked like?

"Ugh," Margaret said as they all sat there in shocked silence. "This is why I didn't want to tell you guys yet. You all look so ... sad."

Even as she looked up, a tear made its way down her left cheek.

Hannah was the quickest to recover. "We're not sad," she said. "We're just surprised, that's all. I'll admit, I thought you were acting strangely, but I figured you just had, you know, a serious boyfriend. And you were having phone sex several times each day."

Margaret gave a little laugh, and Mama Katherine reached over to squeeze her hand.

"Or, you know," Sarah said, "that you were working on ironing out the details of an awesome new job, and you were going to surprise us when you inked the deal."

"I wish it was something like that," Margaret said. "But, alas. It's not."

"So that's why you didn't get a rental car when you came to our house this summer," Sarah said. Margaret nodded, and Hannah said, "And that's why you took a taxi here instead of renting a car, too."

"Yep," Margaret said. "And why I wanted one of you to drive me to the store the other day for plasticware."

For a moment, no one spoke. Then the questions started.

"Will you be completely blind?" Hannah wanted to know, and before Margaret answered, she said, "How long do you have?" and Sarah said, "How did you realize something was wrong?"

"I know you all are going to have lots of questions," Margaret said.

"And I do, too. I promise that when I have answers, I'll tell you. Which won't be for a few weeks as I begin seeing the specialists. Now. I'm going to shower. I expect the rest of you to soldier on."

She stood up, pushed her chair in, and walked out of the kitchen.

"Well," Sarah said. "That's not what I expected."

"What are we going to do?" Hannah said, and Mama Katherine said, "All we can do is be there for her. She'll come through this. She doesn't have a choice."

For some reason, Sarah found Mama Katherine's practicality devastating. Her first inclination was to lock herself in the spare bedroom and cry; mourn for Margaret's loss, purge herself of any strong emotions so she could carry on with her day—without anyone else knowing. She'd always figured she had good reasons for keeping things to herself: she didn't want to stress everyone else out. Now, she thought this might be a good opportunity to share something with Donny, even if it was a burden. She was sure there was some saying about shared burdens, but she couldn't remember it just now.

"I'm going to go outside for a while," she said, and as she went looking for her husband—she'd use that title for as long as it still applied—she realized she couldn't count the number of times she'd encountered a problem and considered talking to Donny about it, but then changed her mind when she had the chance. The truth was, she'd even begun to feel resentful about carrying the stress, irritated by Donny's good mood while she stewed over some problem: Amelia's bad grade on that Spanish test sophomore year, the time someone keyed her car in the grocery store parking lot, the doctor finding an abnormality on one of her annual exams.

On one hand, she thought she was doing everyone a favor by keeping her feelings bottled up inside, but on the other hand, she blew up at them unnecessarily: when Amelia left a ring of milk on the kitchen counter, when Donny forgot to wipe the mirror after brushing his teeth, when both of them pushed "Play" on the show they were watching before she finished heating her water for tea.

Hindsight was both a blessing and a curse, she supposed.

As she walked along the garden and between corn rows, then past the chickens and goats, she felt a mixture of despair and gratitude. Despair related to Margaret, and gratitude that she could see the cornsilk growing out of the ears of corn, the fat yellow hen pecking the slender white one, and the tiny baby goat bounding around its pen like the earth was a trampoline.

Donny was down by the creek, exactly where Sarah had expected him to be. What she hadn't expected was to find him skipping rocks.

He turned around when he heard her approaching. "Ah, so you're here for a rock-skipping lesson."

"Ha," she said. "Can't teach an old dog new tricks. I don't think I'll ever be a rock skipper."

Still, her eyes automatically began searching the ground for suitable rocks: smooth, round, and flat.

"There's time, yet," he said.

She couldn't help but wonder if that was some kind of innuendo.

"I need to talk to you," she said.

She saw his posture stiffen, just the tiniest bit. He was wary, afraid of what she was going to say. He probably thought she was going to bring up that Romeo and Juliet kiss. She had the urge to tell him, "It's not what you think."

But she didn't. "It's Margaret."

He relaxed, visibly, and she would have found it humorous under any other circumstances.

"Did she finally tell you something?"

Sarah told him what Margaret had said, and he listened intently, skipping rocks all the time.

"What are we going to do?" he said when she was finished.

That simple question, those few words strung together, made Sarah's heart beat just the tiniest bit faster.

"I don't know," she said. "What can we do? I mean, we can't stop her from going blind."

Her voice hitched, and a second later, Donny was in front of her, wrapping his arms around her. "No, we can't. But we can research ways to make her life easier, you know, during this transition."

Sarah put her arms around his waist and laid her head on his chest. "That's a good idea."

Already, she felt lighter.

Donny stepped back and put a hand in his pocket. When he withdrew it, he was holding a perfect skipping rock. "I saved this for you."

She didn't know if he'd really saved it for her, or if he'd just been collecting good ones and storing them in his pocket, but she didn't ask. She thanked him and walked to the edge of the creek. Then she adjusted her grip on the rock and flung it across the water's surface. It skipped once, twice, three times before plopping into the water.

Donny cheered, loudly. Smiling, Sarah shook her head.

"That was luck," she said.

"No, that was skill. Definitely skill."

The two of them walked together back to Mama Katherine's house. They didn't speak much, and Sarah thought about the Immersion stage of Hazel Rickshaw Carlisle's plan to make Philip Carlisle fall in love with her. So far, Sarah had immersed Donny in the family activities here at Mama Katherine's house, but for this plan to really work, she had to spend time with him one-on-one.

And she had to make time for adventure, before they took Amelia to school. After that, he'd be slipping through her fingers, already looking forward to the future. Even while she was thinking about how to win Donny back, panic set in. What if he didn't *want* to be won back? He'd seemed warmer, friendlier, since they arrived at Mama Katherine's house, but that could be a result of them being here, away from regular life.

Maybe Sarah needed to read further ahead in Hazel's journal.

––––––––

DECEMBER 12: One year, five months, and one week after the birth of Baby Benny

––––––––

MY DEAR PAULINE,

––––––––

I HAVE BEEN the most neglectful friend, haven't I? To tell you the truth, being a mother and a career woman has been absolutely all-consuming.

I love my job, Pauline. Things are going so well there. I've been given a promotion to copywriting manager and I manage an entire team of people. My boss tells me I'm a rising star.

Unfortunately, I still don't feel the same way about motherhood. I have never been so bad at anything in all my life. The baby—he's more than a year old and he's walking, so I guess he's a toddler, come to think of it—he still cries whenever he seems me, Pauline. On one hand, I feel this fierce love for the little boy. The mere sight of his dimples and his thick, black eyelashes and his bushy little eyebrows makes me want to cry, out of deep, deep love. But he hates me, Pauline. I don't know how such a tiny creature can make a person feel like such a failure.

Oh! Forgive me, Pauline! I forgot to tell you his name.

It's Benjamin. After my oldest brother.
We call him Benny.

———

SARAH'S INDEX finger jumped to the word *Benny* on the page. That was the name of Mama Katherine's little boy—the one who died. Was it possible … no, surely Mama Katherine would have said something when she saw Sarah reading the journal. Millions of people named their sons Benjamin, didn't they? But did they all call their children Benny, for short?

Dimples, though, and thick black eyelashes: Sarah saw a vision of Hannah, whose dimples and thick black eyelashes had always been a source of envy.

Sarah, her heart beating in her throat, flipped to the next entry:

———

NOVEMBER 11: One month since the accident

———

I KNOW. It's been forever since I wrote. I'll just cut to the chase.
God has decided to punish me. My baby is dead. My son. My little boy.

———

SARAH, hands shaking, kept reading, devouring the words as quickly as she could.

———

THERE WAS AN ACCIDENT. One month ago. Benny climbed out of his crib. The nanny didn't know. Don't blame her, Pauline. She was cooking dinner and Benny is such a sneaky little guy.
It's harvest time, and Benny has been fascinated by all the men and their equipment and the piles and piles of apples.
Well, when he woke up from his nap and escaped from the crib, what do you think he did first? He wandered outside and one of the crewmen ran right over him.
If I'd been here, Pauline, I could have stopped him. I am his mother.

Surely mother's instinct would have alerted me that he was in danger. If I hadn't been at work, mixing midday cocktails for a new client, I would have been able to prevent this tragedy. But I wasn't. "I'm a terrible mother," I said. "He hates me," I said. And now, I say, I was wrong. Wrong about it all. And I've ruined my own life and Philip's.

Since Benny died, things just haven't been the same. I don't know why people use terms like "passed away," or "left us," when they're talking about death, Pauline. Those phrases make it sound so peaceful.

But the fact is, my little boy is gone. He was snatched from our lives in an instant. There was no quiet passing, no leaving. He died.

Philip and I don't talk any more, Pauline. We can't even bear to look at one another. I know he blames me for Benny's death, just as I blame myself.

And for me, Philip is just a painful reminder of our son. I see Benny's dimples, his cleft chin, his bright eyes, every time I glance at Philip's face.

I've decided to leave California. It's the best thing for me, but more importantly, it will free Philip from the disaster that is me.

I'm going to leave the coast and head for the mountains. Somewhere with a wide-open sky. I haven't told Philip. I'm sure he'd try to convince me to stay. Not because he loves me—I ruined that—but for the sake of our business. I'd imagine that a divorce and the subsequent break-up of the union our fathers planned so carefully would just devastate everyone involved.

Maybe I'll schedule a private meeting with one of Fathers' attorneys. Perhaps I can just give Philip complete control of the orchard. I don't want anything to do with it, anyway.

Yes, Pauline, I think that's just what I'll do. And then, under the cover of darkness, I'll leave.

———

SO. Hazel Rickshaw Carlisle was Mama Katherine. There was no other explanation. Sarah wanted to run inside, to confront Mama Katherine, to ask her the dozens of questions swirling around: was Philip Hannah's father? Had Mama ever spoken to Philip again? Was he still alive?

The journal contained several more pages, and Sarah flipped to the next one, searching for answers.

———

FEBRUARY 25: Three months since leaving California

———

I'M PREGNANT. Four months along. I must have conceived just before the accident. I'd believed things couldn't get any worse. I, of all people, should recognize the blessing that a baby is, Pauline, but I am absolutely terrified. I am a newly single woman, living in an old farmhouse in Wyoming, without a support system to speak of. No one knows where I am, and you'd better believe I aim to keep it that way.

All I can do, Pauline, is be the best possible mother. I won't make the mistakes with this new baby that I made with Benny. I am a phoenix, and I out of the ashes I will rise.

———

"I NEED TO TALK TO YOU." Hannah's voice startled Sarah out of Hazel's world and back into her own. She was standing at the open door of the RV, her hands on her hips, squinting up at Sarah. Her eyelashes, thick and black, framed bright blue eyes.

"Geez. You look like I just caught you with your hand in the cookie jar." She smiled, and her dimples deepened. Sarah knew, with certainty, that Hazel was Mama Katherine and that Hannah was the daughter of Philip Carlisle.

"Good reading?" Hannah said.

She came up the steps and looked over Sarah's shoulder. Sarah closed the journal.

"I need to talk to you, too," Sarah said. Her lips had gone dry, and she licked them.

"Wow," Hannah said. "You look serious."

Maybe this wasn't the right time to drop this huge bomb on Hannah's existence.

Hannah gestured to the journal. "What's happening now? Intrigue? Romance? Steamy sex?"

"You could say that."

"Huh. Okay, well, I need to talk to you."

"So you said," Sarah said. She laid the journal on the dining table and put her hands in her lap. "All ears."

Hannah took a deep breath, like she was about to make a big announcement. "I think we should take Margaret on a road trip."

"A road trip?"

Sarah blinked. She thought about a line in a book she'd read.

Something about someone blinking owlishly. The shock was making her loopy.

"Yes." Hannah sat down at the dinette, apparently not noticing anything off. "In the RV. I mean, there are some beautiful sights she should see before, you know, she can't, anymore."

Sarah nodded. "It's a great idea."

"But."

"It's not really a, 'but,'" Sarah said, wondering if Hannah had ever asked Mama Katherine about her own father. They'd all known Hannah was Mama's biological daughter, but Sarah had never thought to ask about who'd provided the other set of DNA.

Sarah shook her head, willing herself to focus on the conversation. "I just don't know if she'll go for it. I mean, don't you think we should focus on the practicalities of all of this? Like, where she's going to live? She probably needs a guide dog. There's mobility training she can get. You know, where someone teaches her how to get around. It would probably be easier for her to learn all of that while she can still see."

"That's Sarah talking," Hannah said.

"True," Sarah said. "I'm Sarah."

"What I mean is, we're talking about Margaret. She's the adventurous one. Don't you think she's going to want to have, you know, a big adventure before she loses her vision?"

"She's already seen so many places."

"She's seen big cities. Skyscrapers, city streets, taxi cabs. But has she seen nature's awesome stuff? Monument Valley? Zion? Mount Rushmore?"

"Mount Rushmore is only famous because humans carved faces into it. It's not really nature's awesome stuff."

"Still. You're mincing words," Hannah said. "You know what I mean."

"It's not that I don't agree that a road trip is a good idea," Sarah said.

"But," Hannah said.

"But I think we're both right, here. She needs the training. She's going to want to do the research, herself. You know? She's so independent. I don't think we can assume she'll want to do a fun road trip when there's so much else to be done. I think she'll be afraid of losing her independence."

"I see what you're saying," Hannah said. "What if we went on the road trip, like, right away? And she can do all the research between stops. And then when we get back, she can do the training."

"You're turning this into a lesson plan," Sarah said.

"Kind of," Hannah said.

"Maybe we should ask her," Sarah said.

"Ask who, what?" Now Mama Katherine stood in the doorway of the RV.

Sarah froze. Mama Katherine with the secret identity. In a way, it was easy to understand why she'd never told them about her past. But in a way, it was such a huge part of who she was. How could she *not* have told them? Before Sarah could say anything, Hannah laid out her road trip idea for Mama Katherine.

As she spoke, adding in Sarah's concerns and her own, Mama came up the steps and slid into the other side of the dinette. Sarah snatched the journal before she could see it, and tucked it into the chair beside her.

"It's a solid idea," Mama Katherine said when Hannah finished. "I think it's going to take some convincing, though. I think Sarah's right —Margaret will want to start researching as soon as possible. You're right that she's adventurous, Hannah, but still, I think it's going to be tough to get her to agree to taking a kind of vacation when she's going to want to dive right into the learning and planning. We'll just have to bring it up to her and see what she says."

"Wow, is there a party going on in here? I didn't get an invitation." Margaret climbed up the RV's steps and motioned for Hannah to scoot over. As she sat down at the dinette, Hannah, Sarah, and Mama Katherine exchanged glances.

"Wait," Margaret said. "I know what's going on, here. This is a pity party, and I'm the guest of honor."

"Well, there's no time like the present," Hannah said to Sarah and Mama Katherine, and Sarah thought, *Indeed. This would be the perfect time to ask Mama Katherine about the journal.*

Fortunately, or unfortunately, Hannah plowed ahead. "Don't look so alarmed, Margaret. We just wanted to talk to you about something."

Margaret put her head in her hands. "Bunch of busy bodies. But I do love you."

"So," Hannah said, "Sarah thinks we need to focus on the practicalities. Like where you're going to live and whether you want a guide dog."

"And Hannah," Sarah said, "Wants to go on a road trip. So you can, you know, see nature's beauty."

"Awesome stuff," Hannah said. "Nature's awesome stuff."

"Right," Sarah said.

Margaret was now looking from one to the other, her mouth open. "You guys. I really appreciate the gesture. I do. I am so grateful you want to be involved, here. But right now, we're not even sure what's going to happen. And you're both so busy."

"Not true," both Sarah and Hannah said at the same time. Hannah said, "I'm still on summer break."

"And I just have to take Amelia to school and then I'm fixing to be a single woman, so…"

"And I've got nothing but time," Mama Katherine said. "As you know. Besides"—here she winked at Hannah—"You know your sister won't leave me home alone, anyway."

"You guys don't have to do this," Margaret said. "I'm perfectly capable of getting this all figured out on my own. I don't want to stress you out."

"I'm not stressed," Sarah said. "Are you, Hannah?"

"I'm not stressed," Hannah said. "Are you, Mama?"

Mama Katherine chuckled. "No. I'm not, either. So that's settled."

"But you all have things to do," Margaret said.

"Nothing as important as this," Hannah said.

When Sarah didn't speak, Margaret pinned her with a direct stare. "You should be working on your marriage."

Sarah was tempted to say, "It's a lost cause," but she knew that would bring the focus back to her. "It'll be fine. I promise. So. What do you say?"

"Let me sleep on it," Margaret said. "This may just be something I have to do, myself. You know? It's not that I wouldn't love to spend extra time with you, but I also feel like it's important for me to be independent on this one."

"You always have been an independent little sucker," Mama Katherine said.

The words they didn't say—that Margaret couldn't do much of this on her own, that her independence was already slipping through her fingers—hung in the air, even louder than the ones they did.

CHAPTER TWENTY

In the three days that had passed since Sarah realized Mama Katherine was Hazel Rickshaw Carlisle and Hannah was Philip Carlisle's daughter—and since Hannah and Sarah had proposed the road trip to Margaret—Sarah had agonized over what to do about Mama Katherine.

She almost had to bring it up, have the conversation, tell Hannah about what had happened between her parents. But wasn't it Mama Katherine's right to tell Hannah the story? Maybe she had a perfectly good reason for keeping it close to her heart. Maybe she thought she was protecting Hannah.

Maybe if Sarah could get Mama Katherine alone, she could ask her why she'd kept this secret for so long... and maybe she could even convince her to tell Hannah, herself.

On the other hand, what was the point? What good was it to tell Hannah the story of her past? What if her father was no longer alive? What if this new knowledge caused some sort of strife because she blamed Mama Katherine for keeping her father from her?

In the midst of this internal debate, Margaret had come to Sarah and Hannah with a decision about the road trip.

"I'll go," she said. "But, Sarah, you have to patch things up with Donny before we leave." The light in her eyes and the tone of her voice were both victorious, as if she'd found a way to make everything work.

Sarah had agreed, not necessarily because she thought she could win Donny back, but because she knew it was the only way to make the road trip happen. Now, this morning, as she stood here, watching her husband repair a broken hinge on the chicken coop, she committed to one final push before they left in a week.

She started with the big announcement: "So, I think we're going to take Margaret on a road trip."

Donny stood up and turned around to face Sarah, his hand shading his eyes.

One of the hens—the fat tan one that Mama had named Bessie— poked her head through an opening in the fence and pecked at Donny's shoe.

"I think it's a good idea," Donny said. "What about Amelia?"

"She's practically an adult," Sarah said, as much to Donny as to herself. "We'll let her make the decision. She can go to college, as planned, and sign up for that godawful summer session I signed her up for. Or, she can come with us, on a girls' trip. Or she can stay here with you, and you and I will take her to school when I get back. That is, if you don't mind keeping an eye on the place."

Donny nodded. "It sounds like a great idea."

Sarah hoped Amelia would choose to go on the trip, for several reasons: first, she felt like she should be spending every moment of these final weeks with Amelia, before she left for school. Or, if they weren't actually together every moment, Sarah should certainly make herself available.

Second, she didn't want to leave Amelia and Luke to their own devices. The impending tragedy of Amelia leaving for college just might push the two of them into bed. And an unexpected pregnancy —okay, even Sarah could recognize when she was getting ahead of herself.

Third, Donny wasn't as good as Sarah was about making sure Amelia got her vegetables.

"Wow," Donny said. "I can see those wheels turning. What are you thinking about?"

Sarah laughed, the sound high and brittle.

"It's nothing," she said.

"You're wringing your hands."

"It's nothing," she said again. "This is going to be great."

Before Donny could respond, Margaret sauntered up, a smug smile on her face.

"I have a surprise for you two. I booked an overnight for you."

Donny looked at Sarah, who was too busy glaring at Margaret to look at him.

"Didn't you tell her—" Donny said, pointing at Margaret.

"Oh, I told her," Sarah said.

"She told me," Margaret said. "But one of my final wishes is for you two to spend an overnight together. I'd like to see you together one last time. That's why you're leaving tomorrow morning."

"You're not on your deathbed," Sarah said. "I'm not sure it works like that."

"My vision is on its deathbed," Margaret said. "So it absolutely works like that. Because I said so."

Donny cleared his throat. "So where is this overnight?"

Now Sarah looked at Donny. Was he actually considering going?

"What about our road trip?" Sarah said.

"We'll go after," Margaret said. "Your overnight is in Jackson Hole. Just a hop, skip, and a jump from here. I rented you a car. And I booked a hotel room. And a river rafting experience. You'll be back before our road trip. And it's all nonrefundable, so..."

"So we have to go," Donny said. "Or *you* have to go."

"I already gave your names for the reservation. I used your credit card. There is no turning back."

"Wait. You used my credit card?"

"Just to hold the reservation. I stole it out of your wallet. I'll give you cash to pay for everything."

As if he didn't believe her, Donny pulled his wallet out of his pocket and examined the contents.

Margaret pulled the card and several hundred-dollar bills out of her pocket and held them up. "This is to pay for the room when you get there. And the rafting."

Donny tried to look stern, but Sarah could see a smile tugging at one corner of his mouth. He'd always had a soft spot for Margaret, and she knew it. She was using that to her advantage right now, grinning up at him like she had countless times: when she convinced him to steal the remaining cookies from the cookie jar, since none of them were tall enough to reach it, even when they stood on chairs; when she sweet-talked him in to hosting a huge party in his parents' cornfield because she didn't want Mama Katherine to know about it.

Now Donny looked at Sarah. "Did you know about any of this?"

Sarah shrugged. "Nope."

After handing Donny the wad of cash, Margaret waltzed into the house. Sarah stood there for a minute, frozen in surprise, then scurried after her sister. By the time she got inside, the house was empty.

"Impossible," she said to herself. "She's like a ghost."

Sarah had to get Margaret alone and convince her to cancel all the Jackson Hole reservations. This was absurd. They couldn't leave Amelia right now. She was about to leave for college. They should spend every moment they could with her. *Although,* a voice in the back of Sarah's mind said, *she's been spending most of her time with Luke as it is.*

It would be so uncomfortable to stay in the same hotel room with Donny. To go around Jackson Hole like they were a couple. Which, technically, they were, but not for long.

But Margaret was nowhere to be found.

As she went from room to room, Sarah weighed the options. She and Donny could just not go. They could call and cancel the reservations. But the deadline to cancel had probably passed, which meant the hotel and river rafting companies would probably still charge them. And Margaret had said they were nonrefundable, anyway.

"She did this on purpose," Sarah said.

Almost, Sarah thought, as if Margaret knew the third phase of the project was Adventure.

Well, this didn't have to be weird. They *could* go to Jackson Hole and request a room with two beds, or a suite, even. Which was dumb, since they'd been sharing a bed for years. Or, they could just get another room. They could drive off together and then spend the entire weekend separately. That might work. But how could she propose that to Donny without sounding like she didn't want to spend time with him?

CHAPTER TWENTY-ONE

They went. The morning after Margaret handed Donny his own credit card and a stack of paper money, Sarah and Donny loaded into Mama Katherine's truck, a shared suitcase in the bed and travel mugs of coffee in hand. Margaret, still wearing that smug smile, waved from the front porch as Donny backed the truck out of its spot.

They headed down the long driveway and Sarah sighed.

"That was genius," Sarah said to Donny.

She hadn't meant to say it, because it could only lead to a conversation about Sarah's plan. But being here in Wyoming, away from the PTO and the laundry and the dishes, her guard was down.

"What was?" Donny said.

He sounded a little absent-minded. Maybe she should change the subject.

"Your backing-out job."

"Ha," Donny said. "I know that's not what you're talking about. You're talking about Margaret sending us on this adventure."

"Yeah," Sarah said. "And then I went to confront her about it and she'd disappeared. I still don't even know where she went."

"She went in the back door and out the front door," Donny said. "One of her old tricks, remember?"

"I can't believe I forgot that, especially yesterday."

"She used to do it all the time," Donny said. "And then last night she went for a long walk. I saw her when I was setting up camp."

So he'd seen Margaret, and he hadn't tried to get out of today's adventure, Sarah thought. Or, maybe he had, and it hadn't worked.

He wouldn't say anything about that. Sarah tucked that thought into her cap to consider later.

Donny's use of "adventure" made Sarah think of Hazel Rickshaw Carlisle's three-step process: *Discovery, Immersion, Adventure.*

As they'd packed that morning, Sarah had decided this would be the perfect opportunity to talk to Donny about the journal, Mama Katherine's secret past, and Hannah's secret parentage.

"I wanted to run something by you," she said to Donny.

Belatedly, she wondered if he'd think it was strange that she was seeking his advice now. Then she decided it didn't really matter.

"Lay it on me," Donny said, with no apparent hesitation, and Sarah did. She told him how she'd found the journal inside the recipe box, how she'd immediately felt like she was reading the words of a friend (no wonder, considering what she knew now), and how she'd eventually realized her own mother was the journal's author—using a completely different name than she'd used in her previous life.

The words tumbled out, one after the other, and Sarah experienced a profound sense of relief at having brought the story out into the open.

"It's all so much to take in, I know," Sarah said. "Mama Katherine's baby died. And she never told any of us about her past. At least, not that I know of. And Hannah has a dad. And I don't think she even knows. And I'll bet *he* doesn't even know."

Sarah stopped short when she realized she was rambling. At first, Donny didn't respond. He drummed his thumbs on the top of the steering wheel, and Sarah looked out the passenger-side window as the trees went by.

Finally, Donny let out a breath. "Wow."

"I know," Sarah said. She wanted to speak again, to say more, but she waited.

"I mean, maybe you could talk to Mama Katherine about it, alone. Give her the chance to tell Hannah, on her own. I can just imagine what she'd say about you finding the journal."

"That's no coincidence," Sarah said, and Donny added, "That's good, old-fashioned serendipity."

They both chuckled, and Sarah wondered how long it had been since they'd shared a laugh.

"Good advice, though," Sarah said. "I think I will try to get her alone when we get back. Thanks for listening."

"Always," Donny said.

Sarah knew he meant it—and she also knew she hadn't given him many opportunities to listen over the course of the past several years. What was wrong with her?

They rode in silence for a while, and when the landscape changed, Sarah enjoyed looking at the lush green fields with their tiny shacks and their grazing horses. As they came down through the mountain pass, she rolled down her window. Donny did the same.

"I miss this air," she said.

"Me, too," Donny said.

"I can see why you want to move back. The desert has nothing on this place."

"But it's a dry heat," he said.

"Ha," Sarah said. "Right."

When they'd first moved to Arizona, the proponents of the move—his parents—had answered their heat-related concerns with, "It's a dry heat. You won't even notice it."

It *was* a dry heat, but they noticed it! No, Arizona didn't have the below-freezing temperatures or the driving winds of Wyoming winters, but the heat was its own animal.

"Remember our first summer there?" Sarah said. "We thought we were going to die."

"We did," Donny said. "I think we practically lived in the swimming pool that year."

"We lived in the swimming pool, and we survived off watermelon coolers with lemonade and vodka."

Sarah didn't know if Donny was remembering the same image she was—the one of them making love in the pool one sweltering evening after downing several watermelon coolers each—but he practically confirmed it when he said, "Those were the good old days."

"They were," she said, hating that a wistful tone had crept into her voice. It was embarrassing—no, scratch that: it was humiliating to lay her heart on the line. Her emotions on her sleeve. Whatever.

Silence descended again. They passed by sheer cliffs and churning waterfalls.

"Want to stop at Jenny Lake?"

"It's kind of out of the way, isn't it?" Sarah said. "Past Jackson Hole?"

"Yeah, but we're on vacation. We're already halfway there. And it's your favorite place."

She shouldn't be surprised that he remembered that.

"Sure," she said. "Donny, do you think Amelia's okay?"

"Why wouldn't she be?"

"I don't know. Because we left her there. Alone."

"She's hardly alone, with that Luke fellow hanging all over her," Donny said.

"Did you just call him a 'fellow'?"

"Why, yes, I did. And she's got your sisters and your mom. She'll be fine. Plus, in a few weeks, she'll be on her own, all the time. We won't be able to keep tabs on her at all."

"You're right," Sarah said.

"You're just going to have to trust that we've done a good job, given her the tools to make good decisions. And survive."

"You make it sound like she's going to a remote desert island."

"That was the point," Donny said. "And she's not. She'll be fine today, and she'll be fine at school. She's a good, responsible kid."

Jenny Lake was just as Sarah remembered it. They'd brought Amelia here when she was four, and she'd played with the colored rocks at the lake's edge, her perfect silhouette reflected in the clear water, jutting towards the center opposite the snow-covered mountain peaks.

Sarah climbed out of the truck and stretched. Donny followed her down the path to the edge of the lake.

"Beautiful," he said.

When she turned to look at him, to agree with him, she was surprised to find that he was looking at her. "It is."

"You know," he said. "You always wanted to do that Alpine slide in Jackson Hole. Remember that?"

"Yeah, I remember." I was too scared to let Amelia ride it. I thought she'd find a way to fall over the edge."

"Let's ride it today."

"Today? Didn't Margaret make rafting reservations?"

"Yeah," Donny said. "But not until later. We can eat our picnic breakfast here and then go up to Jackson Hole, ride the slide, have lunch, and river raft."

"Wow," Sarah said. "I don't think we could pack much more into this day if we tried."

"Too much?" Donny said.

Under normal circumstances, Sarah would have said it was too much, that they'd be rushed and over-tired. "Nope," Sarah said. "It's great. Let's do it."

Margaret had thought of everything: the picnic basket she packed contained breakfast sandwiches wrapped in foil, a Thermos of coffee, and a fruit salad.

"She even packed a tablecloth," Sarah said.

Donny helped her to spread the cloth on a picnic table, and then Sarah laid out the food.

"It's been so long since we sat down to a meal, just the two of us," she said.

"I know," Donny said. "It's been years, possibly."

"Wait," Sarah said. She tried to infuse her voice with a playful tone, but thought she might be failing at it. "Seriously? Years? That can't be. I mean, Amelia's gone out with friends here and there, and surely we've eaten dinner together on those nights. Or breakfast together when she sleeps over at someone's house."

Donny just sat there, his sandwich in his hands, and looked at her, waiting. And, like she knew he was expecting her to, she searched her memory of the recent past for any proof that they had, in fact, eaten a meal together.

"What about homecoming? Every year Amelia would go work on the float. Right?"

"Right," Donny said.

"And I'd sit a couple of blocks away, cell phone in hand, waiting for her to call to be picked up."

"You didn't want—"

"I didn't want to make her wait."

Donny took a bite of his sandwich, and his eyes smiled as he looked at her. It almost looked like he was issuing a challenge.

"You're enjoying this," Sarah said. "I'm going to think of one."

Another pause.

Then, "Ooh! I know. That time she slept over at Teagan Garfield's house. Didn't we go on a date that night?"

Donny didn't answer. He sat there, chewing. Still waiting.

Sarah felt herself deflate. "We didn't. We were supposed to, and we didn't. I messed that up, too, didn't I?"

The humor seemed to have floated away. Donny took another bite.

"When did you, you know, notice?" Sarah said.

While he finished chewing, she looked around again, paying attention to the tiny details: the difference in color between the leaves on the trees, the way the lake rippled in long, uneven lines, the tilt of a goose's wings as it soared from one side of the clearing and landed in the water.

"I don't know," Donny said. "It was gradual, you know? The first few times, I was disappointed, but I told myself you were just being a good mom. Then I started to feel sort of ... rejected. I felt like maybe you'd fallen out of love with me. I did a lot of soul searching, trying to think of what I might have done to push you away. Was it work? Was it that I didn't do the chores you wanted me to do? Had I lost my skills in bed?"

Sarah blushed, and then, because she had nothing to lose at that point, she said, "You never lost those."

He chuckled. "Then I started wondering if you'd found someone else. Maybe a stay-at-home dad on the PTO or something."

"Oh, my," Sarah said. "There's like one dad on the PTO, and it's—"

"Jason Dalmer," they said at the same time.

"So not my type," Sarah said. "He's—"

"He's short," Donny said. "I know. But he's also kid-centric."

Sarah shook her head. "I can't believe you thought I'd have a fling with Jason Dalmer."

"I didn't, really," Donny said. "But I considered it. And then it finally hit me, I think it was last school year, Amelia's junior year. We hadn't dated in several years. We hadn't spent any time alone, really. And it didn't seem like you even noticed."

Having lost her appetite, Sarah set her sandwich down on the tablecloth. It was one of Mama Katherine's favorites—blue flowers on a white background.

"I didn't," she said, making eye contact with him again. "I didn't notice. Honestly, Donny, I don't know what I was thinking. Yes, I was trying to be a good mother to our daughter. And you were just always there, steadfast, you know? And I didn't even realize I was losing you."

The conversation ended there. A young family walked up the path, and distracted Sarah and Donny long enough for Sarah to find her appetite and finish her sandwich.

"Coffee?" Donny said as she brushed the crumbs from her palms. Sarah nodded, and Donny poured coffee into their travel mugs while she cleaned up.

At first, they rode without speaking, sipping their coffee, and Sarah fiddled with the radio. Every time she found a station, it was playing some sad country love song. Finally, she clicked it off, and they listened to the noise of the truck's engine and the tires on the road.

"They put in a new slide," Donny said. "It's called the Cowboy."

"Very fitting," Sarah said, "considering everyone's taste in music down here."

More silence. More road noise. More thinking. Sarah wished she could turn her brain off. Now that Donny had put her thoughts on this track, she was remembering time after time that she'd foregone spending time with him in order to "be there" for Amelia.

If she was alone, she would have whispered, "Stupid, stupid, stupid," to herself. But she wasn't, so she thought it. Finally, they arrived at the lodge where they'd ride the alpine slides. When they got out, Donny offered her his arm.

"Shall we?" he said.

She nodded. "Absolutely."

After paying for their tickets, they rode the ski lift up to the top of the slide. As Sarah drank in the view, she thought that she'd make the best of this. It didn't matter what happened afterwards. A few moments later, as they came flying down the slide, she realized there was no need to make the best of this. This *was* the best.

The slide curved one way and then the other, zipping past trees and through shady spots, dropping them down the side of the mountain. Sarah felt so *alive*. Her eyes stung and she couldn't tell whether it was from the wind or from emotion. Donny had insisted she go first, and she waited for him at the bottom. When he slid to the end, he jumped up, his face as bright as Amelia's on any Christmas morning.

"That was so awesome!"

"Again?" Sarah said.

They climbed aboard the ski lift for a second time, and the second ride down was just as exhilarating.

"I wish they sold an all-day pass," Donny said.

But, because they didn't, Sarah and Donny ate lunch, got back into the truck, and drove back to Jackson Hole for their river rafting trip. Sarah hadn't river rafted in years. Since Amelia was born, she thought as they checked in and the guide helped her with her vest.

A wry smile tugged at one corner of her mouth. It was like she'd turned into a weird, overprotective mama bear the moment the nurses placed Amelia in her arms. Lots of kids went river rafting. But she'd read somewhere about one incident where the raft flipped, sending a bunch of kids into the river. That particular trip had been on a slow stretch of water and the adults had quickly fished out the kids—who were all wearing life jackets—safely.

Today's trip was just as tame. Sarah figured Margaret, knowing Sarah's preference for safety, had asked for a mild adventure. She looked over at Donny as they floated along, the water sparkling and the trees pointing at the brilliance of a perfect summer sky, and he was grinning at her. It was a silly, oversized grin, the same one he used to flash at her at dinner after they'd had rowdy sex, or when they shared some kind of secret they planned to reveal later.

"I'm famished," Sarah told him a few hours later, while they were checking in their gear.

It was dinnertime, and Margaret had made reservations for them at an upscale-but-low-key steakhouse just down the road.

"It's walking distance from your hotel," she'd said to Sarah before they left Mama Katherine's that morning. Her voice was conspiratorial and she raised one eyebrow. "Have a bottle of wine, on me. Oh, and here."

She'd pressed a bottle of wine into Sarah's hands. "This one's for after."

Sarah had just shaken her head, unsure of how to let Margaret in on the fact that even if they did drink wine, nothing exciting would happen.

If she hadn't thought of that moment, of Margaret's face when she handed Sarah the wine, she wouldn't have thought about anything other than how hungry she was. But now, she was thinking about wine. And getting Donny naked.

The steakhouse was an all-wood building, a kind of lodge over-looking the same river on which they'd just rafted. Even though it was late in the day, the sun still shone brightly. The hostess offered them a table at one end of a large, shaded riverside deck, and now Sarah felt like she was in some sort of treehouse.

"This is pretty spectacular," Sarah said.

"Yeah, it is," Donny said. "We're going to owe Margaret, big time."

"We are," Sarah said. "Although I don't know what we can do for her, before she loses her sight."

"Her life's not ending, Sarah." Donny reached across the table and took her hand. "It's tragic, yes. And it's going to be a huge adjustment. But lots of people live life without being able to see, and they have rich, wonderful lives."

Sarah nodded, swallowed, and took a sip of water. "You're right. I know you're right."

"Now," Donny said. "Although we definitely must thank your sister for this day, I forbid you from thinking about her situation for another moment. I promise you that we'll help her get through this. But I know, because she told me so, that she wants you to enjoy this day. So enjoy it."

Sarah laughed. "She told you so?"

Donny looked down at the table. "Yes." Now he made eye contact.

"She told me that this trip cost her a small fortune and I'd better not mess this up."

"She didn't use the word, 'mess,' did she?"

"She sure didn't."

———

THE FIRST BOTTLE of wine made Sarah tingly in all the right places. The hotel room, with its views of the river and the forest made her slightly lightheaded. It had been forever since she felt this relaxed and warm inside.

"I never get tired of watching the river," she said to Donny, who had emerged from the bathroom and come up behind her.

"Me neither," he said. "Want to sit on the balcony? Then we can hear it, too."

"That would be great," Sarah said. "Let's."

"Want to open up Margaret's wine?"

"Boy, do I," Sarah said. "She sent us with a bottle of that stuff she got in Napa, that cabernet? It's so good."

"Well, it goes down pretty smooth, if I remember right."

"Oh, you remember right."

Sarah drank almost an entire bottle one night when Margaret came to visit. It had gone down almost too smoothly, and she'd apologized over and over for drinking so much of it. Margaret had laughed it off, saying it was worth it to see Sarah relax for once. Sarah had been very strict with herself since then, having a maximum of two glasses per evening any time there was wine in the house. Now, Donny opened the bottle, and Sarah opened the balcony door and pulled out the chairs.

There was a knock at the door, and an announcement that room service had arrived. "I'll tell them they've got the wrong room," Donny said, but when he opened the door, the man on the other side made a sweeping gesture with one hand and said, "Compliments of Ms. Margaret Bradley."

He removed the cover from the tray to reveal an impressive lineup of cheeses and crackers and grapes and strawberries.

"Wow," Sarah said. "She really went all-out."

"She did," Donny said.

He carried the tray out to the table on the balcony, and Sarah grabbed the wine and glasses. They arranged everything on the table, and then sat down. Sarah sighed, more loudly than she'd meant to.

"Everything okay?" Donny said.

"Yes," Sarah said. "Absolutely. I just feel so relaxed. You know? I guess I really needed this."

"Me, too," Donny said. "It's been a great day to unwind. Think the wine's had long enough to breathe?"

When he'd filled the glasses, he handed her one and held up the other. "Cheers to a great day."

"Cheers," Sarah said.

She watched as Donny took a drink, and then, without warning, a memory came striding to the forefront of her mind: the two of them, at seventeen, on a picnic blanket by the creek. Why she'd thought it was a good idea to disrobe in the middle of a field was beyond her now, but that was beside the point, wasn't it? Donny had managed to finagle a bottle of Boone's Farm wine. Was it strawberry-flavored? Sarah couldn't remember now.

Very creative for a seventeen-year-old, Donny had trickled the wine down Sarah's torso and licked it off, repeatedly, trickling it lower and lower each time until he was between her legs.

The present-day Sarah gave a little shudder.

"You're thinking about the Boone's Farm, aren't you?" Donny said.

Sarah was glad twilight had finally started settling in; maybe he wouldn't see the blush that bloomed fiercely on her cheeks. Rather than give herself away further by croaking out an answer, she nodded.

He chuckled. "What a day."

Then, because she'd had wine and she was relaxed and she wasn't thinking about yesterday or tomorrow or Donny leaving or Amelia growing up, she said exactly what came to mind, which was, "We could never do that with Margaret's wine."

There was a beat of silence, and Sarah immediately second-guessed herself. Why had she said that? Things were just starting to feel normal. But then Donny said. "I suppose not."

Sarah exhaled. She was about to speak, about to change the subject and erase the tension she'd caused, but Donny beat her to it.

He said, "But what if we ordered another bottle?"

Every single nerve ending in Sarah's body went on high alert. Her brain went into overdrive, as if someone had pressed the accelerator and the tires were throwing gravel all over the place. Did he mean it? Did he want to have sex with her? And if so, did that mean he wanted to try again? If not, could she live with the aftermath? Was he saying this only because they'd been drinking?

She knew this was a Moment. With a capital M. The way she

responded here had the potential to fix everything or ruin any chance they ever had of staying together, permanently.

"Would you like that?"

In a move so unexpected it made Sarah laugh out loud, Donny grabbed her hand and put it on his crotch, where she could feel an erection straining against his shorts.

"What do you think?"

"Wow," was all she could manage.

"I'll call room service," he said, "but you have to answer the door. For obvious reasons."

Sarah nodded, and he got up, quickly, and rushed back into the room. "You're like a teenage boy," she called after him.

She heard him laugh before he picked up the phone. In the few moments it took him to order, Sarah wondered whether they'd change their minds when the wine actually showed up. How long did it take for room service to arrive? Ten minutes? Thirty? It was just a bottle of wine, so no cooking required. And it was the middle of the week, so the kitchen probably wasn't too busy.

Donny came back out and sat down. "Can you wait five minutes?"

"Five?" Sarah practically choked. Was she ready for this?

"That's what he said."

Someone knocked. "Room service."

Donny looked at Sarah and grinned that same grin from earlier. He inclined his head as if to remind her that she'd agreed to answer the door, and she stood up and took a deep breath.

"Sarah," he said, grabbing her wrist as she started to walk past him. She paused and he said, "Don't be nervous. This is going to be fun."

She took another deep breath, nodded, and went to retrieve the bottle. When she turned around, Donny was standing in the doorway to the balcony, leaning against the doorjamb.

"Want me to open that?"

She knew he was giving her control of the situation. He was offering her a chance to back out. He'd probably ask her permission at every phase. She wasn't sure whether she liked that. Part of her wanted him to just take control, to stop asking her, to want her so badly he couldn't stop himself. But he was probably afraid to.

So she said, "Yes," and left it at that.

"Should we let it breathe?" he said, giving her the opportunity to put off the action.

"Oh, I don't think we need to," she said.

"There's just one problem," he said.

Sarah's stomach dropped. She licked her lips. Maybe this wasn't a good idea.

"We're both still dressed."

Now, he came towards her, took the wine out of her hands, and set it on the nightstand. He brought his hands up to cup her face and kissed her once, long and deep, before running his fingertips down her arms. He grasped the edge of her shirt and pulled it over her head. He unhooked her bra clasp, nudged the straps off her shoulders, and then his hands found her breasts. She gasped. He kissed her again. She removed his shirt and unhooked his belt. He stepped out of his pants and unbuttoned her shorts.

It was like a dance, she thought, one to which she'd almost forgotten the steps. They were coming back to her now, in bits and pieces, flashes of sensory memories: the feel of Donny's skin under her palms, the way the muscles in his shoulders felt as he brought his hands up her back, his unshaven cheek against her face.

Donny backed up towards the bed, and when Sarah laid down, he laid down next to her. They were face to face. He tucked a strand of hair behind her ear and whispered, "You're so beautiful."

For once, Sarah didn't brush off the compliment, because she actually felt beautiful. After spending this day with Donny in the sun and the fresh air, she felt like the woman she used to be.

"Shall we?" Donny reached across her to pick up the wine bottle.

Then, instead of pouring it over her body like she'd expected him to, he took a big swig and wiped his mouth with the back of his hand.

"Nice," she said. "Really classy."

"Want some?"

"Sure." Sarah followed Donny's example and took a drink straight out of the bottle.

"That's how we used to do it with the Boone's farm, remember?"

"Boy, do I," Sarah said. "I haven't felt this young in ages."

Sarah was overcome with laughter, the kind that bubbled up from deep inside her belly. Donny took the bottle from her and took another drink, which only made her laugh harder. She shook her head when he offered it to her again, and he set it on the nightstand. He kissed her again, so thoroughly that she stopped laughing and kissed him back.

"There," he said. "That's more like it."

This time when he picked up the wine, he did drizzle it, pouring it between her breasts so that it ran down her stomach. She made a tiny yelping sound as some of the cool liquid ran down her sides, and Donny expertly licked it off, sending shivers skittering over her skin. So it *was* possible to recapture some of the passion of their teen years, Sarah thought. She ran her fingers through his hair as he continued to lick the wine off her torso.

Although, as kids, they'd spent what felt like hours going through that bottle of Boone's Farm, Donny seemed anxious to get down to the real business, and he brought his face up to Sarah's after only a few moments, entering her with an urgency that almost made her explode right there on the spot. They began to move together, the rhythm as natural as if they'd done it thousands of times, and as new as if it were the first. When Donny looked into her eyes, Sarah felt her own tears sliding down her temples.

And a moment later, they both shuddered in release.

———

SARAH'S PHONE rang at midnight, startling both Sarah and Donny out of a coma-like sleep. She startled awake, and the first cognitive thought she had was that it felt so nice to be slung over Donny's body, inhaling his scent. Then she realized that a phone call in the middle of the night probably meant disaster of some kind, and her heart started racing and she climbed out of bed and fumbled around in the dark to find it.

"Who is it?" Donny said, his voice thick.

"Margaret," Sarah said, both in response to Donny and as a greeting.

Her sister's voice came through the earpiece, loud and agitated. "Sarah. Don't panic."

"That's not a great way to start a conversation. Panic ensues."

She was facing the mirror and she watched Donny's reflection as he sat up and rubbed his face.

"I know," Margaret said. "Everything's fine. You don't need to come home."

"Um," Sarah said. "Then why are you calling?"

"Amelia's in the hospital. It's not serious—"

"Wait, what? What happened?"

"It's just a broken arm, Sarah," Margaret said at the same time as Donny said, "What's going on?"

"Hannah and I have it handled. I just thought you should know."

"How in the world did that happen, Margaret?" Sarah pulled the cord out of her phone and flipped on the lights in the hotel room. Donny squinted. When Sarah started pulling on her clothes from the night before, Donny did the same, watching her. Sarah put the phone on speaker.

"The details are still, ah, fuzzy," Margaret said.

Silence.

"What?!"

"She was with Luke."

"This late? You know she has a curfew."

"I know," Margaret said. "Eleven. This, ah, incident, apparently happened around ten p.m."

"And you waited two hours to call me?" Sarah said.

"Ahh," Margaret said. "Well, it took Amelia a while to call us. She didn't want us to worry. And then we took her in, and decided to get x-ray results before calling you. I mean, if it was just a sprain, we wouldn't have bothered you, but it's broken, so..."

"We'll be there in a couple of hours. We're leaving in five."

"Sarah, you don't have to—"

Sarah hung up.

"Amelia broke her arm," she said to Donny.

He sighed. "Oh! Well, that's a lot better news than I expected. How bad is it?"

Sarah laughed, without humor. "Isn't that like asking how pregnant someone is? Either it's broken or it's not broken. Honestly, I don't know. I didn't give Margaret a chance to say."

She sat down on the bed, and Donny came to sit beside her. He put his arm around her and she leaned against him. "Maybe we should call Amelia before we go rushing home," he said. "I mean, she's in good hands. Your sisters are there. It doesn't sound life threatening."

"The reasonable side of me hears you," Sarah said. "But the rest of me is panicking. I mean, she needs us, doesn't she? She probably wants her parents. Auntie Hannah and Aunt Margaret are great, but they're not the same as Mom and Dad."

"They're not," Donny agreed. "But she's older now. She's going to be in college. We won't be able to run to her every time she has a mishap."

"But we can, this time. We're right here. I keep picturing her lying there in a hospital bed, and I just feel like we need to be there."

Donny sighed again. "I'll call her."

When he got up, she did, too, and started packing her things. Her movements were jerky and robotic. Why had she thought leaving

Amelia would be a good idea? She was a parent, first and foremost. And here she was, drinking wine, having a good time, getting drunk, having sex—really, *really*, good sex—while her daughter was suffering in an emergency room. Without her mother.

Donny's phone rang. "Amelia."

Sarah rushed over to Donny's side. He put the phone on speaker. And Amelia's voice came through the earpiece, sounding much differently than Sarah had expected.

"Dad!"

She sounded … fine. Not sad or distraught or in pain or lonely.

"How are you, Amelia?"

"I'm okay, Dad. I'm on drugs for the pain and they gave me something stronger so they can set the bone. I think it's starting to kick in. Listen—am I on speaker?"

Donny looked at Sarah, licked his lips, looked pointedly back at his phone's screen, and said, "Yep."

There was a pause, and then Amelia said, "Listen, you guys. Don't come back here. You just finish out your overnight. Enjoy yourselves and I'll see you in the morning. I've got Aunt Margaret and Auntie Hannah here."

"How bad is the break?"

"Clean through one bone," Amelia said in a voice so loopy Sarah had to smile. "I won't need surgery, or anything. They're just going to set it and put a cast on."

"What happened?" Donny said.

"It was so stupid, Dad. I've dismounted from a horse a million times, right? Luke and I went for a nighttime ride and we were just getting back. We were going to clean up the horses and then he was going to bring me home. On time for curfew, even. See? I was being responsible. When we got to the barn, I went to dismount and I slipped right off the horse. I braced myself, of course."

"Of course," Donny said.

"I'm fine, though, really. You and Mom should go back to bed, sleep in, have nice s—a nice breakfast in the morning."

After a short pause, Amelia said, "Mom's right there, isn't she? She's listening, right now. She can't help herself."

"Hi," Sarah said, infusing her voice with way too much cheer. "You're right. I can't help myself. Are you in much pain?"

"Ha!" Amelia said. "What is pain? I'm on some wonderful drugs, Mom. I can't feel anything."

Sarah turned to look at Donny and whispered (loudly), "See? She's on drugs. She doesn't even realize she needs us."

"I can hear you, Mom," Amelia said. Donny smiled. "Seriously. I'm fine. And I'm going to be in college soon. You guys won't be able to run to me every time something happens."

Donny gave Sarah a look that said, "See?"

"I know," Sarah said. "You're right. But it would just make me feel better."

Amelia sighed. "I'm a big girl, Mom."

"I know that."

Sarah knew that. But all the what-ifs were running through her mind now, bumping up against one another in panic-inducing chaos. What if Amelia had a reaction to the medication? What if the break turned out to be worse than they thought, and she needed surgery? What if the doctor wasn't friendly? (Although, to be honest, if anyone could bring out the friendliness in someone, it was Margaret, Sarah thought.) What if Amelia wanted her favorite coffee drink and Hannah or Margaret didn't know they had to order it stirred, not layered? What if she sounded happy only because she was drugged up? What if, as soon as the drugs wore off, Amelia needed her parents, and they weren't there?

"We'll come up there right after breakfast tomorrow," Donny was saying. "We love you."

"Okay, Dad," Amelia said. "What happened, did you tie Mom up, or something? Put duct tape over her mouth? I know she wants to come up here like, right now."

"I'm here," Sarah said. "We love you."

After a long pause, Amelia said, "Love you guys, too."

When Donny set his phone down on top of the dresser, Sarah went back to rushing around the room, collecting her things.

"What are you doing?" Donny said.

She could hear the exasperation in his voice. "We have go to," she said.

"Sarah, she's fine. Let's just relax and enjoy the rest of our time here."

"I can't. I can't relax knowing that our daughter is in the hospital."

"It's a broken arm, not a head injury! She'll be out of the hospital by the time we get there."

"Will she? What if something goes wrong?"

"What if nothing goes wrong?" Donny said.

Sarah huffed out a sigh. Donny came to stand behind her. In the mirror, she could see his face, and his hands wrapping around her upper arms. His eyes met hers, and he said, "I promise. She's fine. Come back to bed."

She nodded, and let him pull her gently backwards until they reached the bed. Donny turned off the lights. Then he took off his pants and lay down. Sarah lay down, too, but she remained fully clothed. The silence was unbearable.

"What if she needs us?" Sarah whispered.

"She's fine. Go to sleep."

"I can't, Donny. We have to go. I'm going to go. You can come with me, or you can stay here and I'll come get you in the morning."

Which, Sarah knew, was stupid, because it was a two-hours' drive each way. He wouldn't agree to that.

Donny sighed, loudly. Sarah got up and went to the table where she'd set her suitcase. She zipped it up and slipped into her shoes.

"Are you coming?"

Donny sighed again.

"I'm coming."

He packed in silence while she waited by the door, barely able to resist tapping her toe in impatience. When he was ready, he simply walked past her and out the door, still silent. Then, without waiting for her, he walked down the hall.

"You're angry," she said when they finally reached the truck and got in.

"I just feel like you're overreacting," Donny said.

"How can you say that?" Sarah said. "Our daughter is in the hospital."

Donny shook his head. "I'm not going to keep going around and around with you, Sarah. Yes, our daughter is in the hospital. For a broken arm. It's minor. She'll survive until tomorrow, almost certainly."

"It's her first broken bone," Sarah said. "She's probably scared."

"Did she sound scared?"

"No, but she was on drugs. What happens when they wear off?"

"She's exhausted. She falls asleep, and you get up early to make her a huge breakfast, and she sleeps in, only to get up, have a bowl of cereal while your fancy breakfast gets cold, and she leaves the house to hang out with her new boyfriend, who signs her cast. With a heart doodle. And we're both left wondering why we rushed home. That's how it is with teenagers."

Well. That was a point. Maybe rushing back was a bad idea. Maybe it was unnecessary. But still. Sarah would feel better knowing Amelia was okay. Seeing her daughter in the flesh.

Sarah's eyes were gritty, and she closed them momentarily. When she opened them again, she sneaked a glance at Donny's profile, and guilt overwhelmed her.

This whole situation was proving his point: she couldn't be an attentive mother *and* a good wife. Not at the same time, anyway. No wonder he wanted to leave her.

There they'd been, smack in the middle of a wonderful night together, and she'd panicked. She'd ruined everything. The symbolism here was unmistakable. And the irony stood out even more: she'd finally, finally taken the time and put in the effort to concentrate on her marriage, and Life threw her a curveball.

It was no surprise Mama Katherine had stayed single all those years, as she raised the girls. If you nurtured your children, your marriage fell apart. And if you nurtured your marriage, you couldn't be there for your children. Sarah was living proof of that. Why had she tried so hard to get Donny to change his mind about leaving her? Now she was hurting him again. She should have known this wouldn't work out, that she'd revert back to being a mother, first. She'd always be a mother, first. With that thought fresh in her mind, she rested her head against the window and fell asleep.

CHAPTER TWENTY-TWO

Amelia was fine.

When they arrived at the hospital, Sarah rushed into the Emergency Department and saw her daughter through a window. Her natural inclination was to run to her, to embrace her. But she held back and watched her for a moment, first. Rather than looking pale and tiny in the hospital bed, like Sarah had imagined her, Amelia was sitting in a chair, her cheeks rosy and her eyes bright. She was wearing her regular clothes: her dark jeans and the yellow t-shirt they'd picked out at the mall before coming here. Yes, her arm was in a cast—she'd chosen blue and yellow, her new school's colors—but she didn't look upset in any way.

She was chatting up one of the nurses, whose smile was just about as friendly as it could be. Margaret was sitting on the edge of the hospital bed, Amelia's jacket draped over her arm.

All at once, Sarah's worries dissolved, and guilt rushed in to take its place. Amelia and Donny were right: Amelia could handle this on her own. It was just a broken arm. The incident was over. And so was the romantic overnight getaway.

"What are you guys doing?" Hannah had come up behind them. Sarah turned to greet her and saw disappointment on her sister's face.

"Wow," Sarah said. "You don't look happy to see me."

Hannah sighed. Why was everyone sighing?

"Margaret told you we had this handled, that's all," she said. She held up a paper cup as if to illustrate that point. "And we wanted you to enjoy the rest of your date."

"It's hard to enjoy a date when your daughter's in the emergency room," Sarah said.

Now Luke walked up behind Hannah. He was carrying a stack of Styrofoam to-go boxes. "I thought you guys were on a date," he said.

Sarah, not knowing what to say, shook her head and walked into Amelia's room, thinking that at least one person would be happy to see her. But Amelia's reaction was similar to everyone else's. Her eyebrows furrowed together, and she looked at Margaret, who shrugged, and then through the window at her dad, and then back at Sarah.

"What are you guys doing here?" she said. "I told you I was fine. Look. We're already about to head home."

Now Sarah sighed. "I thought we should be here, that's all."

A little gratitude would be nice.

Luke, Hannah, and Donny came into the room, and Amelia's face transformed. "Oh, Luke, you're my hero."

He returned her smile. "Only because I have a cheeseburger in hand."

"Should we blow this joint?" Margaret said. "We can eat when we get home."

"Luke and I'll ride with Auntie Hannah and Aunt Margaret," Amelia said to Sarah. "We can't fit in Mama Katherine's truck with you and Dad, and you guys can pretend you're still on your date. Or you can drive back down to Jackson Hole and pretend this never happened."

With that, everyone else filed out of the room and into the parking lot.

When Sarah and Donny were safely inside the truck with the doors closed, Sarah closed her eyes. "Is it just me, or does everyone seem annoyed that we're here?"

"It's not just you," Donny said.

He didn't elaborate; just pulled out of the parking spot and started driving.

The drive back to Mama Katherine's was short, and when they arrived, everyone was already inside, eating.

"Sorry we didn't get you guys food," Margaret said, and Amelia added, "We thought you were still in Jackson Hole."

"Is it a crime that I was worried about my daughter?" Sarah said. Her voice was rising to a crazy pitch, but she didn't care. "I was worried. Can't you understand that? No, you can't, because none of you have children."

This was enough to make Hannah and Margaret, and even Luke, look guilty. But not Amelia. Amelia said, "Dad has a child, Mom. And I know he doesn't want to be here. I know he'd rather be in Jackson Hole, sleeping, looking forward to a nice breakfast with you. We were all looking forward to the two of you having a nice time together. We've been planning this for, like, a week! But like always, you couldn't just be normal. You had to come back. Even though we told you not to. You ruined everything."

Now Amelia was in tears.

And Sarah was flabbergasted. "*You* worked on this?" She looked at each of her sisters in turn, hoping to get some kind of confirmation, but their gazes were fixed, quite firmly, on their plates.

"Amelia," she said. "What do you mean, *we* have been planning this?"

"Aunt Margaret, Auntie Hannah, Mama Katherine and me. We have been planning the date night, okay? It was a last-ditch effort to get you and Dad back together. And you messed it up. You *ruined* it."

Her glare was accusatory, her eyes rimmed with red and her cheeks bright pink. Although the words were the same—"You ruined it"—as they were when Sarah had accidentally kicked over the block house three-year-old Amelia was building for her stuffed mouse, that tiny little girl was nowhere to be seen.

Behind Sarah, Donny cleared his throat. "I, uh, think we should talk about this in private, later. It's almost three a.m. Why don't you guys all finish eating and get to bed. I'm going to hit the hay, myself."

Everyone filed out, and someone turned off the light, undoubtedly assuming nobody was staying up. The moonlight shone through the window, casting blocks of light on the table. Sarah put her head down and closed her eyes. Just as she was dozing off, someone came back in. Although she hoped it was Donny, she felt profound relief when she saw that it was Mama Katherine.

"Lots of excitement this evening," Mama Katherine said.

"Yeah, you could say that."

"Tea?"

"No, thanks."

Mama Katherine acknowledged that with a grunt. "I think we still have an unopened bottle of wine in the pantry. Let me check."

She came back to the table with a bottle and an opener, which she handed to Sarah, and two glasses, which she set in the middle of the table. Sarah opened the wine and poured it.

"To excitement," Mama said.

Sarah inclined her head, tapped Mama's glass with her own, and took a mouthful of wine.

"Why'd you come back?" Mama said.

Sarah shrugged. "I don't know. It was stupid."

"It wasn't stupid," Mama said. "But I can tell from the way you're acting that you're disappointed in yourself as much as the rest of us are disappointed in you."

"You, too?" Sarah had thought she had at least one ally in Mama Katherine, who, as she made clear in her journal, was a mother above all else, but maybe she was wrong.

"Honey," Mama said, and Sarah felt her eyes start to sting. "You're going to have to let go at some point. Letting go doesn't mean giving up or not being a great mother to your daughter. Amelia is a butterfly, emerging from her cocoon. That cocoon is sitting in the palm of your hand. Letting go simply means uncurling your fingers, just a bit, so that she can finish emerging and spread her wings. Yes, you helped create those wings. You were a huge part of that. And that's even more reason to watch them sparkle in the sunlight."

Sarah put her face in her hands. "I know you're right. I know you are. And I think that's why I'm so disappointed in myself for rushing back here. Not only is she fine, but she also doesn't even want me here."

"It's not that she doesn't want you—"

"Yes, it is," Sarah said.

"Okay," Mama Katherine said. "You're right. It is. She doesn't want you here, because she wants you in Jackson Hole, making magic with her father. More than anything, she wants her parents to be together. She wants to feel like she has a home to return to. No matter where that is, it's not home, to her, unless the two of you are together there."

"And now I've ruined any chance of that happening."

"I wouldn't say you've ruined it," Mama Katherine said, taking another sip of wine. "But you've definitely decreased your chances. I'd like to see what you can do to fix this."

"Is there *anything* I can do to fix it?"

"You're going to have to try," Mama said. "And if all else fails, remember this: you did what you thought was right. No one can blame you for that."

Sarah, deciding it was now or never, took the plunge. "Is that what you did, Mama? Is that why you left Philip Carlisle and moved to Wyoming?"

For a split second, Mama Katherine looked surprised. But when

Sarah pulled the journal out of her purse and slid it across the table, her expression shifted to one of resignation.

"You found Pauline," she said. Her expression wistful, she picked up the journal and rubbed her thumb over its cover. "Where did you find this?"

"It was in a recipe box I bought at the farmer's market."

Mama nodded. "Did you read the whole thing?"

Her throat was clogged with emotion, and Sarah felt like crying, herself.

"Not quite. I just read the part where Hazel—where you plan to leave California. But I put two and two together, Mama. Have you ever told Hannah?"

"No. I never told any of you. I felt like keeping it hidden away was the only way to stop myself from experiencing that tragedy, day after day, over and over again. I blamed myself, Sarah, for what happened to Benny. I couldn't bear to think of it, much less to talk about it. But my story's nearing its end, and maybe it's time I tell Hannah, and Margaret, too. I'll admit, I'm afraid of what they'll think of me."

"You did what you thought was right," Sarah said.

Mama Katherine nodded. "I did. And whether it really was right remains to be seen."

Sarah and Mama Katherine had stayed up talking for a while, refilling their wine glasses until the bottle was empty. When Mama Katherine shook the last drops from the bottle, she laughed her loud, rowdy laugh and pointed at Sarah.

"You're probably three sheets to the wind, aren't you, with your three hours' sleep?"

"Absolutely," Sarah said.

It was sometime before five a.m. when Sarah sneaked back into the room she shared with Amelia and fell into a dead sleep.

CHAPTER TWENTY-THREE

By the time Sarah woke up, it was broad daylight. She had no idea what time it was. Amelia wasn't in bed and Sarah didn't know how in the world she'd slept through her getting up. She wondered if Amelia was in any pain, although the doctor at the hospital had promised the medication he prescribed would keep her comfortable.

Sarah, herself, was far from comfortable. A headache pounded on both sides of her head, just behind her temples. She'd probably had one too many glasses of wine and several too few hours of sleep. Although she'd like to stay in bed and avoid even thinking about everything that transpired last night, she dragged herself to an upright position. Then she laid back down.

A single knock announced someone's arrival, and Mama Katherine bustled in with a mug of coffee in hand.

"I thought you might be needing this, seeing as it's noon and you're still in bed."

"How are you feeling?" Sarah said. "You seem pretty chipper."

"Don't sound so dark and gloomy about it," Mama Katherine said. "But I'm feeling pretty chipper. That wine put me straight to sleep and I slept like a dog."

"Like John Wayne?"

"No," Mama Katherine said. She sat down on the edge of the bed and handed Sarah the coffee. "Like some other dog. Anyway. You'll want to know that Donny's gone."

Sarah's world tilted. She took a drink. "Gone? Like, he went to the store? Or gone, like he left?"

The only other definition for "gone" was "dead," and she assumed that wasn't what Mama Katherine meant.

"Gone, like he left," Mama Katherine said. "He left a note."

"Well, I hope so, seeing as we're supposed to take our daughter to college in just a few days."

"Note said he'd be back in time for that."

"Humpf."

"I thought the same," Mama Katherine said.

"I want you to say something like, 'You had one little screw-up, and he's throwing everything away.' But I had more than one screw-up," Sarah said.

"This was a big one," Mama Katherine said.

"Well, you didn't have to agree with me. Is anyone speaking to me? Besides you."

"You'll have to find out for yourself."

Sarah sighed. "I guess I'd better get up. And brush my teeth."

"I guess you'd better."

Mama left, but not before kissing Sarah on the top of her head. Sarah sat in bed and sipped her coffee. And she thought. She thought about how she had ruined Sarah and Donny's Big Day. Amelia was right: Sarah had made the wrong choice by coming back when Amelia had assured both her and Donny that she was okay.

Sarah reminded herself of all the "what ifs" she'd contemplated in the twenty seconds it took her to decide to leave Jackson Hole, and then she realized it: there was one big "what if" she hadn't considered, the biggest one of all: What if Amelia didn't need her?

Then, there was the follow-up: What if Donny *did*? What if Donny needed her more than Amelia did?

Why hadn't she made that connection? How stupid *was* she? Too stupid to deserve a man like Donny. And now everything was ruined, anyway. He'd left Mama Katherine's house, she knew, just knew, that he was gone from her life forever. He had wanted some sort of proof that she could be a good wife, and she'd gone and proven otherwise.

If anything could make this situation worse, Sarah realized when she eventually made her way out to the kitchen, it was Donny's note, impersonal and completely without detail: *Heading out. Be back before Friday.*

And if anything could make this situation worse than worse, it was the fact that everyone else had left the house, too.

"Your sisters went to the farmers market," Mama said. "And Amelia went back over to Luke's. Glutton for punishment."

"Please tell me they don't plan on riding horses."

"I think they plan on having wild, kinky sex," Mama said, and Sarah rolled her eyes even as a smile crept in. "I saved you some pancakes."

Sarah was going to weigh a thousand pounds if she kept eating pancakes at this rate, but she sat down and ate every last crumb anyway, sweeping up every remnant of syrup with the final bite. Where could Donny have gone? Maybe he was house-hunting. Their failed Big Day had cemented his decision to buy in Wyoming and move back up here. He wanted the house to be bought by the time they came back from taking Amelia to school. Or maybe he just needed a break from her, and from her family, and he'd taken a quick day trip. Or three-day trip. Or maybe he never wanted to see her again, and was only forcing himself to come back so that he wouldn't disappoint Amelia.

"Stop tormenting yourself," Mama Katherine said.

"How did you know?" Sarah said.

"I always know," Mama said. "It is what it is, right? At this point there's nothing you can do about it."

"I suppose you're right."

"Best thing you can do is—"

"Keep myself busy. I know. Let's go work in the garden."

Mama Katherine sighed. "I haven't been wanting to tell your sister this. You know, Hannah loves that garden. But I just don't know if I want it anymore."

"But I thought the garden was your pride and joy."

"It's my pride," Mama said. "It is. It's beautiful. I could feed the whole neighborhood on my zucchini plants alone. But lately, it's not my joy. These old knees are tired."

"We could get you a—"

"A gardening mat, yes. Your sister bought me one. I think she loves the garden more than I do, if that's possible."

"Have you told her?"

"Hardly," Mama Katherine said. "I'm afraid she'll think I'm on death's doorstep."

That was true.

"Well, I'll leave that part to you," Sarah said. "I'll go work on it for now and when they get back you can claim responsibility for all of my manual labor."

"Thanks." Mama Katherine offered Sarah a wry smile. "I think.

Although, I have a feeling she'll know it was you, not me, who got so much done."

Alone in the garden, Sarah knelt down between the stalks of corn and cried. Her head was pounding, and her husband was gone. Even though he'd promised to come back before Friday, she knew she'd lost him for good. Tears plopped down onto her jeans and onto the dirt.

What would she do, now? The logistics of it seemed impossible, insurmountable. Donny had probably already started packing his belongings, but the house was still full of their stuff. She would go back to Arizona, alone. She would have to pack up the kitchen, the dishes, the silverware.

Sarah started pulling the tiny weeds that pushed up through the soil near the roots of the corn plants. Surprisingly, the activity was immediately soothing.

Their wedding photos were on the mantel, and all the photos of Amelia as a baby, a toddler, and a little girl. There was the one where she was missing her two front teeth, and the one where she was standing next to the fish she'd caught (Donny's hand, holding the fish by the tail, was in the forefront of the picture). That fish was so tiny, but the glee on her face was almost palpable. Sarah remembered laughing with Donny that day; first, when Amelia reeled it in, then when she jumped up and down with excitement as Donny pulled the hook out of its mouth, and then when she reached for it and refused to touch it repeatedly.

Having finished pulling the weeds in the first row, Sarah crawled around the end plant and to the beginning of the next row. Here in Mama's garden, Sarah imagined being alone in the house, wrapping those frames in newspaper or bubble wrap, setting them in a cardboard box. Or maybe she should offer Donny some of them.

And what about the gifts they'd received at their wedding? Granted, that was twenty years ago. Donny wouldn't want any of those wine glasses. The only thing he really loved was the cookie jar his Aunt Susie had given them. It was shaped like a rooster. He'd want that at his house. Amelia loved that thing.

Sarah was starting to sweat. Volunteering to come out here in the heat of the afternoon had probably been a dumb idea. She sat back on her heels and wiped the sweat from her forehead. Just as she was contemplating going inside to get some water and aspirin, she heard Amelia's voice. Although she couldn't quite make out the words, she could tell Amelia was talking to someone—probably Luke. They were coming around the corner.

Sarah held her breath. The last time they'd spoken, Amelia had been so mad at her… and she'd been mad at Amelia, too. The anger had dissipated. She could hardly be upset with Amelia for wanting her parents to get back together. Maybe if she just hunkered down here between the corn rows, Amelia and Luke would walk right by.

Wishful thinking: Amelia spotted her right away, and Luke, catching on quickly, said good-bye and made a quick about face.

"Hey, Mom."

"Hey. How's your arm feeling?"

Amelia held up her cast. "It's okay. It's throbbing a little, but I can handle it. Aunt Margaret offered to give me some whiskey but I turned her down."

"Very funny," Sarah said.

Amelia fiddled with her cast and swung one leg forward and backward, kicking up little plumes of dust.

"Sweetheart," Sarah said. "I'm really sorry about rushing back here and ruining the date night with your dad. I was just worried."

"I told you guys I was fine," Amelia said. She must have heard the heat that crept into her voice, because she cleared her throat and said, "I understand, Mom. But you and Dad spending time together was really, really important to me. More important than a broken arm. I told Aunt Margaret we shouldn't call you, but she was afraid you'd be mad if you came home and I had a cast and no one had told you."

"She was right," Sarah said. "I am sorry. I just thought you needed me."

When Amelia took a breath as if to speak, Sarah held up a hand. "Let me amend that. I wanted you to need me. You said you were fine, and I believed you. I wanted you to need me because I'm your mom."

Amelia nodded. Now she was looking at her feet. "I know. I just wanted, more than anything, for you and Dad to be together. I wanted it so much. I guess it wasn't very reasonable of me to interfere."

"It was fine, Amelia," Sarah said. "Really. It was fine. If Dad and I aren't meant to be together, there's nothing you or I can do about it. I have a feeling his mind was made up before we even got here."

Even as she said it, she remembered the night before. She remembered the way he'd smiled at her when she agreed to order that bottle of wine from room service. She remembered the way his tongue felt on her lower stomach. She remembered the way he'd felt inside her, moving in their own rhythm, his lips skimming hers, his breath coming fast.

There was something there. It wasn't over. At least, it hadn't been.

And then she'd lost her mind and insisted on coming back to Walker for Amelia's broken arm.

"What was I thinking?"

"I know," Amelia said. "I said the same thing to Aunt Margaret and Auntie Hannah when you showed up at the hospital. I knew you wouldn't be able to stay away. I love you so much, Mom. I really do. But I was really, really disappointed in you."

At this, Sarah laughed out loud. She'd said the very same thing to Amelia on a few occasions: when Amelia, at age ten, had some friends over for a slumber party and fed them ice cream sundaes at one a.m.—after Sarah had told them lights out was ten p.m.; at sixteen, when she and Payton sneaked a couple of boys into the house after Sarah and Donny went to sleep, not realizing they'd gone into their bedroom only to give the girls the run of the house. They heard the back door slide open, and Donny descended on the group like a—well, Sarah thought now, like an angry father who didn't want a bunch of boys in the house after dark.

"I'm so sorry," Sarah said. "I know how much it meant to you. Your dad and I love you, you know."

"I know," Amelia said. "And I'm sorry he's leaving. I feel like it's my fault. If I hadn't been such a needy kid, this wouldn't be happening."

"Oh, Amelia," Sarah said. "It's not about that at all. It's about me. I neglected our marriage. I guess, subconsciously, I felt like I had to be one thing or the other—mother or wife. My own mother—not Mama Katherine, but my first mother—was terrible, Amelia. I haven't told you much about her, but she was awful. I mean, you thought it was bad if I ran out of time to cook and fed you frozen pizza. My biological mother didn't cook a day in her life. So when I had you, I promised myself I'd be the best mother ever. Ever! And I let my marriage go. It's not about you. Not at all. It's just part of my own life story, I guess."

"I'm angry at Dad," Amelia said. "I'm angry that he said he wanted to leave, and that he's not here, now. Where did he even *go*?"

"I don't know," Sarah said. "I know it's hard to understand right now. And it hurts me, too. But he'll always be your dad, even if he's not my husband."

———

THE NEXT TWO days passed in a blur for Sarah. She'd always imagined spending the last of her pre-college time with Amelia doing something fun, together. She'd pictured them eating ice cream on a bench in town, the sun shining overhead. Or drinking Shirley Temples at the bar of a fancy restaurant. Not that they ever drank Shirley Temples, but the image was nice. Lovely, really. Maybe they would walk along the creek one last time.

But Amelia was like a ghost: elusive and intangible. More like an idea than a real, live human. She woke up early and snagged breakfast from the kitchen before going to Luke's house. The two of them might stop by during the day to get something to eat, but they were gone before anyone could nail them down. Sometimes they were at Mama Katherine's for dinner and sometimes they weren't.

Which not only perfectly matched Donny's description of typical teenager behavior, but also meant Sarah was left to her own devices. The days stretched into eternities—eternities filled with incessant mind chatter. Why had Sarah insisted on coming back from Jackson Hole? Why hadn't she listened to the people in her life who loved her —Margaret, Hannah, Amelia? What was she thinking? She could just kick herself.

She imagined Donny wandering through empty houses, picturing himself alone in them, feeling free in his impending solitude ... while she remained here, dreading that same solitude like someone dreads getting an arm amputated.

Finally, it was Friday morning. When Margaret found Sarah walking along the creek by herself, she said, "You know, Sarah, this could be a turning point for you. It could be an opportunity for reinvention."

Even though Sarah said, "I don't want to reinvent myself. I just want to be the self I was before all of this happened," she thought about what that would really look like.

Visions presented themselves: she could be Sarah, the runner, clad in leggings and a visor, or Sarah, the volunteer, walking rowdy dogs at the humane society. When she shared these visions with Margaret, Margaret laughed. As if Sarah were joking. When Sarah didn't even crack a smile, Margaret said, "Well, that's not exactly what I meant. I meant an inner transformation."

"I don't even know what that means."

Margaret sighed. "I don't, either. I guess I said you should reinvent yourself, but I actually don't know the first thing about it. I'm in for a major reinvention, myself, and the prospect is scary as hell. I thought it would be less scary if we were reinventing at the same time."

"Yours is different," Sarah said.

"Is it?" Margaret said. She picked up a rock and tossed it into the creek.

"Someone made my decision for me," Sarah said.

"Mine's worse," Margaret said. She started walking back towards the house, and Sarah followed her. "Nature made it, and set it into motion long before I even knew about it. It's so cruel. It's like the taking back of a gift—a gift you didn't realize was wonderful until it was too late."

Just when Sarah was thinking that maybe their transformations weren't too different, after all, tires crunched on the gravel. A pickup truck—a brand new one, judging by pristine paint job and sleek profile—pulled into the driveway. When the motor turned off, the drivers door opened and Donny stepped out. Sarah turned to look at her sister, to gauge her reactions, but Margaret was gone.

Donny approached her. "Like it?" he said, gesturing to the truck, grinning like he hadn't just taken off for two days without warning.

He held up the key fob and pressed a button, and the truck chirped.

"It's nice," Sarah said.

"I got a great deal on it."

"You bought it?" Sarah said.

"Yeah," Donny said. "I didn't steal it."

Why was he being so good-natured?

"I guess I thought it was a rental or something."

"Ah," he said. "Nope. Bought it."

Normally, he wouldn't have made this purchase without consulting her, but, she reminded herself, this wasn't normally.

"Does it drive nice?"

"Oh, yeah. It's quiet, it's smooth. It's great."

"That's wonderful," Sarah said. "I know how much you've always wanted a truck."

"I'm going to need it, living up here."

Temporarily mute, Sarah couldn't answer.

Donny looked from side to side, then, and rubbed the back of his neck. "Look, Sarah—can we talk?"

Sarah resisted the urge to sigh deeply and loudly. Here it came. This is what she'd been dreading. He was going to announce that he'd bought a new house, that he'd signed the paperwork, and that he had set in motion his plan to move. Maybe if she walked away, ducked into Mama's house, he wouldn't be able to say it.

Hannah hadn't finished taking laundry off the line. Maybe if Sarah busied herself with that, he wouldn't be able to tell her. And if he couldn't tell her, then it couldn't happen. Right?

"Sure," she said, the word dry and brittle in her mouth. "Let's talk."

"I'm sorry I just left," he said. "When we got back from the hospital." Almost as an afterthought, he said, "How's Amelia? How's the arm?"

"She's fine. It's fine. I've barely seen her, so I guess that's good."

"Good," Donny said. "So anyway."

"Anyway."

"Sorry I just took off. I needed some time. To uh, clear my head."

"It's okay," Sarah said. "I understand. I'm sorry. I'm sorry I couldn't just relax and enjoy our overnight together."

"Sarah."

Uh oh. Here it comes. Sarah braced herself, and Donny continued: "I had so much fun with you in Jackson Hole."

Sarah nodded. "I had fun, too." She looked at the laundry, fluttering on the line, illuminated by the morning sunlight.

"It was so nice to see the old Sarah again."

"Old?" She raised an eyebrow at him, and he laughed.

"You know what I mean. You were so fun and relaxed and—well, just you. The you I haven't seen in years."

"It felt good," Sarah said.

"It did," Donny said, and the timbre of his voice made Sarah unsure whether he was talking about the "old Sarah" or the sex.

When she looked at him again, she noticed there was definitely a twinkle in his eye.

"So I've done quite a bit of thinking during the past couple of days."

Sarah wrapped her arms around her waist, as if that would protect her from the blow he was about to serve.

"Being here with you, in Wyoming, it's—it's reminded me of everything we used to have. Seeing all our old haunts, the school, the barn..."

His voice trailed off. Then he said, "We really had something great."

"We did." Sarah's words came out thick and full of emotion. She swallowed.

She knew what he was going to say, next: he was going to say that it was nice while it lasted and he was ready to move on now, that spending time had cemented that decision in his mind.

"So I've spent the last couple of days coming up with a plan. I've run it by Amelia, and your mom and sisters. And they all think it's a great plan. I just need your final okay on it. I want to make sure it works for everyone."

Curiosity sufficiently piqued, Sarah looked up at Donny. He was watching her like a mouse would watch a snake: carefully, standing by for any sudden movements.

"All right." Sarah drew the words out and she didn't know whether it was to postpone the moment when he'd officially break her heart, or for some other reason.

"You know this plot of land, Mama Katherine's plot, is about five acres, right?"

"Right," Sarah said. He didn't plan on asking Mama to sell it, did he? He wouldn't do that. She loved this place. Amelia loved this place. They all loved it. Mama Katherine was getting older, but that didn't mean she had to be uprooted.

"I know you love this place, Sarah. And you've said before that you would move back in a heartbeat."

She nodded, pressed her lips together.

"And *you* know Mama Katherine is going to need some help, and Hannah is going to be going back to school again soon."

Sarah nodded. Was he about to suggest putting Mama Katherine in an assisted living facility? Sarah stood up a little straighter, ready to defend Mama Katherine's independence and their home. Hannah could continue helping Mama.

"And you know Margaret is going to need some time to adjust as she loses her vision. Right?"

"Right." Where was he *going* with this?

"You know I've always loved you, right?"

"Yes, but—"

"And you know we had really hot sex the other night, right?"

Sarah didn't answer this one. He'd been going down one road, and she'd been following, but now he'd done a three-point turn. Or, maybe he'd turned onto a whole different street.

"So. Here's my proposal. I propose that we build two more houses here. Right here on this property. One for Margaret, and one for us. For you and me. And Amelia, when she's on breaks from school."

Sarah's mouth dropped open.

"There's plenty of space," Donny said. "I've been to the County and they approved it."

"You've been to the—"

"Yes," Donny said. "That's what I've been doing for the past couple of days. We just have to hire an engineer and a builder. Your sister can draw up the plans. And I got a recommendation from the guy at County for a general contractor."

"What about your job?"

"I've already talked with Bill, and he says I can work from here. I'll have to travel to Arizona for a couple of days each month, but that's doable. Totally doable. You can go with me. You can lounge by the pool while I work during the day, and we can have kinky hotel sex at night."

"You're really serious about this?"

"Do I look serious?"

He opened his arms and Sarah walked forward, her body sinking against his, fitting into the mold where it belonged—where it had always belonged.

"I love you, you know," he said.

"I know," she said. "I love you, too. More than anything."

"What about my plan?" he said.

"I love your plan, too."

———

AS THE WARD family rolled into Flagstaff a few days later, Sarah rattled off all the instructions she thought Amelia would need at college:

"Call me if you're ever out late and have to walk from your car to your dorm room alone, in the dark. Don't go into a boy's dorm room unless you've been on at least five dates with him. Don't let a boy come into your dorm room unless you've been on at least seven dates with him."

(Donny shot her a look on this one, and she said, "What? Do we want these young men knowing where our daughter lives?'")

"Eat a salad with vegetables every day. Never drink and drive." ("I don't even have a car, Mom.")

"Study hard. Homework first, play later."

"You know," Sarah said. "I should write these down for you."

Amelia laughed. "And what? Ask me to post them on my dorm room wall? I've got 'em. Up here." She tapped her temple.

"Fine, fine," Sarah said.

"She's going to do great, Sarah," Donny said. "I promise you."

They spent the afternoon shopping for essentials: a shower caddy and shower flip flops, a mini refrigerator, and a coffeemaker. ("Don't drink coffee after five p.m., Amelia. You'll never get good sleep." "Okay, Mom. Got it. Stop worrying." "She's going to do great, Sarah.")

After a nice dinner at a steakhouse ("This is probably the best meal you'll have for months, so eat up."), it was time Sarah and Donny to leave.

"Remember," Sarah said. "Wear your flip flops in the shower. And don't eat any lettuce that looks wilted or slimy. And—"

"I'm going to do great, Mom," Amelia said. "And don't worry. I'm going to call you every week. Probably every day, at first. You'll always be my mom, and I'm always going to need you."

Sarah nodded. After a long three-way hug, Sarah and Donny got into his new truck and drove away. Sarah turned around to look out the back window and saw Amelia, standing on the grass in front of the dorm building, waving, a big grin on her face.

CHAPTER TWENTY-FOUR

*J*ULY *18: Two days after my daughter's second birthday*

DEAREST PAULINE,

I THINK *it's about time I wrote to you with an update. I've been quite busy, as you probably guessed. And I know you didn't ask, but I'll tell you anyway: life is turning out beautifully, after all.*

I've named my new farm the Seedling Homestead. It's a place for starting over. It's a place where people can receive the nourishment they need to grow and thrive.

And that brings me to my second child, Hannah.

I named her after my mother. She's a beauty, Pauline. She looks a bit like my little Benny, but she also has my strong chin, I'm afraid. It's a bit manly.

Hannah is two years old now, and she is the light of my life. Because I'm painfully aware of how quickly things can change, I have decided to be the most devoted mother possible. And I've fallen madly in love with this little girl.

She's at once tender and feisty. Can you believe she already collects the eggs from the chicken coop? At two! I think she's advanced for her age. She marches right in there and scoops them up. She's not afraid of the hens at all, even though they can be a bit peckish.

And when she sleeps, she's the most beautiful thing I've ever seen. Her eyelashes are so long, they rest at the tops of her rosy cheeks like little butter-

flies. Her smile is like the sunshine, Pauline. I sometimes wish Philip could see her.

But then I come to my senses. There's no way he'd forgive me, now. Not for neglecting Benny and not for keeping my second pregnancy—and Hannah—a secret, and not for moving to Wyoming without so much as an adieu. But never you mind about that, Pauline.

I have a big announcement. I've decided that motherhood suits me, after all. I've decided to adopt. I'm just going through the certification process now, but I look forward to welcoming new people onto this farm. Hannah will be the best big sister.

———

JULY 16: My first daughter's fifth birthday—and the day my second daughter came to live with us

———

IT'S FINALLY HAPPENED! My new daughter arrived today, and I just had to share the moment with you, Pauline. Her name is Margaret. She's absolutely breathtaking. Her eyes are the most beautiful shade of green, like the sea glass I found on the beach when I was a child. Her hair is almost-black, curly, and wild, and her laugh is infectious.

Poor little thing's been spooked. She picked a green tomato (after I'd told her to pick a red one) and I could see she was afraid of how I'd react. But she's resilient, I can tell. And Hannah! It was love at first sight. They're going to be the most amazing friends. The girls, and their relationship, are sure to blossom here at the Seedling Homestead.

———

SEPTEMBER 25: Three months after Margaret's arrival—and the day my third daughter came to live with us.

———

I'VE ADDED to my brood. I know, you're thinking I'm crazy, Pauline. I've just exceeded the number-of-hands-to-number-of-children ratio of one-to-one. I have welcomed a third daughter to the Seedling Homestead: Sarah Jane.

Margaret and Hannah went into big-sister mode immediately when she arrived, clutching one of those stuffed animals you win at a fair. Margaret made her a sandwich and Hannah, my little drill sergeant, briefed her on the house and the house rules.

They ran outside to play, and within moments, Sarah Jane, who'd been mostly silent until this point, was laughing right along with her new sisters.

I'll tell you what, Pauline: my heart is full.

———

MAMA KATHERINE HAD ASSIGNED Donny to getting the RV ready for the trip. He was checking the oil when Sarah came out, and he finished up and wiped his hands on a towel before pulling her in for a kiss.

"I'll miss you," he said. "I feel like I just got you back."

"I know," Sarah said. "I'll miss you, too. But we'll be back in no time. You'll be so busy here you won't even notice we're gone."

"Four women, plus our teenaged daughter? I think I'll notice the quiet," Donny said.

Sarah swatted him on the arm, but then became serious. "Are you sure you're ready to live on the same property with those four women?"

Donny feigned a dramatic sigh. "I think I'll survive."

"Very funny," Sarah said. "But really. Are you sure your suggestion wasn't just a romantic gesture you're going to regret?"

"I'll admit, the prospect is a little scary. But we'll have our own space. And, just to make sure, I'll be managing the entire project myself. That's the main reason I'm staying here, you know. To maintain control."

When she swatted his arm again, he said, "Seriously, though. I know this is going to be good for everyone. And we have five acres between us. I think it's going to be fun."

Sarah leaned in, put her head on Donny's chest, and said, "I always knew you were the man for me."

He kissed the top of her head. "You'd better believe it."

"Are we ready to roll?" Hannah stood in the doorway of the RV, a duffel bag slung over her shoulder.

"You're good to go," Donny said. He stepped down, and gave Hannah a hug—then Margaret and Mama Katherine, who'd emerged from the house.

"Safe travels," he said as they all climbed aboard.

"You're sure Donny's willing to hold down the fort while we go on our trip?" Hannah said. She was stowing her bag in one of the RV's overhead bins. "There are the chickens and the garden. Taking care of this place is a two-person job. At least."

Sarah saw the way Hannah's eyes flittered over to Mama Katherine, who shot her a semi-dark look.

"He'll be fine," Sarah said. "I mean, it's only a week. I'm sure Luke will help him if he needs it. And this way he can supervise the grading while the guys get started."

"I still can't believe we're doing this," Margaret said.

"The road trip?" Mama Katherine said. "Or the commune?"

"Very funny," Margaret said. "Both, I guess."

"It's not a commune," Sarah said. "It's more like multiple-family housing."

"Are you expecting a share of the eggs?" Margaret said.

"Well, I suppose I am," Sarah said.

"Then it's a commune," Margaret and Mama Katherine said at the same time.

"Well, whatever you want to call it," Hannah said, "I think it'll be fun."

"So," Mama Katherine said. She sat back down. "Where's our first stop?"

Sarah climbed into the driver's seat and buckled her seatbelt.

"Where do you want to go, Margaret?" Sarah said. "What's something you've always wanted to see?"

For a moment, Sarah thought Margaret might cry. But she took a deep breath and said, with decision, "Zion National Park. Let's start there."

Sarah felt a rising sense of excitement as she started Maude up. With a final wave at Donny, Sarah started the RV, and as she pulled it out of the driveway, Mama Katherine said, "Girls, I'd like to tell you a story."

This might not be a love story, Sarah thought, but it was the beginning of a wonderful adventure.

THANK YOU FOR READING!

If you'd like to be among the first to know about new releases and special offers—and which adventures I'm having when I'm not writing—sign up for my mailing list at www.hilarydartt.com.

Keep reading for a preview of the third book in The Seedling Homestead Series, The Structure of Perfection.

PREVIEW: THE ARCHITECTURE OF VISION

I would so appreciate it if you'd take a moment to review The Composition of Order wherever you bought it.

Also, if you want to be among the first to know about exciting news and updates sign up for my mailing list at www.hilarydartt.com. I promise not to spam you or share your contact info.

Preview: The Architecture of Vision: The Seedling Homestead Series, Book 2

It happened gradually enough that Margaret Bradley pretended it wasn't happening at all, until circumstances forced her to admit it. She was losing her vision—which was the most important thing in the world to her, and to her clients.

She literally couldn't go without it. How many times had someone said, "I love your vision," or, "This is Margaret, our architect. She has amazing vision"? Too many to count.

It was also the one thing that allowed her to keep her promise to her first mama. She'd gone to school and gotten a great job, and now she didn't have to depend on anyone. Ever.

And that's why it was impossible for her to lose her vision.

Driving in the dark became difficult, and then impossible. One night, as she returned home after the grand opening celebration for a building she'd designed—it was the new library in the City of Pine Bluff, Arkansas—she realized she could barely make out the street signs or the edges of her lane. She could see the light from the traffic signals, but just barely. Everything blurred together as if her window was fogged up. Only, it wasn't. She blamed it on the wine, even though she'd had half a glass at most.

But somewhere deep in the recesses of her mind, as she crept along the road at fifteen miles per hour, she knew it wasn't the wine. She knew it wasn't the cold medicine she'd blamed the week before when she drove home from a late meeting in Steamboat Spring, Colorado.

So, Margaret stopped driving at night. She took taxis whenever she needed to, and although this put a slight dent in her pocketbook, it didn't hinder her social life too much ... and it allowed her to have a few glasses of wine on a date.

"Silver lining," she told herself on more than one occasion (especially the occasion where she'd needed to take the edge off a particularly strained dinner conversation with a certain Carl the Cryer, whose eyes leaked throughout the meal while he talked about his ex-wife. Margaret downed three healthy glasses of pinot noir with her spaghetti).

Then, her peripheral vision started to disappear. Not that she needed that for work, or for her social life, which is why she ignored it for such a long time. She became accustomed to swiveling her head all the way to the right and all the way to the left.

Until that day in Seattle, when she almost died.

As always, she was in the city for work. She had a seven a.m. meeting with the owner of a building on Pike Street, downtown. He wanted to turn it into—what else?—a coffee shop. She'd grabbed a coffee from her hotel lobby, and was walking down the street with her folder under one arm, taking in the scenery. She stepped off the curb to cross the street at 6th Avenue.

As she always did before an initial meeting with a client, she was going over her plan, thinking about her vision—yes, there was that word again. The coffee shop would have high ceilings with a row of windows running along the tops of the walls. The counter would stand along the back edge of the space, and she was still working out how to ensure maximum flow as people ordered, waited for their drinks, and then sat down. Deep in thought, Margaret didn't actually turn her head to the left to look for traffic as she started to cross the final intersection before she arrived at the new location.

The next several seconds—which actually lasted moments or even hours, in Margaret's mind—happened in slow motion: someone shouted, tires squealed on pavement, a car horn honked and Margaret finally turned her head, swiveled it all the way to the left, to see a gray sedan quickly approaching. She reacted, still in slow motion, her arm coming up (spilling her coffee) and her body scooting away from the car, which came to a screeching halt just inches from her left leg.

She dropped her folder, to brace herself on the hood of the car. Her drawings scattered all over the ground.

Of course, her first instinct was to gather up those papers. She knelt down right there at 6th and Pike, dirtying the knees of the designer slacks she'd bought at Nordstrom the evening before.

"Geez, lady, I almost ran you over."

Of course, she hadn't seen the driver of the gray sedan get out of his car, but here he was, helping her scoop up the contents of her folder. Now that she was touching the papers, she realized some of them had fallen into the puddle of coffee she'd created.

"Shit." Her face burned with shame, and she said, "I'm so sorry. You don't have to help me pick these up. Really, I'm fine."

"Lady, I gotta get you off the street before you endanger yourself again. Did you even realize you were walking against the light?"

Margaret looked up at the crosswalk signal and realized she couldn't even make out which symbol was illuminated.

"I'm really sorry," she said. "I'm just distracted, that's all. Important meeting."

"Nice drawings," he said, as he handed her the stack he'd collected. "But, lady, nobody's going to see them if you don't snap out of it."

He was right.

She thanked him for his help. Then, with a forced chuckle, she thanked him for not running her over. She thought she made out a smile before she stepped back onto the curb to wait for the next opportunity to cross.

This time, she paid attention—to the sounds of people talking next to her, the flow of traffic—and when those people started walking, she did, too.

Margaret feigned confidence as she walked along the sidewalk, but tears stung her eyes and made their way down her cheeks.

That was the moment. It was the moment when Margaret Bradley, independent professional, architect of great vision, social butterfly, finally had to admit she needed help. She could no longer take care of herself.

As soon as her meeting was over, she walked outside and leaned against the wall.

When the receptionist at the ophthalmologist's office picked up, she burst into tears.

————

"So tell me, Margaret. What brings you in, today?"

Dr. Thomas Lane looked at Margaret from under bushy eyebrows. The lighting conditions here were nearly perfect. Margaret knew because she could make out the color and round shape of Dr. Lane's bright green eyes.

They were sitting in the exam room, and Margaret leaned her head back against the head rest. She'd always thought these huge chairs and all the eye doctor's equipment looked like torture devices.

"I'm having some changes to my vision."

"What kinds of changes?"

Margaret's lips had gone dry, and she licked them. She wondered, for a fraction of a second, whether she had to answer the question. Keeping this problem to herself had kept it from being a problem. Sort of. He waited. She cleared her throat.

"At first, it was my night vision. I couldn't distinguish shapes, you know? I couldn't quite read the street signs or see other cars, in the dark. I stopped driving at night. And then, my peripheral vision went. It seemed like I didn't have any, all of a sudden. That's when I started taking taxis. And now, my regular vision—it's just—blurry. Not all the time. Some days, I wake up, and I can see almost normally. And some, I can't."

"How long have you been noticing symptoms?"

She looked down at her lap, and then up at the two mirrors on the opposite wall. They looked more like blobs against the white background.

She inhaled and answered on the exhale: "A few months. Maybe twenty-four."

"Twenty-four months?" Dr. Lane was incredulous. "Twenty-four months is more than a few, dear. It's two years."

"I know. I just—it just—I didn't think it was serious, you know? And like I said, I can still see clearly sometimes. Plus, it's the twenty-first century. Surely, anything, or almost anything, is fixable, right?"

"I wish that were true," Dr. Lane said. "Do you have a family history of vision loss?"

"I don't know." Margaret shrugged one shoulder.

"Your mother, your father, perhaps a grandparent?"

"It's not that," Margaret said. "I'm adopted. My biological mother is dead. And I don't even know who my father is. Last I saw my mother, she had pretty good vision—and pretty good aim. Anyway. That's the long answer. I don't know if anyone had vision loss."

Dr. Lane nodded. He leaned forward, his elbows on his knees. "I suspect you have a condition called retinitis pigmentosa."

"Sounds like a doozy," Margaret said, because she didn't know what else to say and she wanted to keep the mood light. And because it sounded like a doozy. "Or something out of a magic spell book."

This didn't even earn a chuckle from Dr. Lane, who said, "It's a degenerative eye disease, Margaret. It causes severe vision impairment. Do you know what the retina is?"

"Yeah," Margaret said, dread forcing her to slog through the recesses of her memory for the information she'd learned in high school biology. "It's at the back of the eye, and it converts light into images?"

"Right," Dr. Lane said. "It's a thin piece of tissue lining the back of the eye. It contains photoreceptor cells, rods and cones, which convert light into signals the brain interprets as vision. In retinitis pigmentosa, those photoreceptor cells degenerate. They stop working effectively. People with retinitis pigmentosa *usually* begin experiencing symptoms —similar to the ones you've experienced—in early adulthood. Most of them lose their vision gradually over time. Some cases are more severe than others."

Margaret wondered if this torture chair reclined because she thought she might pass out.

"What's the treatment?"

"Let me get you some water," Dr. Lane said.

Margaret hardly noticed he was gone but a moment later, he was pressing a water bottle into her hands.

"It's open," he said. "Why don't you have a drink?"

She nodded and took a sip. "Don't you have anything stronger?"

This time, he did chuckle. "Not at the office, dear, unfortunately."

A few seconds passed, and Dr. Lane spoke again. "Research is promising when it comes to treatment in the future," he said. "But right now, options are limited."

"Options are limited. What does that mean?"

"Unfortunately, there's not too much we can do."

"So, I'm losing my vision."

"Yes, I think so. I'd like you to see a specialist, to be sure; a doctor who has the equipment to get a really good look at your retina, and your photoreceptor cells."

Margaret started to speak, but Dr. Lane held up a hand. "Now, keep in mind that some cases are more severe than others. Depending on lighting conditions, you may be able to see just fine, at least for a while. Some people with this condition continue to have daytime vision."

"I don't think you understand," Margaret said. "I'm an architect. I can't lose my vision."

"I know this information may be difficult to process."

"It's impossible," Margaret said. "I need my vision to draw plans, to see buildings, to see spaces. To *see*."

"If this were a debate, you'd win," Dr. Lane said. His voice sounded so kind she almost cried. "But, I'm sorry to say, it's not."

"I'm going to get a second opinion." Her hands were shaking. She knew. She knew she could get a second opinion, and that it would be the same as Dr. Lane's opinion. Because, as he'd said, this wasn't a debate. It wasn't about opinions. It was fact. She was losing her vision.

"Like I said, I'm going to refer you to a specialist. She can give you a more detailed exam and, hopefully, advice about how to move forward."

"Where can I possibly go, if I can't *see*?"

Dr. Lane rolled his stool toward Margaret and took her hands in his own. He leaned in, so their eyes were on level, and he said, "Margaret, this isn't a death sentence. I promise you, you still have the opportunity to live a rich and full life, even with retinitis pigmentosa."

"My life can't be rich and full if I can't see," she said. "You don't understand."

Her career was everything. In using it as a vessel for self-sufficiency, she'd foregone all the things other people did: finding a partner, having children, buying a house. All so she could focus on her career.

"I'm sorry, Margaret," Dr. Lane said. He gave her hands one final squeeze, and then rolled over to the desk.

"I'm sending out a referral right now. It's Dr. Marie Rossi. She's good. Very good."

The lying started the next day. It wasn't outright lying, but it was lying by omission. Margaret had already scheduled a trip to Arizona. Her niece, Amelia, was graduating from high school, and she'd promised to be in the stands with pompons.

If the trip weren't specifically for graduation, Margaret would have postponed it until she was able to go to the specialist. Or find some witch doctor who could perform some kind of voodoo and bring her vision back.

But Amelia was one of her favorite people. Her favorite person, actually. And Margaret didn't want to let her down.

Typically, she'd fly into Phoenix and then grab a rental car and jet up Interstate 17 to Flagstaff, where Amelia lived with Margaret's youngest sister, Sarah, and her husband, Donny. Not this time. She paid an exorbitant fee to ride an airport shuttle from Phoenix to Flagstaff, and then called for a taxi to take her to Sarah's house.

The process was cumbersome and—well, whatever the opposite of empowering was. Luckily (or unluckily), Sarah was so distracted by her marriage problems that she didn't even question Margaret's taxi arrival.

They went out for lunch, which, under normal circumstances, would have been a fun activity. But Sarah took her to a trendy little Italian place where low lighting was part of the ambience and for the first time, Margaret couldn't read the menu. The letters blurred together, tiny gray smudges.

Margaret kept Sarah talking. She went as far as to talk about Sarah's sex life, and to insist on going to The Big One, a boutique sex shop a few doors down. Then she ordered bottomless martinis.

And it worked. Sarah didn't notice anything was amiss; at least, not at first.

Then Margaret said, "What are you getting? What's good here?"

"The ravioli," Sarah said.

"I'll have the same," Margaret said.

"You don't eat pasta. It gives you gas."

"I know. I'll get a side salad."

Which didn't make sense. But it, too, worked, because Sarah was distracted. Margaret could see the blob that was her sister shrug one shoulder, as if to say, "Suit yourself," and they moved on to a different topic.

The next day, as they were driving to Amelia's graduation, she and Sarah received a text, simultaneously. Margaret could barely read her text messages, which was why her phone was lying at the bottom of her purse on the floor between her feet. But the only person who would text them both at the same time was their older sister, Hannah.

Sarah didn't move to look at her phone, even though the notification was deafening. She was behaving so strangely that Margaret dug out her own phone, angling it away from Amelia so Amelia wouldn't see the super-sized font Margaret had started using.

Sure enough, the text was from Hannah, and as Margaret read it, her blood practically froze.

Mama just collapsed. Taking her to the hospital now. I know it's Amelia's graduation day ... text me later.

For a few moments, Margaret debated whether she should break this news to Sarah. Then she decided it was better to do it now. She'd hate for Sarah to see the message if she used her phone to take pictures during the ceremony. She had to say Sarah's name several times before her sister responded.

"I just got a text from Hannah," Margaret said.

"And?" Sarah said.

"Mama's sick," Margaret said. "Hannah's taking her to the hospital."

Amelia gasped. Donny cursed.

"What kind of sick?" Sarah said.

"Not sure," Margaret said. She used voice-to-text to ask Hannah for details, and Hannah's response came back quickly. "Unconscious. We won't know anything right away. Possibly a stroke."

They rode the rest of the way in silence. And while Margaret was horrified at this news, she couldn't help but also feel the tiniest bit relieved. Now Sarah and Donny would be too busy thinking about Mama Katherine to notice Margaret's strange behavior.

During Amelia's graduation, Margaret was in the stands, just as she'd promised she would be. And she waved those pompons, even though she couldn't even make out which gowned-and-capped teenager was her niece.

Of course, Sarah and Donny picked her out right away, and when they pointed her out to Margaret, Margaret just waved, hoping her palm was facing the right direction.

And then, midway through the ceremony, Margaret had a terrible realization: if Mama Katherine was sick, she'd have to go see her. She had no choice but to go to Wyoming. And even if she was sick, Mama Katherine would know something was off.

There was absolutely no way Margaret could continue acting like things were normal, she thought as she watched the sea of maroon-clad high school graduates become taller as the kids stood up.

Then, as they threw their caps—maroon dots—into the air, Margaret felt a tear slip down her cheek.

Margaret sat on a comfortable chair in Dr. Marie Rossi's office. The cushions were covered in leather and Margaret was almost positive they were filled with goose down.

While music had played in the waiting room, the only sound in here was the ticking of a clock. Margaret drummed her fingers on her thighs. Is this what it felt like to wait for an executioner? Under different circumstances, she would have laughed at herself. Even she knew she was being dramatic.

Finally, *finally*, the office door opened. Dr. Rossi came in, and Margaret could smell her perfume—floral with a hint of vanilla. She sat down in a chair across from Margaret and leaned forward, her elbows on her knees. Fortunately, she didn't try to make small talk or ask how Margaret was. She cut right to the chase.

"I've just finished reviewing the exam results. Dr. Lane was right. You have retinitis pigmentosa."

Margaret inhaled and then held her breath. She'd gone against her own advice and performed hours of Internet research after seeing Dr. Lane. None of the websites had anything good to say about this condition. She was going to lose most, if not all, of her vision.

This was impossible. She couldn't go blind. Not now. She was too young. There were so many things she hadn't seen. The petroglyphs in Utah, the beaches in Belize, the waterfalls in Costa Rica. And although she'd never wanted a husband or children, she realized with a start that if she did fall in love, and start a family, she'd never see their faces.

She clenched her fists, digging her fingernails into her palms.

"It's genetic." Dr. Rossi's voice was calm, but Margaret didn't feel soothed by it. "Does anyone in your family have retinitis pigmentosa?"

"I don't know," Margaret said. "I'm not in touch with my biological family."

"How long did you say you'd been having symptoms?"

Dr. Rossi leaned back in her chair. Margaret could guess what the woman was wearing, just from what she'd gathered during their conversations: a pencil skirt with high heels and a cardigan set. Her hair was perfectly combed and she probably had that air of authority. She was, undoubtedly, beautiful, with one feature that was just a tiny bit too big. Probably her teeth.

"A while," Margaret said. "I could tell from Dr. Lane's response that he thought I should have come in sooner."

"How long is a while?"

Margaret sighed. "Does it matter? Isn't the prognosis the same?"

Before Dr. Rossi could answer, though, Margaret realized she was acting like a spoiled brat. If she were in the other chair, giving a consult, she'd be offended. She rubbed her eyes, sighed, and spoke. "I'm sorry. I started noticing symptoms about two years ago. At first I thought it was just, you know, allergies or something. Making my vision weird. I kept putting it off because deep down, I was afraid it was something serious. I was afraid it would mean I couldn't work."

When Dr. Rossi said, "I understand," Margaret believed that she did. "What do you do for a living?"

"I'm an architect."

Dr. Rossi took a long moment to respond. "Lots of people with vision loss continue to work full-time," she said.

"Not as architects, though, right?"

"Margaret, I know it may feel like it, but this isn't a death sentence. First of all, as your symptoms continue progressing—and in most cases, they, do, unfortunately—then you'll have good days and bad days. You'll have days where you can see almost as well as you always have, and you'll have days where you can barely see anything."

"And at some point, the bad days will outnumber the good," Margaret said. "And before long, I'll lose my vision completely."

Dr. Rossi made a humming noise. "You still have the opportunity to live a really full life. Yes, it may be different from what you've had, or what you imagined you'd have. This is going to be a transition, but I'm confident that with your determination, you'll be able to do many of the things you want to do."

"I just hate that this is happening. I feel like I'm living a nightmare."

"I understand. It won't always feel this way. Give yourself some time to get your feet underneath you. There are tons of great resources available, and before you leave today, we'll make sure you know how to access them."

"My mother's sick."

"And you're worried you won't be able to take care of her."

"Right."

"Do you have siblings?"

At the thought of Hannah and Sarah, Margaret blanched. They'd insist on taking care of her. Hannah would already be taking care of Mama Katherine. And with Amelia leaving for college, Sarah was finally going to be able to focus on herself. This was so unfair.

"Two sisters," Margaret said.

"I'm going to be honest, here," Dr. Rossi said. "You're going to have to let your sisters take care of your mom. Just for now. Just until you get your feet underneath you, like I said. And then, once you learn how to navigate the world without your vision, you'll be able to help, too. This is going to require a lot of patience, Margaret. Patience with yourself. But I promise you, you're going to get through this."

Then, in a gesture that was completely unexpected, Dr. Rossi stood up, pulled Margaret to standing, and gave her a long hug.

Margaret left the office a few minutes later with a binder full of resources and a tiny bit of hope (which she hadn't had when she walked in). Next step: visit Mama Katherine.

ABOUT THE AUTHOR

Hilary Dartt loves great adventures, whether she's writing, reading, or living them. The author of nine women's fiction novels, Hilary lives in Arizona's high desert with her husband, their three children, her Weimaraner and running partner, Leia, a failed barn cat, and a flock of chickens. She loves camping, exploring in the Jeep, and dance parties with her kids. Learn more at www.hilarydartt.com